VOYAGER OF RIVERSTONE

Voyager of Riverstone

Daughters of Riverstone - Book 3

Mandy Schimelpfenig

This is a work of fiction.

Names, characters, places, and incidents either are the product of the author's imagination or are used fictitiously. Any resemblance to actual persons, living or dead, events, or locales is entirely coincidental.

First paperback edition

Cover design and logo by Covers by Violet
Chapter headings, title page, line breaks, and family tree created in Canva.

ISBN (paperback) – 9781737669647
ISBN (hardcover) – 9781737669654

www.RiverstoneSaga.com

To every woman who refuses to be left behind.

Voyage of The Wayward Azymelina
The Green Mountain
Valley of Horges
The Colony ~ Lakeside
Brandemer Sound
Faldr
Bludek's Bay
Cyfirellon
The Unexplored Islands
Island of the Nameless Finner
Braye's Island

THE ELEJICK ROYAL FAMILY

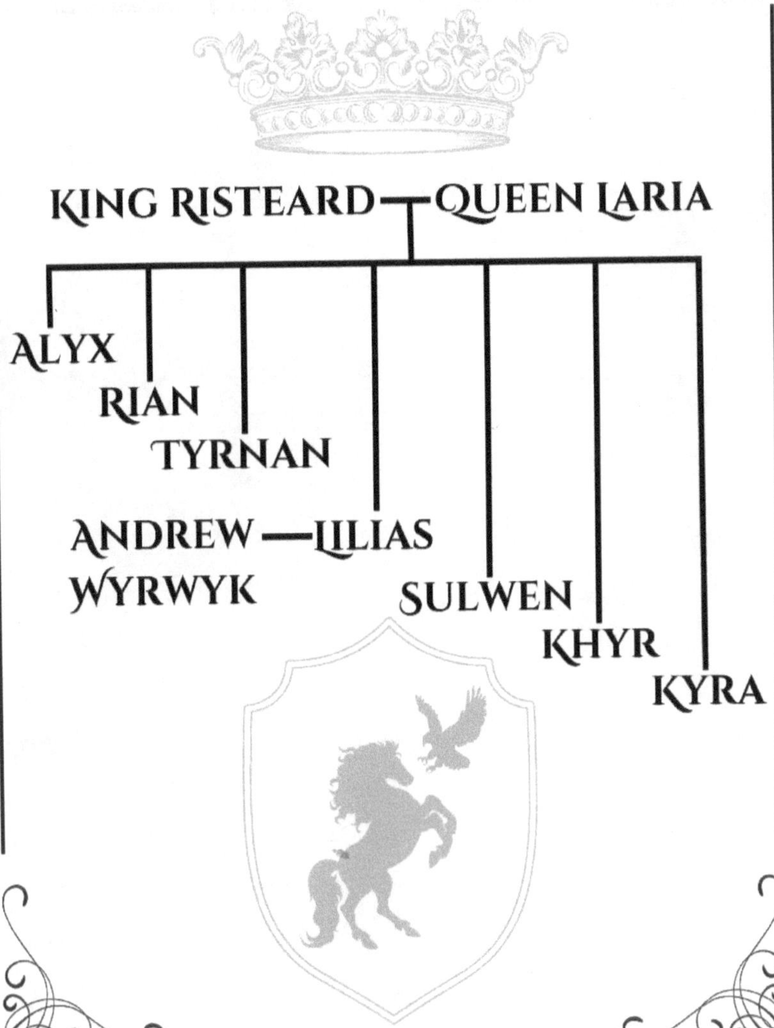

KING RISTEARD — QUEEN LARIA

ALYX

RIAN

TYRNAN

ANDREW — LILIAS
WYRWYK

SULWEN

KHYR

KYRA

A pronunciation guide is provided in the back of the book for those who wish to use it.

PART I

CHAPTER 1

The polished blade of the sword cut through the air at amazing speed. I narrowly avoided decapitation, pivoted, and thrust my sword toward my opponent's stomach. The uneven ground shifted under my weight, yet I maintained my footing when my blade met not the soft flesh of a body but empty space. I gritted my teeth, spun away, and raised my sword to block a downward blow. My arms reverberated with the impact of blade against blade, and sparks showered upon my hair. Sweat dripped down my eyelashes into my eyes, blurring my vision. I hastily brushed the back of my hand across my brow and remained focused on the circling attacker.

My opponent was large, towering at least a head above me, strong, powerful, and highly trained. Yet I never allowed being outweighed or outmatched to slow me down. I kicked up a plume of gravel and dust and took advantage of the resulting sputtering to drive my shoulder into the man's side, knocking him off balance. When he stumbled, I attacked, arcing my sword in a powerful overhead swing. Before I could bring it down, he kicked me in the stomach, knocking the breath out of me and sending me reeling backwards. I recovered quickly, brought the blade high, and charged.

A voice broke through the sound of blood rushing in my ears, "Aim for his right shoulder, Sulwen! It's his weakest point!"

I resisted turning toward the voice but hesitated a fraction of a second. The next moment, I was knocked off my feet. My backside hit the ground hard, and when my eyes flew open, the point of my father's sword hovered above my throat.

"Never let your guard down in front of an enemy. Not even for your mother," the king said.

"Yes…Father," I said between gasps. He reached out to help me to my feet. My mother was covering her mouth, a bemused expression in her eyes.

I brushed the dirt off my breeches and infused every ounce of sarcasm into my voice.

"Thanks for that, Mother."

Laria Elejick, the Queen of Praed, spoke behind her hand. "I was only trying to help."

Risteard Elejick, the King of Praed, whipped around to face her. "By shouting my weak spots to her?"

"A mother would do anything for her daughters," she said, the picture of wide-eyed innocence.

He moved toward her with the grace of a predator. "Even if it means losing her husband to the sword?"

"Eh…" she shrugged. "We've had a good run."

He towered over her, the slow curve of his mouth a sharp contrast to his dark gaze.

Mother's cheeks flushed pink, and she tilted her face up as he lowered his head.

I concentrated on polishing my sword while they fawned over each other. Though I was lucky to have parents so devoted to one another, it didn't mean I had to stomach their ardent displays of public affection.

While I oiled the gleaming steel, my eyes drifted over the courtyard of Praed Castle. Around me, knights were training to keep themselves in top form, though there hadn't been a significant threat warranting such a show of force since I was a little girl. Regardless of the lasting peace, Father insisted his knights and soldiers be prepared. Among them were my elder brothers, Alyx and Rian, practicing drills as Father and I had done. Rian's wicked grin never left his face as they circled each other. His green eyes danced with mischief, but they always gave him away. They flicked toward the right, and the ever-watchful Alyx perceived the movement and blocked it in the same breath. It was amazing how similar my father and eldest brother were. Both shared the same striking cerulean eyes, black hair, and strong jaw. They studied their opponents with a patience I could never hope to possess. Like Rian, I tended to plunge forward on a whim, but Alyx observed and strategized.

Tyrnan, the third eldest prince, sat by watching and offering encouragement. Though Tyrnan himself would also practice with a sword, he was less inclined to duel since fighting held little interest for him. Whereas Alyx and Rian were princes devoted to their training, Tyrnan was a pacifist, preferring books to weapons. My mouth curved in a half smile when Tyrnan surreptitiously glanced around and pulled a small pamphlet out from under his leg and scanned the pages before his brothers noticed.

Mother and Father continued to converse, and I only caught snippets of their conversation. They were discussing my sister, Lilias, and her upcoming marriage. This was a topic I had every intention of avoiding. I didn't begrudge my sister's happiness, but it pained me to lose her, and to be honest, her marriage meant I would be expected to follow. Marriage was the least of my priorities. I closed my ears to their voices and continued to scan the courtyard to distract myself.

I turned my attention to my youngest brother, Khyr, honing his marksmanship. Khyr had never been fond of a blade, but unlike Tyrnan, he wasn't reluctant to wield a weapon. He became proficient in archery the moment he took up the bow. Not many could best him in competition. Arrow after arrow found the center of the target with ease, and my heart swelled with pride at my brother's skill.

Khyr was lean and athletic with dark hair like his elder brothers, but when the sun shone upon him, the strands glowed a deep copper. His eyes were pale blue, the color of snow reflecting the fading light of dusk. In the last year, he'd grown quite tall, surpassing me by at least two inches. In contrast, his twin sister, Kyra, was still shorter than me. She was the youngest daughter and sweetheart of the family. She, too, had brown hair that shimmered auburn in sunlight, but her eyes were such a pale light green they held only the barest hint of color. She was the perfect blend of both our elder sister, the perfect princess, and me, the wild rapscallion. She enjoyed pretty dresses and learning languages alongside penning harrowing stories and racing horses across the prairie.

Among my dark-haired siblings, I was the outcast. Like Mother, I had strikingly bright red hair and moss-green eyes, drawing stares everywhere I went. Mother was used to the attention and ignored the whispers, but I hated being so different and silently wished my hair was dark like my sisters'. I generally wore my unruly locks in a tight braid pulled up and out of the way at the back of my head. This eventually worked loose with activity and stray strands flew about my face like annoying gnats. Sometimes I wished I could just cut all my ginger hair off and be done with it.

My reverie was interrupted by the sound of Father's boots crunching on gravel. Silently, he sat beside me and began cleaning his own blade. We remained thus for several moments, unspeaking but not uncomfortable. My father was a man of few words, though he had plenty to say when any of us got into mischief. We all respected and revered the King of Praed, as did the people subject to his just and prosperous rule. As a father he was patient, loving, and always had time for us. As a girl, I was meant to play the reserved princess, delighting in dances and sewing. But Father did not distinguish roles in terms of gender. He was just as happy to train me in swordsmanship as his sons, and I was grateful to have such an open-minded father.

"Are you going to tell me where I went wrong?" He would offer a detailed critique of my performance eventually, and I preferred to get the lecture over with.

"You mean before you allowed yourself to become distracted by your mother?" He spoke dryly without taking his eyes off his task.

"Yes," I grumbled. "Before that."

"You expose your midsection too much," he said, again without meeting my eye, in that matter-of-fact tone that was neither berating nor sympathetic. "When you swing, keep your elbows tucked. If you're delivering a blow requiring you to raise your arms over your head, make sure your opponent is disabled enough not to counter before you have a chance to strike."

"Fair. Anything else?"

"You're getting faster and more precise. Your practice is paying off."

I smiled, pleased with the hard-won compliment. Father was a strict and demanding teacher, but he always tried to follow-up constructive criticism with a compliment. Once, many years ago, he harshly tore apart my performance and I retreated to my room in tears. He bid entry a short time later, duly penitent. I suspect a stern reproach from Mother had something to do with his heartfelt apology. He still pointed out the flaws in my technique, but he was quick to add a way I'd improved.

I returned my attention to my task, and once the steel was shining in the late afternoon sun, I set it aside to oil the leather scabbard. I glanced at

Father using a whetstone to sharpen a dagger, his sword sheathed at his side.

"I haven't seen that one before." I gave a nod toward the weapon.

"It hasn't been used in years," he said.

"Where did it come from?"

"It's mine."

"Can I see?" I held out my hand.

He hesitated, met my eye for several heartbeats, then reluctantly placed the blade in my hand. He watched intently while I studied it, marveling at the craftsmanship of the hilt, the interwoven strands of leather, and the well-worn blade. Something caught my eye, and I peered closer at the handle. The letters "RE" were carved into the pommel so small I had to squint to see them.

"Your initials."

He snatched the dagger from my hands as if he could no longer bear to be apart from it.

"Why haven't I seen it before?"

"It belongs to your mother now." He spoke quietly, as if he didn't want anyone to hear.

"Oh." I glanced at the dagger, surprised. I'd never seen Mother raise a hand much less a blade. "Does she know how to use it?"

Father's eyes met mine, and my pulse quickened at the darkness rising in their cerulean depths. I'd seen him angry, but the stare he fixed on me went so much deeper than mere ire. It was as if I'd stumbled onto a secret I wasn't meant to know, something terrifying.

"She knows," he said, his words full of hidden meaning. Before I could speak, he added, "Your mother fought fiercely to give you the life you now lead. Never forget that."

"I won't." My lips trembled. I knew a little about Mother's story, how she was raised at Riverstone then forced to become a servant under an evil regime. Though she was reluctant to share any details, I learned from my Aunt Ula how she and Father secretly planned a rebellion, that together they brought down the tyrant King Conall and joined the kingdoms of Praed and Ilano. When I watched the light catch the edge of the dagger in my father's hands and pictured her wielding it, I was overcome with empathy for the cruel situation she labored under, and my admiration was increased ten times over.

"Father…" I hesitated, equally eager to change the subject and desperate to learn more, but I wasn't sure which would win before I completed my thought.

"Yes?" I swore his voice caught as if choking on an emotion he struggled to contain. That was the deciding factor. I couldn't bear it if I upset him, so I changed the subject.

"Do you like Lilias' betrothed?"

He looked up, a mixture of shock and amusement on his face.

"I have no objection to him." How diplomatic of him!

"Even though he's boring?" I smirked.

"He's steady. He suits your sister."

I rolled my eyes and sighed in exasperation. Andrew Wyrwyk was as steady as an ancient oak and just as interesting. He never laughed, rarely smiled, and in general took life way too seriously. I couldn't argue that his personality closely mirrored my proper sister, but to live with such a block of wood? Surely, she was mad to think he would make a good husband.

"Don't you think she's a little young?"

"She's two years older than your mother was when we married." The side of his mouth quirked. "What's really bothering you?"

I lowered my gaze. My father knew me better than anyone, even Mother and my siblings. He could see through my sarcasm and reticence, and he could read my expressions like the lines in a well-loved book. There was always honesty between us as a result, but I still couldn't bring myself to voice my true fear.

"Bothering me? Nothing," I muttered. "I'm happy Lilias found a kind and well-suited fiancé. Not to mention rich."

He looked at me humorlessly. I burst out laughing.

He waved a cautioning finger at me. "Don't ever say that to your sister."

"I won't."

"Come. You'll need to change for dinner." He stood up.

I sheathed my sword and met my brothers cavorting in the middle of the courtyard.

"Don't sulk just because you weren't able to parry my attack," Rian teased Alyx.

"I'm not sulking," Alyx countered. "I'm still puzzling over how you can justify such a sloppy riposte." Rian punched his older brother in the shoulder, and Alyx wrapped his arm about Rian's shoulders before grinding his knuckles into the younger man's scalp. Rian twisted and jabbed at Alyx's sides until they collided into me.

"Aren't you two a little old for wrestling?" I shoved them roughly away.

They laughed, and the next moment my arms were pinned to my waist by a strong grip.

"Aren't you a little too much of a lady for violence?" Khyr's voice teased in my ear. I struggled out of his grasp and drove my elbow into his side, eliciting a satisfying *whoosh* as the air left his lungs. Khyr loved a good teasing and knew everyone's weak spot, including my dissatisfaction with society's restrictions toward women.

"Enough!" Father commanded.

We dutifully behaved as we entered the castle and retreated to our respective rooms to wash and prepare for dinner.

Molli, my lady-in-waiting, was already prepared with a basin of hot water and a gown laid out on the bed. I carefully stored my sword in the chest at the foot of my bed, then stripped off the plain frock I wore for training and tossed it on the floor.

Molli tsk-tsked when she picked up my discarded clothing then sighed in exasperation. "There're three more holes in this dress."

Few in her position would dare speak to a princess in such a manner, but Molli had worked for my family for years and earned the right to comment so freely. I smiled sheepishly at her stern expression and shrugged. "Training is rough on clothing. At least it was an old dress."

A perfect eyebrow rose above Molli's turquoise eyes. She pursed her lips. I scurried to my seat at the vanity and pulled at my braid to hide my grin.

"Allow me, my lady." Molli took over untangling my unruly hair. Her thin fingers expertly untwined the braid without pulling out a single strand. I busied myself with inspecting my broken nails while she brushed the thick locks to a soft shine.

"I think the golden yellow gown with the black embroidery would suit well for tomorrow evening," she said.

"Whatever you think is best," I muttered. Tomorrow evening we were entertaining Lilias' future in-laws, and I'm sure Molli was instructed to ensure I looked appropriately presentable. I wouldn't object, but I wouldn't bother offering an opinion either. Molli was much better at determining the proper attire for such situations. I much preferred our private family dinners, like tonight's, where I could be comfortable in a dress I wasn't squeezed and tied into.

"Stop your pouting," she said. "It isn't becoming."

"I'm not pouting!"

"That jutting chin and furrowed brow would suggest otherwise."

I bit my lower lip and sucked it into my mouth to prove her wrong, but I knew it was pointless.

She smiled kindly, deepening the lines about her eyes and mouth. "It's not the end of the world, Your Highness. You'll still see Princess Lilias very often, I'm sure."

"I'm sure." The truth was it wasn't the thought of losing my sister that troubled me. Yes, I would miss her, but I knew a princess' duty was to marry and leave home to have a family of her own. A fact that was at the core of my consternation. With Lilias married, all eyes would inevitably settle on me as the next in line to be wed, even though I had three older unmarried brothers. But such was the fate of a woman, especially a princess whose life belonged to a crown.

CHAPTER 2

A twitter of birdsong thrust me into wakefulness. I rubbed the haze of sleep from my eyes and blinked up at the window overlooking the mews. A tiny bluebird perched on the sill, pecking at the crevasses between stones. Beyond it, the sky was alight with the golden hues of sun rise.

"Amyl's feathers!" I was late! I threw off the bedcovers and scrambled to pull on an old frock. In my haste, I stubbed my toe and pulled my hair, but I ignored the pain. I braided my hair, shoved my bare feet into my boots, and grabbed my journal.

There was no time to be quiet. I ran down the corridor past my sisters' rooms and skidded into the servant's stairs. I stumbled and almost fell down the last three, but I leapt clear and ran through the kitchens. Maids clutched their floured hands to their chests, and I dodged the head cook in time to miss being side-swiped by a copper kettle.

"Watch whatcher—oh! Beg your pardon, Your Highness!"

I waved a hand over my shoulder. "Sorry, Mrs. Koos! Smells amazing!"

I burst through a back door and raced along the path around the castle. In the days of Mother's youth, the path led to an arena where men displayed their prowess in war games. Jousting, archery, sword fighting, even hand-to-hand combat events were held monthly. Every year, the king's birthday was celebrated with elaborate reenactments of battles. When King Conall conquered Praed, the arena was destroyed, and in its place were erected mews and exercise yards.

The smaller mews for the falcons were a blur as I ran toward a long wooden building stretching along one side of the circular training grounds. It looked like stables, but spires extended from the roof in even intervals connected by woven strips of thinly pounded iron. The cage-like structure formed a dome, and branches poked through the openings. They called it an aviary. It'd been constructed five years ago, and the culmination of years' worth of work was happening this morning.

Besides a few men raking the yard, the place was deserted. Knights wouldn't begin training or exercising their birds until after breakfast, and the head falconer was busy overseeing the morning feedings.

I reached the main door of the aviary and took a moment to catch my breath. I wiped my trembling palms down the front of my frock and inhaled the scent of straw and bird dust. I slid the door open enough to squeeze through and carefully closed it behind me. I stood in a small foyer with three doorways. To my left were the flights for three pairs of breeding eagles. To my right was the juvenile holding pen. In Ilano, noble boys and knights entered the pen at the capital and formed a connection to an eagle that lasted the rest of their life. Some eagles, like Aquila, sacrificed their lives for their masters. Father dedicated the aviary to his fallen companion at its grand unveiling.

I pushed open the door directly in front of me and a blast of warm air set my cheeks aflame. I tossed my braid over my shoulder and brushed loose strands of hair off my forehead. Unlike the two wings, this room was enclosed. Braziers were constantly lit, maintaining a balmy temperature reminiscent of hot summer days. Four rows of tables in the center of the room were covered with crates filled with soft materials and precious specimens. At the back of the room was a large desk built into the wall. A man was hunched over a pile of papers. He looked up at my approach, his curly light brown hair already in disarray. He lowered his glasses to peer at me.

"Sorry I'm late, Master Avi." I flipped to a blank page of my journal and raised a pencil. "Did I miss anything?"

"Hmmm…" The head of the aviary and master of eagles pushed his glasses up the curved ridge of his nose. He ruffled his papers, organizing them into a neat pile while I fidgeted. He turned to me and stared, unmoving, for an agonizing thirty seconds. A smile lit up his face, and he slapped the edge of the desk.

"Princess, you're just in time!" He propelled himself out of his chair with the exuberance of a man half his forty years. He gestured me over to one of the crates, his sky-blue eyes shimmering with excitement.

I steadied myself on the table and leaned over the edge of the crate to peer inside. Nestled among scraps of cloth, feathers, and dried grass were two white and black speckled eggs. I hovered a hand over them, feeling the heat radiating from the shells. Each was nearly the size of my hand and just as wide. One of the eggs shifted, and I jumped back, snatching my hand away. Master Avi chuckled softly, and I relaxed.

A *tap tap tap* brought my attention back to the eggs. I picked up my journal, pencil poised over the page. A sharp *crack,* and my heartbeat quickened. I held my breath and tried not to bounce on my toes. The shell broke, and the tip of a tiny, black beak poked through. I sketched the scene with hasty strokes I'd fill in later with the help of my scribbled notes.

"Don't forget to watch, Princess," Master Avi said in his soft, mellow voice. "You can't draw a blank memory."

My pencil stilled, and I raised my eyes to the hatching egg. It would take hours for the eaglet to fully break out of its shell, but the first few moments were the most exhilarating. The chick used its beak to widen the gap and loudly *peep-peeped.* Master Avi and I beamed at each other.

"Come on, Princess." He patted my shoulder and strode toward the door. "We'll check on his progress after."

A surge of excitement jolted through me. *After.* Master Avi held open the door, and I rushed past him into the juvenile eagle pen. This is what I'd been waiting for, dreaming of, for years. The first eagles hatched in Praed were now three years old, the perfect age to bond with people. Today would mark the first time a Praed-born Ilano boy would match with an eagle on Praed soil.

You would think such a historical occasion would warrant a crowd, but the bonding ceremony was deeply sacred. Mine and Master Avi's presence alone was in violation of tradition and was the only fanfare the family would permit. The rest of Praed would hear of it soon enough.

I jogged down a narrow walkway in front of the pen, Master Avi's long strides echoing behind me. The boy and his father were already waiting at the pen's entrance. The boy stood on tiptoe trying to look inside, his eyes wide. His father stood rigid, arms folded, the picture of a well-disciplined knight. But his features were soft as he regarded his son, his mouth curved in a lopsided grin. He looked up, and his smile widened. He opened his arms, and without slowing, I crashed into him in a fierce hug.

"Thank you for letting me be here, Olim," I said. "You must be so proud!" We turned to Ru, the thirteen-year-old boy hanging off the door.

He blew a stray blond curl out of his eyes. His cheeks dimpled when he smiled, and the bridge of his nose was dusted with freckles.

"He's been so excited he's stayed up late every night for the past month. It'll be nice to get some sleep for a change." Olim draped an arm over my shoulders, and I leaned into him with a laugh. Olim came from Ilano in the time of King Conall. In the aftermath of his regime's downfall, Olim became close to our family and Aunt Ula's personal guard. He'd been a protective presence our entire lives, watching out for our safety like a big brother. When Lilias came of age, Olim's wife, Duveesa, was elevated from nursemaid to lady's maid.

I tweaked Ru's nose, ignored his eye roll, and peered into the eagle pen. Six juvenile eagles looked back, heads tilted curiously. The smoky gray plumage of chickhood was nearly eclipsed by the black feathers characteristic of the adults. Their beaks and feet were bright orange, a sign the birds would soon be considered fully grown.

Master Avi's eyes were alight with eagerness. "Are you ready, young man?"

Ru jumped off the door, crossed his arms, and thrust out his chin. "Uh huh."

Olim ruffled his son's hair, and the affronted teen slapped away his hand and smoothed back the tangled curls. Olim's lips trembled in a repressed smile. "Good luck, kid."

Biting back a smile of my own, I lifted my journal and sketched out the eagles. Master Avi slid open the door until it was just large enough for Ru to squeeze through, and the eagles chirruped and flapped their wings.

"They probably think they're getting fed," Olim said.

Ru hesitated, and I nudged him with my elbow. "Don't worry. They usually don't eat little boys."

Red flushed up the back of Ru's neck to his cheeks. "I'm not little," he muttered. He clenched his fists, took a breath, and walked into the pen.

Olim winked.

Master Avi closed the door, and we huddled against the window to watch. Ru's shoulders were hunched, and I could tell he was breathing hard. The birds scattered at the intrusion. Two flew to the opposite end of the enclosure and hid in the foliage. Another panicked, flying to the top of the pen and hanging from the ironwork. Master Avi's sharp intake of breath was the only sign of his distress.

"Easy, Ru." Olim's calm voice eased the tension in all of us. Master Avi released a deep sigh, and Ru's shoulders relaxed.

The boy took a tentative step forward, startling another eagle into retreat. The remaining pair stood their ground, their feathers ruffled. Slowly, Ru crouched, and bowed his head. Olim's breathing was even and controlled, but his fingers tightened on the window frame. My pencil flew across the page in my hurry to capture the scene. Master Avi rested his chin in his palm as if this happened every day. How could he be so calm? My stomach churned, and if something didn't happen soon I was going to vomit. Or worse.

Ru lifted a quivering hand. I stilled, drawing forgotten. He stretched toward the eagles, and their keen eyes locked on his small, naked hand. When the knights trained, they wore heavy leather gloves to protect themselves from the eagles' inch long talons. But during the bonding ceremony, a boy presents himself at his most vulnerable. I chewed at the skin along my thumbnail and waited. Olim held his breath, and Master Avi lifted his head.

The larger bird cried out and lunged for Ru. He threw his arms up to protect his face, but the smaller of the pair hooked its beak under its companion's wing, thwarting its attack. Affronted, the large eagle nipped at the other's chest, then flew away. Ru lowered his arms, and the lone eagle chirruped. Ru offered his arm, and the bird hopped forward. I'd never seen the thirteen-year-old hold so still.

"Come on." Ru leaned closer, arm outstretched. "I'll take care of you." The eagle wrapped one taloned foot, then the other, around the boy's skinny arm. It blinked up at him as if it wasn't quite sure how it ended up perched there.

The pencil snapped in my hand.

Olim squeezed my shoulder and shook Master Avi's hand. He beamed with fatherly pride, and I thought tears shimmered in his eyes, though he turned away before I could be sure. Ru's focus was solely for his eagle, and tradition would dictate they'd spend hours getting to know one another before the boy left the pen.

I gave Master Avi a parting nod and hurried back into the hatchery to check on the egg. The top of the shell gaped open, revealing the damp gray feathers of the chick. It rested in the material, panting from exertion. I ran a finger along the warm body. One day, this eaglet would choose a Praedan as its sworn companion. What adventures would they have? Would they see war? Spill blood?

I made a few notes in my journal and hoped to make it back to the castle in time for breakfast.

CHAPTER 3

We were stretched out on Lilias' vast bed while she was painstakingly dressed and powdered in anticipation of the arrival of her betrothed and his family. Kyra and I had long since been dressed and styled, but Lilias required several hours of preparation before she was deemed ready to be presented to her future husband, a fact I found slightly irritating. If he truly loved her, she should be able to face him in rags without fear of him withdrawing his proposal.

To pass the time, Kyra read aloud from her latest story.

"Brax awoke from a muddled sleep unaware of his surroundings. He was certain he fell asleep in his tiny dwelling in the woods where friends told him it was foolish to settle. Brax feared neither man nor beast, his yearning for solitude stronger than his sense of mortality. But when the sun's sparkling light warmed his face to coax him from his slumber and his vision finally cleared from the haze of sleep, Brax was afraid. All around, the ground was covered with lush, emerald green grass, dotted with crystal streams and flowers of every brilliant color imaginable. In the distance, purple mountains rose into the unnaturally blue sky that bore not a single cloud. The delicate chirping of birds prompted him to look around in search of another living soul. But the sounds seemed to come out of the very earth and trees, for he saw not a flutter of wings nor a rustle of branches. His mother warned him of such places, that they were meant to tempt mortal men into complacency so monsters could strike and drain them of their living essence. Brax scrambled to his feet and made to run, but where would he go? He spun in a circle, but he did not recognize a way out. Without taking another moment to think, Brax dashed blindly from the idyllic clearing into the trees, for the first time fearing for his sanity and his soul."

"I like it! Very well done, Kyra," I told my younger sister as she lowered the paper with her perfect penmanship scrawled across it. She was an excellent weaver of stories, and I told her several times she should collect them into a book, but she was too shy for such a venture.

Lilias wore a magnificent, crushed velvet burgundy gown with a square neckline and tight bodice billowing into a full skirt that opened to reveal a panel intricately embroidered with inlays of tiny pearls imported from Faqur. The sleeves hugged her upper arms before flaring into a wide cuff resembling a trumpet lined with fur. Her lady-in-waiting, Duveesa, styled her hair in an elaborate pattern of crisscrossing braids that would hold a silver circlet delicately woven with more pearls.

"You do have a vivid imagination, Kyra," Lilias said without moving a single muscle apart from those essential to speaking. "Will the monster be very frightening?"

"You'll see." Kyra tucked the pages into her portfolio. She wore a modestly cut light blue dress with long, bell-shaped sleeves trimmed with embroidered white feathers. Though her gown was simple whereas mine was comparatively elaborate, she was still far prettier, and I was willing to bet she could breathe easier without a tight corset.

"Will it resemble a marionette with ears like wings?" I asked.

Lilias shot me a dirty look, and Duveesa patiently turned her head back toward the mirror and fixed me with a warning glare of her own. Duveesa was our nurse before ascending to the role of lady-in-waiting, so she earned the right to scold me, even silently. It was wicked of me to poke fun at Lilias' fiancé, but I couldn't help teasing her. He *was* quite tall and lanky, and she couldn't deny he had ridiculously large ears.

Kyra ignored my comment and Lilias' restrained ire. "You'll find out in the next installment."

A loud growl issued from my stomach when Lilias at last deemed herself acceptable as a future bride. Kyra stifled a giggle and Lilias rolled her eyes and rose gracefully from her chair to inspect herself in the mirror.

"It's late and I'm starving," I said.

"Can't you think of anything besides your stomach, Sulwen?" Lilias turned her head to ensure not a hair was out of place. She smiled approval at Duveesa, and the three of us hastened out of the room before we were late to greet our visitors.

The rest of the family was gathered on the steps of the castle. Mother eyed us when we hurried to our places, but she didn't remark on our tardiness. A few moments later, a grand carriage rounded the corner followed by a modest equipage. A groom stepped forward, and Lilias took a deep breath as the door to the larger carriage opened. A gentleman climbed out and extended a hand to accept the delicate gloved fingers of Lady Wyrwyk. The Lord and Lady of Thistledon moved aside, and a young man emerged from the carriage and stretched his long legs as if he'd been folded up like a fan. The three ascended the steps and bowed to my parents. Behind them, another trio I didn't recognize alighted from the smaller carriage and joined us on the steps to await their turn in paying their respects. I studied them as they talked amongst themselves, noting the man was significantly older than the lady, who was probably near Mother's age. She was a wisp of a woman with pale skin and black hair hinted with gray, and her eyes remained downcast when she spoke. The man, whom I assumed was her husband, was thickly built with silver, thinning hair and a dark gray beard. A shiver ran down my spine, and my eyes drifted to the young man lingering behind.

I'd never seen him before, but he glared at me as if I'd wronged him terribly. I narrowed my eyes and glared right back, and we became locked in a stand-off I couldn't account for. He was tall beside his diminutive mother, with brown, wavy hair and dull blue eyes. His features were angular, his cheekbones high, and if he weren't looking at me as if he could murder me with his eyes, I might be persuaded to call him handsome.

"Sir Chester," Mother said, a strange tightness to her tone, "And dear Noraa. I am glad to see you so well."

"Your Majesties," Sir Chester said. The pair bowed.

"And this must be..." Mother swallowed and continued, "Your son?" Her voice came out barely above a whisper, and I glanced down to see Father briefly squeeze her hand.

"Yes. This is Ailbert." Lady Chester's voice was high and timorous. She waved the young man forward, and he tore his gaze from me to bow at my parents.

"An honor, Your Majesties," Ailbert said, his tone lacking conviction.

"You're all welcome," Father said with equal flatness. "Come." He extended his arm to Mother, and they led the large party into the castle.

"Do you know that man?" I whispered to Lilias with a nod toward Ailbert Chester.

"We've met once or twice. He's Andrew's cousin."

"I don't like him."

She started grinning but quickly composed herself. "You don't even know him."

"I know I don't like the look in his beady eyes. He hates being here and I feel like he hates *us*."

"Kyra isn't the only one with a vivid imagination." Lilias raised her chin and followed everyone into the Great Hall.

I looked over at the head table with a mixture of longing and resentment. The third course had just been served, and I wasn't sure I was going to make it through dinner without screaming. Mother was pleasantly engaged with Lady Wyrwyk and Lady Chester to her left while on her right Father listened politely to Lord Wyrwyk and Sir Chester expound on goodness knows what men of their age must talk about. Whatever it was, Father was bored, though he hid it well. I sighed, wishing we didn't have to perform to guests but resigned that this was our lot in life. At least their seating arrangements were reasonable. Alyx sat at the head of our table with Rian and Tyrnan on either side. Lilias sat to my left and Andrew Wyrwyk sat across from her. To his left sat Khyr followed by Kyra. Who did I have the misfortune of being stuck with on my right? Ailbert Chester. The fates really could be cruel.

I tried to be the good hostess and engage the taciturn Ailbert in conversation, but he either didn't answer my inquiries or offered monosyllabic mumblings, so I eventually gave up. Lilias was too absorbed in delicately eating tiny morsels of food while demurely gazing across the table through lowered lashes to bother talking to me, so I was out of luck passing the evening with her company. Essentially, I was stuck at a table between two people so self-absorbed I might as well have been by myself. Even Khyr, sitting across from me, was on his best behavior and refrained from making faces with me. I resorted to stabbing at my food and lamenting that no one knew how to have fun anymore.

"Could you please stop that racket before I go mad?"

The voice beside me barked so loudly everyone in the vicinity heard it and froze. I spun in open-mouthed shock toward Ailbert Chester. He glared at me as if I'd insulted his mother. A flush of color painted his cheeks and a muscle twitched at his jawline.

I blinked. "I beg your pardon?"

"That infernal tapping. It's annoying and frankly, rude."

My eyes darted around the table, and I noted everyone ignoring the outburst in nervous embarrassment. I sat up straighter, gripping my fork, and gritted my teeth. Before I could issue a biting retort, fingers dug painfully into my thigh. I looked at Lilias, and she shook her head slightly yet firmly in a plea for me to hold my tongue. My shoulders drooped in resignation, and I dropped my fork with a loud *clang* onto my plate.

"Fine," I muttered.

I clasped my hands in my lap and refused to speak to anyone for the rest of the meal. For me, that's an incredibly long time. Seven whole courses. Plus, dessert. At one point, Lilias even poked me in the ribs to make sure I was still alive.

There was a brief reprieve when dinner ended, and the ladies retired to the sitting room. At least, that's what I'd hoped it would be. The moment the ladies were sitting comfortably with their ice wines, the conversation focused on the upcoming wedding.

"How is the bridal gown coming along?" Lady Wyrwyk asked Lilias. "I understand it's quite lovely."

"It's nearly finished," Lilias said. "The dressmaker is doing a wonderful job."

"I certainly hope the weather cooperates." My sister's future mother-in-law glanced toward the window and took a long sip from her glass.

By the time the gentlemen joined us, my mind was a haze from the wine. Thankfully, no one seemed to notice. They were so absorbed in Lilias and Andrew's upcoming nuptials that I was effectively ignored. Until, that is, when Lilias rose to entertain us at the piano. I stepped out of her way and onto Ailbert Chester's toes.

"Ow! Watch it!" He hopped on one foot, a bit of an over exaggeration if you ask me.

"I'm sorry!" I said.

"Clumsy," he muttered darkly. "Some princess you are."

I socialized only for as long as propriety dictated before begging to be excused.

"If you insist," Mother said. "Don't forget we have an early start tomorrow."

"I won't." How could I forget? We were all parading through Praed so the people could celebrate the happy couple. After the wedding, the spectacle would be repeated in Ilano. It wasn't that I didn't enjoy mingling with the people. I dreaded the inevitable speculations on when *I* would marry.

A cool hand touched my arm, and I looked down into Lady Chester's wide eyes.

"Please, Your Highness," she said quietly. "Forgive my son his foul temper this evening. He's usually much more pleasant. It's just that he's had a trying few days."

"Indeed," Mother said coolly. "I hope everything is all right?"

"Yes, of course." Lady Chester smoothed a hand down her dress and twisted her fingers in the fabric. "It's nothing serious. I suppose every young man goes through certain crises of identity when finding his way in life."

"Why do men always feel the need to find themselves?" I wondered aloud before I could stop myself.

Mother looked at me sharply.

Lady Chester cocked her head in consideration. "I suppose it's because they can."

"Everyone goes through times like that," Mother said gently. "It can be stressful at that age."

"Yes." Lady Chester tipped her head back and drank the last of her ice wine.

Mother turned to me. "You may go to bed," she told me with a dismissive wave.

I took a few steps backward, unsure how to feel about the exchange. Mother began conversing with Lady Wyrwyk about adornments for the bride and appeared to be completely unphased. But as I was about to turn toward the door, movement caught my eye, and I looked in time to see Mother squeeze Lady Chester's hand. The lady returned the gesture ardently, her eyes shutting tightly as she held back tears. Just as quickly, she released Mother's hand and schooled her features as if nothing happened. It seemed there were many secrets to be discovered in Praed.

The door barely shut on Molli's retreating form when someone softly knocked. I threw a robe across my shoulders and called out for the person to enter. Tyrnan strolled in and flopped onto the bed, resting his head on his arms.

"Well…That was an interesting evening."

I flung myself next to him on the bed. "Anything exciting after I left?"

He shrugged. "Not much. A lot of talk about lace and courses and wedding nonsense."

"How dull." I sighed and fell back to lay my head in the crook of his shoulder.

"You certainly caused a stir with what's-his-name," Tyrnan said.

"Ailbert," I grumbled. "He's horrid."

"He is quite unpleasant. He wasn't very sociable when we left you ladies after dinner. Flatly refused to be charmed by any of us."

"Scandalous. He's obviously a monster."

"Even Alyx tried to pry him out of his shell without success."

"You must have been desperate to make friends if you made poor Alyx engage in pleasantries."

"It was less out of desperation and more out of extreme politeness. After all, he'll be Lilias' relation soon."

"And she has our pity for it."

After a moment's silence he said, "Sulwen, how are you handling all of this?"

"What do you mean?"

"It must be difficult having all our attention diverted from you."

I pinched his side, and he tugged on a strand of my hair. "I'm happy for Lilias." I nibbled the edge of my thumbnail. "It's just…"

"What?"

I sighed and gazed up at the ceiling. There weren't many secrets between me and Tyrnan. Regardless, I was reluctant to voice such a personal fear.

"Come on." He wrapped an arm across my shoulders and ruffled my hair. "I won't tell."

"I know." I pushed his hand off my head.

"Are you sad she's marrying a stork?"

I snorted and shook my head. "Lilias has always known she wanted to get married. But I don't. At least, that's not what I want my goal in life to be. I don't want everyone looking at me expectantly after she's married, as if all a princess is good for is marrying off advantageously to some lord or prince to secure alliances."

"I don't think that factored into Lilias' choice. But I understand what you mean. Trust me, Mother and Father won't force you into a marriage you don't want."

"I don't think so either, but there'll be pressure to do my duty to the crown."

"We all have a duty to the crown. But no one said yours was to make yourself miserable in an arranged marriage."

"If not that then what else? I'm a woman after all. You can go off and fight in wars or engage in trade or go on diplomatic missions. But me? I'm doomed to wear a corset all my life."

"Don't be so dramatic. I'm sure you can take it off at night." He tickled my side to demonstrate his point. I laughed heartily, then pointed out we were getting too old for such behavior.

He chuckled. "So you keep saying. You may as well settle down, old lady."

After Tyrnan left for his own bed, I lay awake staring at the ceiling contemplating my life. I wanted him to be right about Mother and Father being supportive no matter what path I chose. But my heart still ached, for I believed the reality of my situation was this: I was a princess, and therefore my choices were subject to the demands of the crown. We'd always been held to higher standards as princes and princesses, so I wouldn't deceive myself into thinking I could do as I pleased. Marriage was my fate, but I didn't want to resign myself to it just yet. There was so much I wanted to see and do before shackling myself to a house and husband, and I was running out of time.

CHAPTER 4

The chatter around the dinner table became as tedious as our days the closer Lilias' wedding drew. The entire castle was consumed with preparations, and I couldn't venture around the corridors or outside without running into someone scurrying to the dressmakers with fabrics and lace, delivering ingredients to the kitchens, or organizing the decorations. There hadn't been a wedding at Praed Castle for years, and everyone was understandably excited. I avoided the hurrying servants as much as possible to keep from accidentally running into them and ruining their hard work. Once, I wasn't quick enough to dodge a seamstress carrying several bolts of fabric, and I caught the edge of her burden on my arm and sent the whole load tumbling to the ground. She was mortified, and I hastily apologized and helped her retrieve the mess scattered over the floor, assuring her nothing appeared torn or overly dirty. The poor girl didn't seem very relieved as she hurried away mumbling about the wrath of the dressmaker. Afterward, I spent much of my time in my room, in the stables, or at the mews.

Tonight, we were all gathered for a cozy family dinner. In general, I preferred these far above the boisterous affairs in the Great Hall because we didn't have to put on a show for guests. Admittedly, it was mostly my own comfort I was concerned with. The delicate dance Lilias perfected as she ate was a masterpiece compared to my clumsy attempts at being ladylike, and my spine throbbed with the effort to maintain a perfect posture. And don't even get me started on the restriction on topics of conversation. I felt more relaxed with my family without prying eyes judging our every move and felt at ease laughing and teasing my siblings. Though I don't think she'd ever admit it, I believe even Lilias appreciated the break from discussing wedding plans.

While we ate, Kyra shared the latest installment in her tale.

"After hours of wandering through dense forests, Brax finally collapsed in an exhausted heap and admitted he was lost. He hadn't seen another soul, whether animal, man, or monster, and every tree looked the same. He looked up at the sky, his breaths coming in harsh gasps, but he could not see the sun through the thick, green foliage. He had no way of tracking his progress nor directing his trek with the movement of stars or the predictable path of the setting sun. What's worse, he had grown terribly thirsty and hungry, but had not found even a single berry or trickling stream to satiate him. Well, he thought to himself, it would be better to die trying to escape than to sit here and starve. He wiped an arm across his brow and licked his dry lips, then stood and froze, one foot poised to leave. There, standing mere feet away in the shade of the trees, was a vision of a woman. She hadn't made a sound, neither when she came upon him nor now. His eyes traced her ethereal form, lingering first on her golden curls, followed by her flawless skin and glowing blue eyes. She was wrapped in a white gown as light as gossamer, and her feet were small and bare. Wordlessly, she extended a white, long fingered hand, and Brax took it as if he had no will of his own. Her skin was soft and cool to the touch, and as he drew closer, he breathed in the scent of warm breezes and fresh rain. He had been warned about monsters and beasts, but no one prepared him for meeting a goddess."

Kyra lowered the page she read from and anxiously looked up for our response.

"Very intriguing," Mother said. "I can't wait to find out what happens next."

Rian flashed a mischievous grin. "If I could make a suggestion, I would like a little more detail when you describe this goddess."

The boys chuckled. Kyra and I rolled our eyes.

"You're indecent," Lilias scolded. "I think she was well described with enough detail to make her alluring and leave a little to the imagination. If one has one that is."

"You have to have a brain to have an imagination." I aimed a pointed look at Rian.

Rian covered his heart in mock indignation. "I have a brain!"

"Correction," Khyr said. "You have to have a brain with room after filling it with women and weapons."

Half the table erupted into laughter, including Rian. He had a good sense of humor, despite his lack of imagination.

"Enough," Father said. His tone was flat, almost bored, demonstrating how often he'd had to rein in our antics.

The laughter faded, but the mirth remained as we resumed eating. I glanced across the table and tried to catch Tyrnan's eye, but he avoided my gaze and had been uncharacteristically withdrawn throughout the meal.

I leaned toward him and whispered, "Is something wrong?"

"What?" Startled out of his reverie, he spoke in a much louder tone than necessary. A few faces turned in our direction, and Tyrnan looked to each one with flushed cheeks.

"You're acting strangely," I said. "Are you ill?"

He gave a definitive shake of his head. "No." He lowered his fork and gazed around the table. "Actually, I do have an announcement I'd like to make. I'd hoped to wait until after Lilias' wedding, but I find I'm unable to."

Each of us wore a mixture of emotions ranging from patience to worry to confusion. Mother's brow furrowed uneasily, and Father retained his stoicism, though I could tell he was unsettled by the tight grip on his fork.

Tyrnan drew in a shuddering breath, and my heart thudded with fear. He looked less afraid and more nervous as he met each of our inquisitive faces.

"A few months ago," he said. "I applied for a position with an expedition to map the unexplored islands west of Faqur. Yesterday, I received a reply. My application has been accepted."

A tense hush fell over the room. I held my breath as he continued.

"My ship sails from Faqur a month after Lilias' wedding."

Mother narrowed her eyes. "And you didn't think to tell us about this until now?"

"I didn't want to detract from Lilias," he said.

"You didn't want us to forbid you from leaving," Mother said. "This was done in a very underhanded fashion, Tyrnan."

My brother turned red, and my empathy for him nearly eclipsed my heartbreak at the thought of his leaving.

"I thought you might be excited for me," Tyrnan said, his voice small. "It's always been my dream to embark on such a voyage."

"What's the name of the ship?" Father asked.

"*The Wayward Aymelina*," Tyrnan answered, his eyes wide with hope. "Her captain is very experienced and has engaged in many successful campaigns. And the route is considered quite safe."

"How long would you be gone?"

"You're not actually sanctioning this?" Mother exclaimed.

As one, my brothers and sisters and I lowered our eyes to the table.

"The alternative is to keep him here and not only disappoint him but tarnish his reputation," Father said. "To retract his application from such an expedition wouldn't reflect favorably on either him or us."

"He's never sailed. It could be dangerous."

"A ship of this nature will have a very experienced crew. He won't be expected to pilot it himself."

I bit the inside of my lip to keep from giggling.

"But," Mother whispered, her voice thick with sadness. "What if the worst should happen?"

"I'm not going to war, Mother," Tyrnan said, his eyes matching the gentle tone of his voice. "It's a voyage of discovery. I could be touching lands no other human has ever seen!"

Mother swallowed and looked toward Father, her eyes imploring.

"We can't hold on to them forever," Father said.

Mother looked away and wiped a hand across her face.

"A toast." Alyx raised a glass. "To Tyrnan and Lilias and their grand adventures."

"To Tyrnan and Lilias," our voices echoed in unison.

As I brought my glass to my lips, I peered at Mother. She hadn't joined in the sentiment and stared blankly at her plate. I glanced at Father. He was watching her, his expression both tender and sorrowful. After several minutes, Mother collected herself enough to go through the motions of eating, but I could tell her thoughts were miles away. She excused herself early, unable to meet anyone's sympathetic faces. Tyrnan watched her leave, chewing at his lower lip and drumming his fingers on the table.

"Don't stress yourself over Mother," Father said. "She knows how important this journey is to you. She will overcome her fear for your safety and will soon be joining in your excitement for this opportunity. Give her time."

"Yes, Father," Tyrnan said. He didn't seem fully convinced Mother wouldn't hold this against him for the rest of her life.

Father rose to follow her, and the rest of us were left to cast furtive glances at Tyrnan, unsure of how to feel about everything that transpired.

Alyx broke the silence. "Father's right. Mother can't expect us to stay home forever. We're not children anymore."

"Exactly," Lilias added. "I'm sure she was just as distressed when she had to let me go, as she will be when Sulwen and Kyra marry."

I held my tongue to keep from ruining my sister's conciliatory efforts.

"You're not leaving Praed," Tyrnan muttered.

"Any of us might leave Praed someday," Alyx said, slamming a fist on the table. "That doesn't mean we won't return. I'm certain when Mother realizes that she'll feel much better."

Tyrnan's shoulders relaxed slightly, and the others started bombarding him with questions about his upcoming journey. I heard none of them. My appetite now gone, I pushed food around with my fork. Not only was I about to lose my sister, but my brother would be leaving as well. Unlike the feelings of deprivation of a beloved sister's company and the general disruption of a changing household, the emotions stirring within me at the news of Tyrnan's departure were much more complex. Next to depression and anxiety was the unmistakable flicker of jealousy. Actually, it was less a flicker and more a roaring flame. I was envious of Tyrnan's freedom to pursue his dreams of adventure and Father's approval of this scheme. If I were to approach Father with such a plan, I was certain to receive a less favorable response, and it was all because I was the wrong gender. It wasn't fair, and the injustice of the situation made me sick to my stomach.

After the meal ended, instead of joining my sisters in the drawing room, I slipped away to be alone. This wasn't an easy task living in a bustling castle surrounded by people who felt it their duty to be at your beck and call. I waved away any servant who asked if they might be of assistance and tried not to be rude when the kitchen staff tripped over themselves as I tried to sneak out the back.

Once I was outside, I took a moment to breathe deeply the night air that still carried the warmth of the day. I gritted my teeth, gathered the hem of my dress, and ran down the slope at the back of the castle. A few people glanced at me as I raced by, but I didn't care what they thought of the wild princess and her reckless careening down the mountain. I ran past the long rows of mews housing the falcons, past the training yard and outdoor perches, and skidded to a stop amid the large eagle pens. I strode purposefully around the buildings until I arrived at one particular mew. Just as I suspected, Tyrnan was there tending to his eagle, a gentle male named Voltor. I dispensed with pleasantries, stalked up to Tyrnan, and stood before him with my arms crossed.

Tyrnan sighed wearily. "Don't look at me like that. It's been a tough night as it is without you picking a fight with me."

"I can't believe you didn't tell me," I said, unable to keep the pain from creeping into my voice.

"I didn't know if my application would be accepted."

"No, you just didn't want me to talk you out of it. Mother was right. You've been very sneaky."

"That's not true!" Voltor flapped and shifted uneasily. Tyrnan soothed a hand down the bird's back and narrowed his eyes at me. "With everything going on right now, I didn't want to add stress if I wasn't leaving anyway. And I genuinely wanted to wait so Lilias wouldn't feel any attention was being taken away from her."

Though a contradiction stuck in my throat, I resisted voicing it. Tyrnan was indeed a considerate brother, so I didn't doubt his sincerity. I lowered my arms, and his features softened.

"I'm sorry I didn't tell you sooner," he said. "I knew it would upset you, and I guess I wanted to delay that as long as possible. Forgive me?"

"How long will you be gone?"

"I can't say for sure. A year maybe?"

I gasped. "A year? That's a long time, Tyr."

"Like Alyx said, we'll all leave home eventually. That doesn't mean we won't come back. *You* may go off on your own someday."

"Unlikely."

"You need to stop feeling sorry for yourself for being born a girl," Tyrnan said, grasping my shoulder with his free hand. "Mother and Father have never treated you any differently because of your gender. Even if you are a delicate flower."

I punched him lightly so I wouldn't upset Voltor. I chuckled, lightening the mood.

"They may not restrict my activities within the boundaries of this castle," I said. "But they're still bound by societal rules outside of it. I can't just go gallivanting around the continent or sail off to undiscovered islands like my brothers can." My mouth snapped shut, and a niggling thought began to weave its way through my brain, searching for a place to take hold. It was disjointed and unclear, but it tickled my mind and begged to be revealed.

"I'm sorry." He placed Voltor in his mew. He draped an arm around my shoulders, and we walked back to the castle.

"What will you be doing on this voyage?" I asked.

"Charting the islands west of Faqur. Very little exploration has been done in that area, and it is believed there could be valuable land and resources waiting to be discovered."

"And probably pillaged."

Tyrnan ignored my sarcasm and continued. "We could find new allies."

I could hear the excitement in his voice and see the glimmer in his eye. He was passionate about sailing, and this was the realization of all his diligent study. Amid the feelings of envy and loss, I began to feel genuinely happy for him. I didn't begrudge him the experiences of life, and I shouldn't pout and make him feel sorry for me. I took a deep breath and listened to the details of his post, the number of crew members, the history of the ship, and the names of his superiors.

"Captain Romy is reputed to be excellent. He's captained several voyages, and this is the most extensive yet. He's said to have never lost a man to the sea and can read the waves." He made a grand, sweeping gesture I ducked to avoid.

I laughed. "That sounds ridiculous."

"It's a great honor to serve him on my maiden voyage," Tyrnan said with a swell of his chest.

"He obviously has excellent judgment if nothing else." I smiled and leaned in to hug him. "He's lucky to have you, Tyrnan. I'll endeavor to be happy for you amid my jealousy."

Despite the exhaustion of the evening, I was restless and unable to sleep. My stomach churned, and I twisted and shifted in bed trying to find a comfortable position. My eyelids were heavy, but they wouldn't stay shut. I tried reading, but the book lay against my chest, having only read a few words before my mind wandered too much for me to focus. Something about the conversation surrounding Tyrnan's departure stuck in my thoughts, like a seed planted in fertile earth. If I nourished it, what might grow? I closed my eyes and picked through the tumultuous thoughts flitting through my brain, trying to find the one causing so much distress. But I came up with nothing, no matter how hard I searched. Then, I opened my eyes and stared into the darkness, remembering something Mother used to say when I became frustrated as a young girl unable to articulate herself.

"If you want to know the answer to a difficult question, ask yourself out loud, and what comes immediately afterwards is the truth."

"Am I truly happy for Tyrnan?" I wondered aloud.

Yes, came the answer in my mind.

"Then why can't I sleep?"

Because I want to go, too. My breath hitched in my throat at such an obvious answer.

"But I can't, so why bother stressing about it?"

Can't you?

My brow furrowed. There was no way to accompany Tyrnan to Faqur...was there? Before I could ask another question, sleep overtook me at last, my mind apparently settled enough to give itself over to rest. Perhaps in the morning, everything would be made clear.

CHAPTER 5

Messengers from Faqur arrived to deliver Tyrnan's sailing orders. At Father's insistence they remained to alleviate Mother's distress by describing in detail the particulars of Tyrnan's assignment. Namely, that it involved little to no fighting and that the seas were generally calm this time of year, reducing the chances of a storm blowing him off course. Tyrnan could not have been more embarrassed, but the messengers answered Mother's questions graciously and patiently. I suspected she was not the first mother to interrogate them out of fear for her son.

Lilias' wedding was only two weeks away, and we'd met every relation her fiancé possessed. I couldn't remember half their names, but they were kind and appeared genuinely excited to have Lilias become a member of their family. Ailbert Chester made a few additional appearances, but I ignored him, which seemed to please both of us. Between introductions to people I probably wouldn't see after the wedding, we were squeezed and laced into gowns and matched adornments. Even the boys were measured and fitted with new doublets, and I teased that they finally understood what it felt like to be treated like a doll.

I shielded my eyes from the sun's glare and flashes of steel as I watched Alyx and Rian spar in the courtyard. It had been days since we had the opportunity to break away from the responsibilities of castle life to indulge in more pleasant pursuits, and we happily leapt at the opportunity. We'd been confined indoors for too long entertaining guests and meeting with dignitaries.

Alyx and Rian were well matched sword fighters, but Alyx had patience where Rian was impulsive. When Rian feinted to the left, he thrust his sword toward Alyx's right without ensuring his brother reacted as predicted. The move was anticipated, and Alyx easily deflected with a powerful blow, throwing Rian off balance.

"I could have seen that attack from a mile away!" I goaded Rian.

Unlike myself, my brother was not so easily distracted, and he recovered quickly to finish the match with a strong showing.

Rian sauntered up to Tyrnan and me. Sweat dripped down the side of his face and he breathed heavily from the exertion. "Your turn." He grinned widely as Tyrnan shifted and drew out his sword. I pulled a cap over my head, tucking loose strands of hair underneath to keep them out of my eyes, and stood to follow my brother into the practice ring.

"Go easy on him," Rian whispered as I unsheathed my weapon.

I smiled and strode forward, raising my sword respectfully. Tyrnan answered my salute, and the match was on.

Though Tyrnan didn't revel in swordsmanship the way Alyx, Rian, and I did, he was no slouch, and he didn't go easy on me. I could tell by the force of his attacks and the way he gritted his teeth with each deflection that he had plenty of pent-up energy to expel. I had a few emotions to take out in the practice ring too, and I clutched my sword in both hands to bring it down again and again against my brother's, telling myself it wasn't merely him I was angry at. For what felt like hours, we spun around each other trying to gain the upper hand, and I was so focused Alyx and Rian's shouts were muffled in my ears. I swiped my sword across Tyrnan's middle, and when he dodged backward, I kept the pressure on by swinging towards his right. He stumbled slightly, and I surged forward, knocking him square in the chest. He shuffled backward, raising his sword to counter, but I was faster. I drove a knee hard into his stomach, and when he doubled over, I knocked the sword out of his hand. Alyx and Rian clapped and cheered as I knelt before Tyrnan gasping in the dirt.

"Yield?" I asked.

He looked up, panting, his face red and damp with sweat. He nodded with a crooked grin, and I helped him to his feet.

"Stop being so hard on your sister," a voice said from behind me.

Tyrnan and I both turned, and Khyr stopped short when he saw our faces.

"Oh, sorry, Sulwen. From behind, I thought you were Tyrnan." He looked over at our brother. "Not that you look like a woman, Tyr. Just didn't see you down on the ground, and she looked so much like you in those trousers—especially with her hair covered."

Tyrnan struggled to find his voice. "No offense taken."

Khyr and Tyrnan walked toward my other brothers, leaving me alone, my mouth opened in stunned silence. Khyr thought I was Tyrnan. I looked down at my garb. I always dressed in a shirt and breeches when I practiced for ease of movement. And it had fooled my own brother into thinking I was someone else. Not just anyone. A boy. A dangerous idea formed in my mind, a thought like a piece of fruit that had been out of reach I could at long last grasp.

I polished my sword in silence while my brothers conversed, and even when they asked for my input, I answered only vaguely. A plan was developing in my mind, a scheme to get out of Praed and live a little before I resigned to my fate of becoming a wife to some overstuffed lord. If I was discovered, the punishment could be grave, but I was willing to risk it for a chance at freedom.

My family gathered on the steps of Praed Castle for the final anticipated guests. I bounced on the balls of my feet in excitement when a carriage appeared at the top of the mountain, and I waved as it drew close enough to be able to see the faces of its occupants. My joy was second only to Mother's, and she cried out as the carriage stopped and hurried down the steps with her arms wide as a couple emerged. My poor Uncle Finton was practically shoved aside so Mother could gather her sister, my Aunt Ula, into a fierce hug. I flew down the stairs behind her as my cousin, Merrin, alighted from the carriage behind them. Her hazel eyes sparkled in the sunshine when she saw me, and our embrace was matched only by our mothers'. My siblings and Father descended behind us, and I pulled away from the cousin I loved as a sister in time to see her younger brothers jump out of the carriage. The two boys idolized their older cousins, especially Alyx, and their eyes glowed in awe at their approach.

"You've grown taller since we saw you last. And is that a trace of beard I see on your face?" Rian asked as he squinted at fourteen-year-old Cale's face. The young man flushed with pride and soaked up the praise as his younger brother, twelve-year-old Kormac, hid a smile behind his hand and mumbled that it was probably dirt.

Aunt Ula stood next to Mother. "This is so wonderful!" she said. "I can't believe Lilias is getting married. It seems like only yesterday she was toddling around with flower wreaths in her hair."

Mother laughed. "It makes me feel old just thinking about it. If you mention grandchildren, I'm making you get back in that carriage."

Aunt Ula shook her head indulgently while Father approached and nodded in acknowledgment.

"Risteard," Aunt Ula said, smiling warmly up at my father. "It's so good to see you."

"And you." Father gave Ula's forearm a quick, affection squeeze, then extended his hand to shake Uncle Finton's, a courtesy he only afforded his brother-in-law.

Father held out his elbow to Mother. "Come."

We followed him up the stairs. Merrin and I linked elbows and whispered with our heads together as we entered the castle amid the bustle of boisterous young men.

"It's bad enough when there's four of them," Kyra said from beside me. "How are we going to handle six?" She indicated her brothers and cousins.

"At least you have sisters," Merrin said.

Our combined families settled into a private sitting room while we waited for dinner to be announced. Mother, Aunt Ula, and Lilias sat on a sofa to discuss the upcoming wedding while Father conversed with Uncle Finton. Well, Father listened while my uncle did most of the talking. That didn't seem to bother either of them, for my uncle always had a lot of interesting things to say, and Father didn't find him boring. Rian and Khyr gossiped with Cale about the girls to in Hrgun while Kormac basked in the eldest prince's glory. Alyx completely ignored his young cousin while he read intently from a massive tome, his brow furrowed in concentration. His pose was closely matched by Kyra, who sat to my right reading from her own book while Merrin and I chatted animatedly.

"Tell me about the class you're taking," I said. "It sounds fascinating!"

Merrin lived in Hrgun, the intellectual center of the continent. It contained the most prestigious institutions for higher learning, including languages, which Merrin had an affinity for. She studied under a prominent professor who wrote the definitive translation of the Torshul language, and it was rumored he was undertaking a new and exciting project.

"It is! We've been learning about the Kuste and how they speak with their hands and drawings. Professor Ritter has been very secretive, but we think he's planning on organizing a team to visit Kuste to study with them in person. It will take a lot of persuasion on his part because the Kuste are quite protective of their language, but wouldn't it be amazing to be the first to learn it firsthand? He'll hold a competition to see which students will accompany him, and I hope he'll choose me."

"He'd be a fool not to," I said. "You're more brilliant than any of those dimwits."

"Sulwen…" Merrin smiled, her cheeks rosy. "You shouldn't say such things. You don't even know the other students."

"I know you, and that's enough for me. You're the smartest person I've ever known."

Her blush deepened and she brushed back a stray lock of her ebony hair.

A page entered the room, and my stomach growled in anticipation. But instead of announcing dinner, he declared a visitor arrived and bid entry.

Father's jaw clenched and his eyes hardened. "Who?" He didn't like the interruption to our family reunion.

The page bowed. "Lady Audrey, Your Majesty,"

Mother shot Father a look just as he was about to roll his eyes. He checked himself and motioned dismissively, indicating the page should see the lady in.

My grandmother swept elegantly into the room. The gentleman rose to their feet. She dropped a low curtsy, a feat indeed for a woman of her age, then rose to sweep the room with her sharp gaze. Fenella Audrey was the formidable Lady of Riverstone, the birthplace of Mother and Aunt Ula. Her features were stunning, with high cheekbones, ivory skin with the barest of wrinkles, straight nose, and shining black hair streaked with white. She floated when she walked in, a mannerism only Lilias could emulate, with an arrogance earned through the high status of having a queen for a daughter. Mother told me she wasn't easy to grow up with, but the years softened her enough to become a warm, kindly grandmother. She smiled at each of us as she moved into the room, accepting a seat closest to the fire.

"Are you warm enough, Grandmother?" Alyx asked.

"I'm quite well, dear," Grandmother said. She took his hand and gazed adoringly at her first born and, therefore, most perfect grandchild.

"Your visit is unexpected," Mother said tersely, though she tried to hide her irritation with a lilt that oddly distorted her voice.

"Is it?" Grandmother arched an eyebrow. "I wonder that any visit from me could be unexpected. You are my daughter as well as my queen."

"You're here for Ula, aren't you?" Mother asked, though her quirked mouth suggested she wasn't insulted but rather amused.

"I heard your sister would be joining us today." Grandmother's gaze swept toward Aunt Ula. "You're looking well, my dear," she said to my aunt.

"As are you, Mother," my aunt said.

I was already growing bored with this tired exchange, the restrained politeness suddenly gripping my family. Merrin shifted and cleared her throat, unwittingly drawing attention to herself.

"Merrin is looking very well," Grandmother observed. Her eyes traveled down my cousin's still form, and a pleased smile graced her features. "She has developed a fine figure indeed. So thin and graceful." Merrin flushed in embarrassment and lowered her face.

"Lilias is thin, too," I broke in. "So are Kyra and I. Not a portly one among us." I met Grandmother's stoic gaze defiantly, and out of the corner of my eye, I saw Mother turn her head to conceal a smile.

"Indeed," Grandmother said dryly.

Thankfully, we were saved from the interminable conversation by the call to dinner, and by the way everyone dashed to their feet, it looked like I wasn't the only one relieved.

After dinner, we left the adults to themselves in favor of our own pursuits. Poor Lilias was accosted by Grandmother and forced to describe every intimate detail of her quickly approaching nuptials, and I felt a slight pang of guilt for abandoning her. The six boys disappeared outside to enjoy the last rays of the summer day, and Kyra escaped to the library to finish her book. Though I normally would have joined the boys, tonight I had my cousin, and our time together was always filled with laughter and amusement. We lay side by side on my bed making ourselves hysterical with our observations about life, particularly the people in it.

"I thought I might die when Grandmother said to the whole room that I was looking 'thin' as if it didn't sound like I was ill!" Merrin exclaimed.

"A little illness is certainly good for the figure," I said, impersonating Grandmother. "Nothing like vomiting to make a trim waist."

"Stop." Merrin moaned and clapped a hand over her mouth.

"For the daughter of a surgeon, you have a remarkably weak stomach." Merrin's father studied medicine in Hrgun and graduated with the highest honors as a surgeon when I was a little girl. Now, he was a professor of great respectability whose teachings were highly sought after. I really expected more from my cousin with such a father. Who knows what the dinner conversation in that house was like every night?

"He's the surgeon, I'm the scholar," she said with an audible swallow.

"Then I won't ask him to recollect his most disgusting cases when you're around."

She elbowed me lightly and shot me a rueful glare. "How's Marick?"

"How should I know?"

Marick was a nobleman's son who Merrin insisted had feelings for me. I don't know why. We rarely spoke except when his family was invited to royal affairs and parties, and even then, we barely shared a few pleasantries. Merrin said that's because he's shy, but I think it's because he's wholly uninteresting.

"I don't see why you should object to him so adamantly," Merrin said. "He's perfectly respectable."

"He is." It was true Marick didn't possess an angry bone in his body, and he was always polite and respectful. There was much to recommend him as a potential suitor, but that didn't alter my opinion on the matter. "A perfect gentleman. Perfectly poised, perfectly dressed, perfectly wealthy, and perfectly boring."

"Oh, Sulwen." Merrin sighed. "You're impossible."

"I don't wish to settle for an ordinary man." I'd never put much stock in appearance. Sure there were men I'd considered attractive, but though they'd all been tall, I didn't have a preferred hair or eye color. I didn't care about clothes. I desired a man who valued independence as much as I did. I couldn't stomach a suitor who hung on my every word and movement. If I could sit in a room with a man without feeling the need to fill it with idle conversation, I'd be happy. Of course, he'd also have to be eager for adventure, good with a sword, and able to hold his own in an argument. Finding a man with those qualities who also valued them in me had so far proved impossible.

"Well, I hope in wishing for the extraordinary you don't overlook someone who could truly make you happy."

"I'm sure Marick would make a good husband, but I'm not interested in marriage at present, and I don't think he's one who would wait around until I am."

"Perhaps not. But Sulwen, what is it *you're* waiting for?"

I didn't answer right away, allowing the silence to stretch between us while I debated whether to confide my plan to Merrin. She would argue against it and point out all the reasons why it was a terrible mistake, but the secret pressed at my heart, bursting to be said aloud. In a way, telling her would hold me accountable to myself and keep me from losing my nerve. I pulled a lungful of air through my nose and let it out slowly, my hands shaking in excitement. Merrin noticed and covered them with her own, her hazel eyes darkening with concern as she sat up to investigate my face.

"What's wrong?"

"Nothing…not really." I sucked in my lower lip and wrung my hands. "Can you keep a secret?"

"Yes…"

"Promise," I said firmly and sat up. "You cannot tell a soul what I'm about to tell you. Not my mother, not yours, no one."

"Are you in danger, Sulwen?"

"Promise!"

Merrin chewed at her bottom lip as she regarded me, her brow furrowed with worry. I set my jaw and narrowed my eyes, waiting for her to decide.

"All right," she said, her shoulders sagging in defeat. Her curiosity won out over her resistance. "I promise."

"You know Tyrnan will be leaving us after the wedding to join an expedition sailing out of Faqur?"

"Yes. Mother had a letter from the queen, and we were very excited for him."

"I'm going with him."

She cocked her head to the side in confusion. "What? Er…you are?"

"I'm going to join Tyrnan on *The Wayward Aymelina* and sail to unknown islands to discover their secrets. It will be the adventure I've been longing for!"

"But *how?* You're a woman."

"I know that…But *they* won't." I unfolded the plan for Merrin, and she listened with increasing astonishment, her mouth hanging open and her eyes wide. When I finished, she shook her head silently.

"You can't," she whispered. "They'll find out and throw you in prison. Or worse! Sulwen, what if they…" Her voice trailed off and she looked around the room as if someone could hear us. She leaned forward and spoke in a low voice. "What if they defile your virtue?"

"They won't find out."

"You think you're so clever?"

"I am."

Merrin shook her head and sighed in exasperation. "Sulwen, stop this nonsense. It's impossible. Even if you were to sneak out of Praed, the king and queen would go after you the minute they discovered you were missing."

"I thought of that. I'm going to leave a note saying I'm confining myself to my room for solitude. That will give me at least several hours. If I refuse to come down to dinner, that could give me at least a day."

"What about Molli? She'll come to your room to prepare you for bed."

"I'll say in my note that I don't require her services. I will insist on being completely alone."

"A day isn't very long. Especially if they travel faster than you to catch up."

"They won't know I've left with Tyrnan. I'm going to set Nettle loose before I leave so they'll think I've gone off on my own." Nettle was my very flighty chestnut mare who would have no qualms about escaping the stables and avoiding capture. I hated to risk losing her along with my saddle, but I was willing to if it meant throwing my parents off my trail.

"This is madness. It's one thing to talk about risking your life for an adventure and quite another to do it. Even if you make it to Faqur and on board the ship without anyone realizing you're a woman, you know nothing about sailing."

"Tyrnan will teach me. And I'm willing to bet I'm better at a sword than most men."

"Is there anything I can say to talk you out of this?" She feared for my safety, but it wasn't enough to sway me.

"No. I have to do this, Merrin. Before I'm shackled to a house and husband."

She smiled wryly and said, "I don't think marriage is as bad as that. A good marriage anyway. Look at how happy our parents are. And Lilias seems perfectly content."

"I want more than that."

"You always have," she said softly. The fight in her was waning, and I grasped her hand reassuringly.

"Just think. After I do this, you'll never hear me complain again. I'll be resigned to my fate and live the perfect life of a princess."

"I just want you to be happy. If nothing else, I hope you'll learn how perfect your life is *now*."

I resisted the urge to roll my eyes and instead embraced her to hide my annoyance. While I appreciated the sweetness of the sentiment, Merrin couldn't possibly understand my situation. One might think the life of a princess is ideal, but it was sorely lacking in freedom. Yes, it was a life of privilege and comfort, but it was a life bound by custom and lived under the gaze of those who would judge an entire country on the appearance and behavior of the royal family. Though I was granted certain allowances, such as being taught how to wield a sword, there were limits to my ambitions. Where Merrin was permitted to study in Hrgun and journey to distant lands to further her knowledge, I was stuck in Praed, doomed to serve the crown and marry either a Praed or Ilano nobleman. Or I would be used as a pawn in the negotiation of a treaty and married to a foreign prince or dignitary. In that case, I would at least get to see new countries, but at the cost of marrying a stranger with different customs from ours. With my luck, I would unwittingly make some horrible mistake, embarrass my husband and his people, be sent back to Praed, flogged, or worse—executed. Merrin could marry whomever she chose without such considerations, and I envied her that freedom. This was my one chance to satiate my hunger for a worthwhile experience, an experience that would have to sustain me for the rest of my life.

CHAPTER 6

Banners rippled in the cool summer breeze and the air was filled with the perfume of flowers covering the inner courtyard of Praed Castle. Practice targets and weapon racks were removed to make way for seating the multitude of guests gathered to witness the marriage of a princess. Their faces were warmed by the afternoon sunshine, their finery glittering in blinding splendor. The entirety of Praed seemed to be there, from the wealthiest noble to the lowliest stable hand, crammed together to celebrate the first royal wedding in twenty years.

Lilias was magnificent in a corseted ivory gown beaded with precious pearls and thick golden threads along the neckline, curved waist, and bordering the edges of her sleeves where they plumed out like bells. The inside of the cuffs and gown opened to reveal an inner lining embroidered with blooming flowers in shimmering threads of gold. More pearls were woven into the braided strands of her hair, and at her neck was the Elejick family crest set in gold surrounded with tiny seed pearls. The most stunning aspect of her person was the brilliant smile she wore as she waited for Mother to lead her out of the eaves of the castle into the light. Her fiancé shifted nervously standing beside my father under an arbor covered with wildflowers. Father stood proudly in his characteristic black doublet embroidered with his coat of arms and highlighted with a sash of blue. Rays of sunshine danced over his crown, sending beams of light skittering across the earth. My brothers stood beside their future brother-in-law, all of them handsome and well-polished in their new finery. Kyra and I were tasked with following behind the bride to keep her train from touching the ground. A bead of sweat trickled down my back, and I shifted uncomfortably in my own tightly fitting gown. It was too hot for so many layers, and my cheeks were already flushed. If the ceremony didn't commence soon, I worried I'd faint.

Mother finally decided the last guest was seated and she was ready to lead her first-born daughter down a carpet of flowers to be presented to her soon to be son-in-law. Lilias walked with floating steps past the awed gazes of the crowd. Kyra and I moved with her on opposite sides of the long train, and I silently counted steps and carefully placed my feet so I wouldn't trip. Mother placed Lilias' hands into Andrew's after saying something about honoring a princess of Praed or some such. I honestly wasn't paying attention. Father began to speak, and though I tried to listen, the deep timbre of his voice lulled me as it used to when he read me to sleep at night. I swayed slightly, exhausted from the last few days of preparations and the early start that morning. An elbow dug into my side, and my eyes flew open to see the peevish glare of Kyra.

"Try to stay awake," she whispered.

"Sorry," I mumbled. I managed to keep my eyes open, but I couldn't recount a word of the ceremony. Father finally declared the couple husband and wife and the pair sealed their vows with a chaste kiss amid cheers and clapping. Kyra beamed with pleasure and Mother wiped her eyes with a handkerchief provided by Aunt Ula.

Kyra and I resumed our places behind Lilias as she and Andrew left the courtyard and led the guests into the Great Hall for the reception. I was starving, but I feared my dress was so tight I wouldn't be able to fit a morsel of food in my stomach. Lilias and Andrew took their places at the head table while the musicians prepared to play. The king and queen sat to one side and the Wyrwyks on the other. My mouth watered when steaming dishes of poached fish from the Rhyvor were served alongside roasted stag, a variety of cheeses, breads, and fresh fruit candied in honey. Cider and ale flowed freely beside warm equi and kumis, and the clanking of goblets and clattering of plates filled the room amid the laughter and hum of conversations.

I quickly learned my prediction about the forgiveness of my dress was correct when I started eagerly shoving forkfuls of food into my mouth. It wasn't long until I became overly full despite how little I'd eaten. I moodily set aside my utensils to allow digestion to make room for more. I considered excusing myself to loosen the stays, but if Mother noticed, a tight corset would be the least of my worries. I listened in on a conversation here and there but found nothing to hold my interest. My attention traveled to the head table, and I couldn't help but smile at how happy Lilias appeared. She was generally a modest woman who rarely showed any exuberance of feeling, but tonight there was a lovely glow to her cheeks and an easy smile about her mouth.

"I've seen prettier," a voice said over my shoulder. I stole a glance as casually as possible and sneered when I saw who spoke: Ailbert Chester. He was speaking to some crony, another spoiled, useless boy incapable of discussing anything other than women. I didn't know who they were talking about, but I pitied her.

"You lie," Ailbert's companion jeered. "You've never had better than a princess." The hairs on the back of my neck prickled and I gripped the arm of my chair so hard my fingernails scratched the wood.

"Just because she's a princess doesn't mean she's worth having," Ailbert said.

I couldn't listen to any more of Ailbert's disgusting comments. Whether he was speaking of Lilias, me, or Kyra, it was degrading. I channeled all the dignity and poise of my grandmother and rose, my back straight and lips pursed. With careful deliberation, I turned and walked in the direction of the miscreants. The moment they realized I was approaching, they fell silent and focused on their plates. I pretended to walk past, paused, then looked down my nose at them.

"A pity that being the son of a lord doesn't make one worth having either."

Ailbert looked up at me in shock, which quickly dissolved into anger when his companion burst out laughing.

"Shut up," Ailbert snapped. The friend continued to laugh, clutching his sides.

"Serves you right!" the young man exclaimed between chuckles.

I grinned and walked away, ignoring the dark glare Ailbert bore into my back. I wove my way through the throngs of guests until I reached Merrin and related the scene to her in exaggerated detail.

The remainder of the evening was less dramatic, though I did catch Ailbert staring daggers at me a few times. I'm not ashamed to admit I stuck my tongue out at him like a child. I participated in the dancing mostly to please Lilias more than myself. She loved dancing and enjoyed having her sisters join her. She danced every set, much to the consternation of her poor husband. His flushed face and damp brow made it apparent he wasn't used to so much physical exertion. I lost myself in the excitement of the evening, good food, and too much ice wine.

Merrin, Kyra, and I took turns dancing with each other, much to Lilias' amusement, and I even deigned to dance with Marick. Merrin eyed me knowingly when I returned to her side, but I shrugged her off and commented that I was perfectly capable of charity. We celebrated late into the evening until we were exhausted and quite over intoxicated. I didn't overindulge often, but tonight I'd been swept up in merriment.

Merrin and I sat away from the dancers, resting our feet and heads. The room started spinning, and I feared if we didn't rest ourselves, Merrin would either get an upset stomach from the wine or from seeing me vomit. We made casual observations about the couples and laughed when Father was forced to dance with Mother. She'd never been a good dancer, yet she insisted he dance with her at least once at every social event. Aunt Ula was much more graceful and pleasant to watch, but our eyes kept drifting to Mother and her clumsy attempts.

"At least she's having fun," Merrin pointed out, laughing behind her hand.

"I think she's having more fun embarrassing Father than actually dancing," I said.

"Um…he doesn't really seem so embarrassed."

I saw the dance had ended and Mother was wrapped in Father's arms, her head tilted upwards with an adoring smile while he placed soft kisses down the side of her face.

"Ugh!" I groaned. "Can't they restrain themselves in public?"

Merrin rested her chin on her hand and sighed wistfully. "I think it's sweet that they're still so in love."

"Well, of course. But that doesn't mean I want to watch them slobber all over each other."

"You might feel differently about public displays of affection someday." Merrin winked and elbowed me affectionately. "I think it's wonderful to see people in love."

"Oh, yeah? Well, look over there then." I pointed toward a table where Uncle Finton and Aunt Ula sat. We watched Merrin's father whisper into his wife's ear, her resulting blush, and the quick nip of his teeth at her neck. When Merrin turned back to me, I worried she would be sick after all.

"You made your point," she said. "Let's get out of here."

I was sad to see Merrin leave so soon after the wedding, but both she and Uncle Finton had to return to their studies.

"I have to work really hard if I want the chance to secure a place on the Kuste expedition team," Merrin said, her eyes wide with excitement.

"You worry too much." I embraced my cousin. "He's a fool if he doesn't pick you."

"Be careful," she whispered in my ear.

"I will." In only a few short days, Tyrnan was leaving Praed, and if everything went as planned, I would be joining him. Surreptitiously, I packed for the journey, setting aside underclothes, old breeches, and shirts once belonging to my brothers. I would wear a cap to hide my hair and bind my breasts with strips of fabric I pilfered from the seamstresses. In addition to clothing, I packed a few books and blank journals to at least appear as if I belonged on a voyage of discovery. And of course, I would not leave without my sword.

My plan was to disguise myself as a groom to get aboard the carriage and reveal myself to Tyrnan once we were a safe distance from Praed. The timing would have to be just right. I needed to set Nettle loose and hurry to the carriage before it left, and all without being seen. I practiced going through the motions a few times until I was confident I could make it with minutes to spare.

Lilias' departure from the castle after the wedding left a strange hole in our lives. At that moment, once all the excitement passed and we'd recovered after being perpetually exhausted, it occurred to me suddenly that never again would we all live under the same roof. Soon, my brothers and Kyra would marry and establish separate houses and have children of their own. Our close bond would be severed by the inevitabilities of life, and it broke my heart coming to terms with the fact that we were no longer children with only ourselves as our closest companions.

The night before Tyrnan was due to leave Praed, we were gathered as a family for dinner. Everyone, even Mother, was in good spirits and full of well wishes for my brother. I tried to act naturally and join in the revelry, but my nervousness inevitably showed. I spilled my drink twice, bit my tongue, and dropped food into my lap. I drew a few confused glances, but I was able to deflect them back toward Tyrnan. His eagerness was infectious, and the whole table was smiling and laughing as he described his upcoming journey.

"I wish it didn't take so long to get there," Tyrnan lamented. "But I suppose it will give me a chance to prepare. I have a few papers I'd like to study."

Rian's jaw dropped. "What? You mean there's one you haven't memorized yet?"

Tyrnan smirked but made no response, probably because it wasn't far from the truth. Since he was a small boy, Tyrnan absorbed every book written about sailing, maritime expeditions, and cartography.

"I can't wait to hear about the unexplored islands when you come back," Kyra said. "It will be such an inspiration for me."

"What if they turn out to be desolate wastelands?" Khyr asked.

Kyra shot him a withering look. "You have no imagination and are wholly unromantic."

"All of it went to you." Khyr flashed an exaggerated smile.

"Along with all the intelligence and manners."

"Leaving me with all the good looks!" With a flourish, Khyr waved a hand across his handsome face. Kyra rolled her eyes but didn't contradict him.

Instead of participating in the conversations, I took the time to observe my family. I didn't know when I would see them again, and I endeavored to collect as many memories as possible. I wanted to capture in my mind's eye the casual ease of my elder brother, Alyx, lounging in his chair exuding confidence. Though he possessed a regal air, he didn't have a trace of arrogance, but rather the fatherly aspect one wants in a king. He'd always been protective of his younger siblings, taking his role as oldest very seriously, but he was also kind and gentle-hearted, a side of him not many people had the privilege of seeing. My attention was drawn to Rian, the second eldest, as his unrestrained laughter permeated the room. I'd rarely seen Rian angry or sad, for he always chose to find humor in every situation. Even in my dourest mood, I could count on Rian to cheer me up with a teasing jest or self-deprecating joke. This was not unlike my youngest brother, Khyr, whose boundless energy could be equal parts exhilarating and annoying. Though his pranks set my nerves on edge, I would miss him dropping down from the ceiling or appearing suddenly from around a corner.

And finally, there was Kyra. My vision blurred as I regarded her from across the table. Her petite form swayed as she laughed with her twin, and a delicate hand brushed aside a stubborn lock of hair that refused to be tamed. I would miss the sound of her voice telling stories and the mischievous sparkle in her eyes. I vowed to bring her plenty of tales to inspire her imagination.

We retired to the Living Room after dinner. I sat next to Mother, wishing to be near her one last time. I breathed in the familiar scent of her—a blend of wildflowers, fresh hay, and summer wind. A pang in my heart suddenly rendered me incapable of breathing, and I grasped her hand.

She turned to me. "Is something wrong?"

I shook my head, not trusting my voice to be steady. She squeezed my hand and asked if I was sad Tyrnan was leaving. I nodded, feeling that was a safe excuse for my forlorn expression. She wrapped her arm around me and pulled me close. I lay my head on her shoulder as I used to as a little girl.

One by one, my siblings excused themselves for bed, and I tried not to hug them too tightly lest I make them suspicious. I did draw out my goodnight to Tyrnan as would be expected and appeared duly upset.

"We'll be together again before you can miss me," Tyrnan said.

I turned away before he could see the gleam of amusement in my eye.

I kissed Mother on the cheek when she rose to retire to bed and looked up into the familiar comfort of her face. She smiled down at me, the barest hint of age appearing as laugh lines about her eyes and mouth. I had always respected her as both my mother and my queen, a strong, intelligent, and loving woman. But I was also an admirer of her unique beauty. Whereas most people might disagree a ginger could be considered beautiful, my mother's distinct features illuminated her inner attributes, making her glow. Her hair was the passionate fire of her soul, her green eyes shown with determination, and the freckles dusted across her pale skin lent a gentleness to her authoritative air. I hoped one day I could be as secure and confident in my appearance. She wished me goodnight. I watched her leave and sighed heavily, knowing I had one last agonizingly painful goodbye.

Father retreated to his study to read by the dying embers of a fire. This had been his habit since I was a child, and I would often crawl into his lap and fall asleep to the sound of his voice as he read to me. It had been many years since I'd done this, but I would still occasionally join him bearing a book of my own. Tonight, I slipped into the study as silently as possible so I wouldn't disturb him and observed his still form for several moments. His head rested in one hand, the other turned pages in the dwindling firelight, his long legs stretched toward the hearth. He didn't stir as I stood wringing my hands, unsure of how to proceed. The man before me took the title of father more seriously than even the crown. He'd been my teacher, my disciplinarian, my greatest support, and my friend. He would not only fight for me, but he would offer up his life to protect me. And now, I would be leaving him and potentially losing his trust and respect in the bargain. But for my freedom, I would be willing to disappoint the person I admired most in the world.

I shifted closer when he straightened in his seat, but though I stood over him, neither of us said a word. A tear trickled down my cheek, and my breath hitched when I tried to speak. Silently, Father moved his book aside and reached a hand toward me. I took it, and just like when I was a little girl, I curled into his lap. He rubbed my back as I wept into his tunic, my ability to form any coherent speech lost in my grief. He remained quiet while I cried until I ran out of tears, until the only sound was the crackling flames struggling to persist in the waning fire. Out of the stillness came the low timbre of his voice reading aloud, and soon my eyes drifted shut and I relaxed into the comforting embrace. Sleep's persuasive tendrils invaded my body and pulled me into the abyss where dreams are absent and all that surrounded me was vast, empty darkness.

CHAPTER 7

I awoke in my own bed early the next morning. The sun had barely climbed above the horizon, and the house was stirring with servants preparing the morning meal and readying the carriage for Tyrnan's departure. This was my last chance to abandon my scheme, to resign myself to crown and country.

Molli was generally punctual in the mornings, so I had very little time to consider my options. I ran the fabric of an old shirt between my fingers, thinking, when a sound drew my attention to the window. I moved forward carefully to peer down unnoticed in time to see a young woman slap a man across his face. Her angry voice drifted upwards, accusing him of being unfaithful. I could only understand snippets of his reply, but they sounded like excuses. Their raised voices continued as I turned away from the window and began stripping off my nightclothes. As I pulled on an old pair of breeches and grimy shirt, I shook my head in disgust. Relationships were messy, and I was in no hurry to deal with them.

I placed a note on the vanity explaining I needed a ride to clear my head before hefting a canvas pack on my shoulder and sneaking out of my room. I planted another note outside the door asking not to be disturbed before stealthily moving down the corridor. I lowered my eyes as I stalked through the castle avoiding servants before ducking down the back stairs toward the kitchens. This was the busiest part of the castle, especially at this hour, so I acted as naturally as possible to avoid suspicion. I shifted my pack and hastened through the crowded room, mumbling that it would be my hide if I was late reporting to the coachman. Thankfully, I received little notice, and I chanced snatching a piece of unattended bread as I swept by. I let out a *whoosh* of air as I burst out of the door and ran toward the stables, my heart pounding and sweat moistening my brow. Something I remembered my cousin Kormac saying made me stop, and I bent down to drag my hands along the ground. I brought my nearly black palms to my face and rubbed the dirt over my cheeks. It wouldn't be completely convincing as a beard, but at least my bright, clean skin wouldn't draw attention.

Horses were being harnessed to a carriage and an armed escort assembled. The king and queen would take no chances with a Prince of Praed no matter how safe the road to Faqur. I waited, concealed in the brambles, until the horses were saddled and led away by knights and the fully prepared carriage was driven to the front of the castle. By now, my family would be breaking their fast and wondering why I wasn't joining them. They may have even found my note. Time was running out, and there were still too many people loitering around the stable for me to feel it was safe enough to set Nettle loose. My legs ached from the effort to remain motionless in a crouched position, and I gripped a low hanging branch to keep from toppling over. The activity settled, and I hadn't seen anyone for several minutes. Slowly, I extricated myself from the bushes and slunk into the stables. I paused, listening for any sounds besides the munching of hay and swishing of tails. I retrieved my saddle and made my way to Nettle's stall. Her beautifully refined head and slender neck appeared over the door, and her ears pricked forward when she saw me. I put a finger to my mouth to hush her when she began to nicker, which she clearly did not appreciate based on the way her ears swiveled back and the energetic sweep of her tail.

"We have to be quiet," I whispered. I pulled a halter over her nose and led her into the aisleway. I threw the saddle onto her back without bothering to brush her down, made sure it was tight, then rushed toward the door. Nettle's hooves pranced behind me excitedly, the anticipation of a ride putting a spring in her step. I peered around the door to ascertain no one was around before leading my horse into the increasing warmth of the day.

I unhooked her lead line. "Go have yourself a run, but don't get into trouble and please come back eventually." I threw my hands up in the air and shouted. Nettle wasted no time. She tossed her head, dug her hooves into the earth, and took off at a gallop. I took my cue from her exuberance and sprinted to the front of the castle. The knights were formed around the carriage but were relaxed as they waited for the royal family to appear. I strolled forward, drawing very little notice. Just as I was about to reach out to pull myself onto the rear seat, a hand roughly grabbed my shoulder and spun me around.

"What're you doing there, boy?" a large man asked. I recognized him as one of the soldiers, and I lowered my eyes.

"Attending the coach, sir," I said.

"What's that then?" he asked, pointing to where a pair of servants were hefting some trunks. "Going to make them do all the work?" I shook my head and jumped in to help. The servants gave me a quizzical look, probably because they didn't recognize me, but they didn't question my presence. In such a large castle, it would be perfectly reasonable not to know everyone.

My family streamed out of the castle just as the last of the luggage was loaded, and the servants scattered to take their places in line or to disappear. Amid the commotion, I tucked myself out of sight amid the trunks. I held my breath listening to my family's last goodbyes to Tyrnan. My eyes burned to hear their voices, and I covered my mouth to muffle a sob. Finally, footsteps retreated up the steps.

When I thought I'd feel the weight of Tyrnan climbing into the carriage, I heard Father speak. "It's nothing against you. She just doesn't know how to say goodbye."

"I know," Tyrnan said glumly. "I just wish I could see her one last time."

They were talking about me.

"Do your best," Father said. "But don't forget to enjoy yourself."

"I won't."

"We're proud of you."

"Thank you."

The sound of Father's footsteps on stone echoed in my ears and the carriage swayed as Tyrnan ducked inside. I braced myself, and when the carriage descended the mountain, I dared to peek out from my hiding place. My family was lined up on the stairs, my siblings waving as the distance lengthened. My mother was pressed closely to Father, her arms wrapped through his elbow. Her chin was raised proudly, but as I watched, she dropped her face into her hand, no longer able to maintain her composure. Just before they disappeared around the corner and became obscured by the procession of knights, I saw my father take her into his arms and press his forehead to hers. This last loving vision of my parents would have to sustain me in the months to come.

I avoided Tyrnan until we were two days into our journey. With some distance between us and the castle, I felt certain he'd be less likely to turn right around and more inclined to listen to my plan.

It wasn't easy pretending to be a boy. I had to sleep with the other servants and try to act as naturally as possible when they cavorted and undressed in front of me. I maintained my distance, although for a moment, I seriously considered abandoning this scheme. Young men are quite base. And they smell.

We stopped for the night at an estate on the western border of Praed. Though the knights protecting Tyrnan were very dedicated, they relaxed once under the roof of a trusted noble. This wouldn't be the case once we crossed into unknown territory, so this was my chance to be alone with my brother. I intercepted a tray with a decanter of equi and an assortment of miniature desserts and boldly approached his door.

"For His Highness," I said in my mock-boy's voice.

The guard posted there inspected the tray, even going so far as to taste a sweet treat, before waving me inside. I rolled my eyes at his needless thoroughness. There was zero chance of anyone in this house poisoning Tyrnan. The soldier just wanted a snack.

I smiled when I entered Tyrnan's room. He was sitting at a table before the hearth pouring over books and scrolls. I quickly glanced around to make sure there weren't any overzealous guards posted in the room. When I was sure we were alone, I stalked right up to him and set the tray down in front of his face, right on top of his precious work.

"Excuse me!" He looked up, an annoyed grimace on his face. Whatever else he was about to say died on his lips. His eyes widened and the color drained from his face. He leapt to his feet, and his chair teetered toward the floor.

I grabbed the chair before it hit the ground and put a finger to my lips. "Shhh! You're going to alert the guards."

"Sulwen, what are you doing here?" he asked, his voice a strained whisper.

"I'm going with you."

"No, you're not!"

I crossed my arms. "I am. So, either you help me, or I continue by myself."

"This is madness!" I'd rarely seen Tyrnan truly angry, but I could tell by the flush in his cheeks and the darkness in his eyes that this was one of those times.

"Please, Tyrnan." I gave him my most desperate, pleading tone. "Help me."

"I will. I'll help you go home." He moved toward the door, and I flung myself against the frame to stop him.

"This is my one chance to do something on my terms," I said. "I know this is difficult for you to understand, but I have to do this. Please." I made my lips quiver, and my brother's anger faded a fraction.

After a long pause, Tyrnan said, "We could both be in serious trouble if you're caught. Nay, not serious. *Grave.*"

"Don't be so dramatic!"

"This isn't a game, Sulwen. We could be arrested and sent to prison. If the crew found out, it could be very bad for you. Some of these men are at sea for months without seeing a woman."

"Oh, please. Are you saying they cannot control themselves?"

"That's exactly what I'm saying." The seriousness of his tone gave me pause, but I would not be swayed.

"I can avoid that because they won't find out I'm a woman."

"They may very well toss you overboard if they do. Women aren't allowed on board ships."

"That's a little extreme."

"They don't allow certain fruits on board, Sulwen. A woman is regarded as much worse."

I scoffed. "Superstitious nonsense."

Tyrnan took a step back and sighed in exasperation. He stalked over to the table and downed a glass of equi in one swallow.

"I'll be careful. I promise."

"What'll you do? You can't sail."

"Neither can you."

"At least I know the logistics!"

"I'll do what you're doing."

"You don't know anything about making maps, either."

"I can make notes of the new plants and animals. I know a little about that."

He poured himself another glass. "And when everyone retires to bed? You'll probably be sharing space with several other men."

"I'll rise before them and go to sleep after so we're never changing at the same time."

"And what about…?" His voice faded as he gestured toward me, a bloom of pink spreading over his face.

"Oh, these?" I smiled mischievously and thrust out my chest. "I bound them. Can't you tell?"

"I suppose," he muttered and turned away.

I grinned at his back and snatched a sweet cake off his tray. He was relenting. I could sense it.

"What about papers?" he asked.

"Papers?"

"Yes, papers." He reached into a satchel and withdrew several important looking sheets. "Orders? Like mine?"

I pursed my lips. This was something I hadn't thought about.

"I'm guessing they'll ask for them when we board?"

"Immediately. Especially since we're not a part of the usual crew."

"I could sneak aboard?"

"No, you can't." By his tone, I knew not to argue. I had no other suggestions. A few scraps of paper were the downfall to my adventure. Over before it began.

"You know," Tyrnan said softly. "There are men who make fake documents of all sorts. I've heard they practice their trade on the outskirts of Faqur. Perhaps we could employ them to draw up some orders for you."

My heart thumped wildly as hope swelled in my chest. "Can we?"

"It will cost a great deal. I don't suppose you brought any money?"

"I have some."

"Between us, we could probably have something official-looking made."

I propelled myself at Tyrnan, throwing my arms about his neck and hugging him tightly.

"Thank you," I breathed.

"Don't thank me yet. Wait until we're safely home." He reached up and pulled the cap off my head, sending my ginger hair tumbling over my shoulders. "We're going to have to do something about all this hair." He took a few strands in his fingers and pursed his lips in thought.

"That's why I have a cap," I said. "To hide it."

"That won't work for long. It would be better if we cut it."

"No!" I screeched and took a step back, pulling my hair out of his fingers.

"This is what's going to stop you? After all that?"

I gathered my hair into my hands protectively. Hadn't I once wished to be rid of the stuff? And now I was clutching my hair as if he'd suggested we cut off a limb.

"I don't see what the problem is. It'll grow back."

Reluctantly, I released my hair, admonished myself for being so foolish, and sat in the chair Tyrnan indicated. Tyrnan gathered my hair into a queue and placed a blade against my scalp.

"Last chance to change your mind." There was a trace of hope in his tone, and a challenge.

I squeezed my eyes shut. "Do it."

Tyrnan sawed the blade against my hair, and I gritted my teeth against the pain of it pulling away from my scalp. Minutes ticked by, then with a final tug, the last strands were cut. Instinctively, I moved my hand to where moments ago cascades of hair resided. Now there were only uneven valleys.

"I'll even things up as best as I can," Tyrnan said. He held my long hair in his fist, and I was struck at how keenly I felt its loss. My hair had always been a nuisance, an embarrassment, and a curse. I watched him toss the thick locks into the flames and puzzled over how something so insignificant could hold so much meaning. The sickly-sweet smell of burning hair filled the room, flames dancing over the copper locks. Tyrnan trimmed the remaining strands into something resembling a boy's style. It was a sign, I decided; destroying my hair signaled the end of my old life. There was no turning back now.

Tyrnan sent me to bed with a manuscript detailing the parts of a ship and basic sailing terms with instructions to read them and report back in the morning. When I protested such an assignment, he said there were two weeks to teach me what he's spent a lifetime learning.

"You're never going to fool anyone if you don't even know the difference between port and starboard," he said.

My blank stare made his case better than any argument I could muster.

In accordance with Tyrnan's wishes, I tucked myself away with an absconded candle and studied the manuscripts, twirling the newly shortened strands of hair in my fingers. I fell asleep with terms like 'mizzenmast,' 'keel,' and 'forecastle' dancing around in my head. I prided myself on being a quick learner, but this was going to take an inordinate amount of diligence. But I told myself, if I can learn to swing a sword against the King of Praed, I can learn to hold my own on a ship of the mighty Faqur Fleet.

CHAPTER 8

After several days of travel, Tyrnan and I established a routine that garnered little suspicion from the other servants and knights. In the mornings, I'd help prepare the carriage for travel then assist in the delivery of fresh bathwater and food into Tyrnan's room. Tyrnan would dismiss the other servants and I would sit behind a screen while he drilled me on the previous evening's assignment from his bath.

It was rough going at first, and I found the strict teacher side of Tyrnan extremely tiresome. He left little room for error and was very annoyed whenever I couldn't answer his questions correctly. He made me so angry one morning I nearly tipped him over, bathwater and all. During the day's travel, I pored over books and scrolls from my perch at the back of the carriage, and in the evenings the lectures would continue. Eventually, we reached a point where there were no inns to be had, no rooms with locked doors for privacy, and I had to sneak into his tent when the guards changed shifts. It wasn't long until I didn't have to affect a deep voice. I had so little sleep I was becoming hoarse.

"Which sail is this?" Tyrnan pointed to a picture of a ship.

"Foresail," I said, my head resting heavily in my hand.

"What is it set on?"

"The foremast." I yawned.

"How many masts does *The Wayward Aymelina* have?"

"Three." My eyes drifted shut.

"What kind of knot is this?"

I opened one eye slightly, closed it again, and answered, "Bowline."

"Beat to quarters!" Tyrnan cried.

My eyes flew open, and I stumbled to my feet before I heard his low chuckle.

"I hate you," I grumbled.

He smiled. "At least you know *that* phrase well."

"Tyrnan, I'm exhausted. Can we please take a break?"

"You won't get a break on board ship."

I slammed a hand onto the table. "We're not on board yet. If you keep depriving me of sleep, I'm never going to retain all of this."

Tyrnan sighed and ran a hand through his hair. "I'm sorry. I'm worried that if we don't pass you off as at least a rudimentary sailor, you'll be discovered as an imposter before we can leave Faqur."

"I appreciate what you're doing for me." I squeezed his hand. "But I need to retain my strength as well as my wits if we're going to make this work."

"I know." The tension drained from his face. "You are doing well. I hope you know that."

"It would help if you told me once in a while," I said with a wry smile.

Tyrnan relented his grueling course of study, though infinitesimally, as we traveled closer to Faqur. I practiced my knots from my perch on the back of the carriage and watched as the scenery changed from prairie to grizzled trees and rocky outcroppings. The stony projections eventually disappeared, and the air became cooler as we dropped into a valley with golden rolling hills dotted here and there with impressive manor houses and accompanying tenant farms. Tyrnan explained one night they were farming grains, and we would be repasting their labors in the form of hard, dry biscuits. Soon, the smell in the air sweetened from the orchards bearing fruits Tyrnan said would be dried and served on board ship alongside a watered-down wine from the vineyards sweeping along the hillsides. The sight reminded me of Ilano's vast apple orchards, and the familiarity was comforting so far from home.

One morning, I stepped out of my tent and breathed in the floral aroma, soothing my flustered nerves, especially after a long night studying and getting little sleep amid snoring servants. I wandered into the long rows of hip deep plants with purple flowers and picked several stalks, avoiding the bees dancing from petal to petal. I inhaled deeply the pleasing scent. I picked more and folded the plants into my clothing. Just because I was playing a boy didn't mean I had to smell like one. Tyrnan tilted his head to the side when he detected the distinct aroma and commented that sailors generally don't carry flowers on their person, to which I replied:

"A pity. They should."

Tyrnan rolled his eyes but said nothing further.

"We're getting close to the outskirts of the main city," he said. "I've sent a man ahead to make some discreet inquiries regarding a forger. We'll meet with him in a few days."

A shudder ran through me, and I nodded mutely. We were so close now, and my nervous excitement was almost too much to bear. I tried to keep myself distracted by watching the continuing evolution of the scenery from fertile farmlands to rows of stone cottages as we traversed the fringes of Faqur. Everywhere I looked, people were bustling about the modest, thatched roof houses, whether it was tending livestock, mending nets, or cleaning fish. I held a hand over my nose to try and block out the pungent odor of decaying offal and fish scales as our caravan ambled through the village and turned away from the brief, yet intense stares of the locals as we passed. Suddenly, the carriage came to a stop, and I was nearly pitched to the ground. I grabbed ahold of a trunk and peered around the corner to see Tyrnan alight and walk purposefully toward a haggard looking man stringing line through several long pieces of wood. We used fishing poles to catch fish from the Rhyvor, but these were much longer and sturdier. The man looked up sharply when Tyrnan and his trusted valet approached, and he appeared suspicious as he listened. I tensed, wondering if this was the man who would supply my forged documents. I strained to hear their words, but there was too much activity to catch them clearly. Finally, the man was presented with a heavy purse, and he beckoned my brother inside his humble dwelling. Tyrnan glanced casually over his shoulder in my direction, and without thinking, I leapt from the back of the carriage and took several steps forward before being stopped by a knight.

"Stay there," he ordered. "We won't be stopped here long."

I glanced toward the house. Tyrnan and his valet disappeared through the door. I stared up at the intimidating knight, clenched my jaw, and bit back a retort. I proceeded to pace along the back of the carriage while I waited for the pair to return. It felt like hours, and each sound had me jumping to attention, until my brother appeared and strolled nonchalantly back to the carriage. The old fishermen went back to his work, and I almost didn't make it on board the carriage before it pulled away.

We continued toward the heart of Faqur, and the quaint village grew into an immense throng of long warehouses, busy merchants, and impressively tall buildings. The streets were crowded with all manner of people from fishermen to sailors, to well-dressed gentlemen and ladies. As we neared the harbor, I inhaled my first breath of the sea, a pleasing mixture of refreshing salt and earthly moisture I could almost taste it was so thick. The port was lined with shipyards, and the masts of moored ships rose into the sky higher than the tallest trees I'd ever seen. I stared in awe as we came to a stop in front of a massive white stone building with the flag of Faqur flying at each corner. The servants and I hurried off the carriage and were directed next door to the lodging house with orders to unload His Highness's trunks. I helped distractedly, watching Tyrnan speak to a sailor outside what he later told me was the Offices of the Fleet, the main headquarters of the Faqur navy. Across the street was a hospital and several more lodging houses, a blacksmith, and a lumber yard. Men bustled in and out of buildings housing clerks and solicitors. Faqur was a busy place consumed with the business of making a living.

"Get along there!" A knight cuffed me alongside the head.

I glared at him darkly, but he was unfazed.

Grudgingly, I finished carrying Tyrnan's things into his spacious room and started unpacking. As I withdrew a stack of books, I froze. Hidden underneath his precious references was a neatly folded uniform consisting of a woolen blue coat with brass buttons and short tails, a white undershirt, and simple linen breeches. I ran my fingers along the rough fabrics and pictured myself in such attire, feeling a swell of excitement.

"You ruined the surprise," Tyrnan said.

I spun around guiltily, dropping the books in a horrible commotion. Tyrnan winced when they hit the ground, and I apologized for my clumsiness.

"It's fine." He retrieved the books and sat them gingerly on a side table.

"What surprise?" I prompted when he continued to inspect the books like a mother scanning a child for injuries after a fall.

Tyrnan gave me a half smile and withdrew the outfit from the trunk.

"This…" He handed me the clothing. "…is for you. It's the uniform of a science officer, though a very low ranked one, I'm afraid. And here…" He reached back into the trunk and took out a satchel. "This is for your journals and pens for making notes. We must have you looking the part of explorer after all. Your papers are in there."

Reverently, I reached inside the satchel and carefully removed the delicate parchment. Written in a shockingly elegant hand was the commission of a gentleman naturalist to join the crew of *The Wayward Aymelina* for a period of no less than one year for the purposes of documenting previously undiscovered flora and fauna during the ship's voyage among the unexplored isles west of Faqur. The gentleman named below was ordered to report to the ship's captain, Lencius Romy, at such an appointed time before the commencement of the expedition. My eyes skimmed the contents of the document until I reached the name "Symon Red."

"Red?" I quirked an eyebrow. "Really?"

"What? It's not uncommon to be named for a distinguishing feature."

"I hate you."

"Rest well tonight. Tomorrow morning, we report to our captain."

"No lessons tonight?"

"Not tonight. If you don't know it by now, you're not going to know it, and you're doomed anyway."

"Then let's hope I don't make a fool out of myself tomorrow."

"Out of *both* of us."

I couldn't suppress the smile spreading across my face, but it quickly fell when Tyrnan added, "That wasn't meant as a show of solidarity. It's a warning. If they find out who you really are, they'll know I helped you as your brother and we'll both be punished. Please don't condemn us to prison."

"I won't," I said, my brow furrowed in determination. "You have my word as a Princess of Praed."

When the other servants fell asleep, I snuck out of their lodgings and was installed in my own quarters under my assumed name. In the morning, the servants might wonder where I'd gone, but they wouldn't dwell on it for long. They had jobs to do that superseded their curiosity, especially regarding some nobody boy. My room was barely larger than a closet, but I was alone. I enjoyed the solitude, bathing in rosewater and stretching out on the bed without worrying someone would notice my feminine features.

I expected to fall into an exhausted sleep after so many miles of travel, but the anticipation of the next morning kept me fully alert. My head swirled with terms and phrases drilled into me for days, and I mentally named all the parts of a ship I could recall offhand. I retained everything Tyrnan taught me, but that didn't help settle my mind enough to sleep. I flipped through some of the notes I'd taken hoping reading would help make me drowsy, and I came across a phrase I found intriguing. According to Tyrnan, *The Wayward Aymelina* was often referred to by the nickname, "A Mother's Pride," because all three sons of the Romy family served onboard. While I regarded this as tactically irresponsible, the general feeling around Faqur was that the familial bond made for a stronger crew. I wrote down their names and positions so I wouldn't forget, and I traced them with my finger so the memory would be imprinted on my brain. It wouldn't be prudent to stumble over who was who when we met since Tyrnan pointed out the first impressions of one's officers could set the mood for the entire journey.

Second mate Absalon Romy was the youngest brother at twenty-six, I repeated to myself. He was primarily in charge of navigation, and I pictured a skinny young man who constantly adjusted his spectacles with sweaty fingers. The first mate was Evrard Romy, two years older than Absalon. He was the security and safety officer. Having trained with weapons and being practiced in intimidation, he was probably a brutish sort of man. Of course, the man I was most interested in impressing was the captain, Lencius Romy. At thirty years old, Captain Romy was touted as the most accomplished sailor in the history of the country, having ascended to his prestigious status at the young age of twenty-four. This was largely due not only to his supposed intelligence and mystical wave reading powers, but because of his bravery in the line of battle against pirates along the coast of Crif. It had been many years since he had effectively sent the last of the plundering Crif pirates, called "Burdeeds," to the bottom of the sea, and since then he had been lobbying for expeditions to new territories. This voyage would be the realization of all his hard work. It was sweet the way Tyrnan beamed with pride over the captain he had yet to meet, and I only hoped the man lived up to my brother's expectations. For my part, I pictured Captain Romy as a hardened, rough-mannered sort of man, the kind who gives orders callously fully knowing they will be obeyed. He was undoubtedly accustomed to having his own way. I always found it difficult to stomach people like that, and I only hoped I would be wise enough to hold my tongue.

CHAPTER 9

The next morning, I left my room clad in my new uniform and carrying my meager belongings to find Tyrnan anxiously hopping from foot to foot just outside the door.

"Did you think I was going to forget?" I said.

"I thought you might oversleep."

"I should be insulted that you place so little trust in me."

"Later." He grabbed my hand and pulled me down the hallway. "We have to hurry if we're going to make it on time."

I had to run to keep up with his hurried pace. "The shipyard is practically three steps out the door!"

"I want to be punctual!"

I laughed. "You want to be early. To impress the captain."

"Don't forget to keep your head down and not to speak out of turn."

We dashed out of the inn. My stomach rumbled at the smell of fresh bread and sizzling meats, but Tyrnan showed no sign of stopping for breakfast.

Someone carrying stuffed rolls passed us on the street and I asked, "Did you eat already?"

He ignored my question and said, "Name all the masts."

"Foremast, mainmast, and mizzenmast." I panted as we ducked between the beams and dodged workers in the shipyard. "Tyrnan, please, I'm hungry!"

"Stop thinking about your stomach." He reached into his satchel and pulled out a wrapped package. He shoved it into my hand, and the aroma arising from the warm parcel made my mouth water.

I devoured the small pie that was a delicious mix of savory fish and sweet fruit and was still licking my fingers clean when we emerged into the sunshine. I froze at the sight of the massive ships docked at the port along the south shore of the Brasdemer Sound. Water lapped against their hulls, swaying the great structures ever so slightly. Men swarmed the docks and ships, throwing ropes and loading cargo with controlled efficiency. A strange mixture of aged wood, paint, oil, and unwashed bodies mingled with the sea. When I remained still for too long, Tyrnan tugged at my sleeve, and I followed.

I stared at the ships in slack-mouthed awe "I had no idea they were so big."

Tyrnan gave me an odd look and continued to usher me forward. At length he stopped in front of a dark stained ship with a stripe of navy blue painted along the hull and quarterdeck. Three masts stretched into the bright sky like imposing trees piercing the sun. A few men climbed among the masts and worked on deck while others loaded supplies. Along the stern against a black background boldly written in gold letters was the name of the ship, *The Wayward Aymelina.*

The *Aymelina* was immense, a veritable floating castle, dwarfing the riverine barges and skiffs I was used to seeing plying the rivers of Praed. No amount of reading could have prepared me for the enormity of it. Her three masts looked as though they'd scratch the bottoms of clouds. I shielded my eyes and craned my neck to see the cannons mounted on the poop deck. Crews were busy polishing the black iron. Along the gunwales we passed a dozen more cannons stationed at gunports along the quarter deck and beyond, racks of ammunition at the ready.

A queue of men filed up the gangplank onto the main deck where a group clustered around an officer checking papers. I gripped my satchel. The terminology Tyrnan taught me swirled in my head, making me dizzy.

Tyrnan stopped at the bottom of the gangplank and introduced himself to a few of his fellow cartographers, then gave me a final once over.

"Be respectful to the officers by saluting them when they pass and for the love of Artur, don't give yourself away by dowsing yourself in flowers." Tyrnan whispered while adjusting my uniform so the shirt buttons were perfectly aligned with my torso.

"Relax, Tyr." I smiled. "I won't disgrace you."

He stifled a smile before striding up the gangplank and onto the ship.

I took a deep breath and placed a foot on the sadly inadequate piece of timber that was the only thing between me and the frigid water. I closed my eyes, gritted my teeth, and chided myself for being so nervous. I boldly raised my other foot from the dock and placed it firmly in front of the other. Though my knees shook, I continued the slow climb until I was nearly on deck. The wood creaked and swayed beneath me with the movement of the great ship, and I threw an arm out to keep my balance. I heard someone quickly walking up behind me, so I practically jumped forward and onto the deck. I must have looked ridiculous standing there catching my breath as if I'd been running for miles. Self-consciously, I glanced around the ship to see if anyone noticed my strange behavior.

The man who'd been behind me looked at me pitiably. "First time?" He handed some papers over to a stocky, brown-haired man.

I nodded mutely. He slapped me good-naturedly on the shoulder and assured me I'd get my sea legs in no time.

"Papers," the stocky man said gruffly.

"Excuse me?" I blinked in his direction.

He frowned. "Orders. Now." A hand shot out and his color deepened.

"Yes…of course…orders." My hand dove into the satchel, dug around, and produced the documents. I watched the man inspect them, holding my breath and hoping he didn't see through the deception. He scanned the papers quickly, his brow furrowed. He wore fine clothing, starched white breeches and a blue tailcoat hanging unbuttoned to reveal a high-collared red waistcoat. He looked up at me sharply, and I shivered under the intense scrutiny of his light brown eyes. Was this the captain?

"You don't look old enough to shave let alone join an expedition of this nature."

I gave him my fake low voice. "I get that a lot, sir. I keep wishing for a beard, but they don't grow well on gingers." I pulled off my cap to reveal my shorn locks, and his eyes widened. It was a lie Tyrnan and I came up with to explain away my perpetually smooth face.

He shoved the papers into my hands. "My condolences. You'll be lookin' like a boy for the rest of your life." He jerked his head toward a seaman waiting to show me to my quarters. He had the same lean frame and wavy brown hair as Tyrnan, though he tried to tame the strands with a generous application of oil.

I saluted Mr. Surly and followed the young man into the forecastle where dozens of men were busy claiming their beds and chatting. The beds were like nothing I'd ever seen. Just as Tyrnan described, they hung in rows from the beams so they wouldn't slide across the floor but sway with the movement of the ship. The seaman directed me to a spare hammock with minimal bedding—only a pillow and a woolen blanket. He kicked a locker.

"Put your things in here," he said. "They'll be safe enough. We don't take kindly to thieves, so let us know if anything goes missing. We'll toss every inch of the place looking for it." He gave me a pointed glare, and I had the sense this was a warning rather than a reassurance.

"Understood."

"You're with the trippers?"

"The what?"

"Those with their eyes in the dirt and on their papers. Never look up and trip over their own feet. Not one of the crew."

"I suppose you could say that, but of course I intend to do my fair share of work."

He looked at me dubiously, though I couldn't account for his distrust. I had an uneasy sense of foreboding, and a quick glance to my side confirmed the other men were quietly watching us.

"I'm Erec. If you need anything, you can apply to me. Put your things away and be on the main deck in five minutes."

"Yes, sir." I saluted.

He sneered. "You don't have to do that. I'm not an officer."

"Right. Of course." My cheeks flushed.

Erec spun on his heel and walked away without another word, leaving me to smile sheepishly at the men still silently staring. I tucked my things into the locker, ignoring the growing unease and whispers. I stood to leave, but an imposing figure blocked my path.

"We don't care to associate with your kind," the man snarled. "So you better stay on your side of the ship and out of our way."

The color drained from my face and my knees buckled. My kind? What did he mean by that? Has my secret been discovered so quickly? I swallowed hard and looked into the eyes of each man as he stared blankly back.

"My k-kind?" I wished my voice wasn't so small.

"Gingers." He stabbed a meaty finger into my chest. "They're back luck. Mark my words, if we run into any trouble, I'll know who to blame."

I sighed in relief when he and the others finally filed out of the forecastle. If it was my hair they didn't like, I could handle that easily. In fact, it served my ends to have the men isolate themselves from me. The less time we spent together, the less chance they would discover how dissimilar we truly were.

When I came up to the main deck, I was ushered forward with the cartographers and historians, well ahead of the crewmen. They glared as I walked by, but I bore it with all the dignity I could summon. There must have been fifty men on deck. Standing above us on the quarterdeck was the surly, brown-haired man I'd seen earlier. Now, his coat was buttoned, and he wore a tall, black hat. Beside him stood a man dressed similarly, but instead of red, a green high-collared waistcoat peeked above his blue tailcoat. He was a little shorter and wore delicate, silver-rimmed spectacles. His rounded cheeks and mess of dirty blond curls escaping from underneath his hat lent him a youthful air. The second mate, Absalon Romy, no doubt. Beside him, wearing a blue coat like mine, white breeches, a short-brimmed hat, and yellow waistcoat, was a man I recognized all too well. I could not prevent the sharp gasp, nor could I keep myself from staring in horror at Ailbert Chester. What nightmare was this? I sensed Tyrnan shift closer to me, but he didn't speak. Surly man started speaking, and my mouth snapped shut.

"Captain on deck!" he yelled. As one, the crew stood at attention, backs straight and chests out.

A man strode onto the quarterdeck. He was already tall, but the sail-shaped black hat he wore made him tower over his brothers. His black tailcoat was draped over impeccably white breeches, and lights danced in front of my eyes when the sun glinted off his gold buttons. The collar of his white waistcoat grazed the sharp angle of his jaw as he silently swept the crowd with his gray-blue eyes, not sparing more than a moment to inspect each face. Even if he wasn't attired so distinctly, I would have known this was Captain Lencius Romy by his commanding presence that bespoke of confidence and self-satisfaction.

"Gentlemen." His voice was unexpectedly quiet and soft, and I leaned forward to hear him properly. "Many of us have served together before, and I thank you for your continued loyalty. This shall be the greatest undertaking of my career, and to have the finest crew I've ever had the privilege of leading on such an expedition is an honor."

I glanced around at the men. It was a short speech, but they clearly appreciated the sentiments.

Captain Romy turned to the dark-haired man, who I now believed to be the first mate, Evrard Romy.

"Stand by to set sail," Captain Romy said.

"Lay aloft and loose sail!" First Mate Evrard commanded the waiting crew. There was a burst of activity as everyone ran across the deck toward their stations. I grasped Tyrnan by the shirt before he could dash away.

"Did you know?" I whispered, nodding toward Ailbert Chester.

"No." He tried to pull away, but I wouldn't relinquish my hold. "Sul—er, I mean—" he paused and cleared his throat. "He's dressed as a bosun."

This did not bode well. I recalled this was a position of some authority. A bosun looked after the maintenance of the deck, the rigging, and the sails. This was not a position he could purchase, so he must have some experience.

I thought back to his rude behavior at Lilias' wedding. "Did he ever mention that he was a sailor?"

"No, but he wasn't exactly forthcoming with personal details."

I let Tyrnan go when it was clear he wanted to help prepare the ship for departure, and I thought it better that I, too, join in the work before I drew more ire from the crew. I strode forward to help tow the rigging for the foresail, but a large hand clamped down hard on my shoulder. I buckled under the weight and was roughly turned to face the large man who had confronted me below deck.

"Where do you think you're going?"

I pointed toward the men hauling ropes across the ship's bow, and the man shook his head, a twisted gleam in his eye.

"No, no. Slight lad like you? You're going up." He pointed toward the men climbing the ratlines up the masts to loosen the sails.

"Go on," he urged. "Up you go!"

He gave me a little shove, and I numbly gripped the thick rungs and climbed high into the cool air. The wind pushed against me halfway up the mast, and I clutched the ratlines when my foot slipped. I cursed under my breath and glanced downward to ensure no one saw my misstep. That was a mistake, for I was surely hundreds of feet up, above me vast sky and below a rough landing. I pinned my body against the ropes and squeezed my eyes shut. Taking a deep breath, I pulled myself upward, staring straight ahead until I reached the top of the sail. A sailor nodded his head toward one of the riggings, and I pushed away from safety and into thin air.

I hoped no one would notice my hands violently trembling as I shuffled along the yard. The only thing separating me from a long fall was a single line of rope under my feet. To my right, a sailor was busily readying the sail to be let loose, and I mirrored his actions with one hand while grasping the yard with the other until my knuckles were white. When finished, I looked up into the steady gaze of the sailor. I looked past him down the line and noticed the other men were watching me, too. To my relief, they didn't appear angry. A short nod radiated down the line until all acknowledged each other. Then, as one, we released the sail. It was a small accomplishment—it only dropped a few feet—but it was exhilarating. Further up the mast, the other sails were released, and orders were shouted below. I took a moment to gaze across the sea and watch sunlight glitter over the waves. The sun was warm on my face, and I closed my eyes and enjoyed the heat and the tangy bite of salty air against my cheeks.

"It never gets old," the man to my right said. I opened my eyes and saw he'd shuffled close and was peering out over the water. He was old, or perhaps he merely appeared so because of his wind-battered skin and unshaven face.

"Pardon me—old?" I said.

"Looking out over the sea from up 'ere. The salt gets in yer blood and sends a thrill through ye. No other feeling like it. Well," he amended with a twinkle in his eye. "Unless yer talkin' to my wife. Then she's the only thrill for me." He laughed and slapped me on the arm. I suppressed a cry and wrapped my arms around the yard to keep from falling. He waved toward the ratlines, and I followed him back down to the deck.

On the order of the first mate, we worked to lower the sails fully so they caught the wind. It was like watching a flower blooming. Captain Romy gave the order to weigh anchor, and I was ushered along with the old man to where several men were inserting bars into the capstan, a device that was rotated to haul the massive anchor up into the ship. I helped push the heavy bars until my arms ached and sweat poured down my back. When the task was done, my arms hung limp and I could barely walk.

"There's not much to ya, but you're a tough young fella," the old man laughed. "I'm Hrod." He held out a hand to me, and I took it with a grateful smile.

"Sul—" I coughed to cover the slip my brother almost committed. "Symon," I said firmly. "I'm here to document the plants and animals we find."

He nodded sagely. "A worthy cause."

"Have you served with Captain Romy before?" I asked.

"Oh, aye." A wide smile revealed several gaps, but it didn't detract from Hrod's outward friendliness. "Many years. You won't find a more skillful skipper or fair master. This your first time?"

"It's that obvious?"

"Stick with me, lad. I'll show you the ropes, so to speak." He draped an arm over my shoulders and led me onto the main deck to show me how to secure the rigging for the sails. We garnered a few stares but no comment. I had a feeling Hrod's experience carried some weight with the crew. He might be the only friend I'd make on board, but it was more than I had this morning. What's more, I was relieved to have someone other than Tyrnan to guide me. The less time we spent together, the greater the chance we could sail through the unexplored isles with the crew blissfully unaware that they possessed a prince *and* a princess on board. If they hated me as a ginger, I couldn't imagine how they might feel to discover a woman amongst them.

CHAPTER 10

My heart soared as *The Wayward Aymelina* sailed out of the harbor and into the Brasdemer Sound toward the ocean. Once we caught the wind, there was nothing for me to do but brace myself against the railing and lean into the spray barely licking up the hull into my face. The water splashed into white-crested waves as the ship cut through the narrow opening between the northwest tip of Faqur and a lone island covered with nothing but rolling grasslands. I looked back toward the harbor and watched the ships slowly shrink as the distance grew between us. For the first time in weeks, the tension drained from my body. No one, not Mother or Father nor a bevy of knights, would be coming after me. I couldn't help my ridiculous grin. Frankly, I didn't care if the entire crew thought I was mad. I was free.

Men moved around me either working or talking amongst themselves, but for the most part, we ignored each other. Vaguely, I registered voices coming close, and I froze when they neared enough for me to overhear their conversation.

"If the wind continues to be this favorable, we should arrive in nine days."

From the corner of my eye I saw the captain and the first and second mate striding toward me. Second Mate Absalon had a leather-bound book open wide and was showing the captain his notes. The captain seemed unimpressed.

"Eight and a half," Captain Romy replied.

"No, I said nine," Absalon corrected.

"I know." Captain Romy stopped and faced his brother pointedly. "I want to be there in eight and a half." I swore I saw a half smile, but I couldn't be sure. The younger man's mouth became a grim line as he eyed the captain with evident frustration.

"Can't you make it happen?" First Mate Evrard challenged.

"I can't control the wind. Why don't you apply to the hero over here?" Absalon gestured toward the captain. "Maybe he can bend the sea to his command like he did at the Battle of Temluc."

The captain chuckled softly as they passed me. I shrank back hoping they wouldn't acknowledge me beyond a nod at my salute. To my relief, the captain and second mate barely glanced at me, but Evrard made eye contact and held it as they passed. All the blood in my body drained to my feet, and my legs nearly gave out when he turned away without speaking. I sensed the first mate didn't care for redheads either.

"Is there a reason you're so idle?" a voice called from behind me.

I whirled around, a hand to my forehead in a salute. Before I could stop myself, I cast a surprised look at Ailbert Chester.

He looked me up and down with a disapproving scowl. "When a superior asks you a question," he said. "You answer him, boy."

"I'm not idle, sir."

He took a few steps closer, and I dared to hold his dark stare.

"You're one of those useless, book toting trippers, aren't you?" He spat at my feet and straightened his coat.

My lip curled. "I'm here to further our knowledge of natural history. An undertaking that may be difficult to understand for those unwilling to learn."

He stepped closer, looming over me. He scrutinized my face, then narrowed his eyes. "Do I know you?"

"No." I hoped my voice wasn't as tremulous as I felt.

"It's not often one meets a person with ginger hair."

"We are a rare breed, indeed, sir."

"Endangered, I should like to think."

"Not unlike civility it seems." I bit my tongue, but it was too late.

Fury blazed in his eyes. He closed the space between us, his arm raised. I stared back without flinching, angering him further. He raised the back of his hand to hit me, but a voice stilled his blow.

"Is there a problem here?"

I wouldn't be surprised if both Ailbert and I had the same look of horror on our faces.

Ailbert dropped his arm. "An insubordinate boy, Captain."

I spun around and hurriedly saluted the captain, whose eyes flickered to me briefly before settling on Bosun Chester. The first mate stood by, hand resting on the hilt of his sword. The gesture struck me as odd, and I wondered if Chester had given them trouble before.

"Did he pay his respects?" the captain asked calmly.

"Yes, but—" Chester started.

The captain continued. "Did he offer you insult?"

"Well." Chester looked down at me, and I raised an eyebrow. "No," he grumbled. "But he—"

"Then don't let him keep you from your duties, Bosun Chester." The finality of his words made it clear Chester was dismissed, and he wasted no time scurrying away. I lowered my eyes and prepared to slink away myself.

"So, you're the naturalist?" Captain Romy said.

I looked up in surprise. He regarded me blankly, his hands clasped behind his back. First Mate Evrard's hand dropped from his sword, and he shifted impatiently.

"I am, sir," I said, my voice hoarse as if I'd been without water for days.

He nodded perfunctorily, and the pair left me alone. I blinked dumbly as I watched them leave, realizing he must have heard most, if not all, of the conversation that passed between me and Ailbert Chester.

At the close of the first day, the atmosphere below deck brimmed with excitement. While we dined on hard biscuits, salted pork, a strange green mush, and weak wine, we were entertained by stories from the older sailors. Once the plates were licked clean, several instruments were produced, and a raucous celebration commenced. I laughed at the cacophony of song and music permeating the inner hold. After a long day of work, the men relaxed in their hammocks, their limbs sprawled languidly as they swung with the movement of the ship. Though the noise was loud enough to reach land, many were already snoring. I couldn't sleep unless there was complete silence. I tried to read, but I found quiet was necessary for this as well. I contented myself with laying back and listening to the merry—though vulgar—music. Beside me, a pair of sailors were discussing a maid in graphic detail, but when I turned away to block them out, a half-naked man stood there scratching himself below the belt. I almost retched. Men, I decided, were disgusting creatures.

"What's your story, then?" A sailor grabbed the bottom of my hammock and almost tossed me out of it. My arms flew out to clutch the sides, evoking hearty guffaws from him and his companions.

"Jumpy little guy," one of the men observed. They were all fairly young, though it was difficult to estimate anyone's age on this ship. Years at sea made them lean and weather-beaten, and if they weren't nourished properly, disease rotted their teeth and hollowed their faces. The men before me could be no older than I.

"No," I said. "I was just...lost in thought."

"Sounds dangerous," the first man said, eliciting chuckles from his friends.

I glared at them but said nothing.

"Maybe he *thinks* he's too good for us," another said. He leaned over me, his hot, sour breath blowing over my face with every word.

"Not at all," I said with what I hoped was casual ease. My heart thudded and I gripped the hammock tighter. The four men stepped closer, and I shrank back instinctively.

One of the men inspected my hands. "You have very smooth skin," he said. It was less an observation and more of an accusation. "Not suitable for work, I'd say."

"Not *used* to work at any rate," his friend added.

I raised my too-smooth hands in surrender. "I don't want any trouble. Truly, I just wish to do my share like everyone else."

"Like everyone else?" the first man echoed. "We'll be working while you scratch notes in your little book. Which is the better cause?"

I dropped my arms and narrowed what I hoped was an intimidating glare. "I don't see what everyone here has against furthering our knowledge. The whole world doesn't want to be as ignorant as you."

Antagonizing him was a mistake. He wrenched me forward by the collar, twisting the fabric until it dug painfully into my skin. A mixture of foul odors wafted from his mouth. He was so close I could count each hair on his unshaven face and see the flecks of gold in his brown eyes, like glowing embers.

"Are you calling me stupid?"

"No," I said, my voice unbearably tight. "Just unwilling to learn."

I don't know what's wrong with me.

The man tightened his grip, and I gasped for air. I clawed at his hands to loosen his hold, but he showed no sign of relenting. His mouth twisted into a snarl, and he bared his teeth like a rabid dog. I vaguely heard his companions' raised voices, but the noise was a dull throb behind the rush of blood in my ears. Time slowed as he pulled back a balled fist aimed right at my face. I closed my eyes and braced myself for the blow.

"Telken!" a voice barked.

The man dropped me. The hammock flipped over, sending me crashing to the floor. I looked up, rubbing my sore neck. Erec gave me a cursory glance before addressing the burly man—Telken—again.

"You know the captain doesn't abide fighting," Erec said. "Surely, this little scrap of a boy isn't worth your trouble?"

"No." Telken looked down at me and sniffed disdainfully. "You're right. He's not." He shook himself and stalked away, his cronies close behind.

Erec extended a hand to help me up. "It would be in your best interest not to insult your fellow crew members."

"They started it," I grumbled and brushed myself off.

He quirked an eyebrow, a gesture so like Mother I felt a pang of homesickness.

"These are simple, hard-working men," he said. "They deserve as much respect as an educated boy like you."

I didn't miss the fact that he kept calling me a boy despite my nineteen years.

"Understood," I said, though I didn't believe men who tormented a defenseless young man warranted respect of any kind.

Erec nodded curtly and walked away. I clenched my fists, annoyed at having to be rescued and then given a lecture. I sighed and dropped into the hammock. For the next several minutes, I watched the beams above sway back and forth and listened to the fading notes of music.

The sounds of boisterous men slowly ceased, and the whispers of conversation ended, leaving the quarters still and silent. I lifted my head to look down the rows of beds. No one appeared awake. Carefully, I eased out of the hammock and stripped off my clothing, unwound my bound breasts, and threw on nightclothes. I climbed underneath the blanket and rubbed my aching chest, relieved I'd made it through my first day without detection. I was asleep within seconds and passed the night in a dreamless, exhausted slumber.

The next morning, I barely woke in time to dress without being seen. I'd just finished buttoning my breeches when Telken knocked his shoulder into me as he passed. I managed to maintain my footing, but that didn't stop him from laughing at me.

"You'll get your sea legs in time, boy," he said. His friends erupted in exaggerated laughter. I took Erec's advice and ignored them.

A meager breakfast of fish stew was served before we reported for duty, and though I tried to soften the hard biscuit accompanying it, chewing it still took considerable effort. I caught a glimpse of Tyrnan when I came on deck, but he was too busy examining the rigging to notice me. Before I could get his attention, someone grabbed me, and I whirled around.

"Time to earn your keep." Ailbert Chester thrust a bucket and scrub brushes in my hands before I could salute. "Clean this deck until it shines."

I grumbled acquiescence and set myself to task. All the while I could feel the bosun's eyes boring into me.

Instead of wallowing in self-pity at being forced to perform such menial labor, I was determined to make the most of the journey. After all, I would rather be cleaning bird waste and grime off the deck of a ship than sit and embroider. The thought made me pause, a smile fluttering across my mouth. Mother was terrible at embroidery, but Lilias inherited Grandmother's talent, and when I gave up on my own work, I would watch her design such beautiful scenes as would make the weavers of Ilano jealous of her technique. I sat back on my heels, thinking how acutely I missed Kyra's imagination, Alyx's proficiency with a sword, and Rian and Khyr's humor. I missed Mother's teasing smile and Father's stern glare whenever we made mischief. This was the longest we'd ever been apart, and I felt sick from it. A tear stained the deck, and I quickly scrubbed it away and wiped a sleeve across my face.

"I hope you're not prone to sulking."

I looked up into Seaman Erec's face. His eyes flickered from my face to the brush clutched in my white-knuckled grip, and his lip curled as if he worried I was about to vomit. Or worse, sob.

"No. I'm not," I said.

"Good. Because there's no one here who will mollycoddle you."

"I don't want to be mollycoddled. I want to be left alone."

He laughed at me, actually laughed, and before I could stop myself, I was on my feet and inches from his face.

"You all act like a bunch of children." I gritted my teeth. "You posture around like puffed up roosters and bully anyone who isn't like you. You claim seamanship is something to be proud of, but when someone comes on board your ship willing to learn, you rub their inexperience in their face. I don't care a whit if you don't read books but stop stomping on those who do just because they don't have saltwater in their veins. We're all here for the same thing, aren't we? To find adventure on unexplored lands? Doesn't that make us equal?"

He glanced away and back so quickly I almost missed it, but there was no mistaking the voice that spoke behind me.

"It does, indeed, naturalist," Captain Romy said.

I winced and slowly turned around to salute the captain, who stood as stoically as if I hadn't insulted his entire crew.

"I hope you haven't been receiving any trouble?"

"Nothing I can't handle, Captain."

"So I see," he said flatly.

"Just a little bit of getting to know each other, Captain," Erec said. "We're not used to having so many trippers on board after all."

"See that nothing goes beyond words, Seaman Erec." Though the captain spoke to the man behind me, his eyes never left mine, and I shrank inwardly knowing he meant this for me as well.

"Of course, Captain."

Satisfied, Captain Romy strode away with all the confidence and authority of a seasoned seaman.

I leaned closer to Erec and whispered, "That keeps happening to me. Does he always appear out of nowhere like that?"

"He always knows what's happening on his ship," Erec said.

For the love of Artur, I hoped that wasn't true.

CHAPTER II

For the next five days, we followed the same monotonous routine. I arose early to dress before everyone stirred, then was forced to perform whatever arduous and demeaning task Bosun Chester could devise. Despite my frustration, I didn't argue nor complain. If he kept treating me like a common sailor, it meant he believed I was, and I didn't want to give him a reason to think otherwise. Telken and his friends continued to glower in my direction, but they made no comment nor threatened me with violence. Hrod was the only person who showed me any kindness, and I regarded him with the same admiration and affection as one would a grandfather. He was quick with a smile and an anecdote to ease my frustrations after a long day of being ordered around by a tyrant.

Between working on the line and consulting with his fellow cartographers, Tyrnan was busier than I was, so we rarely spoke. One morning before Bosun Chester had a chance to track me down, I managed to steal a few uninterrupted minutes. We looked out over the vast ocean undulating in blue and green iridescence.

"How many more days, do you think?" I asked. "The view is getting a little boring."

"Another three or four days," Tyrnan said. "The captain wishes for it to be on the lesser side."

"So, I hear." I smirked. "A bit demanding, isn't he?"

"More like ambitious." He brushed a wayward lock of brown hair out of his eyes and fixed me with a pointed stare. "You know a little about that, don't you?"

My smile widened and I shifted closer to him, needing to feel a connection to home. He ran a hand along the rail, stretching his arm until our shoulders brushed together.

"Do you think of them?" I whispered.

"The family?" He bit his lip. "I try not to. It's been easier the farther away we've sailed."

"Think they're angry?"

"Worried, most likely." He stiffened and gave me the same severe look as Father when he was preparing a lecture. "They don't know where you are."

I lowered my eyes and watched a school of fish darting just below the surface, their scales flickering like gems.

"Will they forgive me?"

"Of course, they will. After all, you're Father's favorite."

"Ha! That's never gotten me out of trouble *before!*"

Tyrnan's features relaxed and he shook his head with an indulgent smile. We lapsed into a comfortable silence, watching the spray lick against the hull. Bosun Chester found me shortly thereafter, and the moment between my brother and I vanished.

The wind died down and with it the relief from the sun's heat. While the crew worked to fill the sails with a less than favorable breeze, I worked the rigging on deck. Pulling, tying, and dragging those heavy ropes was difficult, and by the time we sailed again at a decent pace, sweat trickled down my face. Water had barely touched my lips when Bosun Chester ordered me to help in the galley. It was on the tip of my tongue to argue that I wasn't a cook, but I wanted to avoid being punished for insubordination. I spent the rest of the afternoon in the sweltering heat of the galley, peeling vegetables and washing dishes. Even the cook expressed confusion at my being there.

"They must not be too fond of you," the cook observed.

"Why do you say that?" I asked.

"Why else would they hide you down 'ere below deck?"

"They must be afraid of me." I flashed an impish grin. "I am a ginger, you know."

He laughed and later rewarded my completed work with an extra ration of dried meat.

While the rest of the crew lounged in the cooler temperatures on deck, I escaped to my quarters. The only people I encountered were those snoozing in their hammocks before their night's watch started, so I was essentially alone. I retrieved a carefully wrapped bundle from my storage locker and unrolled it to reveal my precious sword. It was in dire need of polishing. The process of returning the steel to a brilliant shine was cathartic, and I was soon lost in a world where only myself and the blade existed.

"Where'd you steal that, boy?" an all-too-familiar voice asked.

I continued to rub the metal free of debris and answered without making eye contact. "It was a gift."

"Oh, yeah?" Telken leaned over my shoulder and peered closer.

My hand tensed on the grip, but I didn't hesitate in my ministrations.

"Decent looking blade. Who gave it to ya?"

"My father," I said. Emotions tightened my throat, and the words were squeezed from my lips.

"Oh, aye," he said with an astonishing amount of sympathy. He moved away from me. I glanced over my shoulder and saw his friends accompanying him. They pulled their chairs closer, forming a half circle around me.

"My father taught me everything I know about sailing," Telken said. "And he learned from his father. That kind of learning you can't get from books." The malice disappeared from his tone as he lapsed into nostalgia. There was a wave of nods from the men assembled. It was true, I conceded. There were many lessons in life one could not learn from books.

"My father gave me his lucky knife," another man said. "Plunged it into a nasty fish that got caught on my line and made to sink its teeth in me. Got lodged in its bones and I weren't fast enough to grab it before it flopped off the boat. Wish I still had that knife, 'specially now I've lost Pop."

"My pa served with Captain Romy's father," added a young man, probably Alyx's age. "Said there wasn't a greater honor for him. 'Trust your captain,' he said, 'because to him, you're family, and he'll take care of you as such.'" A murmur of assent echoed among the men, and a small smile spread across my face as each added their memories and experiences with their fathers. It was the first time I felt a connection with the crew, a sense of comradery over a shared love.

Telken pointed at my sword. "Did he teach you how to use that? Your father, I mean."

"He did," I said. "I'm not nearly as proficient as he is, but I'm still learning."

"We're always learning." Telken's gaze sharpened. "Even if some people think we don't."

I blushed at his comment, but I kept my mouth shut.

The men reminisced while I continued to polish my sword until I found it acceptable. By that time, the evening meal was ready, and the quarters quickly became deserted as hungry men answered the dinner bell. I was afforded a few minutes to myself, and I took the opportunity to attend to my toilet, shaking with fear at every creak and noise despite not being discovered for several days. As I hurried toward the galley tucking my shirt into my breeches, I collided with another sailor. I threw my arms out defensively, knocking the man in the face.

"I'm sorry!" I gushed an apology, hoping the figure wasn't the hateful Chester. My eyes adjusted to the dim light, and I sighed with relief when I recognized the voice speaking out of the darkness.

"Watch what you're doing!" Erec rubbed his nose. He sniffed several times and looked down at his fingers to check for blood.

"I didn't hurt you, did I?"

"You struck me in the face," he answered dryly. "But no. No harm done it appears." I could feel his glare though I could barely make out his face. "Food is being served and you're usually the first in line. What were you doing?"

I mimicked the coarse language I'd heard around the ship. "Can't a man take a piss in peace?"

"Go on then." He jerked his head toward the galley.

I let out a relieved breath as I brushed past him, my heart thudding in time to my brisk pace. I'd come close to being ruined. I prided myself on how careful I was in concealing my secret, and it was humbling to see how easy it would be to lose everything. Knees shaking, I accepted my bowl of fish stew and hard biscuit. I found a place far away from everyone else so they couldn't see my hands trembling.

"Are you okay?" I jumped and nearly spilled my food at the sound of Tyrnan's voice. I pressed a hand to the table to steady myself and took a large bite of biscuit before answering.

"Fine," I said around a mouthful of food. "You know how it feels to have normal body functions without fear that someone will catch you and either throw you in the brig or have their way with you?"

"I do," he mumbled.

"That makes one of us." I continued to shove food into my mouth as he picked at his food pensively.

"I knew this was a horrible mistake," he whispered.

"Relax. I was just being dramatic."

"That doesn't make the situation any less real. I hate that you always have to be on your guard."

"It's getting easier. Don't worry about me." I nudged him with my shoulder, and he reluctantly smiled. We finished our meals together, and I had to bury memories of dinners at Praed Castle before I grew homesick. I wasn't lying when I told Tyrnan I was becoming more comfortable aboard ship, but I was looking forward to the freedom afforded by dry land. Once we reached the first island, I would be able to sneak away if I needed privacy. I'd grown accustomed to the sway of the ship, but I was eager to put my feet on dry land again.

As dawn broke, Hrod and I watched the rhythmic rise and fall of the waves as they turned golden yellow and pink. We stood high above the deck in the crow's nest, keeping a lookout for stray vessels and signs of pirates, which Hrod assured me was a remote possibility.

"No pirates been seen in these water for years," he said. "Not since Captain Romy fought the last of 'em." His chest was puffed out proudly, as if our captain had singlehandedly destroyed the entire band of Crif pirates. I smiled indulgently at him and allowed him to continue weaving tales of heroics featuring our magnificent Captain Romy.

I'd volunteered to keep Hrod company on his night's watch and listening to his stories helped pass the time. I wasn't prepared for how cold it became on the sea at night, and the thin blanket didn't help. Hrod shuffled closer when he noticed my teeth chattering, though he didn't pause in his storytelling. His constant stream of conversation not only kept him awake, but also prevented his face from freezing. I took a cue from him and added my own questions and commentary, and it worked to take my mind off the biting wind and the flapping sails until the sun finally made its appearance.

"It's beautiful," I breathed as the sun rose higher, illuminating the blue sky and turning the clouds orange.

"Always is," Hrod said. "No two sunrises are alike, and every one is a beauty. Almost enough to make a man weep."

"Surely not a hardened sailor like yourself."

He chuckled and drew a pipe from the inside of his vest, which he packed with an aromatic blend of herbs. Without a flame to light it, he merely rested the mouthpiece against his lips as he contemplated the rising sun. The morning grew brighter, casting shadows along the deck. I watched them recede completely, making way for the light of day. When the deck was fully visible, we descended to start the morning work.

"Only a few more days until we reach our first destination," I said. "What do you look forward to most?"

"Fresh meat. Gods willing, there'll be some tasty critters to feast on."

I laughed at such a simple hope and dropped to the deck with a loud *thwack*. I managed to make it through most of the morning without a run-in with Bosun Chester, who seemed in a particularly distracted mood.

"The cleats need polishing," he said. I had the sense he was either grasping for something for me to do, or he was just as preoccupied with our impending landing. He placed a rag and polish into my hands and left.

I'm not ashamed to admit I stuck my tongue out at his retreating form.

The tedious work allowed me to consider what I most wished to see once we reached land. I was also excited to eat fresh food like Hrod and to feel solid ground below me. But I mostly anticipated filling the blank pages in my book with sketches of new species and adventures. My mind wandered as I pictured what this new place would be like. Would there be vast prairies and rocky hills like Praed? Lush grasses and fertile fields like Ilano? Or perhaps I would see something I couldn't even comprehend.

Raised voices and shouting drew me out of my musings, and I followed the noise until I came upon a semi-circle of men surrounding a pair dueling with short, rough-hewn swords. I leaned against the mast, crossed my arms, and watched them parry and thrust awkwardly across the deck amid the cheers of their friends. One man seemed comparatively better at wielding a sword, and he quickly gained the upper hand, sending his opponent stumbling back into the railing with a lunge any decent swordsman could easily deflect. The men howled and clapped, and the victor helped the loser to his feet.

"Next?" the winner asked, his arms spread wide. "Who is brave enough to challenge me?" There was a smattering of laughter, but no one accepted the invitation.

"You, boy!" The voice was Telken's and he was addressing *me*.

"Huh?" Sweat broke out on my palms. I worried that I wasn't supposed to be watching the men when I should've been working.

"Go get that sword of yours and teach this boasting fool a lesson!" His friends nodded enthusiastically at the idea.

I locked eyes with the stocky man standing in the center of the crowd casually swinging his sword. He broke into a sly grin, no doubt thinking me an easy victory.

"Go on then, boy. I'll wait."

My jaw clenched. Again, calling me *boy*? I dashed below to the sleeping quarters, vowing to wipe that self-satisfied grin off his face and show him what a proper sword can do.

CHAPTER 12

The men were murmuring among themselves when I emerged on the deck buckling my belt and adjusting the scabbard. Something transformed in me when the weight settled on my hips. I approached my opponent confidently and stood, straight backed and square shouldered, waiting for the signal to begin. His eyes registered the well-oiled leather of my belt, its gleaming silver buckle, and the hilt of my sword.

"Shall we?" I waggled my eyebrows up and down.

The man shook himself and smiled. "On guard, as they say." He raised his blade.

I drew my sword from its scabbard, the blade scraping metallically as it cleared the leather. I held it before my face as my brothers and I did. This sign of respect was lost on my opponent.

"What's that mean?" he asked.

"Never mind." I twirled the blade, the sunlight playing off the steel in blinding glory.

He came at me clumsily, using his bulk as a primary means of attack. As he lunged forward, I grabbed his wrist and pulled him forward. His momentum launched him onto the deck. In his favor, he kept hold of his sword, but his exposed back was an easy target. I pointed the tip of my blade between his shoulder blades.

"Yield?"

He growled in response and rolled away, throwing up his arm to knock my sword away. I leapt backward and swung downward. He met the attack with a decent block, but he hadn't gained his feet. I took advantage of his prone position and pushed hard against our locked blades. He kicked out, and I brought up a knee to block the blow. The force knocked me off balance, and he pushed up on our locked blades, unleashing a guttural sound at the back of his throat. He tucked his feet under himself and smiled triumphantly, but before he could stand, I pushed our tangled swords to the side and kicked him in the chest. He fell backward, the breath *whooshing* out of him. While he lay panting, I carefully placed a foot on his neck, my sword level with his eyes.

"Yield?"

Unable to speak, he nodded. I released him and extended a hand to help him up. He took it begrudgingly and stood, rubbing his neck.

"Where'd you learn to fight like that?"

"My father," I said. "I would be happy to teach you."

He nodded and slapped me good-naturedly on the back.

"Tomorrow," he said. "I'm spent. Name's Rex."

"Symon."

"Three cheers for young Symon!" Rex called out and draped an arm across my shoulders. The men answered in kind, and my cheeks flushed with the sudden outpouring of attention.

"Fancy work," Telken said. "I've got coin says no one can beat him."

My eyes widened and all the blood drained to my feet as Telken goaded his fellow crewmates into challenging me. When someone took up the bet, Telken whispered that I'd have a share in any coin if I won. To be honest, I agreed to fight not for the money, but for the sake of Telken's eager face and the chance to make peace with the crew.

The man I sparred with was less aggressive though no less passionate than Rex. He was quick on his feet when we circled and clashed. He wisely studied my feet as we moved, but I used this to trick him into thinking I was going to quickly move to the right. When he raised his sword to deflect an attack from that side, I swung down and to the left, catching him under the arm. He froze and looked down at my blade.

He guffawed. "I guess they'd call that a killing blow. Well done, boy."

Three more men answered Telken's challenge, and all were beaten, drawing a larger and larger crowd of clapping and jeering men who traded coins at the end of each round. I strutted around the deck, though the accomplishment of trouncing such undertrained men was poor compared to besting my brothers. Tyrnan joined in the spectacle, and though I sensed his displeasure, he, too, became swept up in the fun and bet coins in my favor. Inevitably, Telken's call to arms went unanswered. I was left with a sheathed sword and a sharp grin.

"What's the matter?" I wiggled my shoulders. "Too afraid to lose to a boy? Come now. Is no one brave enough to stand up to me?" There was some shaking of heads and muted laughter, but no one took the bait. I was counting myself the undefeated champion of *The Wayward Aymelina* when everyone suddenly dropped their gleeful expressions and shot to their feet, their hands to their foreheads in salute.

"I believe *I* am."

My heart thudded to a stop. If I were a lesser woman, I would have soiled my breeches at the sound of the distinctive voice. I slowly turned and looked up into the placid face of Captain Romy, his hand resting on the hilt of his sword. Behind him, First Mate Evrard scowled. I swallowed nervously. I didn't know if what we were doing was permitted, and I predicted a sound reprimand in my future if I'd broken some unknown rule.

Captain Romy removed his hat and handed it to his irritated brother, then unsheathed his sword in a smooth, practiced motion.

"If you're not too afraid," Captain Romy said, so low only I could hear.

My expression hardened and I answered him by raising the blade of my sword. He mimicked my salute, and with a sideways swipe of our blades, the duel began.

Not surprisingly, Captain Romy proved to be a much more challenging opponent than the crew, moving quickly and precisely. He easily deflected all my well-practiced attacks. After a while, it felt like he was toying with me. I gripped my sword tightly, took a breath, and told myself to wait and watch. I studied the movement of his feet, the placement of his hands, and the intensity of his eyes until I could anticipate every subtlety. His abilities nearly matched Father's.

Our blades clashed again and again, sparks falling into my hair, eliciting gasps from our audience. More men gathered to watch, but I shut out their voices and faces and focused solely on Captain Romy. I raised my arms, making my midsection vulnerable, and he didn't hesitate to strike. When he lunged forward, I brought my blade down with all my strength, sending *his* plunging toward the deck. I stepped on it and thrust my sword toward his chest, but he threw his other arm out and flung my wrist away. I brought my elbow up toward his face as I was propelled sideways, but he leaned back and pulled his sword out from under my foot. I stumbled but didn't fall. I spun around, my sword raised in defense. Sweat poured down my face and into my eyes, but I was pleased to see Captain Romy out of breath.

He raised a finger and I nodded. He took a moment to remove his coat and vest. While he loosened his neckcloth, I threw off my own coat and wiped a hand across my brow. Bets were placed among the men, and I only hoped my brother at least was bidding in my favor.

After Captain Romy divested himself of several layers of clothing, I shocked myself by admiring his lean physique. He strode forward on long and well-muscled legs. My gaze traveled up his lean torso, over his broad chest, and down his toned arms. He held his sword at the ready. I squeezed my eyes shut and mentally slapped myself for being ridiculous. I opened them again with the determination to prove myself equal to that of a legendary hero. I made several quick movements to distract his attention, but he was too steady for that. He towered over me, but instead of being dismayed, I used this to my advantage. I raised my blade high, and when his eyes flickered toward it, I dropped to my knees and swept my sword toward his midsection. He barely dodged the attack, and I boldly thrust my sword forward as he tipped precariously backward. He grabbed my wrist, and I gasped as he pulled me close to his body.

An embarrassing flush inflamed my cheeks, and I frantically struggled to break free. My bound breasts brushed his chest, and heat spread from my neck to the tips of my ears. A breath shuddered out of me, and I faltered.

The point of his sword pressed my side. Anger flowed through my veins. I gritted my teeth and drove my free hand into his abdomen. A *whoosh* of air blew over my ear, and his hand tightened painfully on my sword arm. He wrapped his free arm around me, then entwined one of his legs around mine. We tipped backwards, and I hit the deck, pinned beneath him. I could barely breathe, but I didn't relent my hold on my sword. The coolness of steel touched my neck, and I looked into Captain Romy's stormy gray eyes.

"Yield?" he asked between breaths.

I sighed in resignation. Enough was enough. I nodded, and he pushed himself to his feet. I accepted his offered hand and rose wearily to my feet.

"What would you have done if I wasn't your captain?" he asked.

"I would have broken your nose with my forehead," I said without thinking. A smile flitted across his face, and I offhandedly noted he'd grown a sparse beard since we left port. It was very quiet, and I peered at the crew out of the corner of my eye. They sat in stunned silence, observing our exchange.

Captain Romy reached for his discarded clothing. "Don't you have work to do?"

Everyone scrambled to their feet and scattered like mice across the ship. I bit my lip to keep from laughing and inspected the blade of my sword to hide my smile.

"Well met, Mr. Red," Captain Romy said as he buttoned up his coat. He extended a hand to his brother, who handed back his hat, an even deeper scowl on his face. "You've taken lessons from someone with considerable skills."

"Yes." I cursed the hollowness in my voice. I swallowed back the emotions threatening to reduce me to a blithering mess. "My father taught me. He was a knight of the highest caliber. No man could match his skill in battle."

"Was?" There was an unexpected amount of tenderness in his eyes, and I realized how my words sounded.

"He's...retired."

"Ah." He smiled with evident relief. "Please send along my compliments when you speak to him again."

"I will, sir."

He nodded dismissively and strode away with Evrard trailing closely behind.

"Well done, indeed, boy." Telken placed a few coins in my hand. "Never saw a thing like it."

"A skilled swordsman?"

"Nah. Someone comin' to blows with Captain Romy."

"They lose more quickly than I did?"

"Nah." He shook his head. "He never joined in the fun before. Must have thought you were more worth fightin' than us."

"I'm honored," I said flatly.

Telken extended a hand. "No hard feelings?"

I blinked dumbly. Really? If I'd have known all it took to earn Telken's respect was to win him a few coins, I would have picked a fight long ago. I took his hand, and he shook it in a crushing grip.

"I'm too agreeable to hold a grudge."

Telken laughed and slapped me hard on the back before returning to his work. I looked down at the coins in my hand and slowly closed my fingers around them. It made me happier than beating five men in combat, for the weight and feeling of the cool metal against my skin was a tangible representation of the acceptance of the crew. Before leaving Faqur, I didn't expect to make friends, but I hoped not to draw too much bullying. A turning point had been reached, and I predicted from this point forward, my life on board *The Wayward Aymelina* would be greatly improved.

The next day, I remained true to my word and commenced teaching Rex how to properly wield a sword. He wasn't much taller than me, but his shoulders were broad from years of working at sea. His lips were chapped and his cheeks permanently windblown. His hair was luxuriously thick, sun-bleached, and fell in waves to his shoulders, though he usually tied it back. He turned out to be a dedicated student. He respected my knowledge, and in turn I listened to his advice when it came to navigating the crew.

"The more you keep to yourself, the more they think you're too good for 'em," he explained.

"Telken tried to pick a fight the moment I stepped foot on the ship because of my red hair," I said. "What did they think I'd do?"

"Bah." He waved my concerns away as if they were nonsense. "A lot of posturing to sort out what kind of man you are."

We sat together in the warm afternoon sunshine polishing our blades after a grueling lesson. I listened while he talked about sailing twice before with Captain Romy and fighting the Crif Burdeeds. Prior to becoming a sailor, he'd been a successful fisherman with his father and brothers. But adventure called to him, as it did to many of us, and against his family's wishes, he abandoned his birthright and became a sailor.

"Why didn't they want you to become a sailor?"

"Dangerous," he said. "Though no more so than wrestling a big fish, as I told 'em. I guess it's natural they should worry. Family does that."

"Yes," I said. "Have you a family of your own?"

"Aye." He beamed, revealing a crooked but surprisingly full set of teeth. "Thank the Gods my wife stayed with me. She was just a young thing then. We've had a few little ones since."

I opened my mouth to inquire further, but Erec approached and interrupted our conversation.

"The captain wants to see you," he informed me without preamble.

Rex met my eye and smiled at my pallid expression.

"Not to worry, Symon." Rex patted my shoulder. "If he were angry, he'd send his first mate."

"I hope you're right." I sheathed my sword and rose to follow Erec. The seaman wore a stony expression that gave nothing away, and my anxiety steadily increased as I was led aft toward the captain's cabin. Erec stopped before the door and rapped his knuckles lightly against the wood.

"*Am* I in trouble?" I asked.

Erec shrugged. "I don't know. Like Rex said, Captain Romy wouldn't have sent *me* if you were. He doesn't like to perpetuate rumors and speculation among the crew." A call to enter came from inside, and Erec threw open the door and indicated for me to precede him. The moment I was inside, the door slammed shut. Erec had abandoned me.

Daylight streaming through the large windows lining the stern lit the great cabin like a beacon. To my left stood a table surrounded by chairs and an impressive map at its center. Bulkheads were fitted with shelves of books and scrolls and hung with an assortment of medals and accolades. I repressed a snort at such an obvious display of valor and allowed my eyes to drift around the room. There were a few paintings, but otherwise the panels were plain polished wood. Toward the back of the cabin was an expansive desk, and sitting at it was Captain Romy, patiently waiting for me to finish my perusal. Behind him was the characteristically perturbed First Mate Evrard and the ever-pleasant Second Mate Absalon.

"Please." Captain Romy indicated a chair opposite him. "Have a seat, Mr. Red."

"I much prefer Symon," I sat uneasily before the imposing men, wringing my sweating palms on my legs. The first mate raised an eyebrow in reply and the second mate smiled, dimpling his cheeks. The captain said nothing. His silence made me even more nervous, and I had the sudden feeling that's what he intended.

"Have I done something wrong?" I asked.

"Your captain hasn't addressed you, boy," Evrard snapped. "Hold your tongue."

Captain Romy raised a hand toward the first mate. "You've done nothing wrong. Aside from a little impertinence." The corner of his mouth twitched, and I sank further into my chair. "I have a proposition for you."

I raised an eyebrow but took the first mate's advice and made no response.

"You've proven yourself adept with a sword. Would be willing to use your skills in a more productive capacity than simply winning a few coins?"

"What sort of capacity?" I asked.

"Security," he said.

"Working for me to put it bluntly," Evrard said. "Your captain thinks you'd be useful to me in certain situations."

"Such as?"

"Using your skin to protect the captain and crew. You and I would be the first to scout new territories for signs of danger, eliminate any, and cover the men from attacks."

I cocked my head. "In other words, a human shield."

"Not quite so grim," Captain Romy said. "But your abilities in swordsmanship could be beneficial in the event we encounter hostiles."

"In time," Evrard added. "You'll be training with me daily until I decide you're good enough to join me on dry land."

"You have less than two days," Captain Romy said. "We'll be laying anchor at our first island by then, at which time you will accompany First Mate Romy ashore as the first team to scout the area." The first mate in question opened his mouth to protest, thought better of it, and pursed his lips. His dislike of this plan furthered my unease.

"While I appreciate the honor," I said, careful to remain respectful. "I don't believe I deserve to be so singled out. I fear the crew might perceive such an assignment as favoritism, and the last thing I want is to foster resentment."

"The crew will respect the captain's orders without complaint," Evrard said. We locked eyes for the briefest moment, and though his features were hardened, I could sense his meaning. I nodded slowly and looked back at the captain.

"I understand your hesitation," Captain Romy said. "If you require some time to consider, I will grant it. But we cannot wait long. First Mate Romy is eager to begin your training. He doesn't like to delay." A snort of laughter burst from Absalon before he could stop himself, and I had to bite the inside of my cheek to keep from giggling at his feeble attempt to hide his amusement. His brother glared, his lip curled in disgust.

My gaze wandered over the surface of the desk as I considered the offer. Unlike Father's disarray of papers, Captain Romy's desk was neat and orderly. There was hardly anything upon it, and what little there was had been sorted into piles perfectly aligned with the edge of the desk. There were no adornments save one: an aged compass. Though the shine of the metal had dulled, the face was as pristine as if it had been painted that morning. The needle hovered just to the left of the prominent N, and I found myself mesmerized by the slight shift and sway as it teetered along the points of the star radiating from the center. A hand covered the compass, and I blinked back into reality as Captain Romy brought it to his face.

"It was my father's." He ran a finger along the curved edge like a caress. "I understand from Seaman Erec that your father gifted you with something precious, too."

"Yes," I whispered. Captain Romy met my eyes, and I hoped he didn't see the pain of missing Father on my face.

"Did he intend for you to leave your sword to rust in a footlocker?" he asked.

Oh, he was good. Despite my best efforts to keep a straight face, a smile quirked up the corner of my mouth. "Are you a father yourself, sir?"

His brothers' eyes widened in shock at my impertinence.

"No," Captain Romy said. "Why?"

"Your impressive abilities at manipulation and guilt. They're frequently used weapons in a father's arsenal, are they not?"

"Yes." I could tell he was amused, but he still didn't smile. Maybe he didn't know how, poor thing. The first mate cleared his throat and reminded the captain that he was very busy. The captain stood and prepared to dismiss me.

I hurriedly got to my feet and blurted out: "I'll do it, sir. The security. I make a very good human shield."

"Good." Captain Romy responded without hesitation, as if expecting my acceptance. He glanced over his shoulder at his brother. "Evrard, I leave the boy to you."

The first mate cast a dark glare in my direction. I swallowed the lump in my throat.

"On deck in five," he growled. "Don't be late."

I barely saluted and sprinted from the room, almost tripping over my own feet as I scrambled out the door.

CHAPTER 13

I'd always thought Father was a strict and demanding teacher, but just one day of training with First Mate Evrard left me wondering if Father had been too easy on me. I'd been sent crashing to the ground hundreds of times only to be yanked to my feet and instructed to try harder. By the time the sun slipped below the horizon, I was drenched with sweat, bleeding, and exhausted. But my determination to prove myself propelled me forward, holding nothing back as I swung at his exposed side in the hopes of drawing blood.

My blade swept across the first mate's torso, and he barely dodged the tip before I repositioned myself and sliced the air in front of his chest. His sword met mine, and he pushed me backward with so much force I almost fell. But I was too stubborn to lose and attacked with such ferocity the larger man stumbled. My sword met his again and again, faster and harder with each stroke as I released my pent-up fear and anger. When First Mate Evrard was backed up against a mast, I lunged toward his middle, anticipating a downward block. But with a clang of steel, he diverted my sword toward the sky and kicked me square in the stomach, driving me backward. I doubled over to catch my breath, and the weight of his sword rested on my back. I was finished.

"Enough," he said once it became too dark to see properly. "We'll resume the lesson tomorrow."

My throat burned as ragged breaths shuddered from my chest, and though I could barely hold up my body, I drew my sword up in a respectful salute. He mirrored my actions, and I collapsed onto the deck.

"Easy, there, boy," a voice said out of the haze swirling around my mind. I looked up as Telken heaved me to my feet, nodded respectfully to the first mate, then dragged me away. Another man stepped in to assist, and together they settled me onto the deck to recover.

"He shouldn't be so hard on him," the other man said as he pried my sword from my hand.

"If he isn't," Telken began, "how can he make him the best he can be?"

The other man scoffed, and Telken left us alone to find me some food. My stomach roiled in anticipation, eliciting a laugh from the sailor tucking himself next to me. He sheathed my sword in the scabbard at my side.

"You've got balls of stone, I'll give ye that," he said. "I'm Luc, by the way." He held out his hand, and I shook it dismally.

"Symon," I said weakly. "Pardon me if I don't bow."

Luc laughed heartily and slapped me on the back. I gasped at the soreness already creeping into my bones. Telken returned shortly thereafter, and I practically inhaled the colorless mush he placed before me.

Telken nudged me with his elbow. "Just so you know, I've got coin says you can put First Mate Romy into the dirt before week's end."

Our eyes met, and a smile spread across my face.

"I'll take that bet!" Luc said. "No offense, Symon. You're good with a sword, but First Mate Romy'd rather swim to Faqur than lose to a tripper."

My grin broadened. "The only offense will be to your coin purse when you lose."

Certain memories elicit a sense of heartwarming nostalgia, such as the birth of a child, a wedding, or a childhood friendship. One of my fondest memories was the day I received my first sword. I'd been play-fighting with a wooden toy for years, sparring with my brothers and losing once they acquired steel blades. I remember sitting in the middle of the training yard after they sliced my wooden sword in half and laughed all the way into the castle. I cried until I couldn't breathe, then I flung the pieces at the wall, splintering them further. Not long after, we celebrated my eleventh birthday, and Father presented me with a newly crafted belt and scabbard. Sheathed inside was a simple yet shining new sword just my size. I wept tears of joy and threw my arms around him, thanking him profusely. It still makes my eyes well up thinking about that day.

I expected nothing could ever replace its importance in my life until one afternoon while I rested my numb limbs after a grueling training session, the sun shone mercilessly on my scorched scalp and reddened face. A call came from high up in the crow's nest.

"Land ahoy off the port bow!"

Everyone dropped what they were doing and raced to the side of the ship, pushing and shoving for a chance to see the first glimpse of land in days. The ship turned until we were parallel to a spit of island unimpressive in size yet everything I hoped it would be. Long fronds of trees covered the area, and the lack of beach would make rowing ashore tricky. We continued, a hushed silence permeating the ship. Another island came into view, and I was relieved to see it was much larger. A lone peak rose into the sky out of the dense foliage, and best of all, there was a long, uninterrupted beach stretched out before us.

"Prepare to drop anchor!" The first mate's voice boomed over the ship. The men instantly beat to their quarters, and for a second, I was left to watch as we drew closer to the island. Other than a slight breeze rustling the trees, there was no movement, no sign of animal or man. My eyes darted between the openings in the thick forest, but I saw nothing. The ship slowed, and I knew I should be helping the crew, but my fingers dug into the railing, suddenly on edge.

"What do you see?"

I should have been startled and abashed at the sound of the first mate's voice beside me, but I was too focused to care.

"Nothing," I said uneasily. "Not even a bird. It isn't natural."

"I agree." He eyed the coastline. "You and I along with a few other men will be the first to row over and make sure it's safe."

"Understood," I said.

"Arm yourself and be prepared to leave in five minutes."

"Yes, sir." I took one last lingering look as the ship coasted to a stop and thought I spotted a flickering shadow. I squinted and peered closer, but nothing was there. I shook my head, ignored the shiver running up my spine, and descended into the crew's quarters to retrieve my sword.

I looked back up at the ship as myself, First Mate Evrard, and three other men were rowed toward the island in a creaking dinghy. The dark blue water lapped the sides as the distance between us and *The Wayward Aymelina* increased. The crew watched us leave, their expressions tense and uncertain. Many of them were anxious to set foot on dry land, but the fear of the unknown tempered their excitement.

I settled my eyes on the perpetually sour Ailbert Chester and bit my tongue to keep from sticking it out at him. He obviously wasn't pleased with the change in my circumstances on board since he could no longer pester me with mundane tasks. Secretly, I thought he might be envious. Although boasting is considered a defect of character, I raised my chin in haughty mockery of his frustration. He stared daggers back at me, his teeth bared. A voice in my head cautioned me to watch myself with this man.

I broke away from his angry glare to search for Captain Romy. Just before the scout team had boarded the dinghy, I'd overheard an argument between the captain and first mate.

"No," First Mate Evrard said firmly, piquing my interest. I'd never heard him use that tone with his captain before. I paused, pretending to check the anchor rope so I could listen. Yes, eavesdrop.

"I'm your captain," Captain Romy stated in a dangerously even tone.

"Exactly my point. You're staying here."

"This is *my* expedition."

"Right. And you must live to tell about it."

"Don't be so dramatic." Captain Romy scoffed.

"We don't know what's out there, and until we do, the captain stays here," he pressed a finger on the gunwale of the dinghy, "with his ship and his crew."

In the ensuing silence, the hairs on the back of my neck prickled, and I chanced a peek. First Mate Evrard stood solidly as ever, unwavering despite the storm in his brother's eyes. The captain's jaw clenched as he stared down the first mate, a slight flush to his cheeks. It was the first time I'd ever seen him break his usual calm countenance. His hand tightened around the hilt of his sword, but his brother did not waiver. I found myself looking from one to the other, openly staring. Finally, Captain Romy relented, and he nodded, though his expression didn't soften. We boarded the dinghy without him.

The captain's perturbation remained visible as we moved further and further away. Eventually the distance was so great the crew were indistinguishable from each other. I turned from the ship and fixed my gaze on the beach as we rowed closer, scanning the shore for signs of life.

"Keep a sharp eye," First Mate Evrard ordered. I nodded, gripping the hilt of my sword. The keel scraped against rock, and with a final pull of the oars propelled us onto the beach. I leapt out of the dinghy and nearly wept at the touch of my feet on the sand. The swelling sea pulsed in my legs as I stepped toward the line of trees. Behind me, the crew tied the dinghy to a large stone.

First Mate Evrard issued commands. He singled out two of the rowers. "You two patrol the beach." He pointed to the steersman. "And you stay near the dinghy and gather wood for fires." The crew set themselves to task, their movements nothing but a blur in my periphery.

No sound came from the forest save the rustle of leaves and the groan of trees swaying in the wind. My attention darted toward each fluttering branch, but there were no creatures scurrying in the undergrowth. "Very strange."

"I don't even hear birds," the first mate mused.

"Shall we take a closer look?" I asked. To my surprise, a glimmer of excitement flickered in his eyes. If I looked closely, I could just make out a ghost of a smile.

"After you, Mr. Red," he said with a jerk of his head toward the trees.

I took a deep breath and stepped toward the shadowy undergrowth. Dried leaves crunched underfoot, and I shuffled them aside to make less noise. It was cooler in the shade of the trees, and a dapple of sunshine played across the ground. A few more steps into the forest without the sounds of birds unsettled me, leaving a hollow, heavy pit in my stomach. The first mate and I locked eyes, and he silently indicated for me to continue. I moved forward and carefully placed a hand against the rough bark of a tree. It was warmer than I expected. My brows knitted and I looked closer. There was nothing remarkable about it, no sign that it held anything special under the scales of greenish brown. I leaned toward a line of sap trickling through the crevices and inhaled deeply. It was sweet. Hesitantly, I ran a finger along the sticky substance and rubbed it between my fingertips. Without thinking, I touched the tip of my tongue to the sap. It tasted vaguely like honey with a bitter undertone.

He cocked his head and his eyebrows lifted. "Well?"

I nodded and smacked my lips. "Tastes good."

I pressed my palms against the trunk and held perfectly still. I blocked out the subtle sound of the first mate's anxious shifting, the rush of blood in my ears, and my own shallow breaths. After several seconds, I was certain I felt vibrations under my hands.

Without a word, I drew my sword and sliced into the tree. The bark yielded easier than I expected, and when the dust settled, we beheld an intricate system of tunnels bored into the wood. Thousands of insects, iridescent in the low light, didn't appreciate being disturbed. Green wings sprouted from their dark bodies, and they swarmed out from the tree, encircling us. We swatted at them irritably, then with increasing desperation once we discovered their sharp sting. We careened wildly through the forest away from the nest, waving our arms frantically as we blindly navigated the unfamiliar terrain. The insects eventually stopped chasing us, and we bent over gasping to catch our breath.

"Well," I said between gulps of air. "That was exciting."

Evrard glared at me and straightened to study the area around us. We were still surrounded by trees, but in the eerie stillness I could hear the steady hum of insects and the soft rustle of leaves. I glanced at the ground. The leaves were moving. I brushed them aside to reveal a long line of bright red ants about half the size of my smallest finger. Carefully, I replaced the ground cover and looked up nervously at my companion.

"We're in for an interesting adventure," I said. "It seems this island may be overrun with dangerous insects."

"Let's not be hasty," he responded flatly. "We've seen *two*, and one only became hostile when you destroyed their home." He scratched at a welt forming on the top of his head and cursed.

I rolled my eyes and peered through the trees. Still no birdsongs, but I heard buzzing and chirping. Looking closely, I saw several different insects concealing themselves among the foliage.

"No signs of people," he said.

"No, none yet. Time will tell, I suppose."

"Let's make our way east through the trees. If the only things we encounter crawl on more than two legs, we'll deem it safe for the rest of the crew and captain to come ashore."

"Lead the way." I took one last look around and made to follow when something caught my attention. Out of the corner of my eye, I swore a shadow shifted among the foliage. I turned toward it, lifting my sword defensively as I did, scanning the area. Nothing larger than a leaf moved. The hairs on my arms and the back of my neck tingled. Something was watching. I could feel it as strongly as when making mischief as a child, I'd look up into a nurse's stern stare.

"What is it?" he called out.

"Nothing," I replied over my shoulder. I backed away from the trees, unwilling to turn away. I caught up to the first mate, and he raised his brow in question.

"Um…nothing." My tone conveyed my uncertainty. I ignored his questioning stare and proceeded with him through the forest.

We encountered nothing so ominous as the dark shape I'd seen in the trees, and First Mate Evrard deemed the island safe enough for the rest of the crew to land. The men cheered as they pulled up onto the beach and felt the ground beneath their feet, but their exuberance couldn't shake the uneasy feeling I'd had since laying eyes on this strange place.

I plastered on a fake smile for my fellow crewmembers, perfected after so many years of being a princess forced to attend social functions where I didn't know anyone but had to make a good impression.

I laughed with my friends as we set up camp and planned the next day's excursions. Out of earshot of the crew, Tyrnan found an opportunity to speak to me and he asked if I'd seen anything worth worrying about.

"Is it that obvious?" I asked in a low voice.

"Perhaps not to anyone else," he said. "But you look nervous, like when you've done something you hope no one'll discover."

I smiled conspiratorially, and he added, "Well, besides that."

"We saw some crawly things." I stared into the darkening forest. The sun was beginning to set, and fires for cooking, light, and warmth were starting to blaze around camp. "No birds or anything furry, though."

"But maybe something else?"

"Maybe…"

I dropped my voice lower, and he leaned forward to hear. "Something." I shivered and shook my head forcefully. "I didn't see anything, but I felt we weren't exactly alone."

Tyrnan nodded and glanced around nervously. "If anyone can protect us against what lurks in the dark, it's you."

I smiled, a feeling of pride swelling in my chest. My brother trusted me with his life, and presumably others did as well. It was a mighty burden to bear, heavier than a crown, but his confidence in me gave my life more meaning than a thousand jewels set in gold.

When he walked away, I turned my attention back toward the trees, my face fixed in determination. I scanned the area slowly, the noises of revelry muffled as I concentrated, but there was no movement. My hand rested on the hilt of my sword, and I vowed it would not leave my side. The dinner bell rang, and as I turned to answer its call, something flashed in my periphery. I froze, staring intently into the blackness. Was I losing my mind? But there it was—a glimmer of yellow—then it was gone. Many animals have eyes that glow in the dark, but was this predator or prey? Time, I reminded myself, would tell.

Chapter 14

Though the excitement of the previous day made me weary with exhaustion, sleep would not claim me. Every snapping twig or rustle of wind sent me bolt upright in bed, disturbing those in my immediate vicinity. I received muttered curses and an occasional pillow to the face. Finally, I gave up, pulled on my clothes, and shuffled out of the tent.

I gazed up into the clear night sky, adjusting my belt, and gripped the hilt of my sword. More stars than I'd ever seen glittered above me. I searched their multitudes in vain for a constellation I recognized. If I could find a familiar pattern, I would imagine them sweeping across the skies of Praed, and my family would be looking up at the same night sky as I was. I didn't believe in the fairytales of messages being delivered by creatures living amongst the stars, tiny beings waiting patiently for whispers between loved ones. But for a chance to let my family know I was alive and missing them, I would project from my mind thoughts that would cross hundreds of miles of sea and land to reach them. I scanned the entire scope of the sky along the beach and out toward the ship but saw not one familiar flicker of light. My shoulders sagged and I closed my eyes as a cool breeze came off the water and caressed my face.

"Couldn't sleep either?" a voice asked.

I jumped and nearly screamed in surprise. The sand muffled his approach. I should have been more vigilant. Had I been on my guard, I could have heard his steady breathing, inhaled the scent of starched clothing, salt air, and aged wood that I'd come to recognize as distinct to him alone. I looked up into the captain's questioning gaze, the darkness casting shadows across his angled features, leaving the barest glimmer from the starlight in his eyes.

"S-sorry, sir." I clumsily lifted a hand to my brow. "No, I couldn't sleep."

"Evrard tells me you've seen something, but you won't admit it. Is that true?"

A wry smile twisted my mouth. Evrard, of course. The first mate was no fool. He noticed the unease on my face every time I investigated the trees, but I wasn't ready to commit myself to voicing apprehension just because of a few shifting shadows.

"I haven't seen anything alarming," I said. Captain Romy nodded, and though he studied me intently, he did not inquire further. I returned my attention to the stars, and we stood together in silence until the sun's first rays crept tentatively over the horizon. Feet shuffled behind me, and the musky odor of sweat and herbs drifted over us as Hrod ambled in our direction.

"You can take the man out of the ship," I whispered, "but you can't take the ship out of the man."

"Yes," Captain Romy agreed, his voice strangely low and rough.

I looked up but he didn't meet my gaze. The low light cast shadows that accentuated his angled features. His beard was still short, but a few patchy areas were filling in. The squared line of his jaw drew my eyes to his cleft chin and the tuft of hair below the swell of his lower lip. He was certainly pleasing to look at. My eyes lingered on his mouth a moment too long. The captain turned at Hrod's approach and caught me staring. I inhaled sharply and lowered my face, hoping the dim hour concealed my embarrassment.

"Captain," Hrod greeted with a salute.

"There's nothing to watch out for this morning, I'm afraid," I told the aged sailor.

"There's still a sea, isn't there? Unless it dried up while I slept," Hrod said with a gap-toothed smile.

"It's still there," I assured him. "And getting brighter." We three stood on the shore as the water turned blood red, and the sky was streaked with the deepest orange as the sun climbed out of the sea.

"That's not a good sign," Hrod mused.

"What do you mean?" I asked.

They both looked at me strangely, as if whatever was going on should be obvious. I shrank back, worried that I'd made a fatal slip. Hrod shook his head indulgently and lay a reassuring hand on my shoulder.

"I forget you're not a sailor by birth," he said. He went on to explain that if the morning sky turned red with the rising sun, it was a bad omen for the coming day.

"Superstitious nonsense," I scoffed. "It's natural for the sky to change colors at sunrise and sunset. It doesn't mean anything ominous."

"So an *educated* man might say." Hrod didn't seem to take offense, yet his emphasis on the word 'educated' held an undertone of mockery. "But those who live on the sea know a thing or two 'bout using the sky to predict the weather."

I considered his statement as the sun rose higher, illuminating the water and casting light across the land. I looked back at Hrod and choked on the words I'd been about to speak. The captain had disappeared, and I had the anxious feeling that I'd offended him.

An apology would have to wait, for once the rest of the men were awake, the business of eating breakfast and preparing for the day superseded any personal issues of mine. A group of men set off with axes to fell trees. We would be staying here for a while if permanent structures were being built. Tyrnan and his fellow cartographers gathered their equipment, and I rushed to the tent to retrieve my own supplies.

I opened the tent flap carrying my pack loaded with books and writing implements and stopped short. First Mate Evrard had been waiting. He drummed his fingers on his crossed arms and said, "Don't be so hasty. Your first duty is to scout for danger. Once you've determined it's safe for the trippers to do their work, you can do yours."

"Yes, sir," I said.

"You'll go with half of them toward the interior and I'll take the rest along the coast. Meet back here in five hours."

"Yes, sir." He walked away and began conversing with Second Mate Absalon, whose excitement was palpable even from where I stood a dozen feet away. I scowled at the first mate's back. Tyrnan came to stand beside me and nudged me with his shoulder.

"Don't let him see you look at him that way," he said. "He'll knock you into the sand for sure."

I smirked. "Not if I best him first. I've got coin on the line that says I can."

Tyrnan shook his head. "You're an idiot."

"Are you ready?" I turned toward the trees. Like the day before, there was no sound but the shivering of leaves shifting in the breeze.

"Beyond ready. Do you think it's safe?"

"I don't know. But you don't have to worry. I'll protect you." He laughed, but I wasn't joking.

I led the group of four men into the dense forest, the light fading under the canopy of foliage overhead. They stared in awe at the massive trunks growing high into the blue sky. I moved confidently through the forest, watching the ground for signs of biting insects. Behind me, there was a steady murmur of conversation as the cartographers made notes and measurements, but I paid no attention to them. My every nerve was on edge, alert to any sound or movement. A large, winged insect fluttered across my vision, and I stopped abruptly to watch it dance on the wind from one delicately leaved plant to another. It landed on thin legs, its wings opening and closing as a long tongue unrolled to drink the last of the morning dew from a leaf. The colors of the body and wings were dull greens and browns, but it was mesmerizing all the same. It was close enough to touch and I held out my hand, imagining the wings soft under my fingertips, but just before I made contact, it lifted silently into the air and out of reach.

"Beautiful," I breathed.

"You should be more careful," one of the men warned. "It could have been poisonous."

"I'll take that under advisement," I muttered and strode onward.

We walked for many miles, stopping occasionally so the trippers could take notes and argue about distances and the appropriate notation of landmarks. All we'd seen were trees and insects. The absence of any other animal gnawed at me, leaving a heavy weight in my stomach.

Where were the birds? With so many insects, there had to at least be birds and small mice to eat them. When we stopped to eat a meager ration of biscuits and dried fish, I took a moment to write some notes in my journal. Something drew my attention to the trees, though I couldn't say what—perhaps a flash of movement or simply a feeling of being watched. Regardless, I lifted my head to peer into the forest. For the first time, I was certain something was there. It wasn't my imagination nor a trick of the light. For an instant, I saw something watching us through the tangle of vegetation, its amber eyes framed in black fur. By the time I got to my feet, my sword unsheathed, it was gone.

Tyrnan looked in the direction I faced and asked, "What's wrong?"

Without answering, I took off running, dodging around thick trunks and slashing at branches with my sword. Tyrnan shouted behind me, but I didn't heed his call. I ran blindly in the direction I'd seen the creature, following it deep into the forest. I stopped after several minutes to catch my breath, my sword at the ready. But there was no sign of it. I held my breath and listened. All I heard over the pounding in my head was buzzing insects. I lowered my sword, took one last hard look into the increasing darkness, and turned back toward the group of men I'd abandoned. One of them would surely report what I'd done, but I didn't care. I trudged back without a word, ignoring Tyrnan's questions and another man's rebukes, and led them back toward the beach.

One of the cartographers, a man called Oryn Thatchett, wasted no time in complaining about his escort racing off on a mad dash through the forest. His tirade was overheard by none other than Bosun Chester, who quickly related the incident to First Mate Evrard. I'd barely sat down to rest when I was summoned to the first mate's quarters to answer for my behavior.

"For the love of Artur." I heaved myself back onto my feet and kicked sand in frustration. To my consternation, I found not only the first mate, but the captain and second mate waiting for me as well. The blood drained from my face, and I raised a trembling hand to salute.

"What did you see?" First Mate Evrard demanded without preamble.

I blinked in surprise and noticed all three wore anxious expressions. I relaxed, aware that perhaps I wasn't in trouble after all.

"I can't say for certain what it was."

"It must have been something threatening," the first mate reasoned. "Otherwise, why would you run after it?"

I looked into Captain Romy's eyes and considered what he must think. If I told the truth, he'd think me mad and send me back to the ship in chains. Or he would strip me of the honor bestowed upon me so trustingly only days before. He must have read the turmoil on my face, for he took a step forward and gazed down at me sympathetically.

"Go on," Captain Romy said. "Tell us everything. We'll believe you." I ignored First Mate Evrard's derisive snort. The captain's gaze shifted irritably toward his brother.

"Won't we?" Captain Romy prompted.

"Of course," Second Mate Absalon said gently. He elbowed the taciturn first mate, who reluctantly nodded.

"I don't know what it is," I began. "But I'm certain it's not a man. It has black fur, moves swiftly and silently, and has golden eyes. I've only seen flashes out of the corner of my eye until today, when I caught it watching us. It ran away when it noticed I saw it."

"It must be intelligent then," First Mate Evrard said.

"And afraid," the second mate added. "Otherwise, why would it run?"

"It's studying us," Captain Romy said as he paced back and forth. "Gathering intelligence." He spun to face me. "You're sure it wasn't a man?"

"Absolutely."

"What do you suggest we do, Lencius?" Absalon asked.

The captain paused to consider, then said, "We will not be frightened away by shadows. We continue with the plan until we're given good reason to abandon it." Was it bravery or pride that kept Captain Romy on course? I hoped it was the former. If his stubborn pride kept us on the island and placed us in danger, I'd lose all respect for him. But the captain didn't strike me as someone who was careless with the lives of his crew.

I was perfunctorily dismissed, but not before being made to swear I would tell no one of our conversation.

"We don't want to scare anyone unnecessarily," Second Mate Absalon said.

By the wideness of his eyes and pallid expression, I guessed the man he was most anxious not to frighten was himself. I refrained from rolling my eyes, but I couldn't stop myself from saying: "I can believe men who shudder at a red dawn have much to fear."

Before the men could respond to my impertinent remark I quit the tent in haste. It was a foolish thing to say, especially as I suspected Captain Romy was already annoyed with me from earlier. But I had no patience for superstition, especially from supposedly intelligent people. And I didn't wish to dwell on the fact that an omen was predicted that morning, on the same day I finally saw the dark figure looming in the forest. The last thing

I wanted was to believe that whatever I saw was a portent of evil. From that moment forward, not only did I carry my sword everywhere, but I lay with it clutched in my hands. The creature would not find me so unprepared the next time I saw it.

It was another week before I discovered the secret to the mysterious absence of any creature besides insects. The cook experimented with some of the local plants he found, adding them to stews and considering himself very successful in supplementing our diets. Fresh fish had become part of the menu, but one day a galley boy collected some larvae from a dead tree and declared them a decent source of protein in many countries. The cook indulged him, but the resulting meal didn't sit well in my stomach. I awoke in the darkest hour of night, clutching my sides as pain shot through me. I stumbled into the forest away from camp, carelessly threw down my sword, and was violently ill for what felt like hours.

When the roiling in my belly subsided, I lay on the ground thickly blanketed with leaves until my breathing slowed. In the ensuing quiet, a strange call pierced the silence, followed by the skittering of feet. I carefully sat up. It sounded again, a screech followed by a low, throbbing hum. I didn't have a torch, but my eyes adjusted to the darkness enough for me to make out a shape scratching its way along the forest floor. It was bulky, but not very large, perhaps the size of a hen. It came closer, and I stilled. Once it was close enough to touch, I sighed in relief and nearly burst out laughing. Comparing it to a hen was a fair analogy. Before me was a squat, wingless bird, cocking its head curiously. It made a strange mumbling noise as it regarded me, and out of the darkness, more appeared, picking through the undergrowth. The night came alive with sounds of bird calls, squeaks, and chirps. I observed the trees and saw the reflections of glowing orbs staring back. The animals of this island were nocturnal. *All* of them apparently. But why? What made the day so dangerous that every creature adapted to coming out only at night? Was it the creature with amber eyes? I hadn't seen it in days, but I didn't doubt it was still out there, watching. What was it waiting for?

I brought a lantern and my books into the forest every night after that to record what I saw. I told no one, not even Tyrnan, about my discovery. For now, I wanted it to be mine, and I guarded the secret as tightly as my own identity.

Chapter 15

After several weeks on the island, a rudimentary map began to take shape. While the officers fawned over this accomplishment, I filled the pages of my book with pictures and descriptions of the creatures I'd come to learn about through hours of sitting still and remaining quiet. It was a difficult lesson in patience for me, but like my dedication to the sword, it paid off.

I learned about the flightless birds roaming the forest floor eating berries and nuts, the agile ones that caught insects in mid-flight, and the large-eyed owls that hunted the furry creatures scampering in search of food. Aside from the mice, most of the furred animals lived in the trees and grazed on leaves or picked bugs out of the bark. None of them seemed overly concerned with my presence and munched contentedly as I drew their portraits. If anyone noticed my nightly wanderings, they made no comment, and I was happy to be left alone. During the day, I babysat the cartographers and continued my training with First Mate Evrard. Sadly, I'd yet to win the bet I'd made with Telken.

One morning, we had set out early toward a lone peak jutting out of the middle of the island. All the cartographers came along, meandering, noses in their books, safe with me and the first mate to protect them. The peak loomed over us, craggy and menacing. The cartographers stopped to take measurements, and I wandered away, mindful of the distance stretching between us. After several minutes, an ominous feeling intruded my senses. The hairs on the back of my neck rose and a shiver prickled up my spine. I unsheathed my sword and stepped noiselessly through a clearing. As usual, there was little sound, and I continued to walk, heedless of how far away I was from the group. I pushed through a grove of trees, the branches low and covered with prickly spines. I cut them down with my sword, aware the noise might betray my presence. The last branch fell away to reveal marshlands tucked against the base of the mountain. The sound of rushing water filled my ears, and I spied a small waterfall flowing out of a rocky outcropping on the side of the mountain. A dark shadow beyond suggested a hidden cave.

A flicker of movement caught my attention, and I instinctively crouched, my sword raised. At first, I saw nothing. The light shifted, and the wind parted the tall grass, revealing a dark shape not more than four yards away. It was so still I thought it was a stump or a rock. But there was no mistaking those amber eyes. It stood on four legs, but the front ones were long like arms, its paws curled into fists. The top of its head barely reached my shoulders, but it was twice as thick as a man. Except for the nose and mouth, it was covered in thick, black fur. Its nostril flared, and it stomped. No sense trying to hide. I raised my hands in supplication.

"It's all right." I placed my sword gently on the ground within easy reach. The creature watched, its eyes tracing the path of my hands, seeming to understand every move I made. "I won't hurt you." My voice startled it, but it didn't flee. "What are you?"

Its chest heaved and it made a low grunting sound. I don't know what came over me, but I mirrored its position and duplicated the sound. The beast shifted backward in surprise, then stepped closer and repeated the sound, which I mimicked as best I could. The thing shook its head, whether in annoyance or aggression I couldn't say. I shook my own head, adding a little flare, and it shuffled closer so quickly I stumbled. It towered over my prone form and watched, expectantly. Closer examination revealed it was unmistakably male, and it emanated a pungent, musky odor. I made the low thrum of a night bird that made the creature cock its head. He pounded his fists into the ground, and I tumbled onto my backside with a yelp. He bared his teeth. I swallowed at the sight of those long, glistening fangs. He grunted in several short bursts, and my jaw dropped. Was he...*laughing* at me?

First Mate Evrard's voice called my name. The creature froze and looked over my shoulder.

I held out my palms to calm him. "Don't be afraid."

He looked down and snarled, but I didn't back away. The first mate came closer, and I risked calling out to him to stop. But it was too late. First Mate Evrard broke through the trees muttering to himself and chastising me for wandering off. He stilled when he saw the creature, the color draining from his face.

I stretched a hand toward him and pleaded, "Don't move."

The first mate's hand went to the hilt of his sword. I shook my head desperately and mouthed 'no.' He must have read the urgency in my eyes, for his hand slowly dropped to his side. The creature huffed at him, took a few threatening steps forward, and opened its enormous jaws to let out a deafening roar. The first mate reached for his sword, but I was on my feet before he could draw it, propelling myself into him. He hit the ground, and I squeezed my eyes shut as the creature loomed over us. Powerful fists struck the ground inches from our faces, then he dashed off into the dense foliage. I watched in awe as it retreated, calling out as it went. Dark shapes I failed to notice earlier chased after it, crashing through the trees in a panic. A moment later, it was quiet, save for mine and the first mate's harsh breaths as we lay sprawled in the dirt.

"What was it?" First Mate Evrard asked.

"I don't know. But it was magnificent."

He shoved me away and got to his feet, brushed himself off, and scolded me for leaving the safety of the group.

"I don't want to deal with the paperwork if you get yourself killed," he said. He hauled me to my feet and waited for me to retrieve my sword before stalking back through the trees.

I smiled at his back. I'd finally knocked the first mate to the ground. Telken owed me some coin.

Less than three minutes after I settled back into camp, Captain Romy towered over me and demanded I give a full report of what I'd seen in the forest. The first mate waited behind him, arms crossed, staring pointedly. A few of the crew watched, and my cheeks reddened in a mixture of anger and embarrassment.

"We should speak about it privately," I said in a low voice. "Lest the crew become frightened." Captain Romy nodded curtly, and I followed the pair back to the officers' quarters, briefly catching Tyrnan's anxious gaze.

Captain Romy whirled on me. "Tell me everything."

I'd never seen him so agitated, and I wondered if it had something to do with his brother's sullied account of what he'd seen. It was up to me to smooth things over before the captain gathered up weapons and set off to destroy a species.

"I saw the creature again, up close this time," I said.

"That's an understatement," First Mate Evrard interrupted. "It tried to kill us."

"Only because you threatened it!"

"Enough," Captain Romy snapped. "Both of you." He gave his brother a withering stare, and the first mate stepped back and kept his mouth shut. The captain gestured for me to continue. I told him everything, from the way the creature and I interacted, to my suspicions about its intelligence, to the revelation that there were many of them. He listened intently, his gaze making me feel as if I was the only person in the room. The world blurred, sharpening my focus on the captain's unwavering stare. When I finished speaking, he contemplated the tale in silence.

"I don't think they mean us any harm," I said. "If they did, it would have killed me the minute it saw me. It's obviously been watching us for a long time, but from a safe distance. I think it was protecting its home when it lunged at us. Even then, it didn't hurt us. It was like a scare tactic, a bluff show of force to chase us off."

"You can't be taking this seriously, Lencius," the first mate interrupted again. "He's just a boy. What does he know?"

Captain Romy ran a finger back and forth across his lower lip. "He's the naturalist." A short beard had grown on his once smooth face, and he worried the hairs at his chin as he regarded me. The motion drew my attention to the dark blond hair dusting the back of his hand to his tapered wrists. His fingers were lean and tanned, and I couldn't help tracing the line of his fingertips to his full lower lip.

The first mate pushed past me, shaking me out of my stupor. "We should take care of these animals now, sir, before they realize they can't scare us off the island. The next thing you know, they'll be killing us in our beds."

"They won't," I said. "Besides, they don't come out at night." I assembled the facts a second before I spoke. These creatures were the masters of daylight. Other animals waited for nightfall before venturing out.

The first mate sneered, his face inches from mine. "How do you know?"

I didn't back down. "I know."

"You've become very insolent," he said. "Speaking very freely for such a young boy without any experience to his name."

I gritted my teeth at his patronizing tone, but I didn't reply. I didn't have to.

"Evrard," Captain Romy said, in a tone of unquestionable authority. "Leave us."

The first mate looked at his brother incredulously, his mouth moving soundlessly.

"And please," the captain amended. "Tell Absalon I must speak with him."

The first mate's jaw snapped shut. With a quick nod and a sharp glare toward me, he left the officers' quarters. I glanced at the captain, uneasy about being alone with him after ogling his handsome features.

"Do you really think these creatures pose no threat?" he asked.

"I do," I said. "As long as we leave them alone. Like I said, the creature I saw could've easily killed me, but it didn't. It seemed just as curious about me as I was of it."

"I can't risk the lives of these men if you're wrong," he said, but not unkindly. He had a duty to the crew, to all of us, to keep us safe from harm.

"I understand. With your permission, I'd like to observe them, alone, to find out if I'm correct in my observations."

He considered my proposition for a long time, and my stomach churned while I waited for him to decide. He lowered his gaze, and my lungs expelled air as if I'd been punched in the gut. I'd been so transfixed by the intensity of his gray-blue eyes I'd forgotten to breathe.

"Very well," he said. "You may study these creatures for one week. I expect a full account of everything you observe. Do not leave anything out. And let me know immediately if you feel our lives are in danger."

"I will," I said. "Thank you, sir. And sir?"

"Yes?"

"I'm sorry," I said, fully meaning it. "First Mate Romy is right. I've been impertinent…at times. Sometimes I can't stop myself from speaking my mind."

"Apology accepted. But despite the validity of First Mate Romy's claim, you have proven that you have opinions worth listening to."

I couldn't help it. I beamed so brightly my expression might give me away as a flattered princess. I hastily saluted, breathed a 'thank you,' and quit the building before I did something truly foolish, like giggle myself into a puddle. I'd earned the respect of our Captain Romy. I only wished the first mate had been there to hear it.

Telken, Luc, and Rex were waiting for my return. No doubt they'd heard about the afternoon's excitement and my subsequent summons by the captain. Telken and his companions followed me down the beach.

"Well?" he said. "Are you in trouble?"

"Not at all," I said casually, turning to Luc. "But you are."

"Me?" Luc cried. "What for?"

"For losing your coin." I opened my palm to him and grinned triumphantly. He looked at me in confusion, then his eyes widened in understanding and laughter bellowed from the depths of his barreled chest.

"What did I say, lads?" Telken said as Luc placed some coins in my hand. "Balls of stone!"

Five days later, the pages of my notebook were nearly filled with drawings and observations of the family of creatures living in the shadow of the mountain the cartographers dubbed "Solismont," which I was told meant "lonely mountain" in the old Faqur tongue. By now, everyone knew what I was up to when I disappeared for hours every day, but all I received when I returned were curious stares. The captain and his officers must have ordered the men to leave me be. Thankfully they followed without question. As always.

From the safe observation post I hacked into the brush, I counted ten adults. At least four were female because they nursed young, and due to their immense size, two were male. One was the individual I'd encountered several days prior, and he seemed to be the leader of the group. He was always on the lookout, for what I had no idea. I hadn't seen any evidence of predators, but perhaps there was another group of these creatures deeper in the interior of the island? It was merely speculation. A few of the younger creatures were curious about me, but none came close. They chased each other in the underbrush, climbed trees, and swung overhead from branch to branch. The adults ignored their antics and munched on fruits, dug grubs out of rotting wood, and picked parasites out of each others' fur. They reminded me of a family, at times patient and at others combative.

I wasn't as good at naming things as the cartographers, but I took to calling them braxes after the character in Kyra's story who found himself lost in a magical forest. After a while, I could recognize each individual and started naming them. The big one who attacked me I called Brute. His favorite was a small, gentle female I named Isa. He didn't venture far from her side, and he touched her whenever they were together. It was fascinating to watch the creatures interact in such an intimate manner.

Our time on the island ended, for in the eyes of the officers, there was nothing worth staying for. The crew found no trace of precious metals, and aside from acres of timber, there were no other resources to support the establishment of a territory. I was grateful for this because I feared the group of creatures I'd grown to care for would be wiped out to make way for people. On the last day of my week-long study of the braxes, I sat with my book open in my lap, unmotivated to write any observations. I picked up my pen and tried to write, but nothing came of my efforts. I sighed, shut the book, and prepared to leave. I looked up, and there was Brute, standing only a few feet away regarding me with those beautiful amber eyes.

"Hello," I breathed. "And goodbye, I suppose. I won't be bothering you anymore." My voice broke, and I swallowed hard.

Brute sat on his haunches and scratched his belly, apparently bored with the exchange. I carefully set down my pack, and without considering the consequences, I crouched low and shuffled toward him, my head lowered in deference. He didn't retreat, so I moved closer, then extended a hand as I'd seen the young ones do when they approached him. I waited for him to either walk away, rip off my arm, or accept my sign of respect. My legs quaked with the effort to maintain my crouched position, and my hand trembled. Just when I was about to give up, Brute shifted, and I choked on a ragged breath when his soft, furred fingers touched mine. I met his stoic gaze. He grunted the same soft sound he made to the young. Then he heaved his great body to its feet and ambled back to the group. I smiled after him. Brute bestowed upon me a great honor, one that would stay with me for the rest of my life.

CHAPTER 16

We remained on the island long enough to gather fresh supplies of water, fish, and fruit. The structures we'd built were left in case the council of Faqur decided to explore the island further. Everything else was quickly and efficiently rowed back to the ship. Most of the crew were happy to leave since they found little to excite them on the relatively small piece of land. I, on the other hand, had found enough to fill one of the journals I'd brought. Though I loathed leaving, I anticipated the next adventure.

I showed Tyrnan the drawings and explained the dynamics of the group structure of the braxes. Though he seemed genuinely interested, it was clear the subject didn't fill him with as much wonder as it did for me.

"That's a very good sketch," Tyrnan said distractedly before returning his attention to his own notes.

"And very much like her," I said. It was a portrait of darling Isa nursing her newborn. "She loved her baby. She always stroked its fur when it fed."

Tyrnan closed the book in my hands. "They're disturbing to look at. You've made them too human. Like a man with too much hair."

"That's what they look like." I opened the book again. "They're like people in many ways. They're very expressive, love their families, and their paws look like hands."

"They're animals." Tyrnan rose and stretched. The ship traveled along the coastline in search of a passage west. I stood and leaned against the rail to watch Solismont become obscured by fog settling over the island as dusk fell.

"Will Faqur charter another expedition here?" I asked.

"No," Tyrnan said. "It's too small."

I exhaled my relief. The braxes would be safe.

It took three days to reach the tip of the island. When I awoke early on that last morning, I was mortified to find my hammock stained with blood. On the island when my menses had come, it was easy to sneak away to wash myself. But I'd failed to plan how I would conceal this biological function. The other men were still snoring in their beds, so I risked taking down my hammock and stole a length of rope. I snuck on deck, scanning for anyone milling about, and hurried toward the stern. I fastened the rope to the hammock, tied it to one of the cleats, and dropped it into the churning water. Then I rushed below deck and snuck into the surgeon's quarters. I encountered a few tired-eyed men, who barely gave me a second glance as they passed. The surgeon himself was still asleep, and I'm ashamed to say I stole several rolls of bandage material to fashion myself a sanitary rag. When I pulled my hammock out of the water, it wasn't very clean, but the stain was less noticeable. I wrung out the water and hung it back up just as the men stirred. By the time I pulled on some clothing, I was red faced and panting.

"You all right?" Telken rubbed a hand across his face.

"Yeah. Just excited to land on the next island."

Telken grunted. "That won't be for another few days I'd wager." He stretched out his heavy limbs, yawned, and scratched his backside. I turned away, but honestly, I'd seen worse by now.

Telken was right. We didn't drop anchor for three days. Where the last island was alive with lush trees and greenery, this one had ranges of mountains as far as the eye could see. I scanned the shore as the ship drew nearer, and I was relieved to see birds hopping along the ledges of outcroppings and diving into the water. Large, bulbous creatures lounged in the sun, barking like dogs and flashing their teeth when a neighbor got too close. Though the landscape seemed incredibly bleak, I had a good feeling about this place.

The full moon illuminated the deck when I crept among the shadows to the railing. I took another glance around to make sure no one was watching, then dropped my used sanitary rags into the water. I waited to make sure the waves swallowed them up, then turned to go back below deck. My heart plummeted into my stomach when I saw Captain Romy standing there. I studied his face as he stepped closer, but there wasn't a trace of suspicion on his stony countenance. I saluted and ducked my head to leave, but he halted my escape.

"Another sleepless night for you?" he asked.

"Yes, sir," I said.

He held up the journal containing everything I'd observed regarding the braxes. I'd handed it over to First Mate Evrard a few days before and didn't expect to hear anything about it—not from the first mate and certainly not from the captain.

"I read your notes," he said, tapping the journal with a finger.

"You did?" A grin played about my mouth, and I wrung my fingers as I waited to hear his opinion.

"Very insightful. Do you feel their species warrants further study?"

I wanted to say yes, but I hesitated. If I recommended the braxes be studied by real scholars, not just a pretend one, would they come to love them as I did? Would they see them as gentle giants, or would they take one look at the black fur and large teeth and wipe them off the island?

"I think they should be left alone," I said. Captain Romy nodded slowly, and I could tell he was studying me, as if he hoped to read my expression like the pages in a book. I steeled myself, as Father did, and tried not to give anything away. Without another word, he handed the book back. I grabbed it with a little too much enthusiasm.

"I see. Goodnight, Mr. Red."

I spun on my heel and retreated to my sleeping quarters to keep him from seeing the relief on my face. Though he didn't know I was a woman, his valuing my opinion made me giddy. He wasn't feigning interest because I was a princess and he wanted to garner my favor. I'd proven myself through my own merit and earned his respect. Would that change if he knew who I really was?

First Mate Evrard and I walked along the coast of this new island. Rocks shifted under my feet and the fresh scent of salt air and clean water filled our noses. Tendrils of water originating in the mountains flowed and emptied into the sea near where we had breached the dinghy. Though the color scheme of blacks, grays, and whites stretching before our eyes was monotonous, the wildlife more than made up for the dull scenery. The birds had an iridescent sheen to their black feathers, bright orange feet, and yellow striped beaks. We kept our distance from the large beasts with silver-blue fur and black spots wallowing on the beach. They were clumsy on land, when in the sea, they glided gracefully through the water.

"Not as foreboding as the last one," the first mate observed.

"No," I said. "It feels...safe."

"Let's walk upriver a few miles just to be sure."

The river was not as large as the Rhyvor, that mighty torrent that coursed through Praed, but it was just as deep and so clear you could see through it like glass. In the deeper areas, a flash of silver glittered by as fish darted out of sight. Along the banks stood wisps of plants. I bent down to run my hands along the leaves and tiny buds. I brought my fingers to my nose and inhaled the subtly sweet odor. I popped some into my mouth. It tasted like berries just before they ripened, but not in an unpleasant way.

"I have high hopes for this place," I told the first mate.

"As do I," he said, and he smiled. Actually *smiled*. I was so taken aback I nearly fainted.

After we determined the place offered no immediate danger, a party of trippers and a few of the crew assembled on shore and began milling about, pointing and gesticulating, taking preliminary notes. With no trees in the immediate area there wasn't much to be done about building shelters. What little vegetation there was consisted of grasses and scraggly bushes. The river provided an abundance of fresh water and fish. I even overheard talk of slaughtering one of the lazy shore beasts to see how they tasted.

I scoffed and said, "Because that's what we should do when we find a new species—find out what it tastes like."

"It's only natural," Tyrnan said as he adjusted the straps on his bag. "How else would we have discovered the foods we eat now are edible?"

"Are you trying to out-logic me?"

He grinned. "I really don't have to try."

Once the cartographers set out on their first scouting trip, I engaged in a training session with Rex. He was improving, but admittedly, he was heavy-footed and would probably never be a truly great swordsman. I enjoyed the exercise and the company. Rex was straight-forward and easy to talk to. I spent the rest of the afternoon patrolling the shore searching for signs of life. Something splashed into the water, followed by another, and I stepped around a boulder to see a figure throwing rocks into the sea. I moved forward for a better look, and saw it was Seaman Erec. He didn't look pleased. He didn't acknowledge me when I approached, so I picked up a few stones and tossed them into the sea right alongside him. Without conscious discussion, we tried to best each other, throwing farther and farther until someone lost. It was me, though he didn't seem very triumphant about it.

"You have a strong arm," I said, hoping to coax him into speaking. It didn't work. I didn't have the patience for idle conversation. My best strategy was a direct one. "Why are you so angry?"

"I'm not angry!"

Well, at least he was talking. "Liar."

He stopped and stared hard at me, and I smiled knowingly.

"I'm bored," he finally said. "Happy now?" He hurled a stone into the waves.

"Bored? How can that be?"

"What's your purpose here?"

"Purpose?" I furrowed my brow. "You mean here, in this world?"

He fixed me with a dark glare. Apparently, he wasn't in the mood for jests.

"Sorry," I mumbled. "I'm here to record observations of new species."

"And?"

"And use my sword to protect your skins."

"Exactly. You have work that always keeps you busy. Like the trippers, the muscle, and officers. There are no indigenous people here, nor were there any on the other island, so I'm useless."

I cocked my head in confusion. "You study people?"

"No. I speak to them. I'm a translator."

My eyes widened. "I had no idea!" How could I have not known that? I suppose, as he said, he'd had no reason to display his skills. I also realized I hadn't taken the time to get to know Seaman Erec, but he didn't exactly make it easy.

"The last thing I want is for Captain Romy to think I was a wasted investment." I could hear the misery in his tone, and I clasped my hands together to keep from placing a comforting hand on his shoulder. What would a boy do in this situation? Punch him?

"Hey." I gave him a good-natured shove. "I'm sure the captain doesn't think that. You know he appreciates everyone. I'm certain he didn't just bring you here for your stimulating conversation."

He shot me a nasty look, but the corners of his mouth curled in an involuntary smile.

"No, he has you for that, doesn't he?" For a moment, I thought he was annoyed, but then he smirked, and I knew he was teasing.

"Oh, yeah," I said. "He just *loves* to deal with my nonsense."

"You've given him enough."

"I'm sure he can't wait to be rid of me."

"You're thinking of First Mate Romy."

"Oh, right. That man *hates* me."

"He doesn't hate you. He's like that with everyone. Likes to keep a rough exterior."

"I still think he wants me off the ship."

"Regardless of his personal feelings, he does appreciate your abilities with a sword. I just think he finds you—"

"Impudent?"

"Exactly. It's important to remember your place. You can't speak so freely with superior officers."

"Only speak when spoken to," I said.

"If you possibly can." He threw another rock across the water and it landed with a satisfying *plunk*.

I stayed with him a few minutes more watching the reflections of stones flying across the water. Then I abruptly left, kicking the ground as I tromped down the beach. If Erec thought my behavior strange, he didn't comment or call out, and I didn't look back. It didn't matter if I was a princess or a sailor, it seemed. I would be doomed to silence, to hold back, to be less than myself.

Over the proceeding few days, I spent much of my time alone. I would set out early, following the river farther and farther each day, exploring the land in solitude. Though the sun was bright overhead, a cold wind blew down from the mountains, making me shiver under the simple coat I wore. I made notes about the few animals I saw and took samples of plants, but mostly I sat and considered the course my life had taken. I thought about my family far away in Praed and wondered if they were discretely searching for me. If it was made known that I was missing, how would that reflect on the king and queen or on my own reputation? Whatever else might happen because of this adventure, I knew for certain that I would return home with no reputation to speak of. I'd been living among fifty or so men, and it didn't matter if they thought I was a boy. I pictured Mother's tormented face, Father's disappointment, and my siblings unable to meet my eye. Would I consider the consequences worth it?

A rock hit the ground and startled me out of my reverie. A round, furry face looked down at me. It resembled a small dog, with rounded ears, yellow eyes, and silver and white fur. It sniffed the air around me, then flicked an ear backward, let out a series of short *yips*, and slunk away, its paws making no sound on the rough terrain. I smiled, my heart filling with a sense of peace.

It was worth it.

CHAPTER 17

I shifted the canvas pack on my shoulders and followed the three Romy officers up the river toward the mountains. The cartographers and a few of the crew trailed behind me, all of us in search of the source of the river. Second Mate Absalon argued this could take days, but the captain was determined. A party was formed, and we set out early that morning. First Mate Evrard and I were characteristically on alert for danger, but neither of us had seen anything to cause alarm. Tyrnan and his colleagues were giddy with excitement, so much so that one of them broke into song. I laughed, but not everyone found the singing amusing.

"Are we going to have to listen to that the whole way?" Oryn Thatchet grumbled. I still hadn't forgiven him for inciting Bosun Chester against me on the previous island, which we now referred to as "Premet." I found middle-aged Oryn to be quite cranky most of the time. If he didn't enjoy field work, he should have kept himself quiet in a library. If my feminine singing voice didn't give me away, I would've joined in the song just to annoy him.

We set up camp close to the river, and when everyone was settled around a fire eating and drinking ale, I slipped away to wash myself. I found a concealed area in the bend of the river covered with brush, and a quick glance confirmed no one was around. Hurriedly, I stripped off my clothes and waded into the slow-moving current. I hissed as the icy water bit into my skin straight to my bones. A twig snapped on the banks, and the sound of voices followed. I sank deeper to avoid being seen. The shock of the cold hitting my chest ripped the air from my lungs, but I did not dare chance a getaway. I held my breath, ducked below the surface, and swam under the safety of the undergrowth. Tentatively, I raised my head above the water. I clenched my jaw to keep my teeth from chattering and clamped a hand over my mouth to muffle the sound. The voices grew louder, and I recognized the three distinct voices of the brothers.

"According to these early measurements," Second Mate Absalon said, "this island could be quite large. Maybe even large enough to support a population."

"If there isn't one on it already," First Mate Evrard pointed out.

Well, at least I can say despite his cantankerous exterior, Evrard wasn't one prone to pillage.

"Yes, that goes without saying." I could hear the exasperation in the second mate's voice. I pictured him rolling his eyes and stifled a giggle.

"Has Mr. Red reported any mysterious creatures to you, Evrard?" It was the captain speaking now. I held my breath to listen closely.

"He hasn't said much the last few days, actually," the first mate said. "I thought I'd enjoy the change, but I do find it a bit unsettling."

"Why is that?" the captain asked.

"You know, seems Mr. Red is always the first to speak his mind, so when he doesn't, I wonder if something is amiss."

How insightful of him.

"You think he's keeping something from us?" I could hear the concern in the captain's voice, and I felt guilty that they were discussing me with such sympathy. My toes were going numb, and I wiggled them into the riverbed to try to regain some feeling while the conversation above me continued.

"He's gone off on his own several times," Second Mate Absalon added. "But he is a young man. Sometimes they need space."

There was a rumble of laughter I was shocked to realize came from Evrard.

"Enough," Captain Romy said with exasperation. "I'll speak to him…find out if anything's bothering him."

"Are you his father now?" the first mate asked. "You going to let the rest of the crew cry on your shoulder, too?"

"Oh, stop, Evrard." Absalon Romy tsked. "Lencius, please let me know if there's anything I can do. He's such a young boy with so much promise. I would hate to think there's something wrong."

"Aye, Absalon. Thank you."

Footsteps receded into the distance, but only one set. By now, my entire body had broken out in gooseflesh, and I couldn't feel my legs or fingers.

If they didn't leave soon, I'd have to get out of this river in front of them or risk hypothermia.

"Do you agree with Absalon?" First Mate Evrard asked.

"Maybe…Some of the time, anyway," the captain answered evasively.

"The boy's good with a sword, but he has a problem keeping his mouth shut," Evrard said. There was a short silence, then the first mate added, "If there was something wrong, he'd say so. I think we can trust in that."

The captain made a noncommittal noise.

"You've taken an eager interest in the boy. Some might call that favoritism."

"Others might call it guidance."

"Are you planning on guiding him into an illustrious career?"

"All I needed at his age was someone to believe I could be more than I was."

"And now look at you. Summoning sea demons."

The captain sighed, but it was closer to a frustrated growl.

"I'll be considering retirement soon," the captain said. "I want to leave my ship in capable hands."

I clamped a hand over my mouth, my fingers digging into the frigid skin of my cheeks.

"Retirement?" Evrard scoffed. "Father won't like it if you don't pursue admiralty."

"I don't want to spend the rest of my days behind the closed doors of the Assembly Hall."

"You'd rather spend them with your nose in the dirt like the boy?"

Silence. I pictured myself exploring with the captain, the pair of us forging paths through uncharted territories, documenting new plants and animals. I couldn't feel the lower half of my body, but my cheeks burned.

"If he continues to improve," Evrard said, "I think he has a good chance of becoming a fine sailor."

I smiled. The next time First Mate Evrard showed me outward hostility, I'd remember this moment. There was a sound like a hand slapping against someone's back, and footsteps leaving the river.

"Oh," Evrard called back. "Don't you dare tell him I said that, or it'll be *our* swords coming to blows."

"I won't," Captain Romy said.

After that it was quiet, but I knew he was still there. I started feeling dizzy, and my muscles could barely move. I had no choice. I had to get out of the river. I swam away, slowly, grateful that the rushing current was loud enough to drown out the splashes I made. I reached for my clothing on the bank but heard footsteps heading in my direction. I bolted on wobbling legs and dove into the thick bushes. The footsteps stopped. I held my breath. When they didn't continue, I tumbled into my breeches, pulling them over my damp skin with weak fingers. The footsteps resumed, heading away, and I expelled a lungful air in relief. I finished dressing and snuck back to camp, sticking to the shadows before casually dropping next to some of the men in the firelight.

"What happened to you?" Telken asked.

"W-w-what?" I asked. My mind was hazy and slow, and even my vision was blurred from being in the cold water for so long.

"You look as white as death. 'Cept your lips are as blue as the water."

"Um..." I couldn't think of a witty reply, so I opted for an obvious one. "I'm cold."

Telken laughed. "I can see that. Here." He shoved a tankard of ale in my hand, and I drank the warm liquid until rivulets ran down my face.

"Easy there, lad." Telken took the tankard back. "You'll wreck your head."

I already felt warmer. With hooded eyes, I scanned the faces around the fire, and I was relieved that the captain was not among them. I was suddenly very tired, and I braced myself against Telken to get to my feet.

"You need help there, boy?" he asked with barely restrained mirth.

"I'm tired." I pitched forward. Telken caught me under the arms and called out for Luc. Together, they dragged me into the tent and helped me into bed. I was drifting toward a heavy slumber when I felt hands on the buttons of my coat.

"No!" I yelled in a panic. "I'll do it!"

"All right, all right." Telken raised his hands. "Sleep in all your stitches if you want." I collapsed back onto the bed mat as he exited the tent, breathing hard. I'd almost been caught twice in the same night. I'd become too comfortable with my surroundings, and it made me careless.

I told myself to take care, that this was far from over. My eyes drifted shut, and just before sleep claimed me in its warm embrace, I remembered the hard-earned praise from my superiors. It appeared Erec was right. First Mate Evrard didn't hate me after all.

Looming before us, dark rocky crags jutted out of the earth like crooked teeth. A cold wind whistled along the jagged edges of the mountains, casting an eerie mood over us as we surveyed the area. The cartographers and Second Mate Absalon were deep in discussion over our next course while the captain and first mate scanned the horizon, their hands resting on the hilts of their swords. My attention was fixed on where the river plunged, twisting and curling out of the stone. The men argued about going over or around the mountains, but I had a strange feeling that the best path would be straight through. The water had to come from *somewhere*. My feet moved without conscious thought. Step by step, I drew closer to the river, the rushing of the white water drowning out the wind and the voices behind me. From where I stood, it appeared the water was flanked by sheer rock, impassable to human travel. But as I climbed over boulders, heedless to danger, I found that while the river rushed in a torrent out from the rocks, it was calmer here. The sides of the gorge were quite steep, but the ledges worn into the rock appeared passable. I inched my way along the river, ignoring the urge to go back and show the others my discovery. I was determined to go on alone, to be the first to see the source of the river. The thought sent the same thrill through me as the moment I saw the braxes. Though many might follow, none could claim the distinction of being the first.

I held onto the rough stone as I shuffled forward, careful to avoid areas of wet, slippery rock. In some places, the ledge was wide enough to walk normally while in others I had to flatten my body against the cliff face to avoid falling. The air was warmer in the sheltered gorge where sunlight warmed the stone, trapping in heat despite the presence of the cool water below. I looked down, saw how high I'd climbed, shut my eyes, and kept moving. A flutter of motion caught my attention, and I watched a small blue and brown bird dart out of the cliff and skate across the surface of a calm pool, leaving streaks of ripples where its beak touched the water to nab a tasty morsel from a plume of swarming insects. Several more birds followed, snatching up a meal as they dove in and around the rock. I continued, wiping an arm across my sweaty brow, my shirt sticking to my back. It felt like hours before the air changed, the temperature dropping several degrees. The gorge widened, and I descended toward the riverbed. I jumped down the last several feet, the ground crunching underneath my boots. Black rocks shifted and cracked under my feet as I walked toward an opening in the narrow space. I stepped out of the shelter of the mountains into the open air and gasped.

Nestled in the center of black mountains surrounded by a shore of dark sand was the source of the river: the bluest, purest, and most extensive lake I'd ever seen. Nothing marred the smooth veneer, not a projecting log or boulder cutting the pristine surface. It seemed to stretch for miles. I gazed in open-mouthed wonderment. A slight breeze swept along the valley, disrupting the glassy lake. I walked toward it reverently, past the mouth of the river, and touched my fingers to the crystalline surface. The icy water was likely fed by snow melting off the mountains. I could see the rocky floor beneath the cobalt blue water. Without a second thought, I sat on the shore and pulled off my boots, rolled up my pant legs, and waded into the lake. I stood for a moment, the current tugging gently against my legs. Slowly my body adjusted to the temperature. I scanned the area, noting very little vegetation save for a few tangled bushes with tiny leaves and bright red berries.

As I looked closer, the wind blew again, rustling the branches and exposing a shape crouched amid the leaves. I held perfectly still as a creature scurried along the rocks. It was very small and round with fur the color of sandstone. It paused a few feet away, rising on its haunches and sniffing the air, its tiny whiskers twitching. It froze, and quicker than a heartbeat, it bounded away. But not quickly enough, for a silver-white predator—the dog-like creature I'd seen previously—appeared as if materializing out of the rock itself. It studied me, ears erect and meal dangling from its jaws, before disappearing into a hidden den.

"Well," I said. "Never a dull moment at least."

I saw fury in Tyrnan's eyes when I returned to the group, though he couldn't voice his anger. First Mate Evrard, however, had no such constraints and certainly no qualms about tearing into me the moment I showed my face.

"Where have you been?" he demanded. "You've been missing for hours. Explain yourself!"

"I found a way through the mountain," I said. His anger no longer frightened me. Seaman Erec was right about the rough exterior belying his honorable nature. I'd heard the evidence myself the night I nearly froze to death in the river.

Captain Romy raised a hand to halt the first mate's tirade. He turned to me, eyes intent. "Where?"

"I'll show you." I led the team into the gorge. Though it was much slower going, we made it to the lake without anyone slipping off the rocks. I watched everyone's expression as they stood in awed silence on the shore and repressed a satisfied smile. They fanned out to explore the periphery of the water, and a hand squeezed my shoulder.

"Well done, Mr. Red," Captain Romy said.

I bowed my head to hide my reddening cheeks and silently berated myself for the foolish display of feminine weakness. If I were going to blush every time I felt flattered, I would be in danger of losing more than just my dignity.

We made camp along the shore that night. I wandered off alone again, climbing atop a rocky outcropping on the east side of the lake to watch the sunset. The sun dipped lower in the sky, illuminating a vast mountain range in shades of orange, pink, and red. Below me, I heard someone scrambling on the stones. A smile broke across my face as my brother hefted himself beside me, sweaty and panting.

"You're out of shape." I waited for him to catch his breath.

"You and Rian were always the better climbers."

We watched the sun sink lower below the horizon, and I thought of my older brother's antics. "How big do you think this place is?"

"Big," Tyrnan said. "I wish we had more time to explore. Based on preliminary measurements, we estimate it could be large enough to sustain a population. But, as I said, we have a schedule to keep." The last he mumbled irritably.

"Yes we do. It seems the captain doesn't like to stray from his plans. A slave to his schedule, that one."

"I'm sure he has good reason for it."

"Do you trust him so blindly?"

"Don't you?"

Our eyes met in the fading light. I opened my mouth, but the joke on my lips receded with the waning day.

"Yes," I admitted, hearing the surprise in my own voice. "I suppose I do." I shook off the strange feeling creeping in my veins and added, "He's never given me a reason to *dis*trust him at any rate."

"He's placed a lot of faith in you."

"He's obviously an excellent judge of character," I said smugly, my smile much too wide. Tyrnan looked away, shaking his head, and my smile fell.

"Don't do anything foolish." Tyrnan said it so quietly I almost missed it.

"Like…?"

He looked at me again, and I was struck by the dire seriousness in his eyes. Shadows filled in the angles of his face and made his brown hair appear black.

"Like fall in love with him." There wasn't an ounce of teasing in his tone.

I pushed him so hard he braced himself to stop from sliding down the side of the mountain. I stood and clomped hastily back toward the lake.

"Fall into a pit of fire and burn!" I called back over my shoulder. Tears burned my eyes and my fists clenched. How dare my brother say something so vile! He knew me better, knew I wasn't a lovesick maiden desperate for a handsome suitor. Why would he have said that? And about the captain of all people!

Distantly, I heard him follow and call out my name—my real name—but I ignored him. I wanted to forget what he said, and I couldn't do that if I turned around to face him. I stalked into camp, firelight dancing across the figures of the men preparing the evening meal. I brushed past Rex, disregarding the look of concern he gave me as I ducked into our tent. Tyrnan wisely did not follow.

I paced around the cramped space, breathing in and out slowly to gain control of my temper. I pressed my palms to my eyes to stop the flow of bitter tears and whispered a slew of insults directed at my brother and my own fragile composure.

"You all right?" Rex asked.

"Fine." I turned away and wiped the back of my hand across my face.

"Homesick?" His voice was gentle and understanding.

"Uh, yes. I was thinking of my home as I watched the sunset just now. I used to do the same with my family. You must think I'm ridiculous." I forced a laugh and finally turned around. There was nothing but sympathy in Rex's gaze.

"Nah." He draped an arm across my shoulders. "It's hard leaving for the first time. It gets easier." I nodded, and he sighed. "Sometimes, I get a whiff of flowers and a fresh cooked meal and remember the dear wife I left behind. She's the best cook in all Faqur." He led me out of the tent and patted me reassuringly on the back.

"It's nothing to be ashamed of, lad." He poured out a mug of ale and placed it in my hands.

I took a long drink, hoping the liquid slipping down my throat would make me forget.

Chapter 18

Over the ensuing week, I childishly avoided both Tyrnan and the captain as much as possible. I wasn't angry anymore, but still annoyed at Tyrnan's misogynistic presumption that I wouldn't be able to control my emotions around a handsome man. Just to prove I had no feelings beyond the respect of a sailor due his captain, I didn't engage in conversation when the captain was around and answered any questions he asked shortly and succinctly. While I treated *him* with aloofness, I did the opposite with my fellow sailors. I joined in all their games, helped with the work, and devoted extra time to training with both Rex and First Mate Evrard. If anyone noticed my strange change in behavior, they didn't comment. I still went off alone on occasion to observe nature, but I never stayed away long enough to be missed. The pages of my journal were filling rapidly with drawings of plants and animals, and like Tyrnan, I suspected this place to be larger than we imagined.

Toward the north end, we discovered a river trickling in to feed the lake's massive size. We journeyed upstream for several days, but we found nothing except a barren expanse of rocky prairie devoid of trees and greenery. Thick fog blanketed the area, obscuring our ability to gauge our surroundings. Yellowed grasses sprang up in random patches, and the only signs of life were the small creatures I'd seen near the lake, insects, and, rarely, a snake. With no sign of the river in sight, I overheard Second Mate Absalon caution the captain from wandering too far as our supplies were beginning to dwindle. The captain agreed that it was time to turn back. That night, something miraculous happened.

The fog dissipated, becoming thinner and thinner as the day wore on. By the evening, when the sun began its arduous descent toward the west, one could finally see several miles in each direction. As evening fires were being lit, I climbed onto a boulder to see the rays of the falling sun pierce the last remnants of fog. There, rising out of the wisps of dense air like a beacon, was the tallest peak I'd ever beheld, larger than the mountain where Praed Castle was perched. I couldn't fathom how we'd missed it, but its looming presence graced the valley, rising upward to touch the first stars blinking into the night. I slid off the boulder and hit the ground hard. Ignoring the pain in my ankles, I hastened back to camp. No one else seemed to notice the mountain as they busied themselves with work, nor did they mark my mad dash to the officer's tent. Without requesting permission, I burst inside and headed straight for the captain.

"Sir!" I gasped, struggling to speak.

First Mate Evrard confronted me, fists on hips. "What's the meaning of this intrusion?"

No time to explain. I grabbed the captain's sleeve and pulled him outside amid protests from all three.

Despite his demands for an explanation, the captain offered little resistance as I dragged him toward the outskirts of camp beyond the glow of the firelight. I released my grip on his arm and without a word, pointed north. He looked, and his lips parted in surprise when he saw the mountain. His brothers came up beside him, and he wordlessly directed their attention to the black shape blocking out the sky.

"By the gods," Second Mate Absalon said. He hurried back to camp and returned with the cartographers. Once they overcame their astonishment, they jotted down hasty notes.

The first mate was duly impressed, though decidedly more reserved.

"Huh. The source of this river, I assume." He scoffed. "I can't believe we missed it, even with the fog."

The second mate shivered. "Aye, it was an unnatural fog to be sure."

Evrard turned to the captain. "Impressive, but by my estimation, I think it's too far away." He had the tone of a mother preparing her child for disappointment. "We don't have time."

The captain regarded the mountain with a thoughtful gaze. "What do you think is on the other side of it?"

"Adventure," I whispered. I looked up at them. The first mate's expression was passive, but the barest of smiles graced the captain's lips.

I turned away in embarrassment and was promptly ignored as they talked amongst themselves. What lay beyond such a formidable mountain indeed? The possibilities were vast, and my mind danced with imaginings of waterfalls and lush forests, of blue lakes and curious creatures. My feet twitched with the urge to set off toward it, but though I didn't move, I'm certain the longing in my face was readily visible.

"Mr. Red?"

I blinked out of my reveries at the sound of the captain's voice and looked up.

"Well done." His voice held no reproach, nor did his features after my disrespectful interruption.

"Thank you, sir," I said.

He returned his gaze to the north, the firelight bright against his back, cloaking his face in darkness.

"I wish we had more time," he said, though I wasn't certain if he was talking to me or himself.

"Can't you make time?" I asked.

"This expedition is mine," he said. "But I belong to Faqur and therefore am subject to the high council's wishes."

"Which is…?"

He looked down and I mentally kicked myself for continually ignoring my resolution to keep my mouth shut.

"To return to Faqur swiftly and safely before year's end," he said.

"Really?" My brows knitted in confusion. "That doesn't seem like enough time to thoroughly explore these islands." I gestured into the distance.

"Time is money." He looked away and his expression transformed from an exasperated man back to a stolid captain. He said no more, but I inferred from his irritation that he felt himself being placated by the Faqur council. I understood his frustration. Both of us were beholden to the demands of our stations.

We stood together in silence while the bustle of the men behind us echoed across the valley. The cartographers discussed preliminary estimates on the size of the mountain and the need to take measurements in the daylight. The distinct tones of First Mate Evrard speaking to his brother could be heard over the general camp din, but I could not distinguish any of their words. It was quite dark now with little light coming from the sliver of moon among the stars. The dinner bell beckoned, and the voices receded as the men returned to camp, yet the captain and I remained until we were surrounded by darkness and an easy silence.

"How much longer do we have?" I asked.

"Not long enough. We'll have to weigh anchor before month's end to stay on schedule."

I bit back a retort, remembering the conversation Tyrnan and I had regarding the captain's strict adherence to his itinerary. This recollection reminded me of the reason I hadn't spoken to my brother since, and I shifted uncomfortably.

"Well," I said, my voice much too loud. "I'm hungry." I abruptly left, walking quickly toward camp before my embarrassment became apparent.

Damn Tyrnan. Damn him and his stupid comment. How could I ever hope to look at Captain Romy without thinking about Tyrnan's remark and turning into a mumbling idiot? I had an urge to find Tyrnan and punch him in the teeth, but I settled for pouting in the firelight and picking at my food.

I lay stretched out on my belly on the dark gray stone along the periphery of the mountains. Beyond the rocky shore below me was the sea sparkling in the afternoon sunshine, warming my back as I patiently waited, my eyes trained on an opening in the crevasse of the stone. My heart thudded in anticipation, and I held my breath as a black nose hesitantly poked out of the darkness, followed by a round face of silver and white fur. Yellow eyes scanned the area as its ears swiveled back and forth. Though I lay downwind, it could probably detect my presence. Regardless, it inched out of the den, surveying its surroundings. I didn't move when it let out a high-pitched trilling sound. Four small, fluffy faces appeared, the soft fur like goose down gently swaying in the wind. The pups tumbled out of the den, cavorting around their mother and pouncing on one another playfully. The mother watched over their play, periodically reprimanding one of the pups when it was too rough, and occasionally grooming herself. After several minutes, another adult arrived and was instantly set upon by the pups. They licked at his face, rolled around on their backs, and whimpered as they pawed at him. To my disgust, the newcomer arched his back and retched, vomiting up the contents of his stomach as a partially digested meal for the pups. They devoured it hungrily and noisily while I swallowed down the bile threatening to rise.

The adults raised their heads in alarm, and with a sharp bark, they herded the pups back into the den. I sighed at the sound of approaching footsteps, irritated at the interruption. I didn't turn around, expecting Tyrnan was taking advantage of the solitude to reconcile. I still hadn't quite forgiven him for what he said, but I found I was ready to speak to him again.

"Come here to grovel?" I spoke quietly so I wouldn't further disturb the creatures. I hoped if we remained still for a while, they would re-emerge. Someone stretched out and lay beside me, and every muscle in my body seized when I realized it wasn't Tyrnan.

In a hushed voice Captain Romy said, "I've never had an occasion to grovel. How does one go about it?"

I winced and bit my lip to stop me from cursing. "I'm sorry. I thought you were someone else."

"I expected so, unless I had somehow unknowingly offended you."

"No." I kept my eyes trained on the dark opening in the stone and said no more. What was he doing here? I recalled that he had agreed to speak to me privately to ascertain if something was wrong. That had been days ago, and the dreaded heart-to-heart hadn't happened.

"What are we waiting for?" he whispered.

I raised a finger to my lips. "You'll see." After waiting in silence for what seemed like hours, a nose poked out of the den, sniffing the air. Without realizing it, I whispered encouragements to the little creature, urging it to come out. This was the larger one, the one I suspected was the male. He eyed us suspiciously, then hurried off in a flash of silver fur.

"That's the sire," I said. "He's off to find more food."

The rest of the family emerged into the sunshine. The mother led her pups away, glancing back periodically to make sure we didn't follow.

"She takes the pups over that rise to teach them to hunt. There's a large system of burrows up there full of fat rodents."

"Have you ever seen these animals before?" Captain Romy asked.

"No." I made notes in my journal. "They act a little like wolves, sharing the responsibility of raising young. But they don't live in packs. They don't seem to get along with other adults at all."

"Interesting."

The way he spoke made me truly believe he found it so and wasn't just making idle conversation. Might as well get this over with. "Did you need me for something?"

"No," he said matter-of-factly. "Unless you consider yourself a decent fisherman? The men are replenishing our supplies from the river."

"Probably making the fish go extinct," I muttered.

"We have to eat. And there aren't enough of us to decimate the population so quickly. Extinctions take years."

"Now who's the naturalist?" I smiled wryly.

"I actually did want to speak to you," he said.

I took a deep breath. Here we go.

"First Mate Romy feels you've been elusive lately. At first, I disagreed, but it seems you've barely spoken more than three words to any of us. And I have the strange sense that you've been avoiding *me* in particular."

He was perceptive, I'll give him that.

"If I have, it wasn't intentional." I cast a furtive glance at him. He was studying me. I met his unwavering stare boldly, and one corner of his mouth curved upwards.

"There. That's more like you," he said. "Any trouble from the crew?"

"No. Not for a long time."

"You'd tell me if there were any problems?"

"I... don't know that I would, sir. I can handle myself. You have enough to worry about." This time, he smiled with his whole face, a gentle, fatherly smile.

"Worrying is one of the burdens of being a captain."

"I suppose you can't afford any discontent." I didn't mention the word *mutiny*—Tyrnan said it's bad luck—but the intention was clear. His expression darkened at the implication, but I didn't shrink away.

"Discontent…No, I cannot. To be fair, no captain can."

"Have no fear," I said. "Your crew is quite loyal to you. Almost comically so." I wished the words unsaid the moment they left my lips. What was I doing? I had to stop this conversation immediately. I hastily rose to my feet, shoving my journal into my canvas bag as I did, and avoided meeting his eye as he stood to follow.

"You find their devotion humorous?" He was much taller than I, so my frantic strides were easily matched by his long-legged gait. I detected more curiosity than annoyance. As a sailor and now a captain, loyalty was no laughing matter.

I plastered on a smile. "No. I find the stories they insist are real amusing, that's all."

"Ah. You don't think I summoned a sea god to capsize an enemy ship and send it plunging into a watery grave?"

"It's a trick I'd like to see to believe. Well told, though."

"What are stories, but tales told to delight and amuse? They don't have to be real."

"They *are* made up then?" I released a dramatic sigh. "How disappointing. I was looking forward to meeting a sea god."

We reached the outskirts of camp, and the smell of drying fish became overpowering. Birds circled overhead to snatch up the discarded entrails left behind by the fishermen, and offshore bulbous heads bobbed in and out of the surf, no doubt waiting for an opportunity to steal a meal.

"I'm sorry to disappoint." He saluted to signal my dismissal. I replied with one of my own, and he moved away toward the officers.

"Disappoint? You haven't," I said softly to his retreating back. I stamped a foot and threw my hands in the air. "Ugh! Tyrnan!" That decided that. I was going to punch my brother square in the nose.

CHAPTER 19

Instead of hitting Tyrnan in the face and potentially breaking his nose, I settled for a swordfight. He knew the moment I placed the blade in his hands that this was retribution, so he acquiesced. Not only did I beat him soundly, I managed to disarm him and send him crashing onto his backside. I held out a hand, and he blew a lock of hair out of his face.

"Are we okay now?" he asked.

I gave a conciliatory nod and helped him to his feet.

"I suppose." I sheathed my sword and walked toward the railing of the ship. The rocky shores of the island receded into the distance. "But I'm still mad about what you said."

"I'm sorry," he said in a low voice. He glanced around to make sure no one was listening. "I didn't mean to imply that because you're a woman, you're bound to lose your head over a handsome face. You know I don't think that about *you* of all people."

"Then why did you say it?"

"Because he's..." Tyrnan considered his words carefully. My stomach twisted, and I suddenly didn't want him to continue. He'd already managed to make me feel awkward around the captain. If he planted ideas in my head, it might get worse.

I held up a hand to stop him. "I don't want to know. Let's just forget about it."

"Agreed." He sighed in relief.

We watched the island disappear into a fog and spoke of mundane things. The air was chilled, and I rubbed my arms to restore heat to my rapidly numbing skin.

I felt a keen loss at leaving that strange place, as if there was so much more to discover and that our time would be wasted elsewhere. Tyrnan shared my feelings, but we didn't speak of it. I showed him the entries in my journal and regaled him with tales of the romping creatures I'd named "petiloos."

"What does that mean?" Tyrnan asked.

"It means 'little wolves' in the old Faqur tongue."

"How do you know ancient Faqur?"

"Seaman Erec told me." I rolled my eyes in exasperation. "May I continue?" He eyed me dubiously but nodded and listened as I described their daily life in vivid detail, even the part about the vomit dinners. His skin flushed as green as I'm sure mine did when I witnessed it firsthand.

Three days later, First Mate Evrard and I were once again leading a team onto the beach of a speck of land covered in long, yellow grass and trees burdened with fruit. There was no sign of danger. The only signs of wildlife were no bigger than a hen. We spent several days collecting fruit to supplement our diet, and I'm not ashamed to admit I, as well as some of the other crew members, spent most of our time lying on the beach enjoying the sun's hot rays.

"Soak it up, boys" Telken pulled off his shirt. "I'm starting to lose my color!"

The men chuckled and followed his example, revealing sun-browned skin.

"Don't be shy." Rex settled onto the sand next to me. "Get some color on ya! Will put hair on your chest, too."

"Can't," I lamented. "I'll burn."

"Maybe a little at a time? It'll make you less blinding in the sun." Rex elbowed me good-naturedly, but I shook my head.

"Trust me. You don't want to hear me moaning in pain all night long. And how will I get a girl to like me if I blister and scar?"

"Boy has a point." Telken lay back and rested his head in the crook of his arm.

I'd been telling the truth. I didn't tan, I scorched. It was the curse of being a ginger. My cheeks reddened off and on during the journey, but when the skin healed, left behind were more freckles dusting the bridge of my nose and cheeks.

When the ship's holds were sufficiently full of fresh supplies collected from the last three islands, we once again set sail for what proved to be a longer stretch on the water than I expected. We sailed west, across a barren sea. The monotony of the view was tiring, and I couldn't imagine how some men could spend months at sea, see nothing but water, and not go mad. At least the weather was favorable, with clear skies and fair winds both night and day. I resumed my visits with Hrod in the crow's nest during his night's watch and kept him awake with stories from the islands that he missed out on when he elected to stay on board. I asked him why on earth he would prefer the confinement of the ship to the space and freedom of land. He smiled indulgently at me.

"The ship's like my home," he said. "Don't care to leave it more than I have to."

"But why sail at all if you don't want to explore new places?"

"Every day on the sea is different and exciting. You're young and eager to see everything you can, lad. There's no shame in that."

"I know."

"Just don't forget you can put your foot on every type of soil, but none will feel as good as when you're walking on your home turf."

"And you consider *The Wayward Aymelina* as such?"

"I'm lucky enough to have two places I call home." Hrod had spent more years on the sea than I'd been alive, and I valued his sage wisdom and experience, even if I didn't fully understand the implications. I'd been so willing to leave Praed that I went to great lengths to conceal my departure and perpetuated a fraud to stay away. I missed my home and my family, but I admittedly thought of them little when exploring new places.

Another crew member who remained on board while we mapped out new territories was Bosun Chester, ostensibly because he was placed in charge of the ship while the captain and the first and second mate weren't aboard. The crew whispered that Chester took this job very seriously, even to go so far as to parade his authority around like a rutting stag. He constantly criticized the crews' performance, gave contradictory and excessive orders, and generally made himself a nuisance. Despite his abhorrent behavior, there was relatively little the crew said against him. Whether this was due to respect for his position or fear of reprimands I couldn't say, but I took their cue and didn't perpetuate any gossip. The temporary promotion left Chester with a terrible ego. As bosun, he oversaw the deck maintenance, which involved not only directing the crew, but a certain level of manual labor on his part. By the time he'd been in charge for three island visits, Chester had effectively delegated all his duties to others, leaving himself idle. And when Bosun Chester felt idle after several days of easy sailing on the open water, he grew bored.

I sat on the deck with Hrod, learning how to mend nets and thinking my embroidery lessons were finally good for something, when a shadow loomed over us. I looked up expecting to see one of my friends but saw Bosun Chester glaring down at me. I don't know why he'd taken a sudden and thorough dislike of me, but his feelings were written firmly in his face. Perhaps a part of him recognized me as Sulwen, a part that wasn't communicating with the rest of his brain. I suffered under his dominant rule to prevent him from putting the pieces together. But I'd been a member of the crew for months now, in a position of some standing, and I wasn't in the mood to show deference to Bosun Chester's demands.

"Sir." I saluted respectfully and returned my attention to the netting, weaving in a new line to replace a tear.

The whole section was ripped from my hands. The thin rope sliced my fingers, leaving several streaks of open skin. Blood seeped from the cuts. I shot to my feet.

"That's better," Bosun Chester barked. "You show some respect when an officer is present." His eyes darkened, and the wind blew a lock of his wavy brown hair across his forehead. The angle of his jaw bulged as he clenched his teeth. He'd taken care to keep his face smooth whereas other men grew beards.

. My fists were balled up at my sides, as if my body were looking for an excuse to strike him. "Was there something you needed, sir?" I asked.

He stepped closer and leaned forward, his nose nearly touching mine. I smelled the remnants of his afternoon meal on his breath and the faint odor of shaving soap. I resisted the urge to step back, not wishing to appear submissive.

"You've become much too brazen," he said loud enough for anyone to hear. "Do you know what the punishment is for failing to acknowledge a superior?"

My lips pressed in a firm line. "I do. Which is why I showed you the respect that was your due."

His face reddened. If nothing else, at least he was sharp enough to detect a subtle insult.

"You didn't report to me for your work assignment. I could have you flogged for that."

"I didn't realize I was supposed to." My blood boiled. He was trying to lead me into a trap.

"I'm your bosun and you're on my deck." He punctuated his words by poking my chest with his finger. He targeted my sternum just below the hollow of my throat, but if he continued to push me around, there was a chance he'd stumble on my secret. Well, a couple secrets to be specific. He must have sensed the rage rising in me, or perhaps my arm jerked involuntarily. Either way, he seemed to enjoy my discomfort, and smiled wickedly.

"Go ahead," he whispered. "I dare you to strike me. It would make it easier to order the punishment you have coming to you."

"Why?" I seethed. "What could I have possibly done to offend you so completely that you insist on tormenting me? I've done everything you've asked."

"Your presence alone insults me." His teeth were bared, like a rabid animal. "I hate gingers. They're an abomination, a disease that should be wiped out. It's only a matter of time until you bring disaster down upon this ship, and I'll see you thrown overboard before that happens."

My forbearance could only go so far before my temper took control. In a flash, I unsheathed my sword, the sting from the wounds on my hands barely making me flinch. I gripped the handle tightly, until blood dripped off the pommel to pool on the deck, the blade inches from the bosun. He looked down at me in silent satisfaction, but I wouldn't yet admit defeat.

"The bosun has issued a challenge," I said. The crew observing our exchange drew close in nervous curiosity. "Will he draw his sword and follow through?"

"Lad," Hrod said, his voice a warning in my ear. "Don't."

"You should listen to your fellow crewman," Bosun Chester said mildly, that stupid smile still on his face, as if he'd won.

"Why? Because you know I'd best you?"

His smile faltered, but he didn't respond.

"Are you so afraid of a ginger that you won't fight one? Coward." The satisfaction was now mine, for he snarled and finally drew his sword, slamming it down against my blade in unrestrained fury. The crew erupted in a series of shouts, but whether it was in encouragement or pleas for me to stop, I couldn't say. There was no one but the two of us at that moment, and we both had a score to settle.

He was strong, but his anger made him sloppy, and I easily blocked his attacks. I moved quickly, dodging his thrusts and waiting for my opportunity. When he tired and his sword waivered, I drove it toward the deck with a powerful downward blow and pushed my shoulder into him. He stumbled, and I swept my leg under his feet, and he fell onto the deck. The crew were silent. I strode forward triumphantly and placed the point of my sword against Bosun Chester's chest. Before I could claim my victory, a hand grabbed my wrist and wrenched me backward, then twisted until I dropped the sword. I looked up into the furious eyes of First Mate Evrard and paled.

"What is the meaning of this?" he demanded. His grip on my wrist was painfully tight. Blood still seeped from the wounds on my hand, but he paid no attention to my discomfort.

Bosun Chester scrambled to his feet. "Sir, this boy struck me and must be punished. He has continually showed nothing but disrespect and drew a sword instead of following my orders. He has proven himself a disgrace to this ship, and his presence is a dishonor to us all."

"No, sir," I said. I was on the verge of saying, "He started it," but I knew it sounded childish. "Bosun Chester is misrepresenting the facts."

"Are you calling me a liar?" Bosun Chester took a threatening step toward me.

"Enough," the first mate snapped. "We'll settle this off deck." He proceeded to drag me into the bowels of the ship. As we entered the hold, I registered where he was taking me.

"Please don't," I pleaded. But he threw me into a tiny cell before I could say more and locked me inside.

"Until we can sort this mess out," he said.

When he left, the only sound was the creaking of the hull as the ship swayed and the movement of barrels sliding against their moorings. Very little light drifted into the hold from above deck, cloaking me in near darkness. It was several degrees cooler, and I wrapped my arms around my legs and shivered. The full gravity of what I'd done crashed on my shoulders, and I pressed my forehead against my knees and inhaled a shuddering breath. I would be punished for certain, and that meant my secret could be revealed. I'd been a fool to allow my temper to get the better of me, and now I would most certainly pay the price.

I couldn't be certain how much time I spent in that dark hold shivering with cold and fear, but I jumped to my feet when I heard the first mate's distinct footfalls. He opened the cell and pulled me forward without a word, leading me toward the captain's quarters. The few crewmen we passed looked away without meeting my eye. Not only would I be punished, but I may have lost the precious friendships I'd made. The first mate shoved me through the door of the captain's cabin and slammed it shut behind us after we entered. He took his place at the captain's side behind the giant desk at the back of the room. There was no sign of Bosun Chester. Had they already spoken to him?

"Mr. Red," Captain Romy said sharply. He was in no mood to be patient. I stepped forward, swallowing hard, but I couldn't get rid of the lump in my throat.

"Sir," I said hoarsely. I saluted the three brothers and waited.

"I've heard a disturbing account." The captain's eyes pierced me with his stern gaze. "Is it true? Did you draw your sword on Bosun Chester?"

"I did," I said.

"Can you give me a reasonable explanation why?" he demanded.

I considered for a moment, and I honestly couldn't say that my motive *was* reasonable. I'd been provoked, to be sure, but I knew my anger was not a decent excuse for what I'd done.

"I cannot say that it was reasonable, sir." I willed myself not to get emotional. A woman would cry at a time like this, not a boy. Captain Romy sighed, and I hesitantly looked up at him.

"You told me no one had been giving you trouble," he said.

"I said 'not lately,' sir."

"Tell us what happened," he said, not unkindly.

So, I told him. Everything. I told him how from the moment I set foot on the ship, Bosun Chester singled me out, ordered me to perform menial tasks, tried to pique my ire, and had generally been unpleasant despite my doing everything he asked. I told him the truth, that I didn't know why Bosun Chester had found me so offensive. I hesitated, my voice catching.

"Until today, that is," I finished. "I'm not proud of my actions. They were fueled by bitterness and damaged vanity. I accept whatever punishment you see fit, and I promise it will never happen again." I looked between the three brothers, their expressions characteristic to each personality: Absalon sympathetic, Evrard sharp, and Captain Romy intent.

"Hrod told us what Bosun Chester said," Captain Romy said after a moment's silence. "I want you to know I hold my officers to a higher standard, and I will not tolerate such discrimination."

I could only nod in acknowledgement.

"Neither do I tolerate insubordination, justified or otherwise. The punishment for such a crime is flogging."

I shook less at the idea of being whipped and more at the prospect of having to remove my shirt and be exposed.

"However, in this situation, a few days in the hold should be punishment enough. We will reach our next destination at that time." He nodded to the first mate, and I was led back below deck before I had a chance to release the breath I'd been holding.

CHAPTER 20

What a fool I had been to think that two days alone in the dark would be painless compared to five skin shearing lashes across the back. It wasn't the boredom or loneliness that nearly drove me mad, but the silence and the feeling of utter despair in a cramped and darkened space. Aside from the delivery of a hardened biscuit and small cup of water twice a day, I saw no one. The only sound was the groaning of aged wood. When I was finally released, my hair was a greasy mess and a layer of sweat and dirt covered my skin. I squinted in the sunlight. I couldn't meet the stares of the crew. I was too ashamed. I worried what they must think of me, but I was more distraught at the thought of losing my friends.

I stared through First Mate Evrard's chest when he handed me back my sword and remained impassive as the crew prepared to lower the dinghy into the water. The ship was anchored offshore of an island covered in a dense forest. I scanned the rocky shore without seeing it, my heart not yet into this journey. We were given the order to leave the ship, but when I stepped forward, a hand grasped my shoulder. I stilled, then slowly looked toward the man standing to my left. Telken. He squeezed my shoulder, nodded once, and winked. I managed a small smile, and he released me. I resumed my role as a crewman of *The Wayward Aymelina*, a ship whose people were loyal to their friends. No matter what.

The first mate and I splashed through the shallows and beached the dinghy. The trees soared into the sky, their trunks wide and strong. They were as tall as the masts on *The Wayward Aymelina*, and covered in fine, needle-thin leaves. The ground was soft with the memories of fall, a thick layer of brown leaves mingling with fresh grass. Our steps were quiet while exploring the periphery of the shore, listening to the reassuring songs of birds and rustle of animals scampering in the undergrowth. There were no signs of people, and after another hour of exploration, we concluded it was safe for the others to land.

The crew wasted no time felling trees to build shelters, and some of the logs were taken back to the ship to have in case repairs were needed. The warm breeze carried a sharp yet refreshing smell I later discovered came from the sap and leaves of the enormous trees. I tasted them to see if they were as sweet as they smelled, but the bitterness was overpowering, and I couldn't spit them out fast enough.

Life moved on as if I'd never made a spectacle of my temper, but though my friends and the officers treated me normally, I still felt I'd somehow let everyone down. I particularly felt for Tyrnan, for my actions could have led to the discovery of our deception. Though he said nothing to indicate he was displeased, I still believed I owed him an apology. If I was being completely honest with myself, at the crux of my morose mood wasn't worrying over my brother but related to Captain Romy. He placed a lot of faith in me, and I'd taken that trust and torn it asunder. Simply saying sorry wouldn't be enough. I had to go through the painstaking process again of proving I was worthy of such trust.

Over the next few days, I went above and beyond my usual duties. I carried wood, maintained fires, gathered berries, learned how to fish, and generally exhausted myself trying to regain the captain's favor. If he noticed, he said nothing, and I grew increasingly nervous when I ventured out alone and he didn't show up to engage in conversation. I missed his company, but I hated to think he'd given up on me. I eventually abandoned the fruitless plight and resigned myself to once again being the least of his concerns.

The woods were a comfort. The simplicity of the ground beneath my feet, the sunbeams shining through the branches, and the sounds of ever constant life erased my petty worries. The terrain was at times lush grass and others rough stone punctuated by tree roots. Life was everywhere, from the plants growing on the forest floor to the birds nesting in the trees. I feared I would run out of room in my journal documenting it all.

A small party of us traveled southwest along the perimeter of the island and came to a river, and it was decided we should try to discover its source. Such pursuits always proved exciting, but I was filled with trepidation at the prospect of journeying with the officers with so few people to act as a buffer between us.

"I think they're still angry with me," I said to Tyrnan when we had a moment alone.

"I'm sure they got over it way before you did," he said.

"What's everyone else saying?"

"Honestly?"

"Of course." My voice wavered.

"I think most of the crew were happy to see Bosun Chester put in his place. But you didn't hear that from me."

The smile lingering on my face after such a revelation was doubtless apparent to all, but I didn't try to hide it as we moved northward along the river. It was so small, I could easily jump from one bank to the other, and it barely reached my knees. The banks were soft and rust colored, and my boots stuck firmly when I walked on it. Curious, I reached down and played with a bit between my fingers.

"It feels like clay," I said. My favorite cartographer, Oryn Thatchett, squatted next to me to feel for himself. He reluctantly agreed and made a few notes in his book.

"We should take some samples," Thatchett said. As if on cue, a jar was produced, and a hefty glob of earth was shoved inside.

That night, while the men ate and shared stories around the fire, I sat quietly finishing the details of a sketch of a bird I'd observed feeding her nestlings. A smile played at my lips as I basked in the men's exuberance while not taking part in it myself. My belly was full, and my mind was hazy while my limbs were warm and heavy from the wine. One by one, they drifted off to the tents to sleep, until there was nothing but the sound of crackling flames and the call of an owl.

"Anything of note to report?"

I froze, once again shocked at how Captain Romy was able to appear without me hearing him. I met his eyes and watched the reflection of the flames dancing in their blue-gray depths. I blinked and returned my attention to the pages before answering.

"Nothing that would interest you," I said.

"I'll be the judge of that." He sat next to me and held out his hand for the journal.

Reluctantly, I placed it in his outstretched palm and stared into the fire as he read through the pages. I snuck a glance to ascertain whether I could read his opinions in his expressions but found myself openly studying his face while he focused on my journal. His eyebrows were furrowed, and his long fingers tugged at the beard above his chin, drawing my gaze to his mouth. His lips were pulled into a thin line, but they were as pink as blushing cheeks. Mine were chapped from the wind and sun, but his were smooth…soft. My face flushed and I snapped my attention back to the flames.

Damn Tyrnan forever.

After a few minutes he handed the book back. "Insightful as always."

I took it without meeting his eye and shifted away.

"You have a real talent for this sort of work. Have you considered studying in Hrgun?"

"No," I said. I was grateful for the concealment of night, otherwise he might detect my flattery. "It isn't something I'm able to do."

"I see," he said quietly. "Beyond your family's means?"

"Exactly."

"Perhaps your work here will change that." I stared at him quizzically, but he didn't elaborate. Instead, he gazed back with a blank expression and my shoulders sagged resignedly.

"What can I do?" I asked.

His head tilted to the side in puzzlement.

"To help convince you to forgive me and earn back your trust."

"Ah." His expression softened. "So that's why you've been working nonstop from dawn until dusk?"

"It is."

"Why didn't you just ask?"

"I…um." The directness of his question took me by surprise. "I suppose because I didn't feel I'd earned it."

"You promised it won't happen again, and that's enough for me. You're forgiven."

I blinked at his decisiveness. He rose and left the fire for his own tent. I smiled, a broad, stupid grin that I couldn't blame on Tyrnan.

The river led to a lake that although large, was far from impressive. The water was dark, almost brown, and the trees lining the edges sagged toward the surface, casting several areas around the perimeter in cool shade. We filled several water skins, and the cartographers took measurements while the rest of the crew dove into the water to escape the noonday sun. Even First Mate Evrard began stripping off his shirt in anticipation of a swim. When he invited the captain to join him, I promptly left to explore. My thoughts toward the captain had been drifting dangerously close to admiration and seeing him half clothed wouldn't help.

The temperature was several degrees cooler in the trees, and for several minutes, I simply wandered without bothering to take notes. I breathed in the earthy scents of vegetation, dirt, and lingering moisture. There were a few flowers with yellow and white petals dotting the ground, but aside from those, there was nothing but green and brown as far as I could see. I moved silently, careful to place my steps so I wouldn't disturb a rock or a branch. I lowered myself next to a boulder and sat contentedly with my face turned upward to absorb the warmth from the sun filtering through the trees. I stretched my arms overhead and relaxed to the songs of birds. When I decided I'd been gone long enough to avoid any embarrassing situations, I exhaled heavily, releasing my accumulated pent-up tension, and stood. Something crashed through the trees, and I spun toward the sound in time to see a flash of white bounding away. A deer.

I laughed to shake off the surge of fear coursing through my veins and turned around to face a black arrow aimed at my heart. My gaze traveled down the shaft to a slightly trembling hand and settled on a face trained on mine. It was a boy, no older than my teenage cousins. His brown eyes were wide in surprise and terror. I raised my hands non-threateningly, and he stepped backward, though he didn't lower the bow.

"Don't be afraid," I said in a soothing tone. "I won't hurt you."

The boy drew back on the bow and his breathing quickened. Where was Seaman Erec when I needed him?

"I'm a friend." I placed a hand over my heart and smiled to show my peaceful intentions.

His eyes flickered to my hand, then he gave me a suspicious sideways glance. He relaxed his grip, minimally, and spoke in a language I didn't understand. I tried to indicate that I didn't speak his language. He responded by talking louder. I waved my hands to try and stop the torrent of words coming out of his mouth, but he was silenced by a menacing growl rumbling behind me. We froze simultaneously. The boy raised his eyes above my head to the top of a boulder. I slowly turned and looked up to see the largest cat I'd ever seen. At least I *think* it was some sort of cat. It was the color of the clay along the riverbanks, with green eyes and rounded ears. It looked like two hundred pounds of sleek muscle. It opened its massive jaws and let out an eerily human scream. I stumbled backwards into the boy who stood fixated in fear. The beast crouched, and my hand went to my sword, drawing it just as it leapt toward us. When my blade sliced across the beast's face, the boy cried out and took off running through the forest. The animal shrieked and disappeared in the opposite direction. I stood for a moment in disbelief, panting and sweating. I sank to my knees, and everything went black.

I awoke to the sound of voices calling my name, not the one given to me upon my birth, but the name meant to conceal my identity. I groggily dragged myself onto my hands and knees and retrieved my sword. The tip dragged in the dirt as I walked on quivering legs toward the lake. I broke through the forest and saw the officers clustered in a group. The crew shouted and pointed when they saw me. Heads turned toward me just as my knees gave out and I melted to the ground. I recognized Tyrnan's voice, but the faces were hazy.

"Mr. Red." Captain Romy's face came sharply into focus as he shook my shoulders. "What happened?"

I dropped my sword and leaned forward to brace myself against his chest.

"We're not alone," I said. My fingers dug into his shirt as I struggled to remain conscious. He stilled, his own grip tightening.

"What do you mean?"

"People," I gasped. "There are people here." There was a murmur of voices, and someone called out for Seaman Erec.

"Tell me what you saw." He didn't relinquish his hold on my shoulders——he probably feared I was about to swoon. The thought was mortifying. I still clutched his shirt. I slowly let go and bent over, placing my hands on my knees.

"There was a boy." I swallowed hard. My mouth had gone dry. I licked my lips. Captain Romy called for some water, and once a water skin was produced, I drank eagerly. Water trickled down my chin onto my shirt.

The captain finally let me go. I noted the loss of his support and the sudden bereft feeling I was left with, but I was too emotionally drained to give the realization the proper level of embarrassment. I simply didn't care.

"He couldn't have been older than fourteen or fifteen," I continued. "I startled a deer he was hunting, and he shifted his aim to me. He looked frightened. I tried to talk to him, but we couldn't understand each other."

"Would you recognize the language if you heard it again?" Seaman Erec asked.

I shrugged. "Perhaps."

"Then what happened?" First Mate Evrard asked impatiently.

"I heard a growl behind me, and we both turned to see the biggest cat——" I went dizzy thinking about it, but I took a deep breath and continued. "It was enormous. Had to be at least two hundred pounds. It attacked us. I slashed at it with my sword, and it ran away. The boy ran off, too."

"What was he wearing?" Seaman Erec asked.

"I—I didn't notice. I was paying more attention to the arrow pointed at my heart."

"Can you remember *anything*?" he asked, undeterred.

"He had brown eyes and tan skin. Dark hair, too, I think."

"Tall or short?"

"Shorter than me, but not by much."

"What makes you think he was a teenage boy and not a short man?"

"Because he didn't have a beard," I said dryly, eliciting a generalized chuckle from the gathered men.

"Mr. Red has answered enough questions for now." The captain helped me to my feet.

"Deserves a drink, I think," Telken said. He draped an arm around my shoulders. "Settle his nerves." The captain nodded absently, and I was dragged away for the promised libations.

Regardless of the captain's statement, the moment I was seated with a mug of ale, I was inundated with questions I couldn't answer fast enough. Did I really see a big cat? What color was it? Did it have big teeth? Was the boy naked or did he have clothes? What kind of bow did he have? Each new question flew at me before I could finish answering the last. I soon developed a headache.

"Leave him alone now, lads," Telken said as he shooed the men away. They reluctantly obeyed, and I thanked my friend with a grateful smile.

I tapped my fingers against my mug. "I don't think they believe me."

"Of course, they do!" He looked at me in disbelief. "You've never given anyone reason not to take you at your word."

I looked down at my hands, ashamed, because every day I was with these men, I was deceiving them. They trusted me, and without their knowing it, I was giving them cause to doubt me. I shook off the feeling and took another long drink of the bitter ale.

CHAPTER 21

The officers debated the issue of the boy I'd encountered and how to proceed. First Mate Evrard wanted to gather more intelligence by searching out the boy's home and observing at a distance before risking ourselves to potential hostiles. Second Mate Absalon argued that if we were caught spying, it might look suspicious and suggested we make ourselves known immediately. Seaman Erec paced outside the officer's tent while they discussed the matter, eagerly awaiting their decision.

I gave him a knowing smile. "Not feeling so idle now, are you?"

"I just hope they come to an agreement so I can be of some use." He glanced at the tent flap that remained shut.

Less than a day had passed, but the mood among the men had changed dramatically. Everyone cast furtive glances toward the trees and were never without a weapon. Even the most subtle snap of a twig had them all leaping to their feet with swords drawn, only to see a bird flapping away or a rabbit dash into a burrow. Whether they were afraid of hostiles or the large predator, the result was undeniable: the men were on edge. Seaman Erec was the exception, too busy pouring over his notes and testing his language expertise against my memory. Nothing sounded *exactly* like what I heard, but a few came close enough that Erec was confident he could communicate effectively.

In the end, the captain chose caution. First Mate Evrard and I were tasked with finding the boy's home and discreetly observing before approaching them.

When we prepared to leave, I turned to the first mate and asked, "What if they're doing the same thing to us right now?"

All three officers looked at me, then out at the trees, their eyes wide.

"It just seems to me," I said with casual ease. "That a young hunter probably wouldn't wander far from home. He probably reported everything he saw to his own people, and we've seen no sign of them. They're probably watching us right now." I shrugged on my canvas pack and strolled toward the trees. When I noticed the first mate wasn't beside me, I called back, "Are you coming?"

He blinked, regained his senses, and purposely marched toward the forest ahead of me. I suppressed a grin, knowing my teasing was cruel though not far from the truth. I wouldn't be surprised if we were being watched, and I was on high alert for any movement, from either man or beast.

We started from the point where I first saw the young man and headed in the general direction where he'd fled. In his haste, he disturbed a few bushes, broke a few branches, and scuffed some grass off a rock. We followed his trail for several hours, alert to any sight or sound that might indicate we ourselves were being stalked. When we stopped to rest and eat, I mused that the young hunter wandered further than I anticipated.

"Maybe he was lost," First Mate Evrard said.

"Maybe." I nibbled on some hardtack. It was possible, but I believed it unlikely that he was lost. His trail back was very self-assured, indicating he knew exactly where he was going and how to get there, although it was a long way to go for a one-man hunting party.

After another hour, the trail became more and more difficult to track until it eventually stopped altogether. We searched in vain for any sign that a person had passed through the area, but found nothing, not a bent blade of grass nor a scrape against stone. The first mate and I looked at each other in defeat.

"We should head back before it gets dark," the first mate said, disappointment evident in his voice. He was just as excited to find a settlement of people as Seaman Erec. We turned back toward camp, and I froze, my foot hovering in mid-air.

"Wait," I whispered sharply. He looked at me and stilled, his hand on the hilt of his sword.

I inhaled deeply through my nose, and for a moment I thought I'd imagined it. I closed my eyes, listening to the sound of birds chirping. A breeze rustled the leaves, and I smelled it again. Smoke. My eyes flew open, and I quickly moved through the forest in the direction it came from, the first mate close behind. The smell grew stronger, and I crouched low in the foliage.

"Smell that?" I whispered. He inspected the air like a scent hound and nodded.

"Campfires," he whispered. We practically crawled on our bellies through the dense undergrowth until we heard voices. We sank to the forest floor, and my heart pounded so forcefully I worried the vibration would give away our position. I breathed through gritted teeth, my jaw clenched in fear and excitement. Inch by inch, we shuffled along the ground toward the voices, stopping when there was a break in the trees. Carefully, we drew aside a branch. The first mate gave a sharp intake of breath that could've been heard in Praed. I almost clamped my hand over his mouth.

Before us lay a clearing where only a few trees stood, and among the tall monoliths was a scattering of dwellings. Some were long and some short, but all were constructed of stacked logs with domed thatched roofs. They circled the clearing, in the middle of which was a large firepit where several people were gathered. On closer inspection, they appeared to be older women preparing a meal. They wore shimmering gray and dark blue sleeveless tunics that ended just above their knees. I leaned closer, puzzled by the strange texture of the leather. It was scaled. The clothing was made from fish skins! Woven in their black hair were bands made from fish vertebrae and foliage. One woman stirred the contents of a clay pot, another tended spears of fish dripping over the flames, while another stretched dough over a flat stone.

Children clad in knee-length boots and a simple flap to cover their private areas played between the houses and around the trees. Black, shining hair flowed out behind them, and their skin was the same color as the boy's I'd seen the previous day. They giggled and tossed play spears at each other, reminding me of the games my brothers and I used to play. My eyes drifted around the village. A young woman with fish spines woven in her hair was painting a boat red. She wore a skirt made from strips of fish leather, the tails swishing across her thighs. Long, thin leaves were woven into a covering for her breasts. Another young woman dressed similarly scraped a deer hide stretched between two poles. I saw no weapons, and I realized apprehensively there was something else strangely absent.

"I don't see any men," I whispered. The first mate scanned the area intently and shook his head, indicating he didn't either.

"They must be in those houses," he whispered. We observed the scene in silence for several minutes more, until he tapped me on the shoulder and gestured for me to follow. I took one last look at the people, then reluctantly shuffled backward out of sight.

"Or," First Mate Evrard said ominously once we were out of earshot. "They could be in the forest." He stared into the trees tensely, his grip tight around the hilt of his sword.

"We should leave then," I said. "We're on their lands after all."

If we were observed we saw no evidence of it on our way back to camp. Still, I had a strange tingling in my stomach warning me to be careful. When we returned to camp, the captain wasted no time summoning us for a full debriefing. We described the location, how far away and in what direction one had to travel to find it. We gave details on the structures and the appearance of the people. It was all very dry and matter-of-fact. This somehow left me with a feeling akin to shame, as though we'd violated their privacy.

Before I could be dismissed I had to say something. "Sir? Please, if I might speak freely."

He nodded, inviting me to continue.

"I don't think they're hostile."

The captain's features sharpened. "Why do you say that?"

"It's a village with children and women," I said. "People going about their business. I think we should approach them peacefully. Maybe have Seaman Erec talk to them. Make it clear to them we're not here to harm them."

"I have to wonder," he said. "Where were the men?"

"Probably doing what we're doing now, discussing what to do about the strangers in their land. The fact that they haven't attacked us already should speak to their own caution." I tried to control the rising desperation in my voice—the last thing I wanted was for a bunch of worked-up men to get it in their heads that they needed to draw their swords against an imagined threat and slaughter an entire village.

"You had an arrow pointed at your heart yesterday," the captain said. "Isn't that a sign of hostility?"

"He was a *scared* boy," I said. "And he didn't *fire* that arrow if you recall. They're not inherently dangerous."

"Are you drawing on your observations or personal feelings on the matter?"

"Both." I held his gaze, unwavering in my determination. "One does not necessarily preclude the other. You asked me to make observations and I have. I have drawn conclusions. The logical next step."

I could tell the captain was seriously considering my argument, and for that I was grateful. He looked to his second mate and asked for his opinion, and I wasn't surprised that he shared mine.

"Evrard, what do you think we should do?"

"I worry that we didn't see any men," he said. "I think Mr. Red and I should go back tomorrow and observe them and see what more we can learn."

I was shocked at this conservative approach, but also very appreciative. I couldn't help smiling at him.

"Very well," the captain said. "Report to me afterwards and I will make my final decision."

The next day Seaman Erec accompanied us on our outing, and I couldn't hide my amusement at the awe in his eyes when he first saw the village. It appeared much like it did the day before, except our early start meant the fires were yet to be lit, and the women were occupied with other chores such as mending clothing and chasing after errant children. A mother scooped up a small child in a rust-colored dress with a *whoop* of laughter and tickled her, sending a pang of longing through my heart for my own mother.

We witnessed an uproar of activity, and the three of us pressed ourselves to the ground. The children rushed forward in loud, boisterous excitement. The men finally appeared through the trees, a few carrying the boats we'd seen the day before, now wet and dripping. The men also wore clothing made from fish leather. Some were bare chested wearing long necklaces made with teeth draped over their torso and wrapped around their waists. They carried stone-tipped spears and long bows carved with intricate designs. I recognized the black arrows packed into the quivers at their backs.

The women came forward to receive baskets of fish and a small deer hanging by its legs from a thick branch. We watched the women prepare the animals for consumption and the men clean their weapons. Several older men retreated into the largest building, and the younger men took up the task of minding the children while the women worked. Seaman Erec gestured for us to retreat, and when we could speak without being heard, he was immediately asked by the first mate if he could understand their language.

"It was difficult to hear clearly at such a distance," Seaman Erec said. "But I believe I could understand a word here and there. It reminds me of an ancient language detailed by the scholars of Hrgun that originated in the Geehai Mountains near Kuste. The peoples who lived there are long gone, but some artifacts and drawings found there were enough to piece their alphabet together."

"Fascinating," First Mate Evrard said flatly. "Does that mean you could talk to them?"

"I could certainly try." The first mate raised an eyebrow and Erec amended, "And most likely be successful."

"Good. Let's go back and report to the captain."

I prepared an eloquent yet strong speech to deliver to the captain upon our return, but as it happened, it wasn't necessary. He listened to our account and Seaman Erec's assurances that he could speak to the people, and without further debate declared that we'd go to the village tomorrow under a white banner.

"I hope they know what that means," I mumbled to Erec.

Telken gave me an extra ration of ale that night saying it "could be my last." Rex asked if he could have my sword if I died. My friends could really instill confidence and glowed with support. I took the ale and informed Rex that only a swordsman skilled enough to put me in the dirt was worthy enough to have my sword. The men laughed, but I admit I wasn't as confident as I appeared. If I was wrong in my assessment, it could mean all of our deaths.

The next day, a party consisting of myself, the three Romy officers, and Seaman Erec planned to approach the camp during their evening meal in the hopes that full bellies would mollify the locals and incline them to look upon us favorably.

We brought offerings of pearls and fine cloth the captain brought especially for just such an occasion. With knees trembling and a great deal of nervous uncertainty, we walked into the clearing under the white banner. The moment we were spotted, a flurry of activity erupted. Women screamed and ran off with their children. Men sprang to their feet and stalked toward us. Seaman Erec stepped forward with his hands raised to show he wasn't armed and spoke loud enough to reach their ears over the din. The villagers hesitated, and we took the opportunity to come a little closer so we could see each other clearly in the firelight. The crew tensed as the captain withdrew his sword and laid it at his feet. We followed his lead, and Seaman Erec spoke animatedly. They looked over us suspiciously. One of them shouted and waved us away.

"He wants us to leave," Erec translated.

"No shit," First Mate Evrard said.

Captain Romy maintained his friend smile and in a low voice commented aside, "I don't think they're open to talking."

Another voice called out, and a young man pushed through the wall of men protecting the village. He was the boy I'd encountered in the woods. I smiled despite the tense atmosphere. He pointed at me and spoke in earnest to the other men, who suddenly regarded me with recognition.

Erec translated. "The boy is saying that you're the one, the 'stranger' he told them about. Seems you were the subject of great debate the last few days."

All the tribesmen looked at me, really looked at me, and I shrank under the intense scrutiny of their dark eyes. The man who tried to get rid of us earlier stepped closer, and the captain tensed beside me when he reached out and tentatively touched my ginger hair. I stood perfectly still as he ran his fingers through it, murmuring to himself, and I nearly fainted when he leaned forward and sniffed the top of my head. Our eyes met for an instant, and I was struck by the keen intelligence reflected in the dark brown depths. Based on the lack of lines about his face, I guessed he wasn't very old, perhaps thirty. His black hair was parted sharply in the front and plaited while the rest in the back flowed freely. He wore tall red boots and a matching leather tunic that draped over his body past his waist. Circling his waist was a belt woven from leaves and accented with fish bones. Another man came up beside him and spoke in a low voice, and the red leather clad man grunted in response. Erec tried to engage them in conversation, but the intimidating one ignored him. Instead, he gestured for the boy to come closer and spoke to him for some time, occasionally indicating to me. The boy answered his questions, nodding several times. Finally, the man turned to Erec and spoke.

Erec listened closely. "I believe he's saying that he sees the debt owed to the flame-haired one and will open his hearth to us."

"Debt? What debt?" I asked. Erec repeated my question, and the man placed a hand over his heart then pressed his palm against the boy's chest while he answered.

"You saved his son's life," Erec translated.

My jaw fell open, and I could feel the officers' eyes on me. The man beckoned for us to join him as he and the others moved back toward the fire.

"Well," Erec said impatiently. "Come on!" He hurried after the woodland people with the first and second mate following with slightly more caution. I swallowed the lump in my throat and stepped forward, but a hand on my shoulder halted my movements.

I looked up into the captain's face, and I was grateful the waning light concealed the flush creeping up my cheeks at the sight of his proud smile. "Well done, Mr. Red." He patted my back which instantly filled me with warmth. I lowered my eyes in embarrassment and joined the rest of the men around the flames.

From what Seaman Erec could piece together, the bolder man was the leader of the village. When I met his son in the woods, it was on the boy's first hunt—apparently a tradition—that for a boy to become a man, he must go out alone to stalk and take down his first deer. He was to eat its heart and bring the rest back for the group to share. I had interrupted this hunt—a poor omen itself—but the subsequent attack by the cat-like beast convinced the people that I was some kind of savior sent to protect the young man. Once word spread through the village, the women appeared, bringing us gifts of jerked deer and mercifully soft bread—a welcome relief from the hardtack we endured on the ship. Children peered around the edges of buildings and trees to get a good look at us. The captain presented his own gifts, which were received with pleasure. Erec secured a meeting for the next day. With torches from their fire, we made our way back to our camp to the evident relief of the rest of the crew.

"We thought for sure you were goners!" Telken exclaimed when he saw us.

"Your confidence is heart-warming," I grumbled.

He laughed and jovially slapped me on the back. "Come tell us everything! There's a place right by me at the fire."

I didn't tell them everything. The last thing I needed was endless teasing over being a "savior." As time went on, I was drawing more and more attention to myself, and I feared any more would result in disaster.

CHAPTER 22

Our meeting with the village leaders proved quite a spectacle for the rest of the people. Everyone was waiting for us to arrive, their faces full of curiosity and fear. They'd likely never seen people like us before, and I'm sure they wondered what our motives were. I smiled at each face I met in the hopes of softening their reserves, but many turned away and pretended not to see. The children were not so shy. They bounded up to us, particularly me, talking over each other and pinching our clothes. The second mate found them endearing and let them see his eyeglasses, but the children dashed away in a flurry of giggles before he could get them back.

"That was my best pair," he huffed.

I had nothing so exciting as a pair of glasses to offer, but when I felt a tug at my sleeve and saw a small girl smiling up at me, I kneeled and rummaged in my bag. With a big smile, I produced one of my quill pens that still had an intact feather and handed it to her. She held it reverently, then tilted her head and spoke in her language, holding out the pen as she did so.

"You write with it," I told her. I ripped out a page in my journal, dipped the pen in a pot of ink, and showed her how to scrawl writing across the page. She seemed genuinely astonished, and I handed her the implements. She promptly disappeared into a pack of children to show them her prize.

The men were waiting in the largest dome-shaped building in the village. A small fire blazed at its center, and a wisp of pungent smoke drifted into the air and out a hole in the ceiling. Several older men sat around it on piles of fur. Bundles of drying herbs hung from the ceiling, and pipes were displayed along the walls. The lack of beds suggested the space was only used for meetings. The leader we spoke to the night before pulled a large strip of dried meat out of a beaded leather bag and bit off a piece. Each person took a bite before passing around the circle. It was surprisingly sweet and vaguely fishy and melted in my mouth. An elderly man with crooked fingers sprinkled dried leaves over the fire, and the air was filled with a pleasing earthy aroma. The talking commenced, and it was many hours before we emerged into the sunlight.

Seaman Erec was extremely impressive during those long hours in the warm, confining space. He was truly proficient in his grasp of languages, and it wasn't long until he understood enough to glean a lot of valuable information. The people were called the Nakwacimek, which roughly translated meant "the people who eat lake fish." Another village was located further north and yet another across a small expanse of water on a neighboring island, but they didn't interact very much. The village leader, whom they referred to as *chief* similarly to the Kuste people practice, was called *Noshluat*, and his son was named *Mukahanu*. When he was introduced, the boy I saved stepped forward, knelt before me, and presented me with a hardened leather sheath with fringes of softer leather. At its center was a painting depicting the big cat that attacked us, a beast the people called *nifo gomman*—"fang of the forest." I withdrew the knife and saw it was made from bone, the blade a dull ivory color, and the handle was woven with fine strips of leather. I replaced the knife and smiled at Mukahanu.

"This is an honor," I said to the young man. "But not as great as the honor of being the man who saved your life. I'm relieved I was there to offer my help." Erec translated my words, and Noshluat nodded approval.

"Noshluat would like Nutamoson to sit next to him at the dinner in his honor tonight," Erec translated when the chief spoke.

"Who's Nutamoson?" Second Mate Absalon asked. Erec repeated the question, and his eyes widened at the response.

"It's what the Nakwacimek people are calling Mr. Red," Erec said wonderingly, looking at me. "It means 'fire hair.'" Noshluat made a motion of flames above his head to emphasize the point, and I flushed the color of my hair, embarrassed at the open stares from the officers. "Noshluat said the people have never seen that color of hair before. It must be a gift from their gods."

"Or a curse," I mumbled under my breath. Aloud I said, "Please thank Noshluat for the honor of a Nakwacimek name."

When we took our place at the main fire, I was handed a pipe containing a substance that filled me with a pleasant warmth and fuzzy head. The men began to play drums and sing while the women danced, and I swayed with the music as the rhythm pounded in my veins. At one point, a young woman pulled me into the circle of dancers. I tried to keep up with their steps, but I was as clumsy as Mother, and I ended up stepping on the woman's feet. She giggled behind her hand but kept dancing. I laughed along with her. On impulse, I grabbed the captain and pulled him into the line, followed by the second mate. The first mate fixed me with a dreadful glare, so I wisely avoided him. The three of us circled the fire to the beat of the drums. I absently noted that I was still holding the captain's hand when the beating stopped. The warmth of his skin sent tingles along my flesh. I wanted to tighten my grip, draw closer, feel the press of his body against mine. I shook my head. Whatever I'd smoked was clouding my judgment. Reluctantly, I released my grip. The young girl next to me kissed my cheek and scurried off into the darkness with her tittering friends. I shoved my hands in my pockets awkwardly as the rest of the group dispersed.

"Well done, Mr. Red," Captain Romy said. He draped an arm over my shoulders and leaned in much too heavily. His pupils were dilated, and he sported a crooked grin. He'd obviously smoked the pipe. I shifted away before my errant thoughts got me in trouble.

I honestly don't know how we made it back to our camp by the lake, but I woke up in my own bed with a puddle of drool soaking my pillow and a pounding headache. The rest of the crew didn't appear to fare much better, for they met the day with squinted eyes and short tempers.

Tyrnan handed me a cup of water, and I drank the contents in one swallow, instantly relieving my dry throat. "So, a productive visit?"

I licked my lips and ran a hand across my mouth. "Seaman Erec did a fabulous job. I didn't realize how clever he was with languages."

"He came highly recommended," Tyrnan said.

We strolled toward the edge of the water and watched a fish break the glassy surface. It was already warm, and I predicted a stifling hot day.

I told Tyrnan what we learned the day before and he filled me in on the progress the cartographers made. They'd explored nearly the entire expanse of the lake and requested the camp be moved further west to try and locate the coast. I didn't know what the plan was regarding the Nakwacimek, but I hoped to record more information. I was so absorbed in merely taking everything in that I'd barely written any journal notes. I wished to remedy that. I spoke to Seaman Erec about this after breaking my fast, and he seemed as eager as I was to visit the village again.

He flipped through the pages of his journal. "I still have so many questions." He'd been a much better notetaker than I. We approached the captain together and asked if we'd be meeting with the Nakwacimek again.

"Not today," he said, rather irritably. Still feeling the effects of the pipe we smoked I'd wager. "We're moving camp."

"The cartographers requested it," I explained to Erec. The captain's eyes flashed toward me, then back to the papers he was organizing into a satchel.

"Can we visit with them once we're settled?" Erec asked.

"Perhaps," the captain said, followed by a quick, "Dismissed." We took the hint and left him alone. Erec had a sour look the rest of the morning.

Erec's mood didn't improve over the next several days. Continued requests to meet with the Nakwacimek were denied. I couldn't account for the captain's reluctance. Surely he couldn't think that the people meant any harm after our visit with them. I was getting frustrated over his stubbornness. Erec was content to obey without an explanation, but I was never one to keep my mouth shut.

I approached the officer's tent boldly and scratched at the side. The word, "Enter," was barely spoken when I wrenched the flap aside and strode in prepared to give the captain a piece of my mind.

"Sir, I simply cannot remain silent—" I stopped mid-sentence when I registered Captain Romy's current state of dress—or rather, *undress*. He was naked from the waist up and the top few buttons of his breeches were undone. He was leaning over a basin of water washing his face, and my eyes traced the path of the water as it ran down his muscled chest toward...

"I know this about you," he said.

I looked toward the ground, my cheeks burning, and I inexplicably forgot why I was there in the first place.

"You wanted to see me?" he prompted when I remained speechless.

"No!" I shouted before my brain could catch up. I winced at my stupidity.

"Are you unwell, Mr. Red?" He walked toward me rubbing a towel over his face. "You look as if you're going to be sick."

"I'm fine." I cleared my throat and focused on anything but him. I squeezed my eyes shut and tried to banish the image of his bare skin, the sparse dusting of hair, and the contoured muscles of his torso leading to the hem of his breeches. Inklings of attraction had been trickling into my brain. Now it was a flood.

"It's just I was wondering why you haven't granted your permission for us to speak to the Nakwacimek again."

"Other matters to consider." He tossed the towel aside and, to my exultant relief, pulled on a shirt.

"May Seaman Erec and I visit them this afternoon?" I hoped he didn't notice the roughness of my voice.

"You may."

My brows furrowed at his casual manner. I had expected a fight and was temporarily flustered at not encountering one.

"Anything else?" he asked.

"No…" I slowly backed out of the tent before my lascivious thoughts resurfaced.

Seaman Erec wasted no time collecting his things before we raced through the forest toward the Nakwacimek village. I'd never seen him smile so openly, and his excitement was catching. I was so full of mirth that I failed to pay attention to the sounds of the forest, to the signs that something wasn't right, until we slowed to take a break. While Erec was drinking from his waterskin, I suddenly realized that the birds were no longer singing. I peered through the trees, but not a leaf quivered. There was no breeze to deliver the scent of danger, yet ice shivered up my spine. I drew my sword on impulse, and Erec's eyes widened in alarm.

"What is it?" he whispered hoarsely.

"It's quiet," I said.

"Isn't that a good thing?"

"No." I turned in a slow circle as Erec backed against a tree, his eyes darting frantically from side to side. A heartbeat passed, then three, and nothing happened. I lowered my sword a fraction, believing myself foolish for being so paranoid, when a scream forced me into action.

Seaman Erec blanched and pointed at the trees to the south. I spun in that direction just as a rust-colored beast bounded into view with a shriek.

A breeze stirred my hair as it leapt for us, and I instinctively slashed with my sword. It stopped short mere feet away, its tail swishing irritably and its ears pinned back. I backed toward Erec, his back pinned against the tree, my sword warding the beast off like a magical talisman. The creature snarled, bearing its enormous fangs, and swiped a paw at us. One side of its face was mangled, an eye missing amid a jagged scar. This was the beast that attacked me previously. *Nifo gomman.* Erec breathed raggedly behind me. I forced myself to stay calm.

"Go," I whispered over my shoulder to Erec. I kept my eyes locked on the creature.

"But where?" he asked in a strangled voice.

"Toward the village," I said through gritted teeth. "I'll hold it off."

He didn't question me further. I couldn't decide whether this was a vote of confidence or a bid to save his own skin. Regardless, he inched his way slowly to the left. The beast watched him with its good eye, a low growl emanating from its throat. Erec took a chance and broke into a run, triggering the predator to charge. I roared a battle cry of my own as I drove forward to cut off *nifo gomman's* pursuit. The animal swerved toward me as if it were made of liquid and swiped at my sword arm. My blade flew into the undergrowth, and I grasped my forearm. Blood seeped through my sleeve and through my clenched fingers. No time to scream in pain as the cat slunk toward me.

I stood my ground, growling through my teeth, air puffing out my cheeks, but *nifo gomman* was not to be intimidated. It crouched, tail swishing, ready to pounce. I reached into my boot as the creature sprang, landing awkwardly on top of me. We tumbled backward and I ended up pinned under its chest. The beast's jaws moved toward my throat, but before the fangs sank into my flesh, I drove the knife Mukahanu gave me into its heart. *Nifo gomman* collapsed in a limp heap. I lay in stunned silence, breathing raggedly.

Under the weight of the big cat, I started feeling light-headed. My hands were cold despite the heat. My eyes closed languidly and opened just as slowly, until I didn't have the strength to open them again. I dimly registered voices, but they were muffled as if the sound traveled through water. A weight was lifted off me, and I mustered the strength to open my eyes. Unfamiliar faces loomed over me. I tried to wriggle away, but someone grabbed me and loaded me onto a padded surface stretched between two long branches. Two men dragged me further into the forest. I made an incoherent sound and tried to roll out of the crude stretcher, but a hand was placed firmly against my chest. I looked up into a face I finally recognized: Noshluat's. He gave me a look that brooked no argument, one Father might give me, and I settled back on a cushion of furs. My eyes closed once more, and this time I did not deign to open them.

When I awoke, I had no concept of how long I had been unconscious. I came alive with a fury of uncertainty and fear, thrashing about like *nifo gomman* was still attacking me. A calming voice spoke, and soft hands soothed my brow and face. My frantic eyes locked onto the face of a familiar young woman, one of the ladies I'd danced with nights ago at the Nakwacimek feast. I relaxed, breathing hard. I couldn't understand her words, but her gentleness spoke a universal language. She coaxed me back under the fur covering and dabbed my forehead with a damp cloth. She smiled and bobbed her head. I nodded back gratefully. She left, and I glanced around at the small space filled with pouches and bags. There was a strange odor in the air, not unpleasant, and several hot rocks steamed in the middle of the floor. I raised my arm and gingerly touched the bandage wrapped from my wrist to my elbow, noting only a dull ache. Seconds later, Noshluat, Seaman Erec, and, to my astonishment, Captain Romy burst through the doorway.

"Mr. Red," Captain Romy said. "How are you feeling?"

"Fine," I said.

"Seaman Erec told us what happened and that you were injured."

"Not badly." I held up my arm. "I'm fit to leave, I think." I rose shakily to my feet and nearly toppled over. The captain braced me under the arms, and I cautiously eased him away.

Noshluat spoke and Seaman Erec translated. "Noshluat would like to invite everyone to a feast in Nutamoson's honor to thank him for ridding the forest of the rogue beast that terrorized their hunters."

"Thank you." I was so overwhelmed with gratitude for what these people had done for me I didn't know what else to say. I didn't feel I deserved such accolades.

The excessive praise was worth it when the rest of the crew joined us at the Nakwacimek fire. Most of the crew hadn't been to the village before and there was not a set of people more out of place. Their furtive glances made their apprehension more endearing. But after a few puffs of the pipe, they relaxed enough to enjoy the feast, which consisted of venison, mixed vegetables, nuts, and a light-colored, rich meat that tasted slightly like blood sausage. I was about to ask what it was, but the question was answered in gruesome detail when a rust-colored skin was presented. It was laid at my feet, and there were still remnants of tissue stuck to the underside. I almost retched.

"For Nutamoson. A token of his victory," Erec told me.

I couldn't very well decline the gift, so I made a great show over presenting it to Mukahanu. The boy's eyes lit up and he looked to his father. The chief nodded sagely, and the boy clasped the skin to his body as if I'd given a silk dress to a high-born lady. The chief looked at me approvingly then draped a necklace over my head. It was a strip of leather, unadorned except for the largest tooth I'd ever seen. It was almost as long as my index finger and heavy in my palm. I didn't require Erec's translation to know it was the fang of *nifo gomman*.

"Thank you," I said.

He smiled slightly, then gestured to a spot away from the others. When we were alone, he fixed me with a serious gaze. He pointed to himself, then his eye, then me, and waited. I mimicked his signs and gathered that he was saying he could see me. I nodded in understanding. He pointed to me and made an unmistakable gesture. I flushed and checked to ensure no one was paying attention. He watched my reaction, then repeated the signs and pointed at me with raised brows, a question.

"Yes." I placed my hands against my chest and made the motion for breasts. "I'm a woman. Please don't tell." I placed a finger against my lips and shook my head, hoping he would understand. His people must have discovered my secret when I lost consciousness from my injuries. I stared at him with pleading eyes, my heart seizing as I waited for his response.

He finally touched a fist to my heart, then his own, and nodded. I smiled shakily and released a long breath. He passed me the dagger his son gave me, the blade clean, and gave me a dark look. I felt his meaning and clenched my jaw. I would use this weapon, I told him with my eyes, if any harm came my way.

CHAPTER 23

We spent two months on the forested island. When we left, I felt the loss as keenly as when we departed the black sand coast of the previous island. We traveled parallel to the southern shore, and I marveled at the size of the trees standing over the island in mute guardianship. We sailed two days before reaching the open ocean, but even then, on clear days I could still make out the very tops of the trees.

The routine of life on board *The Wayward Aymelina* returned to normal, occupying the crew from sunup until sundown. The predictability became monotonous by the third day, and I tried to break up the boredom by stepping up the swordsmanship lessons with Rex and engaging in games with Telken, Luc, and some of the other men. I worked on fine tuning my journal entries and listened to Tyrnan's exuberant accounts, *oohing* and *aahing* when appropriate over the sketches and rudimentary maps he and his fellow cartographers created. How incredibly impressive to think that history had no account of these islands before we left Faqur. By all accounts, they never existed.

"Can you even fathom it?" I asked. "That we are the makers of history?"

Tyrnan grinned. "It's humbling, isn't it?"

I sighed. "I don't know how to go back after this."

"Nor do I," he said quietly.

There were many months left in the journey, but I was already becoming depressed at the thought of leaving the ship. I looked forward to seeing my family again, but I'd carved out a place for myself on board *The Wayward Aymelina.* Not because I was born to it, but because I established myself on my own merits. Tyrnan sympathized with my feelings, but he could return if he wished. Once I disembarked at Faqur, I was certain to be confined to Praed Castle for the remainder of my life.

I found comfort in exchanging stories with Hrod in the pre-dawn hours perched in the masthead. Inevitably, I grew quiet and introspective while he wove tales of ancient adventures on the sea and the lore of their gods. I learned the Faqur believe in higher powers responsible for everything from growing crops to having fair winds. One would speak to whichever god was appropriate for the situation, what Hrod called "praying," in order to receive a desired outcome.

"Why don't you just do the work yourself?" I asked.

"Some things are in our hands, some aren't," Hrod said. "A man can plant his crops, but he can't make it rain."

One morning, Hrod and I watched the sun gently rise above the rippling sea, but instead of the bright yellow and pink of the previous mornings, a bloodred streak blazed across the sky.

"That's not ideal," I said. I normally didn't subscribe to superstition, but now I respected the crew's beliefs in the symbolism of the color of the sky at sunrise.

"Aye," Hrod said, unease in his tone and stance.

A measure of tense anticipation pervaded the crew as they went about their day. Many—including me—cast wary glances at the horizon. Yet the sky remained clear and blue. I was beginning to mark myself a fool. While we worked on the rigging in the late afternoon, a shadow fell across the deck. We looked up into the darkened sky, and my jaw dropped at the tumult of gray clouds that appeared as if by magic. The wind picked up, prompting shouts from the quarterdeck. The crew sprang into action tying up the sails from midship to aft. Our direction changed and we headed into the wind, blowing so hard I could barely stand. A rumble of thunder echoed over the water, signaling the onset of a torrential downpour. We were ordered to batten down the hatches, and I was soaked through within seconds. The force of the storm nearly sent me sprawling across the deck, and I grasped the main mast. I could barely hear over the roar of the sea, but I followed the crew to secure the deck and furl the main sails. I slipped on the main yard, but Hrod grabbed me before I plummeted to the deck. He heaved me back up, and I clung to the ship, shaking harder than I did my first day on board. I leaned over and helped secure the sails tightly in the increasingly tumultuous storm.

With each shift of the wind, the bow broke through waves that splashed over the sides. I consumed gallons of rain and saltwater by the time night descended with no sign of relief. Only the most essential crew members remained on deck while the rest of us were sent below. The rough waters pitched the ship back and forth like a bucking horse, making several men seasick. The overwhelming odor of wet bodies and vomit permeated the hold. I closed my eyes and breathed shallowly through cold lips. The ship tipped violently when a mighty wave struck the hull, and I grasped a beam and lost the battle with my stomach. A hand settled over my clammy fingers, and I looked up into my brother's soft blue eyes, the color of waves in a stormy sea, dark and deep and wide.

"I'm fine," I said weakly. He squeezed my hand, then released it before anyone noticed.

I don't know how I slept, but I awoke propped up against a beam with the ship still rocking in the turbulent waters. The wind howled through the ship, and the rain hitting the deck sounded like rocks falling from my hands as I scattered them along the banks of the Rhyvor. Men came through the hold spreading sand along the floor to soak up bodily fluids. I had to rush outside before I vomited again. Things weren't much better topside, but at least I could breathe the moist air and settle my stomach. A few others came out to relieve the exhausted crewmen who kept us afloat during the night. At the wheel Captain Romy himself stood beside the helmsman. The captain's blue jacket was darkly soaked, and ribbons of water fell from his hat, amazingly still on his head. The helmsman grimaced in determination and his white-knuckled hands gripped the wheel. The captain at his side gave him encouragement and the strength to endure.

On the third day of the storm, the rain relented, but the wind was stronger than ever, blowing so hard and fast the crew could barely keep *The Wayward Aymelina* steadily into it. Only the top foresails and the jib sail remained unfurled, and even those seemed in danger of breaking loose. Bosun Chester made himself useful by checking the rigging every quarter hour, and he saw to it that the dinghies were ready in case the time came to abandon ship. I shuddered at the thought, but I didn't argue when he ordered me to inspect them for damage and fill them with supplies.

Most of the crew kept themselves below deck at this point, including the first and second mate. The captain, however, refused to leave the quarterdeck. The few times I escaped the hold for a breath of air, he was always at the wheel or inspecting the sails and rigging himself. Admirable for him to risk his own life to protect the ship and her crew, but this opinion wasn't shared by everyone. In the middle of the fourth day of the storm, I came up from the hold to witness Second Mate Absalon struggling valiantly to hold himself steady while following the captain across the deck. It was raining again, small pinpricks of ice that sent shards of cold deep into my skin. The second mate was shouting, and I moved closer to hear. He begged the captain to retreat to his cabin but was ignored.

"Please, Lencius," the second mate pleaded. "*The Wayward Aymelina* cannot sail if her captain perishes." A heavy stone settled in my stomach at those words, and I looked to the captain in sudden fear for his life. His eyes were deeply set from lack of nourishment and sleep, but they were bright and determined.

"And what about them?" Captain Romy shouted back, gesturing to the remaining crew on deck. "I won't abandon them."

"Your dedication is commendable, but I repeat: you're no use to them dead."

The captain's jaw clenched, and he angrily brushed off his brother's concerns. "I've survived worse."

"Is that what you're about?" Absalon challenged. "Hoping to add to your legend? Be reasonable, Lencius, I implore you!"

But the captain wouldn't be swayed. He walked away, leaving his frustrated brother to brace himself against the railing when a gust of wind plummeted into him. I surged forward with the force of the wind behind me and grabbed his arm to steady him. He clung onto me with a thankful sigh.

"I'm obliged to you, Mr. Red," he said. "Thought that one would send me overboard."

"You should get off the deck," I shouted.

"I will. I'm more intelligent than some men." He nodded at the captain's retreating form.

I grinned and he stepped away from the railing. Just as he relinquished his hold on the ship, a wave battered against the hull, and we were thrown off balance. Then another massive wave hit us again, sending the second mate toppling over the rail. By the grace of Amyl's feathers, we'd kept hold of one another, and I smashed into the railing, taking the force of his fall. Pain shot through me with every breath, but I didn't let go of the second mate. He cried out in fear, a plaintive sound I will never forget.

"Hold on!" I screamed. I grabbed onto his other hand and strained against the pain in my weakening arms. The ship righted itself at last, but I wasn't strong enough to pull him onto the deck by myself. I shouted for help, hoping to be heard over the wind and rain. He groped for a hold in the hull, but his feet failed to find purchase on the wet wood. I saw desperation in his eyes through the water drops on his spectacles. My grip floundered, and I called on every ounce of strength to keep from letting go. My arms burned with the effort, and it was tears rather than rain stinging my eyes. Just when I thought I would either lose my grip or tumble over the side, a pair of arms wrapped around my chest.

"Hold on, lad!" Telken. I was too relieved to feel embarrassed over the intimate contact—the bindings I wore would hide any evidence of my gender.

Telken pulled me away from the railing, dragging Second Mate Absalon further up the side of the ship. Then he released me to grab ahold of the dangling man. Together, we heaved backwards to prevent the second mate from plunging to a watery grave. He collapsed onto the deck, and I fell over in exhaustion, both of us breathing hard. Telken stood doubled over with his hands on his knees to catch his breath. I smiled numbly at him, too weary to offer a verbal thanks. The captain and a few other crew members witnessed the rescue and ran over. I didn't have the strength to ask what took them so long.

"Absalon!" Captain Romy cried and reached for his brother. "What happened?"

"Wave...over...the rail," he said between panting breaths.

"Are you injured?" The desperation in the captain's voice was heartbreaking. He'd almost lost his brother and knew it.

"Not at all, thanks to Mr. Red and Mr. Crummin." He gave us a tremulous smile as the captain helped him to his feet.

"Let's get you below deck," the captain said, and he half carried his brother toward the officer's quarters without so much as a glance toward Telken and me.

"Will he be all right?" I asked.

"Had a mighty scare, but he'll recover. Thanks to you." Telken winked and gave me a firm pat on the back. I winced. I must've bruised a rib when I hit the railing.

My suspicions were confirmed when I peeked under my shirt the next morning and saw a plume of purple spreading from the middle of my chest to just under my right armpit. It hurt to breathe, but I was able to function, though I couldn't raise my right arm more than halfway up. The ship's movement had lessened significantly, and when I went on deck, I saw with relief that the sky was clear.

The crew set to work unfurling the sails and checking the rigging, but the captain and his officers were nowhere to be seen. When I pointed this out to a passing crewman, who happened to be Seaman Erec, he remarked that they were probably trying to figure out where we were.

"Did the storm sent us very far off course?" I asked.

"It's very possible, especially considering it lasted so long." He scurried off to his post.

I resumed my duties as well, but the question preoccupied me late into the afternoon. Telken, Luc, Rex, and I found a dry spot to rest and enjoy a few bites of food before going back to work, when a figure loomed over us.

"Mr. Crummin, Mr. Red…" First Mate Evrard said.

We got to our feet and saluted.

"Come with me," he added and turned on his heel.

Telken and I stared at each other for an instant before following him into the captain's quarters. The second mate beamed at us as we stood before the captain at his expansive desk.

The captain looked at Telken, then me. "Mr. Crummin, Mr. Red. Second Mate Romy wishes to express his gratitude." He looked back toward his brother.

"Indeed, I do, from the bottom of my heart. No amount of thanks seems adequate. Whatever I can give you is yours, gentlemen," the second mate gushed. "You have given me my life, and I am therefore in your debt."

"I'd settle for an extra ration of ale for the rest of the trip," Telken said.

The barest smile graced Captain Romy's lips. "Very well. It's yours. Dismissed. Ah…one moment." He raised a hand when we both turned to leave. "Just Mr. Crummin is dismissed for now." We looked at each other again, my eyes wide.

Telken nudged my shoulder. "You'll survive."

Captain Romy gestured toward a chair. I lowered myself into it as the door closed behind me.

"Mr. Red, Second Mate Romy tells me that though Mr. Crummin helped bring him back onto the deck, it was you who kept him from falling into the water until help arrived. Is this true?" He focused on his entwined fingers resting on the desk as he spoke, as if he was unwilling to meet my eyes.

"Yes, sir, I suppose." I shifted uncomfortably. "But I don't want anything—"

"Leave us," Captain Romy commanded. I braced my hands on the chair to rise, then realized he wasn't talking to me. At his words, both the first and second mate quit the room, and Captain Romy and I were left alone. My nails dug into the armrests, scratching the pristinely polished wood. He looked at me, and I was astonished to see the raw emotion on his face.

"Mr. Red," he began. "It seems that I cannot turn around without finding myself in your debt." I opened my mouth to contradict him, but a firm look made me snap it shut again. "You have given my mother back her youngest and most precious son. Whatever you want of me is yours."

I swallowed at the intensity of his declaration and the openness in his eyes as he waited. In that moment, I felt for the first time I was seeing past the façade of a captain to the man beneath. I looked down at my hands as if I were considering his offer, but in truth I couldn't bear to look at him when he was so vulnerable.

"Sir," I said quietly. "I don't require a reward, and I don't wish for you to feel indebted. Knowing that Second Mate Romy is safe is enough for me."

"But it isn't enough for me."

I met his eyes over the desk, and from the expression on his face, I saw he wasn't making me an offer out of duty. It came from his heart.

My indifferent mask crumbled, and I nearly wept. He wouldn't be satisfied unless I asked for something in return for saving his brother, but I knew in my own heart that what I wanted he couldn't give. I brushed those errant wisps of feeling away before they formed a cohesive thought and blurted out the first idea that came to me.

"I want to stay," I said. "I mean, I want a permanent place aboard *The Wayward Aymelina.*" What was I doing? I couldn't stay, even if I wanted to. My place was in Praed, not aboard a ship. I was lying to myself and to the captain even if I pretended otherwise.

"Done," he pronounced before I could take it back. "As long as I live and breathe, you will have a place on this ship. You have my word."

My heart pounded, and I couldn't stop a smile from spreading across my face any more than I could the warmth blooming throughout my body.

"Thank you, sir."

"You may go now," he said.

How I managed to leave without tripping over my feet I'll never know, but I held the memory of the look he bestowed upon me, which could almost be called affectionate, close to my heart. Though I told myself nothing regarding Captain Romy belonged anywhere near the vicinity of that organ, I allowed this one transgression in the hopes it would sustain the unfamiliar yet unshakable hunger ever growing within me.

CHAPTER 24

The storm sent us several hundred miles off course. Not only had we missed our destination, but we were further south than expected, and the captain had to decide whether to turn around or continue south to search for an island where we might find supplies. The ship incurred a relatively small amount of damage, but the captain wanted to avoid remaining in the open ocean for long. I wasn't privy to their meetings and only received information second hand, but I gathered there was a lot of arguing between the officers regarding the best direction to take. When the ship failed to alter its course, I guessed the decision to head south won. The captain didn't appear very pleased with this when I saw him on deck a day later. I kept my head down and avoided getting in his way.

Two days into our southern voyage, I found Tyrnan sitting pensively on the deck chewing on the end of his pencil, a journal open in his hands. He didn't acknowledge me when I sat next to him, and when the pencil snapped in two, I worried he was unwell. The half in his mouth dangled there briefly before hitting the deck.

"Tyr." I rested a hand on his shoulder, and he jolted back to reality.

"Sul—" He squeezed his eyes and slapped his forehead at the slip. Something was wrong. My concept of time since we left Faqur was hazy, but I estimated that it had been at least six months since Tyrnan used my real name.

"What's wrong?" I tried to mimic Father's voice and manner when he sought a straight answer.

"This isn't right." He pointed to his journal.

I looked at the incomprehensible scribbles of his notes and arched my eyebrow.

"You'll have to be more specific."

"We've gone too far." He flipped through the pages. "If we're not careful…"

I gingerly took the journal from him and tried to make sense of the disorganized mess. There were several measurements, calculations, and rudimentary drawings with his notations. I tried to piece together the few bits of information I could understand, but the reason for his distress was still out of my grasp.

"I don't understand." I handed the journal back. "What are you so worried about?"

"We've made a mistake!"

"Have you told the captain?"

"I've consulted with Second Mate Romy. He said he would speak to him."

"Then I'm sure everything is well in hand." I squeezed his shoulder reassuringly, but the anxious expression didn't leave his face. I trusted Tyrnan's knowledge, but I also had complete confidence in the officers and felt sure that they would keep us safe. I kept a sharp eye on the horizon after that, but when a day went by without incident, I lost interest and occupied myself with other things.

The weather was calmer, but a persistent fog plagued *The Wayward Aymelina*, so visibility fluctuated from diminished to outright impossible. The lookouts were extra vigilant watching for land and danger, but neither was reported. It was a pleasant change when the sun finally shone and burned off the fog. I turned my face skyward to absorb the rays. I hadn't fully recovered from the chill of being soaked through for four days, so the heat was a balm on my aching muscles and frigid bones. The warmth circulating in my veins made me feel heavy and tired, and my eyes drifted shut. I think I fell asleep for a few moments, for when a shout from the crow's nest echoed over the ship, I was jerked back to reality. Footsteps thundered over the deck as men ran toward the railing. My mind was hazy with confusion, until someone shouted:

"Ahoy! Ships off the port bow!"

I stumbled to my feet and propelled myself into the fray along the port railing. The officers determined the best course of action to deal with the newcomers floundering nearby. These ships were galleys, long and narrow, usually driven by oars though none were visible. Their sails were furled as they bobbed and drifted with the current. We saw no one aboard, no movement on the deck. An uneasy feeling crept over me, raising the hairs on my arms. Curious, I moved through the crowd of men toward the officers and overheard their conversation.

"I don't like it," the ever-suspicious First Mate Evrard said.

"They could be in trouble," Second Mate Absalon said.

"They haven't hailed us for help," Captain Romy said.

We watched and waited, the atmosphere tense as the officers debated what to do about the wayward vessels. They were very close now, and still there were no signs of life, until movement caught my eye. The boats shifted as if a string pulled them toward us. Oars emerged from the hulls, struck the water, and propelled them rapidly forward. Their main sails unfurled, revealing a black circle against two bold stripes, the bottom one sandy orange and the top sky blue. I'd seen such a pattern, but only in books: the flag of Crif! My chest tightened in fear.

"Beat to quarters! Run out the guns!" First Mate Evrard ordered.

The men scattered across the ship, and I followed to the gun deck and helped push the heavy cannons through the gun ports. Before I could blink, the cannon was swabbed clean, powder ball loaded into the barrel and rammed home. First Mate Evrard called out directions to aim. I covered my ears when he shouted, "Fire!"

My ears rang in the aftermath of the cannon blasts. Smoke filled the deck, and I fanned it away to try and see if we'd hit the enemy. One of their boats was split in two and sinking. But a second was still coming fast, and several pirates were now visible brandishing weapons and preparing to board us.

I helped aim the cannon at the remaining boat and barely let go when the first mate gave the order to shoot. The explosion was deafening, and the hearing in my left ear was never the same. The canons were loaded and fired twice more, and when the smoke cleared, a pile of detritus was revealed, drifting on the current. Cheers echoed throughout the gun deck, vibrating the deck as the crew stomped triumphantly.

A thunderous crash from the starboard side interrupted our celebration. The force sent men flying. We quickly took up arms and ran to man the starboard guns. Something inside urged me to return to the main deck, where I found myself swathed in chaos. Men shouted and dashed around aimlessly.

I grabbed the sleeve of a crewman as he ran by and asked what happened.

"They came out of nowhere! Rammed us!" He was gone before I could ask more questions.

The deck was barely passable as I dodged and scrambled toward the railing to peer over the edge. Below were three other Crif boats, their bows fashioned into battering rams. They'd plunged into the hull of *The Wayward Aymelina.* Figures crawled out of the boats and climbed up the side of the ship like ants, and the crew were slashing at them from above. I'm not ashamed to admit I nearly lost control of my bodily functions at the sight of the Burdeeds, for I was sure that's who they must be. My fingers dug into the wooden railing, pushing splinters underneath my fingernails. My eyes were drawn to the captain and first mate shouting orders and jumping into the fray, and courage surged through my veins. I gripped the hilt of the sword given to me by a king and charged into battle like a valiant knight.

It's difficult to describe with any great accuracy the melee that ensued, even from the perspective of one who experienced it firsthand. The voices were too loud, the movements too quick, and there was no time to think as disorder rained upon us like falling stars, blinding us in the brilliant light of clashing swords. Many Crif Burdeeds boarding the ship were cut down, but there were too many to fight off all, and they soon swarmed onto the deck like rats. I'd never seen anyone from Crif before, but I couldn't lose myself in curiosity and amazement at the billowing fabrics of deep orange and red draped loosely over their lanky frames. Like many of the crew, their skin was deeply tanned, but their heads were bald. I raised my sword in defense when one came after me with a curved sword, the likes of which I'd only heard about. Sparks flew when our blades connected, and I tapped into all my training to counter his strikes.

For the first time, I fought not merely to win a bet, but to protect my life. He fought hard, but his attacks were frantic, fueled by anger and with little strategy. I used his frenzy to my advantage, allowing him to believe he was beating me down. I dropped to one knee, convincing him he'd won. He swung confidently for a killing blow, carelessly leaving his midsection unprotected. I sliced across his knees, and when he pitched forward in shock, my steel plunged into his stomach. He slid the length of my blade until our faces were inches apart and I watched the life fade from his dark brown eyes. It was the first time I'd seen anyone die, let alone by my own hand. I hurriedly scrambled out from under him and wrenched my blade free. I stood over the body, breathing heavily while the battle raged around me. I looked down at my blood-drenched clothes, and my vision blurred. I would like to say that I threw down my sword and refused to take another life, but I didn't. This was my home, my people, and it was under threat. With a growl, I ran into the tumult of men and defended my ship side-by-side with my fellow crewman.

Time had no place on the deck of *The Wayward Aymelina* on that day. Neither had mercy. I did not regret the lives I took, but for the first time I understood the lengths one must go through to protect their own. The deck ran slippery with blood, and it became a struggle to maintain a footing while avoiding the fallen. I did not search the faces for friends. There would be plenty of time to mourn later. Nor did I look for the captain. If I saw his lifeless body, I would throw down my sword and surrender. I stood back-to-back with Rex, the two of us fighting valiantly despite the ache in our limbs and the sweat blinding our eyes. As one, we spun toward an enemy from opposite sides, slicing into the man's torso and cutting him nearly in two.

"I'll have to remember that move," Rex said. He took a second to catch his breath. I gave a short, breathy laugh, and was stunned at his sudden wide-eyed stare. I glanced over my shoulder but couldn't account for his reaction. I turned quickly back to see his mouth sagging open, and blood poured from his lips.

"No!" I caught him in my outstretched arms and carefully lowered him onto the deck. A red plume gushed around our bodies, and my tears fell onto his pale cheeks.

"Symon," he whispered.

"Don't talk," I said. "You're going to be all right. I'll get you out of here." I tried to lift his heavy frame, but he clutched at my arm and squeezed.

"My…wife," he rasped haltingly. "Love…her." I saw the silent plea in his eyes, and my breath hitched.

"I'll tell her."

His face slackened, and the light disappeared from his eyes. His hand dropped from my arm. I reached up and lowered his eyelids, closing his eyes forever.

A deep laugh permeated my grief. A tall man stood over me, his sword dripping with blood. Rex's blood. He continued to laugh as I gently lowered my friend onto the deck. I rose without fear, my heart hardened, and my fist clenched. Unlike the other Burdeeds, this one was clad in light blue, with a ring of gold piercing one ear. His skin was the color of fresh tilled earth, his eyes black as pitch. He stopped laughing when I stared boldly and hefted my sword. He sneered and said something in his native tongue before coming at me with impressive speed. His skill was easily ten times greater than any other I'd fought, but I called upon my years of training to retaliate. The longer we fought, the angrier he became, as if my efforts were an affront to his dignity. I slashed his arm, and the wound instantly welled with blood. He bared his teeth and growled like an animal. He threw himself at me wildly, knocking me off balance. I recovered in time to deflect a downward blow. He kicked me hard in the stomach, sending me tumbling into a mast. My head struck the hard wood and I clung tenuously to consciousness. My eyes opened and closed lazily as I struggled to regain control. In my helplessness, he brought down his sword.

Knowing I would soon die, a strange peacefulness settled over me. I felt warm all over, like when Mother would wrap me in a blanket and cuddle me. I felt a deep, abiding love, and it filled my every pore down to my soul. My lips spread in a smile, but just when I expected my life to end in searing pain and endless blackness, a sharp *clang* struck my ears. My eyes cracked open in time to see the Crif pirate's sword fly away from me, and a hand pulled backwards.

"Stay back," a voice commanded me—Captain Romy. My head was still reeling, and I clung to the back of his shirt to keep from falling over.

"Kabtan," the Crif pirate said in a low timbre. I peered around the captain and saw the pirate's face fixed upon him with a determined grimace.

"By the gods' blood," the captain said. "Zubhod wa Mara. I thought you were dead."

"Sorry to disappoint." The Crif pirate grinned, revealing sharpened teeth.

"My disappointment will be short lived."

I felt the muscles in his back brace and stiffen, ready to charge. I almost didn't let go of his shirt to avoid being pulled into the fray, but I regained my balance and clutched the mast as their weapons clashed. It was difficult to track their movements, but I could feel my strength slowly returning.

The Crif pirate flicked a gaze toward me once or twice, but Captain Romy remained focused on his enemy. The pirate suddenly stepped back and shouted in his native tongue, gesturing toward me. In an instant, I was roughly pulled to someone's chest, fingers tight in my hair and a dagger at my throat. The blade pierced my skin and a trickle of blood ran down my neck.

"Surrender!" the Crif pirate ordered. "Or he dies!"

At his words, silence fell over the deck as men on both sides froze to witness the scene.

First Mate Evrard strode forward with his own hostage.

"Do it," he said. "And I kill your son." The pirate glanced unflinchingly toward the first mate, looking as unconcerned as a sailor setting off on a sunny day.

"I care not," the pirate said. "I have more." The first mate and the captain locked eyes—they had no doubt of the man's claim.

The pirate strolled toward me with the captain close behind.

"Let him go," the captain demanded. "He's just a boy. Your quarrel is with me."

"A strange boy," he said, stroking my hair. "I shall take his scalp when he dies and bring it home to show the king."

"You want a trophy? Then take me," the captain said.

"Nooo…" I groaned. My captive tightened his hold, the dagger pressing deeper into my flesh.

"You?" The Crif pirate raised an eyebrow in curiosity.

"Yes," the captain said. "Take me, then leave the ship and her crew in peace."

"It's a very nice ship." The blackguard cast a glance up the masts and rigging, considering, then ran a hand over the rail now tarnished with drying blood. "I have a better idea. You and your men drop your swords and I'll take her to Crif with all aboard. Once we reach my homeland, the crew can leave, and you will stay. Or…" He pushed the dagger further into my skin. I winced but didn't scream. "I kill the strange boy whom you risk your own life to save."

Captain Romy's eyes met mine, and I silently pleaded with him not to give himself up for my sake.

"Lencius," First Mate Evrard rasped. But before he could say more, the captain pitched his sword to the deck, and he was set upon by pirates, putting up no resistance while they tied his arms behind his back. The blue-robed Crif pirate chuckled deeply.

"Such honor, Kabtan," the man said. He raised his sword and called to his men in their language. Their answering cheers filled me with nausea and despair. I was pushed to the deck, and I covered the wound at my throat to stem the bleeding.

"Hear me, Zubhod wa Mara." The captain's voice thundered across the ship, drawing everyone's attention. "If you go back on your word, I will kill you."

"I believe you will," Zubhod wa Mara said with a wicked smile. "Take them below deck and chain them in the hold." The order was carried out, and the remaining crew left alive were hauled off the deck. I tried to keep my eye on the captain as we were led away, but the Burdeed leader gestured for him and the other officers to be led aft and we were separated.

There was minimal struggle when we were led below deck. As the darkness swallowed us, I couldn't help thinking that our current predicament was my fault. The captain allowed himself to be captured to save me. If I had just done my due diligence and died, he wouldn't have traded himself for the safety of the crew. I would be warm, and peaceful, and wholly without fear.

CHAPTER 25

Once we were secured into tiny, cramped cells and left with a guard, we called out to one another in the darkness, taking stock of survivors among us. When I heard Tyrnan call out his name, I nearly cried in relief. All told, we'd lost about a third of the crew and one of the cartographers. The remainder of us were packed into the four cells so tightly we had to take turns laying on the floor curled into a ball.

Time passed with us oblivious of any concept of how long we'd been there. The only light came from a candle on a small table. The rotation of Crif guards gave the only way to mark the passing hours. Men wondered aloud if we should try to escape or trust that we'd be released once we reached Crif. They doubted that Zubhod wa Mara would keep his word, and we leaned toward the possibility that we'd all be killed along with the captain and officers. Once or twice I heard someone try to pick locks with no success. They stopped trying when caught and had their fingers rapped with the hilt of a sword.

Tyrnan and I were not housed in the same cell, but we could reach through the bars separating us. When it was my turn to lie down, I would curl up next to his cell and stretch my fingers inside. Eventually, a hand groped in the darkness, and Tyrnan's fingers entwined with mine.

"What's going to happen to us?" I whispered.

"If their leader is honorable, he will keep his word and let us go once we reach Crif," Tyrnan whispered back.

"And if he isn't?" A heavy silence followed my question, and Tyrnan tightly squeezed my hand.

"I'm sorry," he said. I heard the despondency in his voice, and I couldn't speak past my own melancholy. "It's my fault you're here."

"No, it's not!" I insisted in a harsh whisper. "It's my own stupid fault. I talked you into letting me come."

"I should have been stronger. I should have said no."

"You can't say 'no' to me."

He didn't laugh, but I could feel his smile, even in the dark. I lay next to him until my time was up, and the emptiness I felt letting go of my brother was almost worse than the confinement.

Food was provided sporadically, helpings of bread tossed through the bars. The guards were no fools. They never came close enough for us to grab. The hold reeked of filthy bodies and human waste, and it was becoming a horrendous chore just to breathe. I avoided the privy for as long as possible, but I could only hold my urine for so long until it became unbearable. Thankfully it was too dark to see.

Raised voices entered the hold, and we sensed a shift in the mood of the Crif pirates. Candles illuminated the men as they searched the cells, holding up the light to our faces one by one. We could finally see one another, and it was like looking into the abyss of a nightmare. The crew's faces were streaked with old sweat and dried blood, their clothing soiled, and their faces drawn. We looked like we'd been prisoners for months. Had it been that long?

"There. That's him." I couldn't see the face of the man who spoke, but his voice was familiar.

The candles shifted, there was a jangle of keys, and the door to the cell next to mine creaked open. I gasped when the guards hauled Tyrnan out.

"Stop!" I reached through the bars, desperate to grasp my brother. Tyrnan looked back, but the guards ignored me. "What are you going to do to him?" I shouted.

No answer. I slid to the floor, openly weeping. I recognized the man who handed my brother into enemy hands.

Ailbert Chester.

With my brother gone, I no longer felt I had anything to lose. I sank into despair, not responding when anyone spoke to me and not eating the meager offerings of food. If my brother was dead, I may as well die, too. I failed him and my family, and I couldn't bear to face Mother and Father when they learned of it. Hunger gnawed at my stomach until it faded to a dull ache. My mind grew fuzzy and confused.

"Sulwen."

My eyes flew open at the sound of my father's stern voice. I spun around in amazement at my surroundings. I was no longer in the dark hold of *The Wayward Aymelina*. I was on top of the mountain, high on the cliff overlooking the valley, the air pure and crisp. I wore a clean gown, and my hair billowed long and untamed in the breeze. My father stood before me in his black tunic, his mouth a grim line.

"Father!" I ran into his arms and melted into his embrace, tears flowing freely. "I'm so sorry I failed you."

"Have you?" he asked in a flat voice.

"Yes," I breathed. "Tyrnan is dead because of me."

"The only death that will be your fault will be your own if you continue in this way."

"What?"

He cradled my face in his hands. "Who are you?"

"Sulwen," I said quietly. "And sometimes Symon."

"Who are you?" he demanded, louder this time.

"I am *Sulwen*." I spoke with more conviction.

"Who. Are. YOU?" Father shouted.

"*Sulwen Elejick!*" I screamed and stood up straighter. "Princess of Praed! I am the daughter of Risteard and Laria, King and Queen of Praed and Ilano!"

"Daughter," he said softly, a smile spreading across his face.

My eyes flew open. I gave voice to a pitiful moan. Once more I was cloaked in darkness in a dismal cell in the middle of the ocean. I pressed my hand to my mouth and listened to the even breathing and snores of my companions as they slept. Everyone was at the point of utter exhaustion, and most slept for the majority of the time. Whether this was purely due to being tired or if they were simply looking for an escape from our situation, I couldn't say. However, I was certain about one thing: I could either lay there and die or stand up and fight. But with what? I had no weapons. Even the blade given to me by Mukahanu was confiscated. I had to find a way out of this cell using whatever I had at my disposal.

I whispered into the darkness. "Erec." He shared my cell, so I felt around softly calling his name.

Grumbles of protest greeted my efforts, but finally Seaman Erec grasped my arm. "What is it?"

"I need you to do something." I pulled him to the front of the cell and waited for the other men to fall back to sleep. "Can you speak the Crif language?"

"Yes," he said. "Why?"

"Tell that guard to come here."

"Why?"

"Do it," I hissed.

He sighed and called out something in Crif. The guard ignored him. I told him to tell the guard I had a proposition for him. The guard told us to be quiet. "Tell him I have something he wants," I said.

Erec did as I asked, and the guard finally strode over, though his demeanor told me it was more out of annoyance than curiosity.

"He says there's nothing a skinny boy has that he would want," Erec reported after the guard spoke again.

"Tell him I'm no boy," I said levelly. I sensed Erec's confusion, but he repeated what I said. The guard held his candle to my face and squinted.

"He wants to know what you are then," Erec said quietly.

I took a deep breath.

"A woman."

I resisted the urge to look at the reaction on Erec's face, even when I demanded he repeat what I said. The guard's eyebrows shot up in surprise. He chuckled.

"He doesn't believe you," Erec said.

"He can see for himself if he lets me out," I said. "That's the exchange: my body for my freedom. How long since he's touched a woman's flesh?"

The guard's face flushed when the words were translated, and a lascivious leer replaced his suspicion.

"He says if you're lying, he'll kill you," Erec said. I heard the worry in his voice and assured him all would be well as the guard opened the cell and dragged me out.

The door slammed shut behind me, and he ran the candle over my face to inspect me closely before drawing it down my body. While he was distracted, my eyes roamed over him in search of a weapon. Sheathed at his side was a short sword. I hid a smile. The guard placed a hand against my chest and felt for breasts, but he couldn't quite feel them under the layers of binding I'd meticulously placed to disguise them. His hand roved downwards, and my jaw clenched in embarrassment. He reached the juncture between my legs and grinned in triumph. Before he could blink, my hand darted to the hilt of his short sword. I unsheathed it and drove the blade into his throat. I clamped a hand over his mouth as he slumped to the floor, then pulled the blade free once I was satisfied he was dead. I retrieved the still lit candle where it had rolled away and removed the keys from his belt. I turned toward the cell and met Erec's stunned gaze. I could read the confusion, disbelief, and questions in his eyes.

"Not now." I unlocked the cell and flung the door wide.

He stood there a moment without moving, and my heart sank. I saw in his face he didn't know if he could trust me.

"Come on," I urged. "If we're careful, we can take back the ship before anyone knows we're free."

Hesitantly, he stepped out of the cell and searched the guard for more weapons. He found a dagger hidden in his boot and stood to face me with renewed determination. I smiled at him, but before he could turn to wake anyone, I grabbed his arm.

"If you tell anyone," I said quietly. "I will kill you."

"No need for that." He shrugged me off. "You get us out of here, and I'll lie to whomever you want."

We unlocked the rest of the cells, woke the crew, then searched for anything that could be used as a weapon. The hold was full of supplies and food, but unless we wanted to pummel them with hardtack, we were out of luck. The sound of footsteps halted our efforts, and we hid in the shadows as a Crif pirate came through to relieve his companion. We overpowered him before he could call for help and took his weapons, but it still wasn't enough.

"Well, we could sit here and pick 'em off one by one?" Telken suggested. As impractical as it sounded, it gave me an idea.

"I think we should split up," I said. "You men head toward the forecastle and see if you can pick up some weapons on your way. Most of the pirates are bound to be settled in the captain's quarters, so you shouldn't have any trouble picking off a few here and there. Head on to the deck and loot any bodies that remain." I pointed to the group clustered to my right. "You men scrounge the hold. Grab cannonballs if you must."

"I'll drop 'em on their boats," one of the crewmen said.

"That's a brilliant idea. Sink their only way of escape. They will not be getting off this ship alive." The men murmured their eagerness at this plan. "By now they're probably congratulating themselves on their victory and are deep in their cups. We have the advantage of surprise."

They dispersed to carry out the plan, and I laid a hand on Seaman Erec's arm.

"Come with me," I said. "We're going after the officers and Tyrnan."

"How do you know he's alive?" Erec asked as he followed me.

"I don't. But I have hope."

We slipped cautiously onto the deck and scanned the area for signs of the enemy. A few bodies remained in tucked away places, but for the most part, the dead had been disposed of. I listened for voices, but the ship was quiet. This was very unusual for such a large vessel, for it required constant attention. My eyes traveled up the masts. The sails needed attention. The pirates clearly didn't know how to properly sail this ship. Approaching footsteps forced me to drop back into the hold. Erec and I held our breaths as they came closer. It sounded like two people. They moved away just above us, then stopped.

"They're upset," Erec whispered. "Seems their leader has been indulging in our wine stores while they're stuck sailing the ship by themselves."

"Perfect," I said. Slowly, I peered out and saw Burdeeds talking a short distance away. If I wasn't careful, they could easily spot me in the fading light of dusk and warn the others. I took the risk and eased onto the deck, slithering on my belly like a snake. Inch by terrifying inch I moved closer until I could read the expressions on their faces. They were so engrossed in complaining they didn't notice. Before I lost my nerve, I stood abruptly and slit the throat of the closest man. The other fumbled at his sword and cried out in confusion, but Erec covered his mouth and drove his dagger into the man's side. He bled out quickly, and we scavenged the bodies for more weapons. I dropped the sword on the deck for the crew and pocketed the dagger, then made my way to the captain's cabin. The door was unguarded. How arrogant of them to believe they didn't need one. Raucous voices came from inside, and I could almost smell the wine. I reached to open the door, but Erec grabbed my wrist to stop me.

"What are you doing?" he whispered harshly.

I thought it was obvious. "Going to help the officers, of course."

"By yourself?"

"You're here, too."

"You don't know how many are in there. Let's wait for the rest of the crew." I glanced at the door uneasily. What if Tyrnan was injured? I blocked out any thoughts of the captain before I lost control, shaking my head to clear my mind.

"You wait," I said. "I'll sneak in and see if I can take out the leader."

"Are you crazy?" His voice was taut, desperate to stop me.

"Crazy? No. I'm *furious*."

I eased the door open a tiny crack and instantly the noises of celebration were louder and more disjointed. I spied at least ten men inside, some still drinking heavily and singing while others lay passed out on the floor. The usually orderly room was in disarray. Books scattered over the floor, the table that held the massive map was covered with stains and empty goblets, and the beautiful desk was occupied by the leader himself, his heavy boots propped on the once pristine surface. No sign of Tyrnan or the officers but propped in the corner looking very perturbed was Bosun Chester. Men shoved him and tried to put wine into his hands, but he unceremoniously brushed them off.

"Come now, young lord," Zubhod wa Mara cajoled in his thickly accented baritone. "Why not enjoy the fruits of your labor?"

The bosun didn't answer, which amused the Crif pirate immensely.

I eased the door shut and wondered if waiting might be the best course. Soon, none of them would be standing. But I'm never very patient. I saw no sense in trying to sneak in because there was nothing to hide behind. The best course was to go in fast, with intent, so they wouldn't have a chance to recover their senses. I wished I had my own weapons, but I would have to make do with the dagger and short sword I picked off the Crif guard. I took a deep breath and prepared to burst into the room when Erec tentatively touched my shoulder.

"What's your real name?" he asked.

"What?" I snapped. We didn't have time for this, and I tried to convey this in the hardened expression on my face.

"If I'm going to die beside you, I would like to know your real name." His gaze was steady and sympathetic.

My fierceness melted.

"Sulwen," I said. "My name is Sulwen." I smiled, and he smiled back, briefly, before nodding toward the door.

CHAPTER 26

A loud *bang* resounded in the room when we kicked open the captain's cabin door. The Crif froze in stunned surprise. In the space of a heartbeat, I stepped inside and threw the dagger at Zubhod wa Mara sitting behind the captain's desk. The wine slowed his reflexes, but not by much. He shifted just as the blade left my hand, so instead of hitting his heart as intended, it struck below and to the left of the target. There wasn't a second to lose in bemoaning missing the mark with the rest of the Crif fumbling for their swords. I drove into the pirate on my immediate right while Erec went to the left, and we killed both without much effort. We relieved the passed-out men of their swords and fought what our hearts knew could be a doomed battle. The Crif were intoxicated, but we were malnourished, making us well matched.

A searing pain pierced my side, but I ignored it and concentrated on fighting the man in front of me. The familiar coolness of a blade touched my throat, but instead of yielding, I drove a newly confiscated dagger into his arm. He dropped the blade and screamed. I whirled around as he fell to his knees and stabbed him through the eye with my sword. The wet squishing noise upset my stomach, but I was too busy defending myself to care. The other man attacked my back, but just before his blade sliced across my spine, a dagger lodged in his temple. His body slumped heavily on top of me, and it was only then my mind registered the shouts of the crew as they joined in the fight.

I kicked off the Crif's body and retrieved my sword. Together with the crew, we killed every one of those pirates. When it was over, we searched the bodies and found several stolen possessions, but I wasn't looking for trinkets or weapons. All around me were bloodied clothes of orange and red, but not one among them wore blue.

"Zubhod wa Mara's gone." I breathed hard and willed the frantic beating of my heart to slow.

"The captain and first and second mate aren't here either," Telken said.

"Or Tyrnan," I added.

"Let's ask *him* where they are," one of the crew said as he hauled Bosun Chester out from where he'd been hiding under the desk.

I placed a dagger against his throat and leaned in. "Where are they?" He didn't answer right away, so I pressed the blade further against his skin, and he flinched. I read fear in his eyes. He knew I would kill him.

"Officer's quarters," Bosun Chester said.

"Of course."

Without a second glance, I took off to head deeper into the ship, not caring if anyone followed. I didn't bother with stealth. When I reached the sleeping area of the captain and his officers, I threw open the door.

The first and second mate were tied to chairs but appeared relatively unharmed. The captain hadn't fared as well. He was also tied to a chair and still clad in his uniform. Water dripping a steady rhythm from his coattails. I'd read about water torture in one of Tyrnan's books, and I shuddered to think that the man I respected and revered had to endure such an atrocity. Blood ran down the side of his face, and he drifted in and out of consciousness. My attention was diverted by a muffled cry. Tyrnan lay on the floor, bound and gagged, focused on me in wide-eyed desperation.

"Drop your weapon," a voice commanded.

I looked back at the captain. Zubhod wa Mara stood over him. He wrenched the captain's head back by his hair, exposing his throat, the curved blade of his sword hovering just above his skin. Captain Romy stared at me in confusion. There were two other pirates in the room, their swords threatening the first and second mates.

My voice was firm and resolute. "No," I said. "Even a blind man could see you hate Captain Romy. I don't care why, but I'm not an idiot. You'll kill him whether I surrender or not."

Zubhod wa Mara chuckled that deep laugh I'd come to despise. A sheen of sweat covered his brow. I looked closer. His sword hand shook. Was he afraid? I doubted it. A man willing to sacrifice his own son fears nothing. My gaze shifted toward the floor. A pool of blood was forming around his feet. A satisfied smile graced my features. I hadn't killed him instantly, but he was slowly bleeding to death from the dagger I threw.

"You are a brave boy," Zubhod wa Mara said. "I would have you on my crew."

If I kept him talking, he'd eventually pass out. "Your crew? Me? I think not. I'd always be on my guard for fear of my scalp."

"It is…strange." He squinted. He was having a difficult time focusing. It wouldn't be long now.

Calmly, I stepped forward, my sword lowered. The Crif pirate let go of the captain and gripped the back of the chair for balance.

"Are you feeling cold yet?" I asked, as a mother might a child playing in the snow.

Zubhod wa Mara pressed his blade to the captain's throat, but he lacked the strength to do any real damage. The other men were speaking now, and though I couldn't understand their words, I sensed their confusion. I heard the crew of *The Wayward Aymelina* at the threshold but kept eyes on Zubhod wa Mara. He was not to be trusted. He'd killed my friend, Rex, he threatened the life of a beloved brother, and he used me to capture Captain Romy and our whole crew. I pushed all my disdain and hatred for him into my eyes.

His lips curled into a snarl and moved to strike me with his sword. I brought my hand up and grasped his wrist, holding it with a strength I never knew I possessed. Though he was losing blood, he was still determined, and the sword inched closer and closer. Casually, as if I'd grown bored of playing a game, I plunged my dagger into the soft flesh of his belly. The fabric of his clothes ripped open as the blade sliced downwards. Portions of his innards spilled onto the floor. The sword dropped from his hand, and he crumbled to his knees. I knelt before him, my limbs feeling as cold and numb as his no doubt were. The crew took care of the other two pirates before they could flee, but I was barely aware of their fate—the sounds muffled and distorted, as if underwater.

"Strange boy…" Zubhod wa Mara said in a strangled voice, blood spraying from his lips. He grasped my shoulder, and finally, slowly, he slumped forward. I gasped when a blade pierced my left side. The bastard had concealed a knife up his sleeve. I quickly grabbed his hand before it became fatal. He breathed his last, and I shoved him aside.

The blade had only gone an inch or so into my flesh, but my shirt was drenched in blood. I lifted the hem. Just above the small wound from Zubhod wa Mara's knife was a deeper gash. I'd been wounded earlier and hadn't noticed. Blood oozed down my side, and I pressed a hand against the slash to stem the flow. By now, the first and second mate were released and untying the captain and Tyrnan.

"Mr. Red!" Captain Romy said in a distressed tone I'd never heard him use. I looked up into his hovering face and realized I'd collapsed and was in his arms. I smiled despite the direness of the situation and allowed my eyes to drift shut. I heard my brother's voice ordering people out of his way, and I opened my eyes again to gaze up into his face.

"Symon," Tyrnan said, his voice tinged with desperation. There were tears in his eyes, and his face was pale and gaunt. He wrenched me away from the captain, regardless of how this might look to the crew.

"Tyr," I whispered, smiling.

"You idiot."

A tear fell onto my cheek. "Don't let me fall asleep."

"I won't."

"Tell them to keep me awake when they fix me."

"I will."

"Don't leave me."

"I will never leave you."

I didn't care if this exchange was confusing to the crew. I was determined to live, but if they put me out to suture my wounds, I would be finished.

I managed to stay conscious by the sheer will of myself, Tyrnan, and, amazingly, Seaman Erec. We were bound together by the dangerous secret I kept, and he bravely stepped in to protect me. The surgeon was insistent that I be drugged, but I flatly refused, and Tyrnan told the poor man that I would bleed to death rather than be rendered unconscious. So instead, I was filled with wine and examined semi-intoxicated. The blade hadn't perforated my intestines, but he had to tie off a few damaged blood vessels and cauterize the wound. To stave off infection, the surgeon prescribed a concoction of garlic, wine, onion, and bile. Gross. I would recover after several weeks of strict rest.

I nearly passed out from the procedure despite the copious quantities of alcohol I consumed, but with a monumental effort, Tyrnan and Erec kept me awake throughout, ensuring I wasn't stripped and my shirt was only raised high enough for the surgeon to work. The surgeon thought this strange, but Tyrnan mumbled something about me being shy, and he shrugged off the oddness of the situation and finished his work. Once my surgery was deemed a success, I was placed in a hammock and finally allowed to sleep.

Tyrnan informed me later that the crew did a wonderful job taking back the ship. They had indeed dropped cannonballs onto the boats drifting along beside us, and the impact was enough to punch through their hulls and send them and the pirates on board sinking into the cold water. They overpowered whomever they encountered on their way to the captain's cabin. The ship was purged of Crif bodies, and our men were given proper burials at sea. The deck was scrubbed clean of blood. The ship was in sore need of repairs but was able to set sail.

"And the captain?" I asked. "Was he badly injured?"

"No," Tyrnan said. "They needed him alive. They tortured him, but Captain Romy is not a man to be easily broken."

"No, I would think not," I said.

Tyrnan shifted uneasily. "Bosun Chester is being held below deck. He'll be tried for treason."

"What was he thinking?"

Tyrnan explained that Ailbert Chester made a deal with Zubhod wa Mara. Like the rest of us, he believed that the pirate would not let us go once we reached Crif, so he made a deal in exchange for his life. Ailbert Chester handed over a Prince of Praed, a valuable hostage that would mean a great deal of ransom money, and in return he was to be given a boat and allowed to leave. It didn't quite go as he planned, as evidenced by the fact that we caught him enjoying the pirates' merriment.

"I knew he was trouble the moment I laid eyes on him," I said bitterly. "His poor mother will be heartbroken."

"Yes."

I squeezed his hand reassuringly and reminded him it was over, that we were free now. His eyes were glassy, and I noticed that his skin still retained an unnatural pallor.

"Are you all right?" I tried to sit up straighter.

"I'm fine." He placed a restraining hand on my shoulder. "Just tired, that's all. I'll be happy to step onto dry land."

"Will it be soon?"

"Within a week. It's our last stop before heading back to Faqur."

Back to Faqur. This filled me with a mixture of relief and dread. I longed to see Mother and Father, but I didn't look forward to the punishment awaiting me.

I awoke again. Not to eyes the color of a stormy sea, but to a pair of blue gray hue, reflecting the coolness of polished silver. I struggled to sit upright, but the captain pressed his hands to my shoulders and pushed me back onto the bed.

"There's no need for that," Captain Romy said. "Rest yourself."

"Sir?" I hadn't seen him since the recovery of the ship, a fact which left me somewhat resentful. But now, here he was, in characteristic tidiness, his uniform clean and pressed. He still retained his beard, but it was neatly trimmed. The only evidence of injury was a healing wound above his brow.

"Mr. Red, how are you feeling?"

"Fine," I said sharply, "but you didn't come here to inquire after my health."

He blinked, startled at my presumption. The stuffiness in his shoulders eased visibly. "Correction," he said. "I didn't *just* come here to inquire after your health. It was my chief concern, but not the only one."

"Go on." I was somewhat mollified by his outward concern.

He cleared his throat. "I've pieced together what happened the night you and the crew took back *The Wayward Aymelina*, but I'm a little hazy about one thing. Everyone agrees that it was *you* who let them out of the cells, but I can't explain how you yourself escaped."

"I asked Seaman Erec to speak to a guard on my behalf."

"And tell him what, exactly?"

"That I would give him money in exchange for releasing me. I told him I had some hidden on my person."

"And he believed you?"

I gave a palms-up gesture. "He must have, because he opened the door."

Captain Romy eyed me speculatively, and I could tell he didn't quite believe me. He asked no more questions about my escape.

"Regardless," he said. "You have saved the life of this ship and her crew. I am once again in your debt."

"We're even," I said. "You saved my life in exchange for your own."

"Fair enough."

I couldn't help but glow at how pleased he was with my actions. His smile faltered, however, and he asked in a graver tone, "Had you ever killed anyone before this voyage?"

"No."

"I'm sorry you were forced into the position where you had to take lives to survive, but I promise you will not be judged for it. And I promise any guilt you carry will fade."

I nodded. In truth, I felt very little guilt in what I had done, especially in killing Zubhod wa Mara, but I feared others' remarks. Captain Romy patted me on the arm and rose to leave.

I had questions of my own. "Who was he?"

Captain Romy paused and lowered himself back into the chair beside me. I stared, waiting, knowing he required no further explanation. He knew exactly whom I was referring to.

"When I was a young man and newly-made first mate," he began, "our ship was charged with patrolling the coastline in search of enemy vessels. Historically, the Crif were poor navigators, and their ships unsuited for long travel on the open ocean. My captain was a very competent man, but he was also very arrogant. He didn't believe a group of savages could best a ship of the Faqur Fleet. I worried our forays into Crif territory would incite an attack, but the captain welcomed one openly. He was daring the Crif to start a war so he could wipe them off the face of the earth." His eyes flashed with angry memories. "He got his wish. We were attacked in the middle of the day by five boats, very much like the assault on *The Wayward Aymelina.* However, this attack was not as well organized. We were able to fight most of them off when they tried to board us, but more were waiting right behind them. Our captain was slain by Zubhod wa Mara, a lord of one of the Crif tribes. He was notorious for preying on ships up and down the coast and was regarded as a fearsome and relentless warrior. When I saw the captain dead at the enemy's feet, I realized that now *I* was the captain. The moment that registered, I raised my sword to the sky to rally the men. I'd seen what happens when morale is low. Losing a captain is a great blow to a crew. Zubhod wa Mara came after me, and our fight extended the length of the ship. Evrard was a seaman on the same ship and an accomplished swordsman. He traded blows with Zubhod wa Mara's eldest son.

"A storm that'd been brewing picked up. I'd just pinned Zubhod wa Mara against the mast, and lightning struck. He went flying across the deck, struck the railing, and toppled overboard. His men abandoned the fight, but the sea was raging. They made it to their boats but were claimed by the waves."

"Because of the sea god you summoned?"

He smiled. "Exactly."

"What happened after that?"

"In short, we made it back to Faqur under my direction and the incident was deemed an act of war. It had been years since we'd fought Crif under such a declaration."

"I wasn't two years old during the Great War," I said.

"I was a young boy myself. The Admiral of the Fleet took no chances. Our ships were grouped into one fleet, and within a matter of a few years, we'd sent the remainder of the Crif boats to the bottom of the sea. Or so we thought."

"And you?"

"I was made captain of *The Wayward Aymelina* before I reached my twenty-fifth year."

"So the history books say."

"I don't think I'm old enough to be in history books."

"On the contrary, you're legendary."

He rose to leave, I suspect to hide his suppressed smile, and bid me well. I settled into the covers and allowed myself the indulgence of picturing his eyes looking down at me with such evident kindness. It wouldn't be long until we reached Faqur and I returned to Praed, never to see him again.

The moments I struggled so hard to pass off as the result of Tyrnan's meddling could no longer be denied for what they were. I cared for Captain Romy, beyond the respect he deserved as a captain. There was no sense in pretending, though it only made the thought of our parting more painful. I liked the crew and considered many of them dear friends. I liked Absalon Romy and his infectious optimism, and I even liked Evrard Romy and considered him a cantankerous yet protective older brother. But I held Lencius Romy closer to my heart, and though I couldn't absolutely say that I was in love with him, were I to remain on board this ship, I felt certain I was in very real danger of being so.

CHAPTER 27

"Symon! Symon!"

The sound of my name echoed dimly through my sleep-hazed state. My eyelids fluttered but did not open. Someone roughly shook me, and I flailed comically amid the sounds of sniggering.

"Wake up, you lazy lout!" Telken yelled.

"What's going on?" I mumbled.

"Get yer breeches on." He tossed the clothing at me. "Once yer decent, come on deck."

I waited until he was gone before I eased out of the hammock. The pain of my wounds had diminished, but the ache remained, rendering me almost helpless. I pulled on my breeches inch by agonizing inch. By the time they were buttoned and I was donning my coat, I was gasping for breath. Steadying myself against the hull, I emerged into the sunlight after an eternity in the dark.

I squinted while my eyes adjusted to the brightness. Tyrnan rushed to my side when he saw me. The hand that grasped mine was clammy, and I was shocked to see so little color in my brother's cheeks.

I studied him with undisguised concern. "Tyrnan?"

"Come on," he urged. "We've reached land."

"Land?"

He led me to the railing, and the crew parted for me to see. I eagerly looked out over the first piece of dry ground I'd seen since we left the land of the Nakwacimek. There wasn't much to recommend the seemingly barren landscape devoid of trees or greenery of any kind. Yellow ochre stone jutted out of the earth in jagged relief against the blue sky, and wisps of bluish grass rippled like waves in the breeze. A trickle of water glimmered just beyond the shore, and birds glided among the rocks, diving into the sea or soaring over the grasslands in search of food. A scouting party rowed ahead to ensure it was safe to disembark, and I felt a pang of remorse at being left behind.

When First Mate Evrard deemed it safe for us to leave the ship, the crew wasted no time in setting off. Tyrnan and Seaman Erec remained to help me into a dinghy. My first steps on dry land were like ecstasy, and I thanked Artur for my life. Sun warmed the stone, and I spotted large lizards absorbing the heat through their green and yellow scales. The crew became occupied with the business of setting up camp while the cartographers consulted as if nothing had changed, but there was no ignoring the decrease in our numbers. I wandered away to be alone and explore, tamping down a hiss of pain while climbing over rocky ledges. I found a place to watch the sun move over the valley. The island appeared quite desolate at first glance, but when I looked closer, there was so much life to be seen. This was what I loved most about this journey, and I would miss it dearly.

A shadow crossed my path. I glanced up at Captain Romy. Where once I would welcome his presence, I now wished he was indifferent. The more time we spent together, the more difficult it would be when we parted. "You forgot this." He handed me a journal.

"Thank you." I tucked the book under my leg and returned my attention to the valley, willing him to leave. Unfortunately, he took a seat beside me, and I shifted away in consternation.

"How are your wounds?"

"Fine," I snapped. I felt the intensity of his eyes, but I stared resolutely ahead.

He gave an exasperated sigh. "What is it?"

"Nothing."

"Nothing you can speak of?"

"Nothing I can speak of." Even *I* heard the sadness in my voice.

"I bid you good day then."

At the sound of his retreating footsteps, my chest tightened. I couldn't bear to be near him, and yet I couldn't stomach pretending to be hostile or even indifferent. It wasn't fair to him, no matter how much easier it would make *my* life if I were to drive him away.

I made a concerted effort to avoid Captain Romy over the next few days, ostensibly because I was busy documenting the local wildlife. If only I hadn't been so selfish. Perhaps I could have prevented the turmoil that upset my world more than a stormy sea.

Tyrnan's pallid features weren't lost on me, but I trusted his continued assurance that he was well. Even after spending days in the sun, his color did not return, and soon a dry cough accompanied him wherever he went. I watched to make sure he ate—his appetite was decidedly diminished. Wheezing signaled his approach, and after a coughing fit so fierce he almost fell over, I was finished listening to excuses.

"You're sick," I told him matter-of-factly.

"I know." He wiped his mouth with a handkerchief. "I thought if I ignored it, it would go away."

I rolled my eyes. "Typical."

I presented him to the ship's surgeon thinking it would only be a matter of rest and nourishment, but the man took one look at my brother and ordered him bedridden.

"What's wrong with him?"

"Congestion of the lungs." Straightaway, the surgeon began mixing herbs and pounding them into a paste with a mortar and pestle. He fashioned a poultice and laid it on Tyrnan's bare chest. When he produced a scalpel and bowl, I narrowed my eyes.

"What are you doing?"

"Bloodletting." He moved to slice open my brother's inner elbow.

"Barbarism!" I slapped the bowl out of his hands.

He gaped incredulously. "You fool! We must draw out the bad humors!"

"You'll kill him," I said. My Uncle Finton was a staunch opponent of bloodletting as a medical procedure. He studied the practice closely, and he concluded that it often caused more harm than good. I trusted his judgment implicitly, and I wasn't about to let some low-rate surgeon bleed my brother to death.

The surgeon shouted, "No, *you'll* kill him if you don't let me treat him properly!"

"Doctor!" the captain called out over our argument. "Report."

"The prince is very ill," the surgeon said, "and this upstart won't let me treat him." He glared at me and crossed his arms.

I turned to the captain. "Sir, please. I don't doubt that the surgeon does his best with what he has, but if he bleeds Tyrnan, he will kill him. Look how pale he is already. He can't afford to lose any more blood."

The captain studied Tyrnan for a few seconds, then looked at the surgeon.

"You and I have sailed many times together and I trust your medical judgment," the captain said. "I don't wish for us to be hasty with the prince's life. May we hold off bleeding him as a last resort?"

"Well…" The surgeon glanced at my brother and considered. "I suppose we can wait for a while. But when it comes time," he pointed a finger at me—"keep that boy out of my way."

"I'm sure Mr. Red will not interfere with your duties. Isn't that right, Mr. Red?" Captain Romy looked at me meaningfully, and I bit the inside of my lip to keep the bitter retort from escaping my mouth.

"Yes, sir." I fell heavily into a chair by Tyrnan's side.

I remained close to my brother day and night, forcing him to eat and wiping his damp forehead with a cool cloth. His cough relented, but the wheezing continued, and he fluctuated between burning hot and bitterly cold. I slept next to his bed and only took in enough nourishment to survive. A few of the crew tried to relieve my watch, but I refused to leave him. Over the next few days, his condition didn't worsen, but he wasn't getting any better. Something had to be done.

I found the captain with the first and second mate consulting the preliminary maps drawn up by the cartographers. As the situation was dire, I didn't bother with pleasantries or propriety.

"Sir, I need to speak with you. It's important." I held his gaze and didn't glance at the other two men.

"Go on," Captain Romy said.

"It's the prince. He's very ill." I had to pause a moment to swallow several times so I could speak clearly. "I think it would be prudent to leave for Faqur as soon as possible."

He nodded and looked at his brothers.

"We could have the camp packed up and be ready to depart by tomorrow morning I should think," Second Mate Absalon said.

"We can," the first mate added with a firm nod. "We cannot risk the prince's health. King Risteard would have all our heads should he die due to our neglect." There was no sign of humor in his statement for nothing truer was every spoken. I knew more than anyone that my father could be extremely intimidating and downright frightening where his family's safety was concerned. I left the three men to discuss the details and returned to my brother's side.

Camp was quickly broken down and the dinghies loaded up to return to the ship. The medical tent was taken down last, and Tyrnan was carried on a stretcher and carefully settled onto the last dinghy. I didn't leave him for a moment, and he voiced concern about how this might appear. I insisted I didn't care, but he was so worried about the prospect of people talking that he threw a tantrum and demanded I go to my own quarters. I stomped off, resolving to come back within the hour, but I fell asleep in my hammock and didn't rise until late the next day.

"Why didn't anyone wake me?" I asked Telken when I stumbled groggily onto the deck.

"Figured you needed the rest, and no one was brave enough to rouse you."

We were on the open sea traveling at a decent pace. The sensation of wind whipping across my face and tumbling my hair reminded me of riding my horse across Praed. The pain of my wounds was now only a nuisance, and I was able to enjoy a deep breath without jolts of pain. I studied the scars left behind by *nifo gomman*. I had many stories to tell when I returned home, and I couldn't wait to see Kyra's face when I told her of the wonders I'd seen. The closer we sailed to Faqur, the more I thought of my family, and a strange blend of trepidation and excitement fluttered inside me. I leaned far over the railing and breathed in the distinct smell of the sea and tasted the salt spraying up over the hull. A part of me tugged in the direction of my brother laying miserable in the infirmary, and the other wanted nothing more than to enjoy these last moments.

Duty won out over desire in the end, and I ventured below deck to resume my place at Tyrnan's side. He was sleeping peacefully, and I asked the surgeon for an update on his condition. He wasn't fond of me after my earlier defiance to Tyrnan's treatment, but he was good enough to inform me that the patient was progressing satisfactorily. I eyed my brother skeptically noting the loud, raspy breaths issuing from his lungs and sweat coating his skin.

"Thank you, doctor." I hoped to keep the peace. I washed sweat from my brother's face and upper torso. He felt warm, but not unnaturally so, and he slept restfully enough. I worried over how thin he'd become during his illness, a shadow of his former self. He would need assistance walking for some time.

"Is Mr. Red quite safe? The infection is not contagious?"

I heard the voice through a haze of sleep.

"There is no danger of the congestion spreading, sir."

My limbs felt heavy, and I couldn't bring myself to open my eyes. I listened to Tyrnan's raspy breathing and ignored my sore back. I remained bent over with my head lying next to his side. A hand touched my shoulder and gently shook me, but I squeezed my eyes tighter and didn't respond. It shook me again, and a voice whispered close to my ear.

"Mr. Red, wake up." It was Captain Romy. Feeling his warm breath caress my skin sent shivers through my body, and I jerked away to place some distance between us.

"What is it?" I mumbled in my sleep-laden voice.

"You should go to your own hammock. You'll sleep easier there."

I glanced around the room. A few lamps illuminated the space, and the ship felt very quiet. "Is it night?"

"The middle of it, actually. Go on and get some rest."

"No." I shook my head and gripped Tyrnan's blanket. "He shouldn't be alone."

"I'll sit with him until you return. After a good night's rest and a meal."

"But, sir—"

"That's an order, sailor," he said with a stern look.

I couldn't argue with a direct order, so I relented and vacated my place at Tyrnan's side. Captain Romy settled into the chair, felt my brother's forehead, then laid a cool cloth upon it. From the inside of his jacket, he removed several sheets of paper and leafed through them. I watched him from the doorway, unwilling to break away from the scene of the captain presiding over my beloved brother during his time of need.

"Go to bed, Mr. Red," Captain Romy said without looking up.

I did as I was told, satisfied that my brother was in good hands.

Tyrnan remained ill for the weeks' journey back to Faqur, but I managed to stave off a bloodletting. I knew we were close to port when we were met by one of the smaller ships patrolling the waters off the Brasdemer Sound. I'm almost certain that in addition to the news of our impending arrival, the sloop carried back with it a letter informing my parents of the prince's illness. By the time we reached Faqur, a messenger would be placing the letter in their hands, and from there, it was only a matter of days until they arrived to escort him home. I longed to see them, but I shook with fear at the same time.

"It won't be long now," I told Tyrnan. I coaxed him to eat. His appetite improved for a short time, but now he complained of stomach pains and was reluctant to take in anything solid. I spoon fed him broth with biscuits soaked in it to make a semi-edible paste, but after only a few bites, he turned away and refused any more. I stubbornly tried to force him, but he would only concede to water, which was quickly running out.

"When we get to Faqur—" A coughing fit cut off his words, and he needed to recover before continuing. "You will have to stay with the crew."

"What? No!" I said. "I'm staying with you."

"You'll have to report to the council, especially about the Crif attack."

"I don't *have* to do anything. I can send in a written report if they wish, but I'm not leaving you."

"Don't be a fool." He sighed and closed his eyes. "I'll be sent to the hospital. I'll be well taken care of until Mother and Father arrive."

I chewed at my nails, something I hadn't done since I was a child. I didn't have much confidence in the doctors of Faqur if the ship's surgeon was any indication of their practices. If I left Tyrnan alone and unguarded, there was a possibility they would take one look at him and drain him of blood. The savages. No, I was not going to take that chance. I resolved not to leave my brother's side until Mother and Father came to take us home. If the council needed my testimony so badly, they could wait. Surely they could appreciate the direness of the circumstances. Nothing truly heinous could result from my decision.

Chapter 28

The moment the gangplank touched the dock, the crew flowed off the ship in a wave of excitement, running into the arms of loved ones and inviting each other to the pub for a celebration. They would be permitted a week of freedom to reacquaint themselves with their homes and families before reporting to the Faqur council. We were all reminded when we disembarked, but I had no intention of heeding that summons.

I walked stoically beside Tyrnan's stretcher as he was carried off the ship and loaded onto a cart to be transported to the hospital. His condition remained stable, but I was becoming despondent over his lack of response to the treatment he received on board. I hoped, though I did not believe, that the doctors at the hospital would have better luck. I explained to the attendants that I was the prince's closest friend. Begrudgingly, they allowed me to accompany him.

I looked back to the ship that had become as dear to me as home. The three brothers stood near the bow directing the dock workers as they unloaded supplies. This would be my last time seeing them. I had no patience for tears, but I whispered a goodbye on the wind and hoped it would be carried to their ears.

The hospital was much cleaner than I expected, and the smell of medicine was stronger than the odor of sickness. The building was large with two wings to separate the men from the women. Within each wing was an area to isolate those who were contagious and those who were not. Specialized attendants served each one. The floors were made of stone, but beds were placed on raised wooden platforms. There was an abundance of natural light from the rows of windows, and wood stoves were placed strategically to warm each ward. There were several cabinets containing instruments and medicines, and doctors and nurses moved about the space with quick efficiency. Tyrnan was installed in a private room specifically for personages of great importance (a fact which I will never tell him) and given prompt care. I introduced myself to all the staff, explaining that we were childhood friends and that I served Their Majesties the King and Queen of Praed. They gave me every courtesy after that, and I was allowed to remain by his side.

The doctor who examined Tyrnan declared that though the ship's surgeon did well in keeping the prince alive, he was not satisfied with the patient's progress in fighting the infection. A treatment plan was ordered that included hot baths in lavender and mint leaves, herbs to reduce the fever, a foul-smelling root that supposedly would break up the congestion, and juice made from a combination of fruits and vegetables. After many days of this regimen, Tyrnan's condition improved markedly, and I felt comfortable enough to leave his side for an hour at a time to sleep and eat. I'd neglected my own health to care for my brother, and it was showing in the circles under my eyes and protruding ribs. An obliging nurse removing my sutures eyed my thin frame. Extra helpings were given to me at mealtimes thereafter.

I received a notice to attend the upcoming council and give my account of the events that transpired during the long voyage. A council of this nature would last for days, but I simply didn't have the time. Tyrnan asked about it once, but I gave him a withering look and informed him everything was in hand. He didn't bother to ask again after that.

The opening day of the Faqur Assembly came and went without me, and I didn't worry that my absence was missed. Tyrnan was managing his treatments well and was finally eating solid foods. However, his cough had gone from a dry hack to a wet mess that produced all manner of disgusting fluids. The doctor assured me this was a good sign, but I was wary of leaving Tyrnan's side should he suddenly take a turn for the worse.

The next morning, heavy footfalls echoed through the hospital. A raised voice demanded an explanation for why patients were being so disturbed. I couldn't hear the response, but I closed the book I'd been reading aloud to Tyrnan. The door flung open, and First Mate Evrard strode in. A smile tugged at the corner of my mouth. I was happy to see him, but the look he gave me cast away any pleasant feelings I might have with regard to our reunion.

"What is the meaning of this?" the first mate demanded.

The hospital attendant bowed to Tyrnan. "I'm sorry, Your Highness. He…erm, I mean, the *officer* insisted he be admitted."

"It's all right," Tyrnan croaked and waved a dismissive hand.

The attendant bowed and left the room, leaving the door slightly ajar.

"Sir." I saluted. "To what do we owe the pleasure of this visit?"

"Don't play games with me, boy!" His hands clenched into fists at his side. "Where were you yesterday? And this morning?"

"Here," I said. "Obviously."

"You were given a summons by the Faqur Assembly to issue a report. Why did you ignore it?"

I rose to my feet with a royal grace. "Because my place is here."

"You have been commissioned as a guard and are a sailor of Faqur. Your place is with the crew of *The Wayward Aymelina*. The prince is in capable hands and no longer requires you to sit at his bedside and read every minute of the day." He was angrier than I'd ever seen him, and yet I did not waiver. I stared steadily back. His nostrils flared and his eyes flashed.

"I am staying. Right. Here."

His face reddened, and I held a hand up to silence Tyrnan's protest. "Understand this, sir. I will not come with you. I am perfectly willing to issue a statement, whether in writing or when His Highness is recovered enough that I deem it safe to leave him for the day. But that day is not today."

"And you should understand," he said darkly. "That the punishment for insubordination is flogging. If you do not come with me, even the captain will not be lenient."

I flinched at his words, but I had had enough.

"I will not be bullied."

"Don't. Please," Tyrnan said behind me.

"I am giving you an order!" The first mate was almost screaming.

"I am a Princess of Praed, and I do not take orders from you!"

He stepped back in alarm, blinking dumbly at my bold declaration.

"You idiot," Tyrnan breathed. He sat up in bed looking between us in fear and desolation. The first mate's eyes went from mine to my brother, his lips set in a firm line.

"Is this true?" he asked Tyrnan, his voice strangely weak.

My brother's face was answer enough.

The first mate turned back to me, his eyes taking in my raised chin, the way I held my shoulders back, and straight posture. I stood before him as a royal and he knew it. Without another word, he threw open the door and quit the room. I listened as his footsteps receded into the hospital. I calmly closed the door.

"That could have gone better," Tyrnan muttered. He fell back against the pillows.

I shrugged. "It could have been worse."

"It *will* get worse, Sulwen."

I smiled, enjoying the sound of my name once again.

"They'll come for you."

"Let them come. Let them try to take me from you."

They came for me sooner than expected. The following day, armed guards entered the hospital and demanded I come with them. I refused. They tried to take me by force, but I resisted. I only went by my own volition because of Tyrnan.

"It will look better if you comport yourself in a manner befitting a princess," he said.

I sneered, but I knew he was right. I shrugged off the guards and raised myself to my full height, meeting their glares with a regal indifference that mimicked Grandmother's. I glided out of the room and through the hospital, looking every bit the perfect princess amid armed ruffians. Everyone stopped to stare as we passed, and whispers followed in our wake.

I was shoved into a barred carriage and trundled down the busy streets toward the Faqur prison located next to the Assembly Hall. I propped my forehead against the bars and bit back tears. People glanced toward the passing carriage, and while some tried getting a closer look, most couldn't be bothered with a criminal. Little did they know this particular criminal was royalty. Had they known, I'm certain the streets would be clogged with gawkers.

I turned away from the window, ashamed. I'd been imprisoned on the ship, but this felt wholly unjustified. What's more, my parents, the crew, the officers…the captain…they'd all find out what I'd done. How could I look them in the eye again after breaking their trust?

The carriage jolted to a halt, and the door was flung open. A guard gestured for me to come out, but I didn't move fast enough. He grabbed my arm and yanked me down from the carriage. I stumbled, a sharp retort at my lips, but the feel of cool iron encircling my wrists shocked me into silence.

"Get on with ya." The guard shoved me toward the prison. Another guard waited, holding open the door as if I were a welcomed guest.

I held my shackles up to the guard's face. "Is this really necessary?"

"Want to be treated like a man? You'll be bound like one. Git!" He pushed me through the doorway.

I tripped over the threshold and landed sprawled out on the floor. Sharp pain shot up my knees, and I hissed as my palms scraped against the rough stone.

"Careful, will ya?" the other guard said. He mumbled something about incurring the wrath of King Risteard, hauled me to my feet, and led me through the entryway to a large desk. An austere man wearing a long gray tunic buttoned up to his chin peered indifferently at me over half-moon glasses.

"Name?" The man lowered his eyes to a thick ledger, quill poised.

"Princess Sulwen Elejick," I said.

The man raised a bushy eyebrow, then studied me from head to foot. He shrugged, then wrote my name.

"I'm Thamir, the warden," the man said. "We've been expecting you."

"Ah, then I assume you've drawn a bath and ordered my favorite pastries?"

"If I were you, I'd take this seriously, young lady." He stepped from behind the desk, and from a thick belt jingled dozens of keys.

I ground my molars but kept silent as he unlocked a massive door to the right of his desk. It swung open on thick iron hinges, and the smell of straw, waste, and stale bread hit me like a wall. I gagged and tried covering my mouth, but my chains were tugged forward, and I followed Thamir into the prison. The guards were close behind, their breaths hot on my neck. Torchlight illuminated rows of cells, some occupied with several men. None of them paid us any attention.

We descended a set of stairs, and the air thinned and grew colder. On either side of a narrow hallway were smaller cells just large enough to fit a cot and a chamber pot. Thamir stopped outside of one and unlocked the door. The guards ushered me inside, and I'd barely made it before the door slammed shut with terrifying finality. Thamir waved me over and tapped on a slot in the bars.

"This'll be where you'll take your meals," he said. "Put your hands through."

I maneuvered my hands into the opening, and a guard unlocked the shackles.

"You'll do the same when we need to shackle you again," Thamir said.

"Is that really necessary?" I asked.

"Standard protocol. For *all* prisoners. Until you're released, you'll abide by my rules. No shouting, no attacking the guards, no trying to escape. You'll be ready to take your meals twice a day. If you're not, you don't eat. Understand?"

"You're enjoying this, aren't you? Must be thrilling ordering a princess around."

"I take no joy in this, Your Highness. Frankly, I find it a waste of my time."

He left without another word, taking the guards with him. Little light filtered into the cell, and though I was used to darkness, I'd never felt more alone.

"I was expressly told no visitors, sir. I could lose my job."

"I won't tell if you won't."

The hushed voices pulled me from a dreamless sleep. I lazily opened my eyes and watched reflections of torchlight dance across the stone wall. Footsteps came closer, and I turned over on my cot to see who was coming. The voices were silent, and they hadn't spoken long enough for me to recognize them. Certain the visitors couldn't be here for me, I sighed and buried my head in the thin blanket that did nothing to stave off the chill.

The footsteps stopped at my cell, and I recognized the warden's voice saying, "Five minutes."

One set of footsteps walked away, and I curiously peaked over the covers. A man was silhouetted in the torchlight, his features hidden in shadow. But I would know him anywhere, his scent of sea and salt air, his bearing, and the way my heart fluttered when he was near. I threw off the covers and rushed toward him.

"Sir!" I cried, my voice hoarse. I gripped the cold bars and willed myself not to cry.

He stepped closer, the torchlight throwing half his face into startling clarity. He was clean shaven, blank-faced, and impeccably dressed as always. But there was a wariness to his gaze that broke my heart.

"Please forgive me," I said. "I know I don't deserve it, but please—" I choked back a sob and drew in a steadying breath. "I never meant for it to go this far. I just wanted…" I groaned and pressed my forehead against the bars. It wasn't enough. I could never explain my actions well enough to make amends.

"I regret deceiving you, but I don't regret the voyage." My tone was calm, resigned. I smiled in the darkness, unable to meet his eyes. "I got to taste freedom. I'll be grateful forever for that. Thank you."

His hand covered mine so briefly I could've imagined it. Then he was gone. I sank to the floor in a boneless heap, too miserable to cry.

Because I was a princess, they couldn't very well leave me in prison. Within two days, I was housed in the best room of an inn to await the arrival of my parents and subsequent trial. A contingent of guards was installed at the inn "for my protection," and only a few staff members were allowed to attend me. I had nothing to wear aside from my uniform and boy's clothes, so a seamstress was brought in to make me more presentable.

An official of the Faqur Assembly visited to inform me of the charges: disregarding social conduct—by which they meant wearing men's clothes——and fraud. Both crimes were considered very serious under Faqur law, and the chief prosecutor of the continent was brought in especially to preside over my trial. There was some talk as to whether I would face a jury, but the official assured me the trial would most likely be a private affair in order to avoid any embarrassment. I kindly asked him to leave after that.

When I was finally left alone, I sat in my modest bedroom staring at a sputtering candle contemplating the sharp direction my life had taken. I did not pretend that it wasn't my fault, but I also believed it was unfair. All this turmoil could have been avoided if women were permitted to serve, if society didn't dictate that our only role in life was to be wives and mothers. I came here because I wasn't content to be married off. My thoughts turned to the crew, who had been my friends. What did they think of me? What did Captain Romy think of me?

I couldn't hold back the flood of tears I'd withheld since revealing my secret. I buried my face in my hands, wept long after the candle burned out, and fell asleep perched at the vanity.

I spent my days sitting at the window staring at the street in anticipation of my parents' arrival. Every night when I went to bed, I was disappointed not to have them with me. I longed for Mother's warm embrace and Father's comforting presence. They would fix this mess, and Tyrnan and I would go home. I received no letters and had no visitors during those lonely days. A part of me hoped Captain Romy would visit, but that would no longer be proper now I was once again a woman. The easy manner in which we conducted ourselves was a thing of the past, and there it would remain. I'd lied to him, no doubt angered him, and I had no right to expect him to show up with an offer of continued friendship. I'm ashamed at how much I cried at this realization, and I fell asleep with an ache in my heart and a puffy red face.

A voice gently called my name, and cool fingers caressed my warm cheeks. I stirred in my sleep, trying to hang on to this pleasant dream. But the voice persisted, and slowly I became aware that the voice was real and someone was stroking my hair. My ginger locks had grown some during the voyage, but I'd kept it relatively short. Fingers ran through the shorn locks, and the sensation felt so wonderful I sighed and snuggled deeper into the pillow.

"Sulwen," the voice said, more firmly this time, and I finally recognized it. I bolted upright. There, sitting on the edge of the bed smiling tenderly at me, was Mother. I threw my arms around her with a sob and clung to her.

She hugged me back just as fiercely, rubbing small circles on my back. I didn't want to let her go, but she pulled away and gazed lovingly at me. She ran a hand over my shorn hair and smiled, a mischievous gleam in her eyes.

"It suits you," she said through her laughter. I laughed, too, and it felt like a balm to my tortured soul.

"I'm so glad you're here."

"So are we."

"Have you seen Tyrnan?"

"We have. He told us where you were and what happened. Well, the short of it anyway."

"I'm so sorry." I lowered my face in shame. "You must have been so worried."

"Let's not speak of that now. Right now, we have to find a way to get you out of this mess. Your father is trying his best, but I fear we may have no choice but to proceed with the trial." My heart clenched in fear, and Mother placed a hand against my cheek as she sensed my unease. "Don't worry, my love. It will be a private trial. Your father has ensured that at least."

"I've made a terrible mistake," I sobbed.

"I hope that's not true. Otherwise, what would be the point in trying to salvage your good name?"

"You mean my reputation. No one will want to marry a soiled woman."

"That's not what I mean. It's not any marriage I'm worried about. It's your life."

I looked away, unwilling to see her dissatisfaction with me. She took my hand and urged me to look at her, and when I finally found the courage to raise my eyes, I saw neither anger nor disappointment in her face. Her green eyes were shimmering with unshed tears, and a soft smile graced her lips.

"Come on," she whispered. "Let's get you dressed. Your father is eager to see you."

Father's eyes settled on my short hair briefly before I launched myself into his arms. I buried my face in his doublet, inhaling the scent of leather, horses, and polished steel that was distinctly his. He rocked me like a child. Mother came up behind me, and I was cradled in the embrace of both my loving parents. Whatever fears I'd held about punishments were gone. There was a lot to apologize for, but I was secure in the knowledge that I hadn't lost their love and affection. Father kissed the top of my head, then unwrapped one arm so he could hold Mother. He nuzzled her hair and kissed her temple, and she looked up at him with shining eyes and a smile proclaiming her relief. I no longer felt the urge to avert my eyes, but rather felt overwhelming tenderness at their open admiration for each other. At that moment, I knew everything would turn out well.

CHAPTER 29

"This is preposterous!" I slammed my thick drinking glass on the table. My parents had been in Faqur for three days, and it seemed certain the trial would occur no matter what Father tried. "Aren't you the King of Praed and Ilano? Shouldn't they do whatever you command?"

"We're not in Praed or Ilano," Father said flatly. "We managed to secure a private hearing with the chief prosecutor, but the Faqur Assembly insists a trial be conducted in the interest of public relations."

I folded my arms and sat back in a huff.

"Face the facts, Sulwen." Father leveled a finger at me. "You will have to pay the consequences of your actions."

I sank further into my chair, knowing full well he didn't just mean the trial.

Mother ran a hand down my arm and squeezed my wrist. "I'm sure they'll be lenient."

"Because I'm a *woman?*"

"No," she said, and now the irritability was hers. "Because of all you did on board that ship. Tyrnan told us about the lives you saved."

I looked from Mother to Father. My heart swelled at the pride in his eyes.

"You can tell us about all that later," Father said. "For now, we have to get you out of Faqur."

My parents went back to their breakfast. I picked at my meal. After months of eating semi-palatable food, the rich spread was too much for my stomach.

"How is Tyrnan?" I asked. I hadn't been allowed to leave the inn, even to visit my brother.

"Very well," Mother said. "We look forward to getting him home. Your Uncle Finton is traveling down from Hrgun to take over his care."

"Will Merrin be with him?" I asked hopefully.

"Not this time, darling. She's been awarded a place in her professor's expedition to Kuste and will be busy preparing for it."

"That's wonderful!" I beamed. "I told her she was certain to be chosen."

"She'll have some adventures to share herself when you see each other again," Mother said.

"So just how angry are the both of you at me?" I had to ask.

They stared at me, Father's food poised halfway to his mouth, and I stared back without trepidation. Father was right, I was going to have to face consequences sooner or later. And I'm certainly not one to be very patient.

"We were very worried," Mother said, her voice on the verge of breaking. "We didn't know where you were. Your father organized a search party. Nettle was eventually recovered several miles away. We worried that you'd been thrown, but no sign was ever found. I eventually wrote to your aunt hoping you'd run away to stay with her. I knew you'd been upset recently, and I thought perhaps you needed some space. She wrote back and said you weren't there, but that Merrin knew where you were."

"I shouldn't have forced her into a confidence," I said. "That wasn't fair. Did she tell Aunt Ula where I was?"

"Not entirely. She kept your secret, but she assured us you were alive and well, though she hadn't heard a word from you either. We satisfied ourselves with that until we had more definitive information. You don't know what a relief it was to arrive and find out you're alive and were with Tyrnan the whole time." She reached across the table and took my hand, and I could tell it took a monumental effort for her to refrain from crying.

"I wanted to contain you to the castle for the rest of your life," Father said. "But your mother thought that was too harsh."

A small chuckle escaped my lips. "I expected you would."

Our companionable breakfast was interrupted by a messenger delivering a letter into Father's hands. Mother and I watched him read the missive in strained anticipation. Once again I found myself chewing at my fingernails. He looked up at us with a sigh and handed it to Mother.

"What does it say?" I asked.

"The chief prosecutor has arrived and set your trial for the day after tomorrow," he said.

"So soon?" I said.

"This is for the best," Mother affirmed. "We'll get this over with and be on our way home by week's end."

"You better be prepared to defend yourself, young lady," Father said.

What could I say? *Your honor, I decided to leave home, dress as a boy, and commit fraud because I didn't want to get married.* It sounded ridiculous, even though it was essentially the truth. However, I came to realize that my journey was less about running away from a potential marriage and more about my desire to discover a world beyond Praed, to live a life full of excitement and new experiences, and to be more than just a princess. I indulged in a fantasy, and it brought me everything I could have hoped for. My journals were filled with a lifetime of adventures. I did not regret a single one.

My parents procured a light blue gown fit for a princess for the occasion of my trial. I fiddled with the gold embroidery stitched along the cuffs on the way to the Assembly Hall where the chief prosecutor awaited. Mother clamped her hand on my knee to keep me from bouncing the carriage with my fidgeting, and a dark glare from Father ceased my nail-biting. Permanently.

When we arrived, I stared up at the imposing white stone building already feeling like I'd been judged and sentenced. We were ushered inside amid a swarm of onlookers, but I held my head high as they whispered. Word must have spread that a princess had masqueraded as a sailor, and everyone was eager for a glimpse of the disgraceful girl. The building itself was largely empty, no doubt by my father's royal command. He might not have the ultimate rule here, but he still knew how to use his authority to get his own way.

Our escort led us through an open foyer and into a small chamber near the great hall. The walls were lined with shelves filled with aged leather books and a large desk with a throne-like chair on one side and three smaller ones on the opposite. We were seated in the smaller chairs with me closest to the desk and my parents placed behind me. This would be an incredibly intimate trial.

"Chief Prosecutor Ekhane will be with you momentarily," our escort said before leaving the room.

My parents gaped in shock.

"Did he just say *Ekhane?* Surely he doesn't mean…" A man strode into the room, cutting off my words, and took a seat behind the desk. He had a vague familiarity, a face I couldn't quite place. He was young, with sandy brown hair and dull blue eyes that peered out placidly from behind thick-lensed spectacles.

He addressed my parents with a respectful bow. "Your Majesties." He turned to me and inclined his head. "Your Highness."

"Gerrid, what an unexpected surprise," Mother said pleasantly. "It's been a long time. How are your parents? Is your father well?"

My jaw dropped and my heart sank into my stomach. The last time I saw Gerrid Ekhane I was a toddler sinking my teeth into his calf. I was in deeper trouble than I thought if he oversaw prosecuting my case.

"They are well, thank you," he said, his voice devoid of emotion. Either he'd forgotten or was a master at disguising his feelings. He tapped a sheaf of papers against the desk to even out the edges, sorted them into two piles, then folded his hands neatly atop them.

Oh, dear Artur. I was doomed.

"Princess Sulwen," he began. "I have reviewed the evidence presented to me regarding the charges of disreputable conduct and fraud. To be perfectly honest, the main issue here is not the fact that you dressed as a boy, though it is certainly frowned upon for a lady to do so. The real crime here is the fraud perpetrated against the Fleet of Faqur and the officers of *The Wayward Aymelina.* You impersonated a sailor with forged documents and misrepresented yourself as a naturalist in order to gain passage aboard the ship. The presentation of yourself as the opposite gender not only jeopardized your safety, but placed yourself in a compromising position, namely in procuring valuable information pertaining to the movement of Faqur ships and the management thereof."

My eyebrows shot up at this last statement. It was refreshing to be charged with an actual crime as opposed to some nonsense regarding my femininity and virtue.

"These crimes," he continued, "carry the penalty of having all the money you earned under this guise revoked, a substantial fine, and imprisonment for a minimum of five years."

Mother stifled a gasp, and I could hear Father breathing heavily through his nose. I gripped the arms of my chair and maintained my composure. I had been through worse than imprisonment in a Faqur jail, but I had no wish to be away from my family or stripped of my freedom for so long.

"Do you understand these charges?" Chief Prosecutor Ekhane asked mildly.

"I do, sir," I said.

"What do you have to say in your defense?"

"I have thought for many days of what I could say to try and convince the chief prosecutor that I deserve to go home without punishment," I said coolly. "But the fact is, everything you said is perfectly true."

"Sulwen!" Mother interjected. Father placed a restraining hand on her arm.

"I did dress as a boy and obtain false documents to gain passage on *The Wayward Aymelina*. I don't know that I was necessarily privy to sensitive information, but I certainly placed myself in a position where I could have been. My intentions were honorable though admittedly selfish. Yet I conducted myself respectfully as a sailor and trusted guard. I won't sit here and tell you everything I did in service to the crew for I'm sure you're well aware. Nor will I try to use these events as reasons for why you should let me go free. I did deceive the crew, the first and second mate, and most regrettably, the captain. The king said I should accept the consequences of my actions. I am prepared to do so in recompense for my behavior toward the men who trusted me with their lives."

Chief Prosecutor Ekhane regarded me thoughtfully. During our brief acquaintance as children, we'd come to despise each other, and I feared that fate brought us together so he could have his revenge. My stomach twisted, and I swallowed to keep from vomiting. Outwardly, I was as composed as a princess should be under duress.

"I am aware of your conduct," Chief Prosecutor Ekhane said. He flipped through a few pages. "You saved the lives of the three officers on separate occasions and were instrumental in the retaking of the ship after it was commandeered by Crif pirates. However, I agree with your assessment that this does not erase nor diminish the seriousness of your crimes. It did prompt me to collect accounts from the crew as witnesses to determine the severity of your punishment."

He placed one of the stacks of paper in front of him and read aloud:

"Mr. Red, or Princess Sulwen as it were, was hard to sort out when he first came on board, but he proved his ability as a sailor through hard work and a swing that nearly put the captain into the deck."

I stifled a giggle. He looked at me over his glasses, then continued:

"His sword saved our hides and the ship from pirates. Boy or girl, I would consider Mr. Red one of my closest friends for life. Telken Crummin."

Dear Telken—he was a true friend indeed. The Chief Prosecutor read a few more along the same vein from other members of the crew, then he came to the first letter that truly moved me.

"To Whom it May Concern. I didn't think much of Mr. Red when he first came aboard. As an inexperienced sailor, he worked hard, but he spoke much too freely and seemed to always be in trouble. But upon closer acquaintance, I found him to be friendly, delightful to the crew, and very intelligent. I appreciated his dedication to his work and his abilities with a sword, but I was most moved by his staunch support for basic animal and human rights. He never looked upon a new species or peoples with fear, but with curiosity, and he was crucial in the development of a relationship with a native people we encountered on one of the islands we explored. I owe Mr. Red my life, and hold him in highest respect, but never more so than when he sacrificed his greatest secret in exchange for the safety of the crew. It was from then on that I considered Mr. Red, or rather Princess Sulwen, as one of the bravest people I know. Respectfully, Seaman Erec Voxe."

I could barely make out Chief Prosecutor Ekhane's features for the blur of unshed tears. I wasn't given a moment of recovery before he continued:

"To the chief prosecutor. I could expound on the virtues displayed by Princess Sulwen during her tenure here, but the simple fact is that she saved my life and asked for nothing in return. That fact alone marks her as a person of exceptional

integrity, and I would be proud to serve with her again. Second Mate Absalon Romy."

Dear, wonderful, Absalon!

"Chief prosecutor. I admit that my anger over the revelation that Mr. Red had joined us under false pretenses eclipsed any regard I may have had for him. Her. But I cannot deny that she was invaluable to us, and we owe the preservation of The Wayward Aymelina *to her quick thinking and tenacity. I never cared for her willfulness nor her strange humor, but taken as a whole, I may say that she impressed me. First Mate Evrard Romy."*

Typical of the man, but I appreciated his support.

When Chief Prosecutor Ekhane failed to continue, I asked, "Is that all?"

"These testimonies were persuasive, and shed light on your character in general, but taken together, I wasn't inclined to be overly lenient. Until I read this one."

He took up a sheet, and I leaned forward to hear his every word.

"There is much I could say regarding Princess Sulwen's conduct aboard The Wayward Aymelina, *but the facts could easily be discovered via witness testimony, the captain's log, and diaries of the officers. What cannot easily be expressed is the appreciation of those who owe their lives to the princess, the gratitude of their families, and the respect earned through continued displays of performance above and beyond expectations. Princess Sulwen impressed me with her astuteness, her compassion, and her fearlessness. In the whole of my career, I have never met a sailor more capable. But these facts alone do not influence the declaration I hereto make. It matters not that she is a woman. I made a promise, not to a boy or a girl or even a name. I gave my word, as long as I live and breathe, to the person who saved the life of my brother, that they would have a place on my ship. That vow stands. Should Princess Sulwen choose, she will be granted a commission in her own name on* The Wayward Aymelina *with my regards. Captain Lencius Romy."*

Try as I might, I couldn't control the tears. Father placed a reassuring hand on my shoulder, and I drew in a shuddering breath and wiped a hand across my face. The captain's words filled my heart with hope that he didn't hate me, and even if I was sentenced to a lengthy prison term, I would go willingly with such knowledge. I stared unflinchingly at the chief prosecutor's blank face and waited for his final judgment.

"Princess Sulwen, I have considered Captain Romy's perspective. I asked myself, what would my judgment be in regard to these charges were it a man before me and not a woman? And in all fairness, I admitted that the accounts of which I have read and the events reported would greatly influence my decision. But none more so than Captain Romy's assertions that despite the fact that you committed fraud against himself and his ship, he is still willing to allow you to be among his crew."

I held my breath and dug my nails into the armrests to keep from shaking.

"Therefore, I declare all your wages forfeit and sentence you to time served. You are free to go."

All the tension in my body vanished amid Mother's relieved sigh. My smile was painfully wide, and I lost the ability to form words. Mother pulled me into her arms and hugged me while Father leaned across the desk and shook Chief Prosecutor Ekhane's hand. He looked just as shocked as Mother and I were.

"Thank you, sir," I managed to say and grasped his hand. He flushed in embarrassment. No doubt he wasn't used to the people he prosecuted expressing such glowing appreciativeness. If not for the desk between us, I would have been tempted to hug him.

"You're welcome, Your Highness." He smiled with such warmth I was temporarily rendered speechless. Here was no longer the angry, spoiled boy I knew, but a kind and fair man.

"May I ask you something—that is, if you're allowed to answer?"

"You may." He eyed me cautiously.

"Are you in charge of Bosun Chester's case?"

His features darkened. "I am."

"What's going to happen to him?" My parents became very still waiting for his reply. My mother went pale, and father's eyes were as dark as the chief prosecutor's.

"He committed treason," Chief Prosecutor Ekhane said simply. "He's been imprisoned and will be tried for his crimes."

"Here?"

"And Praed."

"Will he be found guilty?"
He hesitated. "It's a distinct possibility."
"And if he is?"
"The penalty for such a crime is death, Your Highness."

CHAPTER 30

We had little time to enjoy the relief of avoiding imprisonment because Mother immediately set about planning our departure. Tyrnan was recovering from his illness, but Mother was anxious to take him home and place him under my uncle's care. I was just as eager to see my brothers and sisters again, and I had next to nothing to pack, so I was ready within a day of being set free. The tension among us over my impending trial was gone, but there was still an undertone of uneasiness hanging in the air, especially with Mother. She brushed off my inquiries in respect to her health and was evasive in general if I brought up her odd behavior. Father wasn't helpful either, and the secrecy drove me mad.

A few days before our scheduled departure, Father was absent most of the day, and when he returned late in the evening, he offered no explanation as to his whereabouts. I restrained myself from asking more questions and excused myself to bed, then snuck out of my room to listen in on my parents' conversation. No, I'm not proud of this, but I was bursting with curiosity, a trait that admittedly was my greatest flaw.

"So, that's the end of it?" I heard Mother say.

"You can't save him from this, Laria," Father said. "He's a grown man who made his own decisions."

"I feel for Noraa. Despite his parentage, he was still her son."

"No one else would have done as much for her as you have. You've succeeded in keeping your promise to her. You couldn't control or predict his nature."

"You predicted it." I heard the smile in Mother's voice and Father's answering sigh.

"Ailbert Chester was given every opportunity to overcome the circumstances of his birth to become a decent human being. It isn't your fault or Lady Chester's if he squandered it. And I take no pride in being proven correct that he would turn out just like his father."

"Liar," Mother teased with affection.

I couldn't fully comprehend this cryptic exchange, but I deduced that there was a secret in regard to Ailbert Chester, a secret spanning years. If I was the gossiping sort, I would guess that perhaps Lord Chester was not his biological father since my parents spoke of questionable parentage. Lord Chester was as average and steady as an ancient tree. Lady Chester seemed meek and sweet, so where had her son acquired such a nasty temperament?

Their conversation shifted and no longer interested me, so I retreated to bed. I expected to fall asleep the instant my head touched the pillow, but I tossed and turned fitfully. My heart pounded with excitement at the prospect of returning home, but I had a strong desire to see my Aymelina friends one last time and say a proper goodbye. I made a comment in passing regarding this desire, and though Mother was sympathetic, she wasn't sure we'd have time before our hasty departure. Out of all of them, I wished to see Captain Romy and thank him for his part in allowing me to go home. I missed him these past weeks, finding that his opinions and acceptance mattered as much to me as Father's. I lay in bed paging through my journals and remembered the look of concentration on his face when he read them. I wished he could read my final notes on the last island we'd visited. But alas, it seemed we were not to meet again, and though I bore the separation with all the grace of a princess, the pain in my heart was greater than a blade piercing my flesh.

Long after the inn grew silent and the night laid its thick blackness upon Faqur, I still hadn't slept for more than two minutes together. I finally decided there was no sense in fighting the inevitability of a sleepless night and tossed aside the bedcovers, donned my sailor's garb, and eased open the door to my room. I listened, and when nothing but silence permeated the space, I snuck from the room and tiptoed down the hall. A loose floorboard creaked, and I froze, holding my breath and hoping my father's keen hearing hadn't registered the noise. When the sound wasn't followed by his heavy footfalls, I hurried down the back stairs before I lost my nerve. I stumbled through the dark kitchens using my hands to guide me until I saw the outline of a doorway.

The streets were nearly empty save for a few stray vagabonds and overworked servants. My drab garb and short hair allowed me to escape even the most nefarious looking scoundrel's notice as I made my way through the narrow alley behind the inn toward the prison located near the Assembly Hall. The front door was predictably locked, but I brazenly knocked and waited for an answer. A shuffling and muffled curse sounded from within. A small opening in the solid wood appeared when a block was slammed aside. A pair of eyes filled the opening, squinting into the darkness and alighting on me in undisguised indignation.

"Whatcho want, boy?" a rough voice asked. Based on the raspy tone and the drooping eyelids, I deduced I had woken the guard from an unsanctioned nap.

"Message for the prisoner, Ailbert Chester," I said authoritatively.

"At this hour? Piss off," the guard said. He moved to slide the block back in place, but I jammed my fist into the opening. I winced but bit my lip to keep from crying out.

"It's from his mother, Lady Noraa." Despite my efforts, the guard tried to force the opening closed. I strained against the pain.

"Tell it to me then," the guard said. His eyes softened slightly, and I took advantage of his sympathy to push the little door open fully.

"It's a personal matter. I'm sure you understand. I was sent with great urgency from Praed and ordered to deliver the message as soon as I arrived on pain of disfigurement. I can't stomach losing my hand, so if you would be charitable enough to let me in, I'm sure her ladyship would extend a payment your way."

His eyes roamed over me suspiciously, but a twinkle in his eyes at the mention of coins assured me the ploy was working. To seal the ruse, I withdrew a small pouch I'd retrieved from my nightstand and dangled it before him.

"Consider it an advancement." I shook the bag and the clinking of coins seemed to make him salivate. He licked his lips and reached out for the bag, but I withdrew it quickly and insisted on being let in first. Begrudgingly, the guard unlocked the door, and it swung open.

"We are to remain undisturbed." I dropped the bag into his hands and strode forward.

"Whatever you say, lad," the guard said. He began counting the coins.

I grabbed a torch off the wall and entered the prison, searching the faces of sleeping inmates as I made my way through the lines of cells. I tried to cover my nose to protect myself against the worst of the pungent odors, but it became so overpowering I had to duck into a dark corner to retch. Someone should really have a word with the high council about the deplorable state of Faqur's prison.

The torchlight illuminated a figure in a cell smaller than the one that held me for days in the bowels of *The Wayward Aymelina*, a figure with wavy brown hair wearing a stained blue jacket. I braced my free hand against the cold iron of the prison bars, took a steadying breath, and whispered into the darkness.

"Wake up," I hissed. The figure groaned but did not comply, so I repeated myself more forcefully.

"Get up, you pathetic excuse for a man," I seethed.

The man rolled over, his eyes squinting in the firelight. Dark blue eyes that had tormented me with their vehemence.

"Who's there?" Ailbert Chester asked, his voice hoarse from sleep. He held out a hand to block the light, and I obligingly moved the torch aside so he could see my face. He sneered and leapt to his feet, and I gripped the bar tighter to keep from jumping away as he drove forward with outstretched arms. He didn't reach through to bars to strangle me, but braced himself as he pressed his face against the hard metal and bared his teeth.

"What are you doing here, Princess?" he growled.

So, he knew. Perfect.

"I wanted to see if you were afraid, as my brother must have been when you spinelessly gave him up to save yourself." I held his gaze as his eyes darkened and his skin flushed scarlet.

"His life is not worth more than mine just because he's a prince," he said.

"No, it's worth more because you're a selfish bastard!" My eyes darted into the dark corridor, but the guard remained in the front room.

"You think I'm selfish?" His steady tone was more frightening than if he screamed in my face. I hoped the shifting shadows created by the flames of the torch hid my pallid features.

"You're repulsive," I whispered. "Without any perceivable reason, you've been nothing but hideous since the moment I saw you. My family has done nothing to you."

"You think you're so clever, but you know nothing. You've grown up in your castle shielded and comfortable with absolutely no idea what real life is like." His eyes were nearly black, and his face was so close I could smell his neglected teeth.

"You're the son of a lord. Don't lecture me about privilege when you grew up with it yourself."

He laughed, a short and harsh sound, then looked at me as if I were a simpleton.

He lowered his gaze. "I thought the same thing once."

I was amazed to realize that he was trying to master his emotions. Perhaps it was beneath me, but I took advantage of his vulnerability to press him.

"Is Lord Chester your real father?"

"I'm going to die," he said with the first trace of regret I'd heard from him. "At first, I felt sorry for Mother, but then I remembered how she lied to me for my entire life, and then I felt only disdain." He moved away from the bars, and I followed his pacing with the torch, stretching his shadow across the floor. I waited, and unhindered by the sound of my voice or propriety or self-preservation, Ailbert revealed what I already knew to be true.

"I suspected the man who raised me was not my father," he said. "He was weak and complacent, and he showed so little interest in Mother I often wondered how he could have possibly found the time, much less the desire, to conceive me. As I grew into a man, our appearances and personalities were so dissimilar I resigned myself to the fact that Lord Chester did not father me. I didn't think about what this meant concerning Mother."

My heart twisted in sympathy for what it must have been like for him to doubt his father. It was especially painful to ponder considering the close relationship I had with my own. If I found out he wasn't truly my father, how would I react? What would I think of Mother?

"One day when she was away, I went into her room and searched through her things looking for proof of what I believed," he continued. "At the bottom of an old trunk, I found a faded letter. A love letter." I heard the disdain in his voice, as if the very thought of his mother in love left a vile taste in his mouth.

"Who was it from?" My voice trembled. I was afraid he would turn on me for asking, or at the very least he wouldn't reveal the truth to a person he had historically despised. He slowly came toward me, closer and closer until he was leaning so close I'm certain he could hear my heart thundering.

"I'm sure the queen knew." An accusation. "We always had special visits from the palace, and Mother often sent reports that I knew were about me growing up. Did you know about them?" I shook my head. "Did any of you?" Again, no. "You've never even heard my name mentioned?"

"Why would we?" I asked. "You are the son of a lord that practically lived as a hermit. He never came to court and neither did your mother. We never saw any of you at Thistledon either. We didn't even know you existed until you arrived at Praed Castle before Lilias' wedding."

"Why?" he seethed.

I flinched both at the level of vehemence and to prevent spittle from hitting my eye.

He gripped the bars and continued. "Because I, too, am royalty, and was probably considered a threat to your crown!"

I recoiled in horror and swore I felt a welt forming on my cheek, as if he'd really slapped me. My mouth opened and closed, but I could not produce any words aside from a breathy, "Wh-wh-wh—"

"My father was the King of Praed before yours murdered him in front of hundreds of people. His father was the king before him. By all rights, I should have been a prince!"

I knew the king he was referring to. Brannon, the spoiled prince who was rumored to have poisoned his father, King Conall, in order to secure the crown. The whole family line was mad. My parents rarely spoke of those dark times, but there were plenty of texts detailing the events. It was true that my father killed the young king, his own cousin, and that afterward he himself was crowned. But though King Brannon was married, he had no children. At least, that's what everyone had been told.

"If that's true," I said, "I fail to see your point. Once my father became king, your claim to the throne was nonexistent. I'm sorry you found out the truth about your parentage, but you've obviously been taken care of, even by a queen who was tormented by your father's family. There is nothing you can say that would excuse *your* crime."

"Maybe not." He shrugged. "But wouldn't it be interesting if this information became public knowledge?"

"It would, indeed. It would expose your mother as the whore of a murderous former king whose line was thought to be exterminated. If you weren't on the verge of being executed for treason, Praed would be calling for your head."

Ailbert winced but made no further reply. He shuffled back to the cot at the back of the cell and fell heavily upon the thin mattress. He lay with his back to me, his arms wrapped protectively around himself.

"I'm sorry," I whispered. He didn't respond, and I had nothing further to say. I left the prison without looking back, waving off the guard's inquiries as to when he would receive the rest of his money.

I didn't immediately return to the inn. My mind whirled too much for sleep. Streetlamps illuminated the main road through town. A few people darted in and out of the light, but I was too lost in thought to notice. It was reckless of me to let my guard down. I was an unarmed woman wandering the streets alone with sunrise on the distant horizon. My lifeless corpse could remain undiscovered for hours.

I shook myself and shoved my hands in my pockets. Even the fear of death didn't turn me around. I quickened my pace and left the safety of the streetlamps behind. The road narrowed and split into tributaries leading to pockets of villages. I stood at the crossroads and allowed my eyes to adjust to the darkness. With little information to guide me, I allowed my instincts to take over. I headed west, along a road that hugged a rock outcropping. I dragged a hand over the rough stone. As long as I kept close to them, I'd avoid a steadily rising cliff on my left.

After an hour, the road dipped toward a valley. Pinpoints of light twinkled in darkened houses. A gust of cold air blew in from the ocean, bearing with it the scent of salt, fish, and wood smoke. The village was quiet. I strolled down the dirt road, searching for a sign that someone was awake. A dog barked, and my ears perked. I headed toward it, and the dog's barking turned into a panicked cacophony of yips and woofs. A man's voice called out, and he threw open his door holding up a lantern.

"Who's there?" His voice was rough from sleep. He rubbed his eyes and tried focusing past the lanternlight.

"I mean no harm," I said, raising my hands.

"Who-who's that?" He blinked and narrowed his eyes. "Boy, whatcho doin' this hour?" He took a menacing step forward.

"Please! I'm looking for someone. If you could only tell me if I'm in the right village, I'll be on my way."

"Up to no good!" He grabbed a fishing spear propped against the doorframe and raised it over his head.

"Stop! I made a promise to his widow!"

The man paused and slowly lowered the spear.

"I'm looking for the widow of Rex Pichur," I said. "We served together on *The Wayward Aymelina*. I promised—" I choked on a sob and swallowed the knot in my throat. "Before he died, I promised I'd give his wife a message."

The man's features softened, turned mournful. He pointed the end of the spear down the road. "Three houses down. Her name is Adie."

I nodded my thanks and sprinted toward the house. I was running out of time. If Father woke up and found me gone, I'll be locked in my room for eternity. I jogged up to the porch and rapped on the door. There was shuffling inside, but no answer.

I knocked harder. "Hello? I'm looking for Adie Pichur. I have a message for her."

A crack appeared in the doorway and a woman's face appeared. She was several inches shorter than me. Several strands of ash blonde hair escaped her kerchief, and her blue eyes were wide with fright.

"I'm Adie," she said, her voice quiet and trembling.

I flashed a friendly smile. "I won't take up much of your time. My name is…Symon. I knew your husband, Rex."

Her eyes filled with tears, and she pressed a fist to her mouth to stifle a cry.

"It was his last wish." I took a deep breath and fought to keep my own tears at bay. "That I tell you he loves you."

She sank to the floor, no longer able to contain her grief. A muffled voice called out from deeper in the house. I jumped off the porch, but only managed a couple of steps.

"Wait!" Adie said. "Please. Did he suffer?"

I turned back. She'd come outside in her bare feet and nightdress. Her hands were clasped to her chest, her eyes pleading.

In Praed, dying in battle was the epitome of honor. In the time of my grandmother, widows thirsted for details of their husband's demise and passed on their tales of glory. But we weren't in Praed, and I couldn't bring myself to recount the gruesome story of Rex's death to this poor woman.

"No," I said. "He died peacefully. In my arms."

She nodded, mouthed a thank you, and went back into the house.

I'd never sneak out of the inn again.

CHAPTER 31

I sat on the windowsill, miserably bored, watching the people outside go about their daily lives. We'd decided that though I was allowed to return home with my freedom, it would be best to avoid being seen in town and inviting questions. Thus I remained behind at the inn with Mother while Father visited Tyrnan and arranged for his transport home. I was anxious to leave, though a part of my heart would remain in Faqur. I'd given up hope that any of my friends or the officers would take their leave before our departure, so I filled my hours catching up on news from home and reading to Mother from my journal. She listened with rapt attention, a touch of wistfulness in her eyes, and I wondered if she was a little envious of my adventures. She assured me that wasn't the case, but I caught her reading a few passages over again.

"Do you ever wish you'd have traveled more before settling into your role as queen?" I asked.

"My place has always been in Praed by your father's side. That's been adventure enough. Look at the wonderful life it brought me." She smiled up at me warmly, and I saw a kindred spirit in her green eyes. She may not have fought pirates or discovered far off lands, but my mother lived her life to its fullest potential.

I moved away from the window with a sigh when a servant entered with a tray of tea and honeyed cakes. Our drawing room was a small sitting area with a writing desk, a few bookcases, and a settee by a fireplace. Mother rose from said settee to sit beside me, distractedly reading a letter.

"Anything exciting?" I dismissed the servant and poured Mother a cup of tea myself.

"Alyx is acting as regent in our absence. He's sent me a very detailed account of all his dealings since we came away," she said.

"Practicing for the day he's crowned," I said glibly.

"I think he shall do very well as king."

"I do, too." I meant it wholeheartedly.

A servant entered and bowed to Mother. "Your Grace, a visitor has arrived and asked to call on Her Highness, Princess Sulwen."

"Oh?" Mother glanced at me in confusion. "Who is it?" We both rose to greet our guest, eyeing each other warily.

"Captain Lencius Romy, Your Majesty. Shall I see him in?"

Mother's eyes widened, and all the blood drained from my body to my toes. I placed a hand against my breast, suddenly short of breath, and reached for the table to steady myself.

"Yes," Mother said. "Do let him in." She leaned close to me and whispered, "Compose yourself." I shakily drew in a breath and straightened my back, clasped my hands together and tried not to faint as Captain Romy strode into the room with easy confidence.

He bowed gracefully to my mother. "Your Majesty." He turned to me, and I couldn't prevent the flush of heat from creeping into my cheeks. He studied me ever so briefly before he bowed and said, "Your Highness." I felt a surge of resentment over his formality, but I couldn't blame him for addressing me thus. I was no longer a lowly sailor under his command. I was now far and above his consequence, though in my eyes I was beneath him in many respects.

"Captain Romy," Mother said with casual ease. "It is such an honor to meet you at last. The king and I have heard nothing but the highest praise of you."

"Thank you, Your Majesty," he replied. "I understand you will be leaving Faqur soon?"

"Yes. We wish to bring Prince Tyrnan home as soon as possible."

"Of course. Please accept my wishes for his swift recovery."

"Thank you, sir." Mother looked at him expectantly, and he shifted his hat under his arm. If I wasn't mistaken, I would say he appeared uncomfortable, but this wasn't a state I'd ever known the captain to be in.

"Your Majesty, might I have permission to speak with the princess?" he asked.

"Of course," Mother answered lightly. She indicated my person with a sweeping gesture and moved to sit on the settee, affording us privacy but still maintaining propriety. He looked at me, and my throat tightened with words I couldn't quite express. As always, he was impeccably dressed in freshly pressed, white breeches, a high-collared white waistcoat, and gold-buttoned blue tailcoat without a speck of dust. He was once again clean shaven, and his sun-bleached hair was oiled and combed back. I couldn't bear to look him in the eye, so I focused on his black boots that were polished to a brilliant shine.

"Sir." My voice strained through everything I wanted to say. "I cannot thank you enough for your testimony to the chief prosecutor. It was instrumental in his decision to let me go free."

"Good," he said. There was a heartbeat of silence, and I tried to read his expression, but he looked at me so blankly I couldn't deduce what he might be thinking.

"And your brothers, are they well?"

"Very well, thank you." I rolled my eyes in exasperation. I despised small talk, especially when I felt too much had happened to warrant such things. I cleared my throat and said, "Let us speak plainly, sir—"

"You always do."

I smiled and felt a little easier.

"Did you mean it?" I asked.

"Mean what?"

"You said I would always have a place on *The Wayward Aymelina?*"

"I did."

"You don't hate me then?" My vision blurred, and I cursed my fragility in that moment.

"No." He reached into his greatcoat and pulled out several sheets of folded parchment and handed them to me. I took them reverently, feeling the delicacy of the paper and running my fingers over the wax seal. It was of an anchor with three suns above the stock.

"What is this?"

"Your commission papers." I looked up at him in awed silence. He continued. "The council has decided that the island with the black shore deserves further investigation. Based on the cartographers' estimate, it could be large enough to support a colony. I've been tasked with leading an expedition to map its entirety. *The Wayward Aymelina* will be in drydock for repairs for the next three months. Should you choose, I..." he hesitated, his jaw working.

"Yes?"

"Should you choose, there will be a place for you on board. I ordered a separate cabin installed for your privacy, and the crew have agreed to respect it. They are...eager...to see you again. But not inappropriately so." I couldn't help but laugh at his amendment, but I quickly regained a respectable mien.

"Will you be leaving as soon as the repairs are finished?" I asked.

"Yes," he said. "You have until then to make your decision. If you are not on board by the time we sail, I will take that as your answer."

"This is very generous."

"I don't offer this out of generosity."

I nodded. "It's out of obligation. You're offering me this because you made a promise that you cannot retract."

"I would have made you this offer without such a promise." His blue-gray eyes flashed with intensity. We stared at each other, our chests rising and falling with restrained emotion. I released a breath, urging myself to be calm.

"Thank you, sir," I said with genuine gratitude. "I will consider this offer."

He nodded, bowed, and took his leave without another word. I felt his absence acutely and stared at the floor where he'd been standing longer than a sane person should. Then I rushed to the window and peered down just in time to see him mount a blood bay stallion and ride away at a pace dangerously close to reckless.

Mother came and stood beside me. "Well?"

"I have a place on *The Wayward Aymelina* should I choose." I maintained my gaze on the street below.

"And will you take it?" she asked, her voice heavy with apprehension.

I looked down at the folded documents, then pressed them tightly to my chest.

"I don't know," I whispered. "How does one choose between the life they were born to and the life that was a lie?"

"Only your name and gender were lies." She rubbed small circles between my shoulder blades. "The rest was you."

"It was a fantasy," I said. "I knew it wasn't meant to be forever." She said nothing while I struggled to maintain an indifferent attitude, but the weight of her studying gaze crumbled my calm exterior.

"Your father and I will not make this choice for you, Sulwen. You are a grown woman, and it is yours to make. We will respect whatever course you think is best."

Should I abandon my birthright and sail off toward unknown lands on *The Wayward Aymelina*? I knew if I did, there would be no coming home. Not really. The call of the sea would permanently run through me, and I would never be satisfied with a normal life. Praed and the crown would merely be an afterthought, a place I visited occasionally to see my family. It would be where I was from, but not where I belonged. Was I willing to make that sacrifice?

Father arrived shortly and informed us that the preparations were ready for our departure the next morning. Mother said nothing of Captain Romy's visit, at least not with me present, and we went through the motions of our day as if nothing so momentous had occurred.

That night, I thought not about my own wants and desires, not of Mother or Father, and not of *The Wayward Aymelina* and her crew. Instead, I considered my brother, Tyrnan. He dreamed of the sea since he was three years old, and this adventure was the chance of a lifetime. Yet he understood that one day he must awaken and return to Praed to fulfill his duty to the crown. I thought of Alyx and how he expertly stepped in to rule a country while the king and queen were away. He knew his role and he performed it without a moment's hesitation and without complaint. Lilias married the son of a prominent lord as a good princess should. Though I didn't doubt she had affection for him, her preference stemmed from her understanding that such an alliance would benefit the country. Even Rian, who in every respect portrayed the typical unfettered prince, dedicated himself to the crown in training tirelessly with the sword.

My brothers and sister accepted their fates happily and with grace. I, on the other hand, looked upon the crown and the responsibility that came with it resentfully instead of embracing the honor that came with it. It had taken a distance of thousands of miles to realize what a gift my life was. True, I would be bound by certain social customs, but like my siblings, I could find a place where I belonged, a place that was mine. But was that place in Praed?

CHAPTER 32

The next morning while we prepared to leave Faqur, Mother's eyes desperately searched mine. She was looking for a hint of my decision, and I wasn't ready to give one. I disregarded her painfully obvious scrutiny and watched our carriage be loaded with trunks. Father assisted me inside. Mother sat across from me and tried to catch my attention, but I staunchly ignored her and gazed out the window as we pulled away from the inn. The carriage behind us was specially outfitted for Tyrnan's comfort. I waited in silence when we arrived at the hospital to collect him. Father volunteered to ride with my brother first, leaving Mother and me alone as we left the main city of Faqur and headed in the direction of home.

I watched the buildings gradually change from large structures to the humble dwellings of fishermen and farmers and wondered whether any of my friends lived in them. A few people stopped to gawk as we passed, but most went about their business undeterred. I smiled at this, for what did the hardworking people of this country care for a foreign king and queen when there were fleets of ships to supply?

I didn't speak for two days, which for me was akin to dying. Though Mother was miserably worried, she didn't press me into confidence. When she could no longer bear to ride in silence with me, she changed places with Father and rode with Tyrnan. The silence between Father and I was easier, less strained, as we understood the importance of self-reflection. He busied himself with letters and ledgers, and I continued to stare at the ever-changing landscape, remembering a time so long ago when Tyrnan and I passed this way. I looked upon the purple hills and gray mountains with a sense of peace, knowing what lay ahead of me now.

When it was my turn to ride with Tyrnan, we laughed over how terrible of a sailor I started out as and the close calls I'd experienced. We recalled our greatest accomplishments and fondest experiences, reading aloud from our journals. Tyrnan particularly enjoyed my passages on the Nakwacimek and thought Kyra would find them inspiring. My heart swelled at the mention of my sister, and I missed her more dearly the closer we drew home. We didn't mention the commission Captain Romy offered me, though I was certain Mother or Father told him of it.

"We estimated that the area beyond Bruyarmont could be vast," Tyrnan said. "That's what we named the mountain we saw that night. Remember?"

"I remember." Captain Romy and I stood together regarding that great mountain contemplating what lay beyond long after everyone answered the call of the dinner bell.

"I wish I was going with you," Tyrnan said quietly, paging through his notes. "What an exciting opportunity."

"I never said I was going."

"Aren't you? Mother said the captain himself presented you with your commission. She expects you to accept."

"I'm sure she does." A guilty blush spread over my cheeks. "But I don't know if I will."

"I see." He took my hand and read some more from his journal, but I could tell he was distracted.

"I have a duty to my family," I argued, though he said nothing more about the possibility of my leaving.

"I know."

"I understand now that I can't afford to act so selfishly."

"Good."

"It's not about what *I* want."

"Not always."

I stared at him, no doubt with consternation clearly written on my face. He stared back. Did I want Tyrnan's permission to accept the commission? Or at the very least, his blessing? He offered neither. He was leaving the decision entirely up to me.

We ascended the White Mountain toward Praed Castle. I bounced on the edge of my seat and beamed. Winter was on its way out, but the ground remained covered in snow, making the last stretch of our journey slow and arduous. As we turned the corner, the castle finally came into view, and there on the steps was my family. Father grinned as I pushed past him, picked up the hem of my dress, and bounded up the steps toward my siblings. Behind me, Tyrnan was carefully unloaded from his carriage, and I heard Uncle Finton delivering instructions to the men carrying him. But my eyes were only for Alyx approaching me with outstretched arms. I threw myself into his embrace, and I wept openly onto my oldest brother's tunic as he rocked me gently, as Father had done.

"Move over and let someone else have a turn!" Rian said.

Alyx relinquished his hold and I was immediately enveloped by the next brother in line. Khyr came up behind me, but instead of pulling me away from Rian, he simply wrapped his arms around us both and squeezed tightly. I laughed amid my happy sobs, relishing the warmth of our reunion.

"Are you quite finished yet?" It was Kyra, and I disentangled myself from Rian and Khyr to look upon my darling sister. She smiled widely, her beautiful green eyes shimmering with emotions she made no attempt to restrain. Our laughter mingled with our tears as we hugged and twirled in excitement.

"Come now. She must be exhausted," Lilias said. "Let her come inside."

Kyra stepped aside at her words, her eyes still fixed upon me. I looked up into the serene face of my older sister gently smiling down at me. She was just as lovely as when I'd seen her last almost a year ago, her dark hair styled fashionably, her ivory skin glowing, and her gown in the newest style. My eyes traveled down her frame, soaking in her presence, when they fell upon the unmistakable swelling of her belly.

"Lilias," I said. She lay a hand against her abdomen knowingly, a tender smile on her face.

"Come inside, Sulwen." She linked her arm with mine, and together we ascended the steps into the castle.

The joy of once again being surrounded by my family at the dinner table was indescribable. I sat back and observed Rian and Khyr's banter with a wistful smile, gazed adoringly at Kyra, and felt an overwhelming love for all of them. As if by some unspoken rule, there was no discussion of my absence, and it was a relief to not be interrogated. Even after we retired to the drawing room, there were no questions, no strange looks, and no judgment. I was welcomed home as if nothing happened, and it was glorious. Tomorrow might be a different story, but tonight I was allowed to relax and settle back into the routine of castle life.

Lilias announced I should be excused to bed, and I stifled a yawn and protested that I wasn't tired. Mother smiled at me indulgently but agreed with my elder sister's assessment. Lilias and Kyra rose with me when Mother pulled me to my feet, and together the four of us left the room to a chorus of goodnights from the men.

"You must be exhausted, too, Mother," Lilias said. "Why don't you let me and Kyra take care of Sulwen and you retire yourself." My mother and sister shared an unreadable look before Mother acquiesced and allowed me to leave with just my sisters as company.

Molli was waiting with a hot bath when we entered my room, and I gratefully sank into the soothing water while avoiding her raised brow. My sisters chatted about events that happened while I was away, from the marriages of people we knew to Merrin's impending expedition to Kuste.

"Perhaps we'll be able to visit before she leaves," Kyra suggested. "I understand it won't be for many weeks."

"Perhaps," Lilias said as she handed me a towel.

They continued to apprise me of the delightful gossip circulating around the castle, including speculation that Rian was infatuated with the daughter of an ambassador who had recently visited from Vyt.

"Do you think it's true?" I was incredulous. Rian was the least romantic among us, and I couldn't fathom that he would form a sincere attachment to any woman for more than five minutes.

"He was very sad to see her go," Kyra reported with wide, amused eyes. "And moped about for at least a week."

"What was she like?" I asked. Molli brushed out my short hair, and I saw her downturned expression in the mirror regarding the shorn locks. I detected a trace of sadness as she ran her fingers through them.

"Very pretty," Kyra said. "She had shining black hair pulled back from her face and styled very elaborately behind her head. She wore enormous headdresses made of gold with glittering jewels and dresses to match in soft fabrics covered in embroidery. She had big, dark brown eyes, and a cute little nose. Her skin was not white nor light brown but rather..." She looked up to the ceiling as she tried to find the right description for the color of the girl's skin.

"You aren't sure?" I asked.

"Like straw that's been left out in the sun," Lilias offered.

"She was very sweet," Kyra said. "Quiet, but sweet."

"I don't think she spoke our language very well," Lilias said.

"What was her name?" I asked.

"My'lan," Kyra said.

"What makes you think Rian liked her?" I asked.

"He always found an excuse to be near her," Kyra said. "And even though she could probably only understand every third word he said, he conversed only with her whenever she was around."

"Well," I said. "If he's found his heart in her, then I'm happy for him." I dismissed Molli and the moment the door closed behind her, the tone of the conversation changed dramatically.

Kyra leapt forward, grabbing the bedpost, a huge grin on her face. "Did you really fight pirates?"

Lilias tutted. "Kyra, don't make her relive something so terrifying."

"I don't mind." I retrieved the journals from my trunk and placed them in Kyra's hands. She hungrily flipped through the pages.

"I wrote down everything I saw with you in mind," I said. "I hope you can find inspiration within these journals for your stories."

"I'm sure I will!" She clutched them to her chest and sighed.

"It must have been so frightening." Lilias squeezed my hand. "Being on board that ship all those months and pretending to be a boy. How worried you must have been at every moment that they would find out."

"More so at the beginning," I said. "Pretending became easier as time went on, but I still had to be careful."

"Did you make friends with the crew? Were they kind?" Lilias asked.

"Not at first, but we warmed to each other. There were several men I counted among my friends, and I will miss them dearly," I said.

"Were they angry when they found out the truth?" Lilias asked.

"I don't know. I never saw them again after disembarking *The Wayward Aymelina*. Well, most of them. I saw the first mate in the hospital with Tyrnan. He was very angry when I revealed my secret. But both he and the crew seemed to forgive me for they wrote testimonies to the chief prosecutor that facilitated my release."

"What of the captain?" Lilias asked. "Did he forgive you as well?"

"The captain..." My voice faded as I pictured Captain Romy standing in the tiny drawing room at the Faqur inn telling me he did not hate me. I swallowed, shook my head, and answered, "If he was angry upon hearing the news that I deceived him, he was no longer when I last saw him."

"What was your favorite part about the voyage?" Kyra rested her head in her hands and eagerly awaited my answer, as if she were a child anticipating a sweet treat.

"I can hardly choose," I said. "I saw so many wonderful things, so many beautiful new lands and animals, as you'll read about. If pressed, I would have to say I'll never forget the moment I emerged from a gorge after climbing along the rock wall and seeing the largest lake I'd ever seen shining like a blue gem." I paused, thinking about how awed I'd felt at several points during the voyage, so many of which occurred on that island. What I'd seen may have only scratched the surface of the secrets it contained, secrets I would never uncover. I stared sadly at the bedcover in the ensuing silence, and Kyra took my other hand.

"Were you quite happy there?" Lilias asked quietly.

"Yes," I whispered. "But I'm happy to be home now, with you." I smiled at my sisters, and Lilias took hold of Kyra's free hand in hers. Together, we formed a circle of sisterly love, a bond that could not be broken by distance or time.

"And." I glanced at Lilias' belly. "I'm happy to have arrived just in time to become an aunt."

"Sulwen..." Lilias gazed at me solemnly, as if she knew I was holding something back.

"Enough." I forced a smile. "I'm tired now. We'll talk more tomorrow." I hugged each of my sisters in turn and shooed them out of the room. Once I was finally alone, I tucked into the luxurious bed and listened to the sounds of the castle for several hours, allowing the familiar noises to lull me to sleep in a bed that was supposed to make me feel as if I'd come home. But it was only a mattress and blankets, a soft pillow, and an empty heart.

"I'm going to stay," I told Mother the next morning. "My place is here."

"Are you sure?" She studied my stoic countenance.

"I have been away from Praed long enough. The time has come for me to take my place in service to the crown."

She couldn't hide her relief, and I couldn't bear to witness her moment of utter joy. I turned away before she could take me in her arms, and I didn't acknowledge the offered commission ever existed.

CHAPTER 33

Once I made the decision to commit myself to Praed, I resumed my role as princess and devoted my time to improving my chances of either becoming a diplomat or securing an advantageous marriage. I joined my brothers in the training yard once more to hone my skills with a sword, and I impressed them with how much I'd learned over the course of my tenure on *The Wayward Aymelina.*

Along with combat skills, I concentrated more on my studies, including those I'd largely ignored, namely embroidery and music. If I was going to be sought after, I reasoned, I would have to be well-rounded in my accomplishments. At my request, Mother began planning a spring ball for the purpose of circulating and meeting new people. She raised an eyebrow at my reasoning for such a party but said nothing against it.

Tyrnan's health gradually returned, and Uncle Finton allowed him to venture outside for fresh air for a few minutes at a time each day. I was usually the one to accompany him on these outings, and we would walk about the grounds with him bundled in a heavy fur coat. By now, he knew I'd declined Captain Romy's invitation, but we didn't speak of it. In fact, we deliberately avoided any discussion of our time on *The Wayward Aymelina.* Mentions of the ship pained me. I'd left Tyrnan out in the snow the last time he spoke of it. Uncle Finton was not pleased.

I spent a great deal of my time with Lilias, whether at Praed Castle or at Thistledon. She said she had about three months left in her pregnancy, and I was determined not to miss another second of it, even if I annoyed her immensely.

"I'm not enfeebled," she laughed as I tucked another pillow behind her back while we embroidered in the Thistledon drawing room.

"I want you to be comfortable," I said, and contemplated getting her another blanket.

"And I appreciate it, but it's not necessary, dear one." We lapsed into a comfortable silence as I concentrated on my work, but after a while, I could sense Lilias was on the verge of asking me something. I avoided meeting her eye, but she finally asked, "Are you happy, Sulwen?"

"Of course," I said.

"You're very restless," she pointed out.

"You know I don't like to be idle."

"This is different." She set aside her sewing and carefully pulled the embroidery project from my hands. "Tell me what you're thinking."

"I am wondering," I said uneasily. "If you've heard about Ailbert Chester."

The look on Lilias' face said everything: anger, shame, remorse, outrage. She knew.

"How is Andrew handling it? And poor Lady Chester?"

"As well as can be expected," she said tersely. "They don't talk about him much, and Lady Chester has kept to her rooms as I understand."

"You know," I said conspiratorially. "I think there's a possibility that Lord Chester is not Ailbert's father." I watched her face as I spoke and wondered if she knew the truth.

She tilted her head in curiosity. "Why do you say that?"

"Something I overheard Mother and Father say. It was a great secret, and I've been scouring my brain trying to figure out who his father might be." I tried to detect a hint of guilt, a turn of the chin, a slant of the eye, anything that might indicate Lilias knew the identity of her husband's cousin.

She shrugged. "I suppose we'll never know for sure." I couldn't tell if she believed my story or was just placating me. "It doesn't do any good to talk about it now that he's been condemned."

She was right, of course, and I never gave Ailbert Chester another moment's consideration. I didn't tell a living soul about his parentage, and I never alluded that I knew the truth to Mother and Father. After all, he was no longer a threat to their crown or my family.

Kyra was the only one with the nerve to ask questions about my time abroad. She'd wasted no time absorbing everything in my journals, spending most nights staying up to read. I indulged her curiosity and didn't lash out as I did with everyone else. Kyra had a voracious imagination, and

I reveled in the notion that the adventures I'd had would feature in her future stories.

A full month elapsed. I felt confident that I'd effectively moved forward from my experience at sea and was now fully invested in my life in Praed. Though I believed I behaved normally, the atmosphere around the dinner table felt strained. I couldn't explain why everyone sent furtive glances my way, but I told myself it was because I'd started comporting myself as a lady. My short hair was expertly styled, I wore gowns in the new fashion, and I sat with perfect posture. The snow was melting, and with the improvement of the roads, it was easier to venture out and visit the less fortunate families of the country as a princess should. I traveled several miles a day and returned exhausted, which facilitated a deep and dreamless sleep every night. Most surprisingly of all, I began encouraging Marick's attention and visits to the castle even though I still found him as dull as ever. I believe it was this act that prompted Father's request one night that we speak in private.

"Sulwen," he intoned as we rose from the table following dinner. "Come to my study."

He left without another word, and I turned a wide-eyed gaze toward Alyx. He smiled gently and indicated that I should follow. I looked to Mother, and her response was similar.

When I entered Father's study, I was shocked to find him pacing. He was rarely discomposed, and I rushed into the room in a panic.

"Is everything all right, Father? Did something happen?" I asked.

"Sit down, Sulwen," he said, avoiding direct eye contact. I did as I was told, and I sat on the edge of my seat as he took his place across from me.

"Sulwen." It took a monumental effort for him to meet my eyes. "Are you happy here?"

"Of course, Father!"

"Do you feel fulfilled?"

"Of course!" He studied me as I responded, and he didn't appear convinced.

"Sulwen." His tone brooked no argument. "Do you want to leave here?"

"Why are you doing this?" I clenched my hands into fists to keep them from shaking.

"Answer me. Do you want to go back to *The Wayward Aymelina?*"

I opened my mouth, but I failed to form words. *Ask yourself an honest question.* "Father," I said, so quietly even I could barely hear it.

"I see what you're doing, and it pains me." He raised a hand to halt my protests. "I would rather see you live unmarried and happy than dissatisfied in a marriage of convenience because you think it would please your mother and me."

"I'm trying to do my duty to my country. And to you."

"I was a father before I was a king," he said.

This was news to me, and I stared at him wide-eyed wonder.

"I loved your mother and married her in secret. Alyx was conceived when she was a servant, alone and friendless. I accepted the crown to protect my family, to give them a life where they could be free from fear. I will not sit back and watch my beloved daughter throw her life away because she thinks it's what *I* want."

"Father." My voice wavered, and I couldn't utter another word.

"I do not wish to be parted from you, to have you journey into the unknown where you may face danger. Yet you have proven that you are capable of the extraordinary. Much like your mother." I'd never heard him speak so passionately before.

"Father." I swallowed, my throat painfully dry. "What do you want me to do?"

"I want you to be honest with me. Do you want to go back to *The Wayward Aymelina?*"

I folded my hands together, looked at the floor, and took a deep breath. "Yes," I whispered. A tear trickled down my cheek.

"Then go," he said. "Go with our blessing."

I launched myself out of the chair into his lap, and I hugged him so fiercely I probably left a bruise around his neck.

"But," I managed to say between sobs, "what about—?"

"Stop," he said firmly. "Everything here will be well in hand."

I fell asleep curled in my father's lap as I had done almost a year prior when I resolved to follow my heart and forge a path against the wishes of my family. Now, I had their consent to leave Praed, and the thought filled me with a contentment that I'd only felt as a child warm in her bed after a winter storm. Tomorrow, there was much to be done, for *The Wayward Aymelina* would be setting sail in less than two months. But for that night, I would devote myself to a peaceful night's slumber devoid of heartache. A sleep that I did not have to bring about by exhausting myself to the point where I couldn't keep my eyes open. A sleep where I did not fear the dreams that might follow.

My siblings were understandably disappointed that I planned on leaving again. Well, most of them. Kyra was excited for me to be off on another adventure and made me promise to write this time. I explained that would be difficult to accomplish on an undocumented island hundreds of miles out at sea. Her response was that if anyone could do it, I could. So now I have that aspect of the journey to sort out. Lilias, who had more reason to regret my leaving than anyone, was surprisingly serene about my missing the birth of her first child.

"I don't suppose you could squeeze it out early?" I asked.

"One cannot control these things, Sulwen. For all I know, it could come later."

"I'll wait as long as I can."

"I don't wish for you to miss your ship. If the child is born before you leave, I will be happy, but if not, I will send you word express with the news."

"And you won't be angry that I missed it?"

"Not at all. Just make your ship, and I will be pleased." She smiled knowingly, as if there was some secret between us that I wasn't aware of. I shrugged it off and continued planning for my departure. Father insisted I take an escort, but I had elected to travel to Faqur on Nettle for expediency's sake. If an escort slowed me down, I informed him, I would leave them behind. He didn't look very pleased at this prospect, so I conceded to a small contingent of guards for his own peace of mind.

I rose each morning with frenzied anticipation and practically stalked poor Lilias for any signs that she was about to give birth. She was enormous at this point in her pregnancy and had confined herself to Thistledon. I visited her daily to check on her progress. But every day I still left 'just

Sulwen' and not 'Aunt Sulwen.' Though I was beginning to irritate myself, she indulged my persistent visits and expressed remorse that I continued to go away dissatisfied.

"Lilias' baby is taking its precious time," I grumbled to Mother one evening two weeks after I'd begun my vigil.

"They always do," she said with a wistful smile.

Meddling babies.

After another week went by without my niece or nephew making an appearance, I declared that if a baby didn't produce itself in another sennight, I would have to leave without making its acquaintance. Mother found this announcement particularly humorous, but I saw nothing amusing about it. I had to make it to Faqur before *The Wayward Aymelina* left dry dock, and I also had to see Lilias' baby before I left. It was the worst predicament to be in. Give me pirates any day.

Unfortunately, the day came when I could no longer wait, and even though Lilias was the size of a horse, her labor pains had not begun. Reluctantly, I set the date of my departure for the day after the next. I declined any pomp and circumstance. No large banquet or ball to mark the occasion, just a simple family dinner. The tension I'd felt previously was gone, as if my decision to leave was a relief to everyone, not because they wished for me to be gone, but because they knew how happy it made me to return to *The Wayward Aymelina*.

None were more delighted than Tyrnan, whom I suspected was a little jealous of being left behind.

"You could always sneak out and become a stowaway?" I said.

"That's more something *you* would do." He grinned. "Besides, my adventuring days are over. For now." Tyrnan's illness was behind him now, but he was still recovering his strength after being bedridden for so long. I hoped when his health was fully restored, he would resume his studies and return to the sea.

I was happy not to leave my family by stealth in the dark. This time, I was able to wave as I descended the mountain without worrying that they would be searching for me. I left them behind without the uncertainty of my absence, but with the knowledge that I was journeying toward destiny. For I knew beyond a doubt that mine could not be found in Praed.

PART II

CHAPTER 34

Nettle's hooves thundered over the rocky terrain at the base of the Gris Hills as we crested the ridge overlooking the purple fields above Faqur. The journey took much longer than anticipated due to an unnatural snowstorm at the closing of the Praed winter months, rendering the roads slick and wet until I left the western outskirts of the country. I'd lost precious days of travel time, and when the terrain finally became favorable, I kicked Nettle into the gallop she'd been longing for. My escort struggled to keep up with her swift pace, but they lagged, and I didn't bother to wait for them to catch up until we turned onto the road leading into the city.

I slowed Nettle to an easy trot so she could catch her breath, and she danced and threw froth from her lips as we passed the simple dwellings of fishermen. My heart swelled to see them again, and I inhaled the scent of the sea and drying fish I'd once loathed.

A guard brought his horse alongside me. "Your Highness, I thought we'd lost you."

"Perhaps you did. But now I'm found." I smiled. "Don't follow too closely. I don't want anyone to think I believe myself in danger here."

He nodded and signaled the other men to drop back several paces.

After being gone almost three months I rode into town with four knights of Praed trailing after me. Once again I was dressed in men's clothing with my short hair pulled back in a simple queue. A few people glanced our way, but no eyes lingered as we passed. These were busy people who had no time to gawk at strangers. The sound of creaking ships grew louder as we rode closer to the docks, and Nettle's ears flicked nervously when her hooves echoed on the wooden planks. I'd planned the journey to Faqur meticulously, but with the unexpected delays, I only hoped I wasn't too late.

I dismounted and untied my saddle bags containing my commission papers, changes of clothes, journals, and proper hygiene tools. Now that I wasn't pretending to be a boy, I certainly didn't want to smell like one. A guard asked if I might rest and take some refreshment before boarding the ship. I declined.

"They'll see to my needs once I'm aboard," I assured him. "Here." I placed some coins in his hand. "Take care of my horse and have yourselves something to eat. Thank you." I took Nettle's face in my hands and nuzzled her soft nose. Her ears pricked forward, and she blew softly against my face.

"I'm sorry I keep having to leave you," I said. "I will miss you." I rubbed circles on her forehead and took one last look into her deep brown eyes before turning away. She whinnied after me, but instead of a piercing sadness in my chest, I felt only affection for the horse that had carried me miles and miles over the course of several years. I was incredibly lucky, indeed.

I walked past the monolithic ships without awing over their majesty. I strode down the dock with purpose, my eyes on one ship only. I nearly wept with joy when I saw the gold lettering against a black stern bearing her name, and this time, when I stepped onto the gangplank, I didn't hesitate to walk onto *The Wayward Aymelina*. Men bustled around me preparing to set sail, and I realized how close I'd come to missing her. I watched them while they worked without noticing me, my eyes trailing along the deck and skywards up the masts as men checked the rigging and the sails. I recognized many of the faces and saw some new ones, but I didn't see the captain. My heart thudded at the thought, and I chastised myself for acting so foolishly. This was going to be a long voyage indeed if I didn't keep my wits—or my heart—in check.

"Orders!" I turned at the sound of the familiar voice, and despite his characteristically sour grimace, I smiled at First Mate Evrard.

"Good morning, sir," I said. I produced my commission papers. He eyed them suspiciously, and my smile grew.

"Cutting it close this morning, are we…?" He seemed at a loss as to how to address me.

"Miss Elejick. But I prefer Sulwen."

He almost smiled, I swear he did, before returning his attention to the papers.

"This is my family's own seal," he said.

"Is it?"

"I don't suppose I can reasonably deny you passage with such a seal." He handed the papers back. "Or question their validity."

"I don't suppose you can."

"Seaman Calux will see you to your quarters," he said with a dismissive wave.

"What happened to Seaman Erec?"

"Accepted another post on dry land. Needed a break from the sea. I can't imagine why."

"Neither can I," I said with a wry grin. I turned toward this new sailor standing casually a few feet away. He had dark wavy hair, brown eyes, and a distasteful looking mustache tarnishing his upper lip. Really, if you're going to grow facial hair, why do it halfheartedly?

"Your Highness*h*," he said with a bow. When he spoke, there was a quirk when pronouncing his 's' sounds, like his tongue became stuck to his bottom jaw.

"I prefer Sulwen," I told him.

He nodded and gestured for me to precede him. But I was not two steps away when I was swarmed by several crewmembers. A momentary trill of fear radiated through me, and I clutched tighter to my saddle bags, my hand itching to reach for the sword sheathed at my side. But their faces were smiling, not menacing, and I recognized one man in particular as he stepped toward me.

"Well met, lad...er...lass," Telken beamed. "Can't say I've ever been more shocked over a piece of news as when I heard you were a girl. Felt a little embarrassed, too. Sorry if I said or did anything to upset your sensibilities."

"There's no need for that," I said.

He smiled wider and patted me on the shoulder. "I don't suppose it would be entirely proper to hug ya."

"No, it probably wouldn't." I hugged him anyway.

"We promised we'd be polite," Luc added as he stepped forward.

"That's a shame," I said. I became reacquainted with my friends and was introduced to the newcomers, many of which averted their eyes when I looked at them. I stifled a laugh, expecting they had a stern lecture with a healthy dose of threats to leave me alone prior to my arrival.

Behind me, I heard First Mate Evrard's annoyed sigh as a sailor scrambled for his papers, and I observed the poor boy's anxious expression.

The first mate wrenched the papers from the boy's shaking hand, studied them longer than necessary, eyed the young man, then stuffed the papers back into his hand. The boy looked lost after that, and I stepped forward with an encouraging smile, remembering my first moments on the ship.

"Are you new?" I asked the young sailor sympathetically.

"Yes, sir…er…miss?" he asked in confusion as he took in my obvious femininity.

"Don't stress yourself." I brought him into my fold of friends. "We'll take care of you." I left the sailor to Telken and finally allowed Seaman Calux to lead me down into the ship.

"You will have complete privacy," Calux assured me as I followed him into the forecastle. He led me to a door and opened it onto a small yet comfortable room with a built-in dresser, bed, vanity, and privy. A smile played at my lips as he described the amenities, and I lay my saddle bags on the bed and started unloading when he pointed out the lock on the door 'for my safety.' I raised an eyebrow at this, believing that I was perfectly safe among my friends, though appreciating the courtesy.

"Did you not bring your maid with you?" he asked.

"Why would I?" He seemed so confused by my question it was comical.

"I don't know if we have someone who can attend to you," he said.

"That won't be necessary. I can take care of myself." I was starting to get annoyed and took no pains to hide it.

"Forgive me, Your—"

"Let us have a right understanding, Seaman Calux." I strode toward him, my hand resting nonchalantly on the hilt of my sword. "When I am on this ship, I am no longer a princess. You will address me as *Sulwen*, and you will afford me the same respect as any sailor on this ship without an excess of idolatry. Do I make myself clear?"

"Yes, madam." I raised an eyebrow, and he hastily added, "*Sulwen*."

"Good." I tapped the hilt of my sword with my fingers. "Are you the new translator?"

"I am."

"The last one was very good." I thought back fondly of Erec. "I hope you measure up to his standards."

"As do I." He smiled, rendering his appearance a little less repulsive— if I didn't stare at the mustache—and informed me that the crew were expected on deck in five minutes. My hands shook when he left, but I tamped down the anxiety and reminded myself that I'd fought pirates. Nothing could be more challenging than that. Except maybe living among a crew of fifty men as the only woman.

I ascended the stairs onto the main deck and wove my way through the assembled crewmen to stand before the quarterdeck. Above me was a new bosun I didn't recognize, and standing beside him was Second Mate Absalon, who smiled warmly when he caught my eye. First Mate Evrard wore his characteristic scowl while surveying the crew. When I thought I couldn't bear the anticipation any longer, he announced the captain. My heart pounded in my ears, and I held my breath when he came forward to inspect the crew. He was as immaculately dressed as always, with an authoritative air that silenced the dwindling conversations. He scanned the faces more thoroughly than I remember him doing last time. At length his eyes fell on me, and I couldn't stop the smile from spreading across my face. His shoulders subtly relaxed, and there was a softness to his eyes before he turned away.

"Gentlemen. And lady," Captain Romy said with a quick nod at me. He paused to allow for the uproar of hurrahs and pats on the back directed toward me to subside, and I flushed with the outpouring of attention. The revelry faded when the captain's features hardened. A few men still gave my shoulders a companionable shake. He focused his ire on me, and I gave him a sheepish grin and mouthed, *Sorry.*

"The Faqur Assembly has graciously requested we chart the island northwest of here to ascertain its habitability. This expedition will possibly establish a new territory, a new home for many people. Let's not disappoint them. As always, I appreciate your service and your loyalty." There was an answering murmur as the captain turned toward the first mate and said the words I'd been longing to hear. "Stand by to set sail."

First Mate Evrard barely gave the order for us to lay aloft and loose sail when I hastened across the deck toward the main mast and climbed up the ratlines toward the sails. I moved with purpose, my muscles remembering the details of the work that were hazy in my mind. When the sail finally unfurled, I could have fallen onto the deck and still would be smiling. I turned my face into the wind as we left port, closing my eyes as the salty air blew heavily over my face. It was a cold wind, colder than before, but I ignored the chill and allowed my cheeks to become pink and chapped until

I felt a hand on my shoulder. I opened my eyes and beheld a gap-toothed smile I'd missed dearly.

"Best get going, lad," Hrod said. "There's still work to be done."

I began climbing down, absently noting that he had called me 'lad.' Surely, he knew the truth? I spotted a small boat being towed behind us, a craft that required only perhaps a handful of people to sail. "What's that?"

"For sending word of our success. Or failure, as it may happen," he said.

"Did you enjoy your shore leave?" I asked as we made our descent.

"Nothin' like a home cooked meal," he called back. "And a bed that doesn't move."

I laughed.

"You?" he asked.

"I enjoyed seeing my family. I don't suppose you heard the truth about me." We dropped from the ratlines to the deck.

"Oh, everybody knows about that, lad."

"But…" I hesitated, confused. "You keep calling me *lad*."

"So? I did before. What of it?"

I blinked in disbelief. "Did…Did you know?"

"Nah. Well, not for sure. Thought you was odd for a boy."

We worked along the deck side by side, him chattering on about what he'd been up to in the last three months and me in stunned silence. In his aged wisdom Hrod had suspected me all along and not only kept it to himself but didn't seem upset and treated me exactly the same. I was simply a member of the crew in his eyes. Boy or girl, it didn't matter.

Hrod and I along with our other friends leaned against the railing when the ship was underway. He turned to me with a crooked grin. "So," he began. "You didn't get bundled off to a husband, eh?"

I flushed red as the men chuckled, but they quickly stifled their merriment when I shot them a dark glare.

"No," I said. "I'm blissfully unattached. And you shouldn't be asking me about such things. A married man like you? What would your wife say?"

The men burst out laughing while Hrod tapped some herbs in his pipe and shook his head, bemused.

"Did we ruin all your prospects then?" Telken asked. There was a touch of serious worry in his otherwise amused face. It warmed my heart he was genuinely concerned about my reputation.

"Absolutely," I said. "And I cannot thank you enough."

They laughed. Telken's eye still held an uneasy look.

"To be perfectly honest," I went on. "How can I ever enter into a mediocre engagement when I have to compare them to such fine examples of manhood?"

"Aye." Telken nodded. "I can see how that would be a problem. Poor, lass. We've made a terrible mistake in being the very standard of manliness. Sulwen will never be satisfied with another."

"There's nothing for it but for her to stay on the ship forever," Luc added. The men nodded agreement, and I leaned over the railing and watched the blue-green water lap the hull and spill over into white-capped waves as we cut through at a brisk pace.

"Luc, I think you're right," I said with a contented smile.

I stood at that same railing at the close of day, staring up at the stars in the clear night sky and marveling at the beautiful sight of the sea as the tiny lights reflected off the rippling surface. Footsteps approached sounding a cadence I recognized as well as Father's. I bit the inside of my lip to keep from grinning like an idiot, but I couldn't stop the blush from rising in my cheeks. Thank goodness for the cover of darkness.

"I didn't think you'd come," Captain Romy said. He stood beside me and looked out over the water.

"Honestly, I wasn't sure that I would either."

"What made you change your mind?"

"Father."

"How so?" He couldn't hide his astonishment. Hopefully, my gaze didn't betray the rapid beating of my heart.

"There's this saying my family has always held," I explained. "Ask yourself an honest question, and what immediately follows is the truth. In this case, it was Father who asked the question, but it still holds true."

"What did he ask?"

I hesitated, seeing his eyes focused and his manner relaxed. I'd rarely seen him not rigidly at attention or on constant alert. He leaned nonchalantly against the railing, hand resting on the hilt of his sword, the first few buttons of his coat undone, his hat gone.

"He asked if I wanted to go back to *The Wayward Aymelina*. And I said *yes*."

"Simple as that?"

"Simple as that. Well…" I shrugged. "After first dealing with my horrible temper for a month and a half. I think he was tired of watching me try to be something I'm not."

"And what was that?"

"A princess." I returned my attention to the sea.

"You didn't get swept up in any advantageous marriage proposals then?"

I looked at him sharply. Had he overheard my conversation with the crew? Though his features were indifferent, there was a glimmer of something strange in his eyes…decidedly not amusement. He seemed intent on my answer. I was intrigued yet a little perturbed. My fists shot to my hips. "Do you eavesdrop on *all* my conversations?"

"No," he said, raising his palms in defense. "I just know everything that happens on my ship."

I arched an eyebrow and looked away. "Not quite everything."

"Well…I've endeavored to be more vigilant." He gave a curt bow. "Goodnight, Miss Elejick."

"*Sulwen*," I corrected. "And you don't have to bow."

He paused, visibly uncomfortable at the idea of addressing me informally. He couldn't before, and certainly not now. "Goodnight, *Miss Elejick*." He turned away without bowing.

I shrugged. Small steps.

CHAPTER 35

Over the next few days at sea, I reestablished a routine of rising early, helping on deck, and becoming reacquainted with friends. I interspersed these practices with the consumption of those meager and bland meals I'd surprisingly missed. Luc asked if I might train him to improve his swordsmanship, and I almost declined since it brought painful memories of my previous student, Rex. Ultimately, I agreed, if for no other reason but to keep my own skills honed. He proved to be a decent student, and soon word spread that I offered swordsmanship training and several others requested I teach them as well.

"It's a strange thing," Seaman Calux said after observing me for several hours.

"What's strange?" I wiped an arm across my damp brow.

"I've never known a woman to wield a sword, much less so skillfully."

"Want to experience it up close?" I raised my blade, the light reflecting off the steel and making him blink.

He raised his hands. "I don't mean offense. Do all princesses of Praed practice combat?"

"No." I resumed the lesson with Luc and ignored the seaman, who continued to watch.

At the evening meal that night, Seaman Calux sought me out and shoved his way beside me. "I really do hope I didn't upset you."

"No. I gave you no more thought after that." I ate a spoonful of fish stew.

"I've never been to Praed," he continued, undeterred. "Is your castle really on top of a mountain?"

All it took to dispel my irritation was for someone to ask me questions about home. I even smiled at him a little when I answered, "A white mountain."

"What's it like there?"

"That's a very long answer, Seaman Calux."

"I have time." He smiled, and I resisted giggling at the way his mustache twisted up like a dying caterpillar. The talk around me grew quiet, and I looked at the men sitting closest to us and saw that they were waiting, too.

"Praed is covered in vast prairie," I began in undisguised reverence. "At times the grass is yellowed and brittle, but in the spring, it's light green and dotted with wildflowers of purple, pink, and white. Hills roll like waves, but the only mountain is the stark white beacon that rises above the marketplace. Atop the mountain is Praed Castle, built from stone quarried from the Kreeg Mountains and the depths of the Rhyvor, the mighty river that flows from the mountain toward the east. Along the banks of this river stands Riverstone, the birthplace of Queen Laria, my mother." A quick glance at the men's faces confirmed I had their rapt attention. They even set down their bowls while listening.

"I was born in the castle," I continued. "Perhaps not the largest structure ever built, but it is the strongest, fortified by the heavy stone and cornered by turrets. When you ascend the mountain, you encounter the stone steps leading to the heavy wooden door, and beyond it you enter a foyer pillared in sculpted river rock polished to shining perfection. The Grand Hall has seen gatherings of the finest dignitaries, including ambassadors from Hrgun, Kuste, Faqur, and even Berg. Praed Castle is where the Great War Council was held many years ago, when the countries united to defeat Crif." The men nodded, many of them remembering that horrible war, some perhaps even serving in it. I moved on to a more pleasant subject. "We have one of the most well stocked libraries you'll ever find. The queen herself personally oversaw its restoration and arrangement.

Our stables are very large—horses hold an important place in Praed society. Aside from working as transport and in farming, horses carry us into battle, feed us with their milk, clothe us with their hide, and are our trusted friends. My father comes from Ilano, and in his country, people rely on birds of prey in much the same way. His family is of the Black Eagle, the largest species of its family. A man will train for years to be able to bear one on his arm, and once he's chosen, he and his eagle will be companions until death." I smiled to myself, remembering how determined I was to have an eagle even though they were only for men. "They're housed in buildings we call *mews* near the stables."

"It sounds very exciting," Seaman Calux said, interrupting my reverie.

"It often is," I said. "My life there was busy."

"Do you have brothers or sisters?"

"Many." I smiled. "Two sisters and four brothers."

"That's a lot of mouths to feed," one man observed.

"Not much of a burden when you're a king, I'd wager," another said. My face fell in dismay. Now that everyone knew I was a princess, would they judge me because of my privileged upbringing? Seaman Calux seemed to sense my discomfort, for he cleared his throat to bring the attention back to himself.

"The king and queen must really love children to have so many," Seaman Calux said.

"Yes," I said. "I think they would have had the same number even if they were paupers."

"Luckily, they ain't," the same crewman said, his tone gruff. I really looked at him then, noting his disgruntled demeanor. I didn't know him from before, and he clearly resented my presence. If he was the only one who did so, I would count myself lucky. But I wouldn't allow him to speak about my parents in such a manner, nor would I allow his prejudice to influence his perception of me.

"No," I said. "They are not." The hardness of my voice threw him off guard, and now the attention was on him. "And I am perfectly aware of how lucky I am to have grown up with the security that my needs would always be met. My parents fought hard to give that to me, as any mother or father would, so do not make the mistake of believing that because they are now king and queen that they have not seen heartache, spilled blood, or scraped by. Money and privilege do not place one man above another, just as poverty does not automatically make a man beneath notice. It is our *opinions* that do that." I stared at him pointedly, and he had the decency to look away, somewhat mollified.

"Besides," I said in a lighter tone. "Nothing equalizes men more than being fathers to teenage daughters."

A general wave of laughter spread through the group, with one man shouting that teenage girls were a sign of the gods' displeasure with mankind. This made the men laugh even harder, and the tension around the table was erased. Everyone went back to eating, even the grumpy one, and I sighed in relief.

"Well said," Seaman Calux commented. "I agree with your viewpoint. A man or woman cannot be defined by their station. My father was a soldier before he became a lord. We must judge people by their actions."

"And how would you judge me?"

His face flushed a satisfying shade of red at the boldness of my question. I calmly ate a few more bites of food while he composed himself enough to answer.

"I'll admit I was...skeptical...about the captain's decision to allow you to come back to *The Wayward Aymelina*. It didn't seem wise to allow a woman on board a ship alone with so many men—both for her safety and the men's sanity."

I shot him a dirty glare, more in response to his casting aspersions on the captain than for his concern for my welfare.

"However," he continued, "having seen how well you conduct yourself with a sword, I can see why the captain had no fear for your safety. And you seem to know your way around the ship competently enough."

"Thanks," I mumbled around a mouthful of food.

"I would judge you're a capable sailor, Sulwen."

I looked up at him expectantly when he didn't elaborate further, but he simply stared back with an amicable smile.

"Is that it?" I asked.

"For now," Calux said. He held my gaze and rose to leave me to my meal.

What an odd fellow.

The tails of the extra coat I wore to combat the cold billowed in the breeze while I stood at the railing watching the black shores of the island come into view. A smile fluttered over my lips, and my breathing quickened. Seeing the island again felt like coming home to a dear friend.

"Did you miss it?" a voice asked.

"Yes." The word emerged on a husky breath before I realized the voice came from Captain Romy. I blinked up at him, my cheeks aflame. At first, he appeared stoic as always, but he stood frozen, like a rabbit when it senses danger. So motionless he didn't even breathe.

"What's wrong?" I asked.

He blinked as if my words woke him up and snapped him back into reality.

"Nothing." He looked toward the shore, and my gaze traveled to his hands gripping the side of the ship. His knuckles were white.

"Are you sure?" I asked.

"Yes." His short tone warned me not to ask anything further.

"Will we anchor offshore at the same place?" I asked.

"No." His voice was devoid of the strangely hostile undertone it had previously. "We're going to sail around and see if we can find an inlet."

"How long will that take?"

His eyes were soft when he looked at me, the corner of his mouth curved up slightly.

"Impatient, are we?"

"Do you think it's obvious to anyone else?"

"Only to everyone."

"I'm all right with that." I stuck my nose in the air and turned back to watch the black shore as we sailed along. The large creatures that basked in the sun the last time were very active, calling out to each other and bearing their pointed teeth. I watched two particularly large brutes rise into the air in a delightful imitation of a ground squirrel then smash into each other repeatedly.

"I wonder what they're fighting over?" I mused.

"Territory maybe," Captain Romy said.

I glanced around the beach. "No. They're all crowded in on each other. They don't appear to have designated places."

"Food?"

"They eat fish. Land isn't exactly prime fishing ground." I deliberately avoided the glare he was probably giving me.

We watched in silence while I contemplated their odd behavior when there was a strange sound coming from my right. Was it...no. Could it be? It was! Captain Romy was laughing. Not in the way normal people did. He wasn't throwing back his head and clutching at his sides. He was barely even making a sound. But a quick assessment confirmed that he was smiling and making a merry sound at the same time, the very definition of laughter.

I couldn't hide my shock. "What's so funny?"

"What else can you think of besides territory or food that an animal might fight for?"

My brow furrowed and I looked closer. "I don't know. What?"

"The same thing a man will fight for."

I rolled my eyes. "Animals don't have money."

"Try again."

"No idea." I was getting annoyed. "Tell me."

Our eyes met, his brimming with amusement while I'm sure mine reflected my exasperation.

"A woman."

My eyes widened and I looked back to the beach. Sure enough, the fighting between the two brutes produced a victor that was currently wooing a smaller sized female.

"Huh. Typical, I guess. Have you ever fought for a woman?" I regretted the words the moment they left my mouth. Not only was it incredibly presumptuous, but I also wasn't sure I wanted to hear the answer. My cheeks burned, my nails digging into the railing.

"Once," he said.

I hadn't expected a response, and the surprise addled my brain. It was the only way to explain why I asked, "How did it turn out?" I risked looking at him. He held my gaze for several seconds of deliberate silence.

"I've yet to decide if it was worth all the sarcasm."

Now, I had two choices at this point: to die in utter embarrassment or find some humor in the situation. In the end, my own nature won out. I nearly toppled over the side of the railing laughing.

First Mate Evrard came up beside me and glared. "You are much too prone to childishness."

I collected myself as best I could, but every time I looked toward the shore, I had to smother a grin. I tried looking at the captain, certain that with his first mate here he would be as stolid as ever. Though he stood with calm poise, humor still sparkled in his eyes. He hid his face when I burst into giggles again.

"I'm sorry, sir," I managed to say to the increasingly irritated first mate. "I shall leave you two alone."

"Actually," First Mate Evrard began. "I was coming to speak to you." He looked over my shoulder at the captain and asked, "Did you mention anything to her?"

"No," Captain Romy said. All traces of the humor we shared vanished. "I thought I would leave that to you."

My panic rose steadily. "Leave what to him?"

"Reinstating your position as a scout and commissioned guard," the first mate grumbled. Though he was tasked with giving me this news, he clearly wasn't very happy about it.

"Truly?" I asked Captain Romy.

He inclined his head. "If you wish."

I considered the generous offer, then turned to First Mate Evrard where he stood glowering.

"Sir, you once said that you considered me invaluable, and I impressed you with my abilities."

His eyes widened and a pink hue colored his cheeks. He obviously didn't think the chief prosecutor would read his testimony aloud and never intended for me to know his honest opinion.

"I know you said those things believing you would never see me again, so I understand if you don't want me here. But I'm not going anywhere. I don't wish to be a nuisance to you, either. If you want me to return to my duties as a scout and resume our training, I'll accept. If you don't, then I'll understand and respectfully decline."

His eyes darted behind me to the captain, but I remained focused on the first mate. I don't know what silent exchange occurred between them, but the first mate returned his attention to me with little improvement of his mood.

"I will do what my captain orders," he said.

"I know you will," I replied. "I'm not asking you to defy his orders. I'm asking for your opinion."

"And you are entirely too free with yours." The first mate's face reddened, and a vein throbbed at his temple. "Now I know why. You can't speak to everyone as if they're subject to your rule. You're not a princess here, Miss Elejick. *I* outrank *you*."

My face burned, and I clenched my fists hard, hoping the pain of my nails driving into my palms would calm my temper. The captain shifted behind me, but he didn't speak.

"I am aware of that, *sir*. I make no claims to the contrary. Yes, I am opinionated and tend to speak my mind, but these are qualities in many people, not just princesses, if I'm not mistaken. I never meant to cause you offense, but it seems clear that I have, and though I'm grateful for what you wrote to the chief prosecutor, I can see now you meant none of it. I therefore respectfully decline the offer to resume my duties in your service." I saluted him with deliberate care, then cast a salute in the captain's general direction before excusing myself from the deck.

CHAPTER 36

I didn't speak to any of the Romy brothers for two days, neither the captain nor the first mate. I had taken to perching myself on the bowsprit whenever my work was finished to watch for signs of an inlet. I avoided the captain, because I was embarrassed, and the first mate because I currently despised him.

I lay on my belly with my head resting on my arms and watched the rocky shores. We sailed past where the river emptied into the sea, the crystal blue water mingling with the green depths to create a beautiful mixture of color and current. The familiar black and white birds with orange beaks nested among the sides of the cliffs that rose higher and higher as we traveled. I feared the entire island was a fortress we couldn't penetrate.

"I beg your pardon!"

The sudden exclamation startled me, and I clung onto the bowsprit to keep from falling. I glared over my shoulder as the 'beg pardons' became 'beg your forgiveness,' and Second Mate Absalon scrambled down the front of the forecastle to join me.

"I didn't mean to frighten you," he said breathlessly. He slid onto the bowsprit and shuffled closer.

"No harm done." I shifted into a sitting position. I bore no ill will toward the second mate, but I still preferred solitude over his company. I resumed staring at the coast, deciding that if the second mate had something to say, he could say it and have done with it. I wouldn't be cruel, but I wouldn't initiate a conversation, either.

"I hope you've settled in well and that the crew are being respectful," he said amiably.

"Yes, thank you."

"I haven't had a chance to tell you, but I'm glad everything turned out well and that you're back here. I don't think it would have been the same without you."

I smiled, full and genuine. I could always count on him to be completely kind.

"Thank you, sir. I'm happy to be here."

"Are you? It's just you've been hiding out here an awful lot the last few days."

I pursed my lips. "I'm not hiding."

"My apologies. I just want you to know that if you need a friendly ear, I am always at your disposal."

"Thank you, sir. You have always been very kind. And I appreciate what you wrote to the chief prosecutor."

"You're very welcome." He smiled, an open, friendly smile, and I almost confessed everything that I had been feeling the last few days. But how could I tell him that the object of my distress was his own brother?

As if reading my thoughts, his features grew remorseful, and he couldn't look me in the eye. He glanced over his shoulder to see if anyone was in earshot, then turned back to me.

"Miss Elejick, I heard what Evrard said to you and am mortified. He's impulsive at times and may say things he doesn't mean."

"It felt…meaningful." I shifted my gaze so he couldn't see my flushed face.

"He's regretted his words since, I can assure you."

"Then why doesn't he say so himself?"

"Pride can be a powerful thing. Regardless, I hope you do not allow his stupidity to ruin your time here."

"I can excuse stupidity, even rash actions, but I fear he truly feels that I think myself above everyone. I can assure you I don't."

"I can see that," he said, his eyes wide and pleading. "And I'm sure he does, too. He's just hanging on to resentment, and I regret he took it out on you."

I smiled wryly. "He's lucky to have such a passionate advocate."

He shrugged. "He's my brother. Surely you understand."

"Very well, sir."

"Anyway, don't take everything Evrard said to heart. He really did mean what he said to the chief prosecutor, even if he's too stubborn to admit it."

"I'll take that under consideration, sir." He rose to leave when a thought struck me.

"Sir," I called out. He turned with a questioning brow, and I asked, "Did the captain ask you to speak with me?"

"No." He raised his hands as if to halt further questions. "And don't tell either of them that I did. They'll call me meddlesome."

I released an inadvertent sharp laugh as he climbed back onto the ship. I looked back toward the shore. The black cliffs seemed endless, and I feared we would never find a spot to drop anchor. I needed space, lots of it, and to fill those empty pages in my journals. I lay back down on the bowsprit and closed my eyes as droplets of saltwater sprayed over my face. The journey had been cold, but now the wind blew warmer. I hoped it was a good sign, and that with the change of temperature came a change in the climate, both on and off the ship.

The scenery on the island eventually changed from sheer cliff to a sloping land mass covered in trees reminiscent of the ones we'd seen on the island of the Nakwacimek. The ship veered around a point of land leading into a bay, and my breath quickened in excitement as I studied the forest that gave way to lush grassland. Could this be the landing point we'd been waiting for?

"See anything of note?" My jaw clenched. First Mate Evrard walked up beside me and spoke casually, as if he hadn't broken me down emotionally only a few days prior.

"No, nothing," I said.

The first mate sighed beside me, and if I didn't know any better, I'd think he sounded defeated.

"Miss Elejick," he said. "I must apologize for my behavior the other day."

"*Must?*"

"I'm not under orders if that's what you were implying. Though Lencius was not pleased." This was said more as an aside than to me.

I reined in my temper and faced him. "Sir, I don't want to be at odds with you despite our differences. You don't have to like me, but I want you to know that I honestly respect the rules of this ship, and I don't want to be treated any differently than the rest of the crew."

"I know," he said. "If you did, you would have brought a royal entourage."

"And a cook. Have you sampled the offerings on this ship? Disgraceful." I gave my hair a haughty toss, and though he didn't laugh, he relaxed incrementally.

"Will you join me when we row out to the island to verify it's safe for our landing party?"

I considered making him say *please* or forcing him to take back everything he'd said or issuing some other ultimatum. But I wasn't a monster, however much I wanted to act like one now. Despite his deplorable behavior, I didn't hate the first mate. If I did, I wouldn't have been so hurt by his declaration.

"Is that what you want?"

"Yes." He rolled his eyes in exasperation.

This wasn't easy for him. I knew he was being honest. If the captain was forcing his hand, he would be angry, gritting his teeth and clenching his fists. He was more annoyed than angry.

"All right then." I peered at the shoreline searching for signs of danger.

The ship dropped anchor a short row from the beach. I would have forced my way onto the shore-bound dinghy even had there been a sword at my throat. I surveyed our immediate surroundings but saw nothing to give me alarm.

Trees rose into the sky from the precipice to our right, but the ground sloped into a valley that was interrupted with a streak of blue from a bubbling creek. The keel scraped bottom as we landed on the grassy bank, and I inhaled the sweet smell of fresh vegetation. I stepped out of the boat and walked a few feet forward, listening to the breeze rustling the grass and scanning the area for signs of life. There was nothing but green as far as I could see. Green grass, and in the distance green hills with scattered trees. Far beyond rose a triangular peak like a beacon, its surface carpeted as lushly as the valley.

"We should head in that direction." I pointed toward the mountain.

"Any particular reason?" the first mate asked.

"Where there's a mountain, there's water."

We walked across the valley, our footsteps silent on the thickly vegetated surface, even on the rocks. I bent down and ran my fingers over the ground.

It wasn't just grass, but a dense moss covering the earth, making it soft and spongy. A rabbit darted across our path, and out of the corner of my eye, a creature with silver fur disappeared into a burrow. I smiled, a refreshing breeze lifting my hair and chilling my cheeks.

Squinting in the bright sun, First Mate Evrard eyed the distant mountain. "Thoughts?" he said.

"I think we should start moving toward the interior immediately," I said. The first mate agreed, and we hurried back to the ship. I looked back over my shoulder in time to see a furry face with rounded ears and yellow eyes watching us before ducking into a dark hole. *Petiloos*, I thought with a smile, the creatures I observed for so many hours the last time we were here. What more discoveries were waiting to be made?

Under the guidance of the second mate and the studious cartographers we made our way into the interior. A great din of excitement and activity accompanied our passage. No stone went unnoticed, no bush unsampled. This was more than just an expedition meant to further our knowledge of the world. I did my own investigating, leaving camp on my own for several hours to document the wildlife. There was no shortage of birds and rabbits, but the petiloos were elusive in this part of the island. There was evidence of their presence in the form of scat and remnants of kills, so I was determined not to lose heart. My old friends respected my solitude when I wandered off on these missions, but Seaman Calux tried to follow on many occasions.

"I prefer to be alone," I told him.

"What if you should encounter a predator?"

I repressed a smile. "I can take care of myself." Was he being overprotective to gain my favor? Having a princess for a friend could certainly open doors for the second son of a lord.

"Might I join you out of curiosity then?"

"No." I walked away briskly. Whatever his motives, I wasn't interested in indulging Seaman Calux. He was nice enough, but the man never stopped talking.

Luc and I grew closer during our sparring matches, and I was happy to note how much improvement he was making. As we moved further away from the sea the temperature was warmer, though there was still a biting wind preventing me from calling the weather favorable. Nevertheless, our lessons left us wet with perspiration, and we would hunker against the cool stone to catch our breaths and drink from our water flasks.

"You're doing well," I told him. "Your movements are still somewhat predictable, though. You have to keep your body steady until you're ready to follow through with your attacks, otherwise I can see them coming. But you're striking with more confidence and deflecting with more accuracy."

"Well, I have a good teacher." He grinned and we toasted our water flasks.

"Out of curiosity." I wiped a dribble of water from my chin. "Why did you decide to join this expedition?"

"Same reason as last time. The captain wants to map new places, and I go where he goes. I wouldn't want to sail under anyone else."

I shifted uneasily at the mention of the captain. I still hadn't spoken to him out of embarrassment from nearly breaking down in front of him. How could he see me as he always had, as just another sailor, if I responded so emotionally, like a woman?

"What do you think of this place?" I said.

"It's nice." He gave a noncommittal shrug. "Very green."

I laughed. "Think you'd like to live here?"

He considered my question for a long time while he scanned the expanse of lush valley, craggy moss-covered stone, and meandering creeks. He squinted as his face turned up to the glacial blue sky bright with sunshine, then he looked over his shoulder at the triangular mountain in the distance.

"There's a lot of space for a man to build a house," he said. "Land to farm, water to drink, and no shortage of food. But it's not home."

"You could make it home."

"I already have one of those. Don't want to uproot it. But for someone setting out on their own or wanting a change, I don't think they could want for a better place to start fresh."

"No." I drifted my hand over the grass, the blades tickling my palm. A family of rabbits tentatively wandered into view, nibbling on the tender shoots. "I think a person could search their entire lives and never find a more perfect spot."

CHAPTER 37

I lay against the soft earth so quietly I barely breathed, taking care to blink only when necessary. After days of waiting and searching, I finally encountered the petiloos. Or rather, they deemed me non-threatening enough not to run away the instant I came into view.

A large, thick-coated silver and white one I guessed was a male, walked carefully over the ground, stopping occasionally to listen, his head tilting this way and that, his round ears pointing to the ground. He arched upwards, his yellow eyes intent, then he leapt into the air with his paws toward the ground. He buried his nose in the soil and came up with a mouse. He ate several rodents in this manner, then he would take the last one and dart into the rocks. I tried to follow, but he was too fast.

It took a few more days until I caught him disappearing into a den, and another before a gray face poked out to receive the offered meal. I didn't see any young, but I figured it was too early in the year for that. When our camp moved too far for me to come back every day to observe them, I admittedly was a little petulant. I reminded myself that this was a different sort of expedition. We were here to plot out a map to determine if the island could support a population, which meant there was no time to indulge in my selfish pursuits.

Our party traveled for over a week when I left my tent early one morning and wandered into the dense line of bushes blooming with yellow flowers to relieve myself in privacy. But when I pushed through the dense branches, I came out onto a patch of earth torn up in a swath of disrupted dirt and foliage. My eyes traced a path stretching for several miles, leading into rocky hills dotted with trees. I knelt and looked closer, running my fingers along the cloven tracks whose numbers were unfathomable.

"What made those?" Seaman Calux asked.

I nearly fell over at the sound of his distinct voice. I stood and whirled at him in a fury, angered that he'd been following me. "What are you doing here?" I snapped.

His face flushed and his eyes darted toward the bushes. "I-I…I was—"

"What?" I crossed my arms over my chest. His blush deepened, and my anger rose when I deduced that I'd caught him sneaking around.

"I needed to use the privy," he blurted out.

"Oh." I relaxed. "I won't disturb you then."

"So what did you find?"

"Tracks." I stooped to the ground. "Maybe from some kind of deer. Thousands of them."

"Looks like they lead into those hills." He nodded toward the trees.

"Yes."

"Should we tell the captain?"

"Are you hungry?"

"In general, or at this moment?" I turned to him with a grin, and he smiled that irritatingly pleased smile he wore when he teased me.

"Come on." I jerked my head toward camp. The men were stirring, and fires were being lit in preparation for cooking. I strode past them with Seaman Calux at my heel toward the officer's tent. I paused at the entrance, suddenly shy about bidding entry.

"What's wrong?" His voice softened and he asked, "Do you want me to go first? Make sure it's…safe?"

"No." I stepped forward and scratched at the tent flap and announced myself in case the men inside needed a moment to make themselves decent.

After a brief pause, the captain called out, "Enter." I stepped inside and noted all three brothers were present in various stages of dress. The second mate was hastily buttoning his shirt over his breeches. The first mate wore a coat, but it was hanging open. The captain was fully and impeccably dressed as always. He was looking at me expectantly, and I almost forgot why I was there in the first place.

"Sirs," Seaman Calux spoke up from beside me. "Sorry to disturb, but we've found something." The captain glanced at the seaman, and I cringed inwardly at his use of 'we.'

Captain Romy's gaze met mine. "Explain."

I swallowed at the hard look in his eyes. Was he angry with me? I stifled a groan. Great, I'd have to figure out what I did wrong this time and make amends all over again.

"A trail, sir," I said weakly. "I think it could be a herd of deer."

"Where?" the first mate demanded.

I gestured for them to follow and led the three officers to the torn-up earth venturing to the tree-covered hills.

"Sulwen thinks there could be thousands of them," Seaman Calux told the captain.

Our eyes met, and I nodded once in confirmation.

The captain turned to the second mate. "Absalon, gather the best archers into a hunting party while we take a closer look."

The second mate ran back to camp while the four of us followed the trail. We kept silent while we searched the surrounding landscape. I examined a pile of round scat and noted it wasn't recent, but it couldn't be more than a few hours old. I put a finger to my lips, and the men and I climbed the hill to get a better vantage point. I resisted the urge to push Seaman Calux off the side when he slipped and dislodged a rock, but his sheepish look spared him.

We made it to the top and crawled on our bellies through the undergrowth to peer into the trees. I couldn't help thinking that the captain's clothes would get dirty as he stretched out beside me and squinted in concentration. He'd stopped shaving again, leaving his face covered in about a half inch of dark blonde hair. I could still perceive the clench of his jaw as he intently scanned the area. A snapping twig startled me out of the inappropriately long scrutiny of his face. I thank Artur we weren't closer together because my arm flung out, and were I mere inches nearer, I would have accidentally grabbed his hand. Instead, my fingers dug into the rich soil as I looked in the direction of the noise. I sucked in a breath through my teeth at what I beheld.

Thousands of deer-like creatures roamed through the trees feeding on the moss growing on the rocks. But they were unlike the deer native to Praed. Those were tall, elegant, and reddish brown, bearing large racks with multiple points at the height of summer. The animals before me were decidedly smaller and had predominantly gray coats with brown backs and a shaggy white ruff. The antlers were still covered in the thick velvet that sheds at the end of spring, but they were obviously long with very few points. They moved silently on wide hooves that displaced their weight over the uneven ground, an ear flicking here and there as they grazed.

"I'll head back to camp and inform Absalon," First Mate Evrard whispered. He began slowly inching his way backward.

I turned to Seaman Calux, who grinned at me like an idiot. I rolled my eyes and returned my attention to the animals, annoyed that I would need his help to come up with a name for them.

After watching the creatures for a few minutes more, I had a strange sense that wasn't quite unpleasant, but it wasn't very agreeable either. I looked around but Seaman Calux was gone. My heart pounded when I realized I was alone. No, not entirely alone. I turned and saw that Captain Romy was staring at me. I tried to swallow, but my throat was inexplicably dry. I couldn't read his expression, increasing my unease.

"Well done, Miss Elejick," he said quietly.

I nearly wept in relief and the tension drained from my body. He motioned with his head for us to leave, and I followed him down the hill. He didn't hover over me as we descended nor hold out his hand to offer assistance. Though his actions may appear to be ungentlemanly, to me they showed that he believed me perfectly capable of handling myself. I dropped down the last few feet, landing on the soft earth beside him, and wiped my hands on my breeches. We walked back to camp in companionable silence and met the hunting party on their way to the trees. Not only would we be eating well from now on, we'd also be teaching a species how to fear a true predator. Man.

I dubbed the small deer "serarb" after consulting with Seaman Calux on the proper translation of 'tree-dwelling deer' in ancient Faqur. They were beginning to rub their antlers on the trees to rid them of the velvety coverings. In Praed, this behavior signaled the beginning of the breeding season. It would soon become dangerous for me to stalk around the stags when their brains were full of does.

The serarb hunts successfully filled our stores for the foreseeable future, a pleasant change from ship's rations and fish to red meat. We gorged ourselves on thick stews and sausages while strips were salted and dried to preserve them for later. The thick furs were prepped for tanning, and I imagined the ruffs would come in handy during winter. The long bones were wrapped and saved to harvest the marrow while the rest was discarded a good distance from camp. I watched these remains for the appearance of scavengers, and while I was preparing to leave on such a task Seaman Calux surprised me with an unexpected request.

"I wish to accompany you, if I may." He wore his pack slung over his shoulder. "I've come to see there is much I might learn from you."

I eyed him dubiously, but he was undeterred by my less than enthusiastic response.

"Please, Sulwen, would you let me come with you? I promise I'll stay out of your way and won't make a sound."

What could I say? I had no valid reason to refuse his company. Besides, his eagerness was pleasing, and I had no objection to sharing my discoveries. I offered a half-smile and nodded, and he grinned broadly in anticipation of our outing. Really, that mustache was too much, the way it stretched unnaturally across his face.

He followed me out of camp, and I reminded him of his promise to stay quiet. To his credit, he didn't say a word as we came to the pile of bones scattered in a clearing. I chose a spot downwind to watch and wait. He patiently sat beside me without so much as a bouncing leg or exasperated sigh while an hour went by with only a swarm of flies buzzing around the remains. I crouched lower in case our sitting position was too threatening, and he stretched out beside me. A bird swooped down, then another, a pair of eagles with brown bodies, black beaks, and white tails. They were smaller than the black eagles of Ilano, but no less magnificent. I hastily sketched out a picture, a pang of loss shooting through me at the remembrance of home, but I tamped down my emotions. The pair squabbled at the best portions before settling in to pick at the bones. While they fed, not another creature showed itself, but the moment they were gone, smaller black birds and white seabirds descended on the scraps.

"Do you think those birds were too afraid of the other ones to come and eat?" Seaman Calux whispered.

"An excellent observation," I said as I made notes. "I think you're right. The first two appeared to be some species of eagle. There's a chance they abandoned the bones in favor of a fresher meal."

"Are they anything like the eagles of your homeland?" he asked.

I paused momentarily, then resumed writing without meeting his eye.

"They're smaller," I said.

"Could you train one?"

"It's not that simple."

"Why not?"

I sighed and set down my pen. "Because the black eagles are raised in captivity around people their entire lives. They're not taken out of the wild and tamed. That's a more difficult process and might not yield favorable results."

"Why is that?"

"Would you be loyal to someone who took you from your home and forced you into a cage?" I gave him a hard stare. "Our eagles are used to their circumstances. These birds are used to coming and going whenever they please."

He considered my statement while I went back to writing in my journal.

"You are very passionate in your convictions."

I glanced up at him, but he wasn't awaiting a response, simply stating a fact, possibly just to himself, and didn't require my input. His attention was on the birds flapping around the bones, his manner relaxed.

He accompanied me on my outings every day after that, and I objected less and less to his presence, mainly because he kept quiet and didn't disturb the animals. He made some good observations and wasn't afraid to crawl in the dirt in search of burrows or nests. Telken jested we were spending a lot of time together with a suggestive wink, but I punched him so hard in the stomach he never said a word about it again. I made reports to First Mate Evrard if I found anything of note, but he was mainly interested in knowing about potentially dangerous animals, of which I had seen none, so our interactions were blissfully brief. The captain was very busy, and since I couldn't think of any excuses to speak to him, we rarely crossed paths. This pained me more than him. He looked upon me with the same passiveness he did the rest of the crew, of which I was equal parts grateful and devastated.

There was no sense denying that Captain Romy awoke something in my heart, and now I was tasked with putting it back to sleep. An alliance between us certainly had its benefits. He was from a good family, and we could form a bridge between Praed and Faqur. But we came from different worlds. Despite his current position of power over me, I was still a princess. We both had our duties, mine to a crown and his to the sea. He'd be gone all the time, and I didn't want to be left behind.

I spent more and more time away from camp as we ventured closer to the triangular peak, which meant my predominant companion was Seaman Calux. He was a decent man, I granted, despite the unruly mustache. He strode beside me asking questions about what I did in Praed while I made a few notes in my journal after observing a warren of rabbits.

"Did you study the animals there as well?" he asked.

"Some. I read a lot. And I helped with the hatchlings."

"Have you considered studying in Hrgun?"

I paused, my pen hovering over the page. "Once or twice. I…" I shrugged one shoulder. "I thought about publishing a book."

"What stopped you?"

"Everything I would have written about has already been done." I smiled. "Until now."

"What did you do for fun?"

"Rode horses, practiced sword fighting with my brothers and father, visited the countryside, avoided playing the piano…" I trailed off as I finished one of my drawings. I answered his questions distractedly, not really paying attention, until he crossed the line from interested bystander to an invader into my privacy.

"Did you…" He cleared his throat before continuing, "have any suitors?"

I slammed the book shut with an echoing *THWACK* and spun around.

"No," I said darkly, holding his gaze so he felt my full meaning.

"I don't mean to pry."

"Yes, you did." I stalked away from him.

"I meant no offense!"

"Let me make myself rightfully understood, Seaman Calux." I prepared to launch into an impassioned speech about not desiring a husband and not to presume I did just because I was a woman, when I stopped abruptly in my tracks. Seaman Calux collided with me but grabbed my shoulders before I fell forward. I was too entranced to voice indignance over his clumsiness or to protest the fact that he was still clutching onto me. I stepped forward and knelt beside the body of a petiloos, resting a hand on the soft, gray fur. It was still warm. I ran my hand down the chest but felt no heartbeat.

"What do you think happened to it?" Seaman Calux asked.

"I don't know." I inspected the body but saw no obvious wounds. There was blood running from its nose and the whites of its eyes were red. Seaman Calux hissed through his teeth when I opened the creature's mouth.

"Well?" he asked, and if I wasn't mistaken, he sounded as if he was going to be sick.

"The jaw is broken," I said. "I don't think it starved to death, though. It looks in good form. It must have died from whatever caused the injury." I ran a hand along its back reverently, feeling for any other clues. When my hand settled on its abdomen, I froze.

"No," I breathed. I turned the body onto its back and felt the unmistakable swellings along its stomach.

"What's wrong?"

"It's a female and she was lactating." I stood and scanned the area in the immediate vicinity.

"What does that mean?" The tone of his voice rose with concern.

I whirled on him. "What do you think it means, you idiot?"

His eyes widened in shock, and he drew up short, obviously because he'd been following too closely again.

"She was nursing pups!"

CHAPTER 38

Seaman Calux helped me search for the den for the rest of the afternoon. It didn't take much persuasion for him to help me, much to my chagrin. I was suddenly very wary and suspicious of his intentions, though to be fair he was always respectful. The sun was sinking low on the horizon when I finally admitted defeat and turned back toward camp. To his credit, Seaman Calux made no comment about how long we'd been gone, even though we missed the afternoon meal.

"Do you think the father will take care of them?" he asked gently as tents came into view.

"No. He would have no way to feed them." I refrained from going into more graphic detail.

"I'm sorry." He lay a comforting hand on my shoulder, and I didn't have the energy to shake him off.

"You look terrible," Telken said. He offered a plate of delicious-smelling serarb. I wrenched it out of his hands and took several bites before he could react.

"Hey now, lass!" Telken exclaimed. "What's gotten into you?"

"She's had a rough day," Seaman Calux said when I was unable to speak around the mouthful of food.

Telken looked sharply at Seaman Calux then shifted his attention to me.

"Come on." Telken draped an arm across my shoulders and pulled me further into camp. "Let's get yer belly filled." He sat me down at a fire and brought me another helping. He handed me a mug of ale and I downed half the contents in one draught.

"When you didn't show up at midday, I thought you'd been injured or worse," Luc said. "I've never known you to miss a meal. A few of us went looking for ya."

"I'm sorry." I wiped grease from my lips. "I didn't mean to worry anyone. We came across a dead petiloos, and I was looking for its den. I was worried it left behind some pups."

"Sounds about right." Telken chuckled. "We almost alerted the captain, but if we had, there would have been a full-scale search for sure and we didn't want to start a fuss if there was no call for it."

"Was about to, though, just before you walked up," Luc added.

"I'm glad I showed up then. I would have hated to inconvenience everyone, especially the captain," I said.

"Bah." Telken waved off my concerns. "No trouble."

We lapsed into a comfortable silence as we ate, but my head was heavy at the thought of those poor starving pups, cold and alone in their den. I wasn't sure what I planned on doing if I found them, but anything was better than slowly freezing or starving to death. Once the sun fully set, the men set aside their plates and began playing instruments and singing merrily, but I had no wish for revelry tonight. I walked away from the fire to the outskirts of camp and stared into the darkness beyond wondering where those pups might be and planning out a system to search for them tomorrow.

"You were gone a very long time today."

Despite my worry, I smiled at the sound of Captain Romy's voice beside me.

"Find anything of interest?"

The brief uplifting of my spirits in his presence crashed.

"A dead petiloos," I said. "She left behind nursing pups, and I spent the rest of the afternoon trying to find them."

"Alone?"

"No." I kicked a loose pebble across the dirt. "Seaman Calux was with me."

"Good," he said, his voice a little loud. "I would prefer no one venture out too far alone, at least until we're familiar with everything that's out there."

"That might take some time."

"I don't wish for anyone's safety to be jeopardized. Do you think you can restrain yourself from wandering off alone?"

He stared down at me with a bemused expression, as if he didn't believe for a second that I could show any self-control in these regards. He knew I valued solitude when I needed it, and I turned away to hide how much it pleased me that he knew me so well.

"I'll try," I said. "But I can't promise anything."

"Then I'll *try* not to worry about you."

My heart thudded so loudly I feared he could hear it. *Had* he worried about me? My breathing quickened despite my efforts to calm myself, and though I'm certain he noticed, he didn't comment. Before I could stop myself, I shifted closer to him, very subtly, as if I were merely distributing my weight from one leg to the other.

In a very serious tone he said, "Promise me you won't go out at night."

"I promise I won't." I had no qualms about making such a promise. I wasn't a fool.

"Not even to search for orphaned pups."

I glanced up at his face, but there was no sign that he was teasing. He fully expected that searching in the dark for nursing petiloos pups was a thought I would not only entertain but an act I would carry out. I couldn't rationally take offense at this assumption. He did know me after all.

"I won't…" I said. "I suppose." I couldn't help but tease him a little, but he didn't look amused.

"Goodnight, Miss Elejick," he said.

I blinked at his abruptness. "Goodnight, sir."

He walked away with his long, confident stride. I sighed at his retreating form. He might be able to read me like an open book, but to me Captain Romy was still a mystery.

I slept fitfully that night, my mind swirling with thoughts of the orphaned petiloos and Captain Romy's strange shifts in mood. I couldn't account for him being indifferent one moment, considerate the next, and seemingly angry. Was he regretting his decision to allow me back? One thing was certain, I wouldn't spend my entire time on this island dancing around the issue. If he continued to act so diametrically, I would force a conversation as to why.

At last, I started drifting to sleep while mapping out a pattern to search for the pups while covering as much ground as possible. I heard a scratch at the tent flap. Groggily, I opened my eyes and listened, hoping it had been in my imagination. But the scratching sounded again, and I sighed in annoyance.

"Who is it?" I called out.

"Seaman Calux," a voice answered. "I'm sorry for the hour, but I couldn't sleep without speaking to you."

"Seaman," I grumbled and rose to a sitting position. "It's late. Can't it wait?"

"I'm afraid that if I wait, I'll lose my nerve."

I stared dumbly at the tent flap. I could almost see his silhouette, and I shook my head at his odd behavior. Had he gone mad?

"Seaman—" Before I could say more, the tent flap was flung aside and Seaman Calux entered the tent. I pulled my blanket over my body, though I was perfectly decent in a long nightgown.

"What are you doing?" I hissed.

"Sorry. I was afraid if I stayed out there any longer someone might see me and get the wrong idea."

"They certainly will if you're found here! Get out!"

"Please!" He sat close to me, his voice pleading. I groped for my dagger, but he reached out and grasped my wrist. "I mean you no harm!"

"Then get out!" I'm sure he heard the panic in my voice, and he released my arm. But he sat regarding me with a desperate expression, and I waited for him to speak with growing trepidation.

"Sulwen," he began, "I don't wish to frighten you. But I find I can no longer hide the passion growing inside me."

Now I was no longer worried. I was annoyed. I rolled my eyes and pointed toward the tent flap, but he remained seated.

"I'm only asking for you to give me a chance to prove my affection for you. I've never met a more fascinating and intelligent woman."

"Please stop," I said. "I don't want to hear more."

"I can offer you whatever life you desire. I have a home in Faqur or we could travel the continent together. I will devote my life to fulfilling your every wish."

"Seaman Calux," I said in the best imitation of Father's stern tone.

He stopped rambling and watched me hopefully. "While I respect you as a member of this expedition, my feelings go no further. Please take this as my final word in regard to your…declaration." I waited for this statement to sink in, and he shook his head in wonderment.

"But I've been very attentive. Surely, you have not mistaken my intentions."

"You mean you weren't simply being nice?" I made no attempt to hide my irritation. "I can appreciate that you probably haven't seen a woman in a while, but don't attach yourself to me simply because you're lonely."

His eyes narrowed angrily. "I assure you that is not the case."

"I don't wish to be cruel, but there is no future that involves the two of us becoming intimately connected. Now see yourself out." I tucked into bed in a bid to appear nonchalant, but I was shaking so badly I'm surprised the sides of the tent weren't trembling. I squeezed my eyes shut and willed him to leave. I closed my fingers around my dagger. If he made a move to touch me, I would gouge his eye out.

"Is it the way I speak?" he asked morosely.

"No," I said. "It's the mustache. Now go away."

To my eternal relief, he left the tent in a huff, pushing the flap roughly aside and stomping away. I hoped no one heard him, but I was too exhausted to check. Truthfully, I felt for Seaman Calux's struggle. Did I not feel my own heart stir in a direction that only meant disappointment? I didn't object to him on principle. He'd been a decent man, the son of a lord. Merrin would point out how foolish it was to throw away a perfectly decent offer, but I wasn't on this island to secure a husband. And if I had learned anything about myself, it was that I wasn't the type to settle.

The next morning, I opened the tent flap warily and looked around to make sure Seaman Calux was nowhere in sight. After last night, I didn't want to spend the day alone with him. When I was certain he wasn't lurking around waiting for me, I left the tent as casually as possible and strode toward the fires where breakfast was being served. I snatched up a slab of serarb and hardtack and immediately headed in the direction of where I suspected the petiloos den might be found.

"Sulwen!"

I winced and resisted the urge to groan aloud at the sound of Seaman Calux's voice. I reluctantly turned. He ran up to me with a hopeful expression. I closed my eyes and sighed in defeat. He'd shaved off his mustache.

"Seaman Calux, it would probably be best if you stayed behind today," I said.

"But..." He looked toward the area where we'd searched yesterday. "You weren't going alone? What if something happened?"

I opened my mouth to issue a firm rebuke, but we were interrupted by Captain Romy's voice.

"Are you ready, Miss Elejick? I don't like to be kept waiting."

He strode forward toward us. Seaman Calux and I saluted. I couldn't hide my bewilderment, but a look from the captain regained my senses.

"My apologies, sir," I said. "Shall we?"

"Seaman." Captain Romy nodded toward the dejected man and held out his hand for me to precede him.

I wouldn't be surprised if he had to run to keep up with my hurried pace. When we were well out of camp, I spun to face him. He drew up short, but he'd maintained a respectable distance and hadn't run into me. A sign of a true gentleman, I mused.

"Thank you," I said. "You cannot know how timely your appearance was."

"I think I can." He strode forward, his hands clasped behind his back. "I happened to encounter Seaman Calux coming from the direction of your tent last night. He didn't look well." The blood drained from my face and then flooded every vessel in a rush, leaving me equal parts cold and hot.

"It's not what you think." My eyes burned as I looked at him, imploring him to believe me.

"Isn't it? Did he declare his intentions and you rejected him?"

"Well. I—" I blinked rapidly and tried to collect myself. "In a sense, yes."

"Is there anything more I should know?" Instead of feeling ashamed, I felt protected. He was asking me if Seaman Calux acted reproachfully, and he was prepared to enact a punishment on my behalf.

"You have me to thank for him shaving off his mustache," I said to him with as much seriousness as I could muster.

"Then I owe you a great deal, Miss Elejick," he said with equal seriousness.

I snorted and resumed walking. To my surprise, he followed.

"You don't have to come with me if you have better things to do."

"I meant what I said last night. I don't want anyone venturing out alone, even someone as perfectly capable as yourself."

I couldn't bring myself to meet his eye for he would surely see how delighted his compliment made me. I pressed forward and resumed the search for the petiloos den, even going so far as to pull out a piece of paper where I'd sketched out the places I'd already scoured.

He peered over my shoulder. "Did you draw out a map of the area?"

I shifted awkwardly. "Yes."

"How thorough of you. Where do we start?"

"There." I pointed toward a stand of trees.

"What am I looking for?"

"Disturbed earth, a hole in the rock, the sounds of tiny, innocent pups whining for their mother."

"Seems straightforward enough." He slowly moved forward, his ear turned to the ground. I watched him and smiled, but just as quickly shook myself for being ridiculous. I had to stop gazing at him adoringly or one of these days he'll catch me and send me back to Praed.

We searched for hours, and my heart was sick thinking about those pups alone in the dark. They must be dead by now, but I refused to give up. Captain Romy was kind enough not to declare the search futile and order me back to camp, but I was certain it was only a matter of time. We split up to cover more ground, and I found myself alone when Captain Romy disappeared behind a ridge. In despair I sank onto a rock, taking advantage of the solitude to mourn for the creatures that life treated so cruelly. Before I could lose myself to weeping, Captain Romy called out.

"Miss Elejick! Hurry!" His voice was a mixture of excitement and desperation, and I tore down the hillside without care of my own safety. He held out his hands to catch me, and I slid to a stop before an outcropping of stone tucked into the lee of a large tree. Together we dropped to our knees to peer into a well-hidden hole.

"I don't hear anything." I reached inside, but I couldn't feel anything either. Without care for my own safety, I dug a larger opening and wriggled my way inside, feeling around as I inched into the den. I closed my eyes to keep them free of dirt, and I ignored the discomfort of soil in my breeches and down the front of my shirt. Shortly my fingers encountered fur, and I gently grasped one of the pups. I called out for the captain to pull me out, and he grasped my legs and hauled me to the surface. In the light of morning, I was able to see the pup in my hand was long dead.

"Miss Elejick—"

"There were more." I set the pup aside gently before crawling back into the den. This time, when my hand closed around a pup, I felt for warmth, for movement, for a heartbeat. But every furry body I touched was stiff and cold. The tears streaking across my face had nothing to do with dirt getting in my eyes. Five times I was disappointed, but I reached toward the back of the den, determined not to fail. Something wriggled against my palm.

"Len—er, Captain!" I yelled, nearly calling him by his first name in my excitement. "Pull me out! Hurry!"

He wrenched me out of the den, and I wiped my eyes free of dirt and tears and saw the creature moving weakly in my grasp. Its eyes weren't open, and it was terribly cold. Heedless of how it appeared, I tucked the pup in my shirt, hoping the warmth of my body would revive it.

"I have to give it some food," I said through a haze of emotion.

"And warmth. Come on. Let's get you to the fire."

Captain Romy helped me to my feet, and we hurried back to camp. I was so focused on the pup clutched against my breast that I didn't register until later that the captain supported me with one arm around my shoulders and the other across my arms where they crossed over my chest. He settled me in front of the flames, ignoring curious onlookers as he added more logs to the blaze.

"Lencius?" First Mate Evrard took in our haggard appearance and my no doubt dazed expression. "What's going on?"

"What do you need?" Captain Romy asked me without acknowledging his brother.

"It can't eat if it's not warm." I peeked inside my shirt. "I think the fire is helping. I'll have to figure out something to feed it."

"What 'it'?" the first mate asked.

"Miss Elejick's new charge," the captain said.

I looked up at him hopefully. Would he let me keep the petiloos pup if it survived?

After a few minutes in front of the warm fire, the pup began to whine and squirm. I laughed in relief, and it poked its black nose out of the top of my shirt in its search for food. First Mate Evrard jumped back in surprise and immediately argued against such a pet, but I paid him no attention. While I waited for the little one to revive, I contemplated what to feed it. I had to act fast to deliver it nourishment.

"Can you have a pot of water put on to boil?" I asked. "And have some long bones brought out. And an egg if we have any."

"That's quite an order, young lady," First Mate Evrard snapped. I bristled at the term 'young lady,' but the captain silenced him with a look and demanded my needs be met. Begrudgingly, the first mate obliged. Once the water came to a boil, I gingerly removed the pup from my shirt and handed it to the captain.

"Just for a minute," I assured him. He made no objection and settled the pup close to his chest.

I broke open the long bones and scooped out the marrow, adding it to the boiling water to make a thin paste. Then I cracked open an egg and allowed the clear liquid to fall into the mixture while saving the yoke. I pounded the shell into a powder against a rock and added it to the paste, then removed it from the flames to cool. When it was no longer hot to the touch, I mixed in the yoke and dipped my finger into the rather unappetizing potage. I brought my finger to the pup's searching mouth, and it clamped onto it and suckled greedily. I wept with joy as it ate heartily until its belly was full, then it fell asleep contentedly in the captain's arms. He handed it carefully over to my keeping, and I couldn't imagine loving something so thoroughly in such a short amount of time as I did that tiny, gray-furred creature.

"You're responsible for it," Captain Romy said.

"I know." I stroked the soft fur of its head and voiced absently that I didn't know if it was a boy or a girl.

"A boy," the captain stated.

"You're more observant than I am." I laughed.

"At times, perhaps."

I smiled, but I had eyes only for the little pup in my arms. He opened his mouth in a wide yawn, his paws trembling with the effort, and snuggled deeper into my embrace.

"Well done, Miss Elejick," Captain Romy said softly. I met his eyes and was struck by the tenderness of his gaze the instant before his features resumed their characteristic stoic poise. He left me by the fire with my tiny charge, and soon the crew drifted over to look. I paid them no heed. It must be what a mother feels the first time her child is placed in her arms: a profound euphoria.

CHAPTER 39

Through my sheer stubbornness and tenacity, the petiloos pup survived. To honor the little creature, I named him Will, for *his* was strong, strong enough to survive cold and near starvation. I remained close to the fire for several days and fed him every three hours around the clock, and though I was left exhausted, he thrived. When we moved camp, my feet dragged, but my heart was full of triumph for the life I'd saved. His eyes soon opened, though they were a hazy blue as opposed to the stunning amber of the adults. His little face poked out of my satchel as we traveled, his nose constantly in the air. When we stopped to rest, I let him out to exercise his wobbly legs as he learned to walk. The men were a mixture of curious amusement and uncertainty, with several voicing that it was only a matter of time before the creature was trying to steal their food. I vouched for the pup's good behavior with a look that brooked no argument.

When the triangular peak seemed so close we could almost touch it, we ascended a ridge and there was a collective gasp of amazement. Below us stretched a valley carpeted in shades of green so vibrant it was almost blinding. It stretched out toward the mountain's distinctive shape rising out of the valley floor like a sentinel standing guard over a magnificent lake fed by three waterfalls. The water was reminiscent of the deep blue we'd seen further south, but this expansive body of water was at least three times larger. From its banks was the origin of a mighty river heading east. Far in the distance, a massive mountain dwarfing the peak before us rose out of a dense fog. The sight rendered us all speechless.

"Looks like a good place to set up a camp to scout from," Second Mate Absalon said.

"We better get down there and get to work then," First Mate Evrard said. He pulled aside about ten men and handed them heavy bundles of supplies before they headed off in the direction we'd just come.

"Where are they going?" I asked Telken.

"They've got to report to Faqur," he said.

The rest of us descended into the valley, and it wasn't long before I felt the cool air from the waterfalls. The temperature was warm, but it was still nothing compared to a Praed spring, where flowers bloomed in the high sunshine that brought hot summers. There was no sign of grazing serarb, but there was no shortage of songbirds and the occasional raptor hovering over the grass in search of prey. A bird dove from the side of the waterfall into the lake and came up with a mouthful of fish. A smile spread across my face. This was a land teeming with life, and I couldn't wait to discover it all.

A suitable area was designated for the building of permanent structures, and the men set about felling trees along the ridge and dragging them back to camp. It soon became apparent that this would be a tedious undertaking. The distance was fairly great, and the men were exhausted by the time they made it back with the timber. I'd overheard the officers discussing the conundrum when I stopped to take a break from clearing the ground to feed Will.

"Why don't you just use stone?" I said. "There's not exactly a shortage of it, and it needs to be cleared to make way for the buildings anyway."

The three officers looked at each other as they considered the practicality of such a suggestion. To my surprise, First Mate Evrard advocated most staunchly for it.

"They would last a very long time and withstand wind and snow," he said. "We don't know what sort of weather we're going to be in for, so it stands to reason to be prepared."

I was pleased that they followed my suggestion but regretted it later when I had to haul rocks from the shore.

A respectable settlement slowly took shape over the following days, including a cookhouse with food storage, a storehouse for weapons and supplies, an officer's quarters, and the beginnings of a bunkhouse. The cartographers were understandably excited to have a base camp and their own space to lay out their preliminary maps and discuss figures. They were gone most of the day while the rest of us worked, but there was no sign of any ill will among the crew, especially once an oven was built and the smell of freshly cooked meals began wafting through camp. The lake was teeming with fish, some larger than my forearm. Fat waterfowl whose feathers were used to stuff new mattresses and pillows also made up a portion of our diet. I worried all the hunting and fishing would put a sizable dent in the wildlife population, but once the first mate deemed the food stores full, he ordered hunting to cease for the time being.

Will now walked with confidence, but every time he tried to romp around my feet, he tumbled, his rump flying over his head. Though he looked ridiculous, I had to admire his spirit, for he simply shook the dirt out of his fur and tried again. His eyes were still blue, but they were clearer, and his rounded ears were becoming more erect. Even the men who'd glared at him from a distance found his antics comical so long as I kept the pup from disrupting their work. The gray-furred creature became something of a good luck charm, and he learned that if he pranced around and wiggled his tail, the men would throw him a morsel. Soon, Will was wagging his tail like a dog and tilting his round face eagerly at everyone, including the first mate, who still wasn't quite sure keeping the animal was a good idea.

"You're spoiling him," First Mate Evrard grumbled one day when Will yipped in protest of being ignored.

"*I'm* not," I said. "But everyone else is."

I took Will with me whenever I had spare time to leave the settlement and explore, letting him stretch his legs to improve his strength and carrying him when he tired. He was generally well behaved and quiet, unless he spied a mouse in the undergrowth. He'd charge after the creature like a bumbling idiot, scaring whatever I was watching and me in the process. I wondered if I should try and teach the petiloos how to hunt, but I hadn't the first idea how to go about it. Luckily, Will was still very young and wouldn't be required to hunt for himself for several weeks.

I stroked Will's soft fur in the firelight after the evening meal, the young pup curled contentedly in my lap as I listened to the crew's raucous song. Out of the corner of my eye, I saw Seaman Calux striding toward me. We hadn't spoken privately since he declared his unrequited feelings for me, nor had he tried to resume our outings together. Now, it appeared he had something to say.

"Sulwen." He sat beside me.

"Seaman Calux." I straightened and prepared to send him away. I didn't expect him to renew his offer with so many people around, but I couldn't be too cautious.

Seaman Calux leaned over to look at Will. "He's getting big. I was so relieved when you found him. I know how much it meant to you to save those pups."

"Yes." I reached down to my little charge and rubbed his ears.

"Sulwen," Seaman Calux said in a low voice. "I hate the way we left things between us. I understand I have no chance with you, but I've missed your company. Is there any possibility that we can put everything I said behind us and be friends again?"

"I can put it behind me, but can you? Truly?"

"Yes, I promise! I'll never speak of my feelings for you again."

"But you still have them?" I'd forgiven Seaman Calux for the disturbing manner of his declaration and sympathized with him. After all, he couldn't help the way he felt any more than I could. But I needed to make it clear he had no future with me beyond friendship.

"I have tried to forget." He lowered his eyes. "But I cannot deny that the feelings I have for you are still there and just as strong."

"Then perhaps it would be best if we stayed away from each other until they're gone. I would hate to inadvertently lead you on or cause you further pain."

He met my steady gaze, his brown eyes shimmering in the firelight. After a moment of silence, he sighed heavily.

"There's really no chance that you might open your heart to me, is there?"

"No, none at all," I said.

"And it's not just the mustache, is it?"

I smiled. "No."

"Is it...someone else?"

"I don't think it's fair for you to ask me that." I struggled against my temper. "Not only because it's none of your business, but why would you want to torture yourself if there was?"

"I just wanted to prepare myself in case I saw you with another man."

"Rest assured, there is no danger of that happening. Even in the unlikely event I formed an attachment with anyone here, there would be no acting on it under the present circumstances."

"If you say so." He stared into the flames. "I will speak no more of this. You have my word. And I'll leave you alone until I can look upon you with indifference instead of hope." He abruptly left. I felt sorry for him, but he'll get over his feelings soon enough. I'm not worth all this fuss anyway.

Telken occupied the seat Seaman Calux vacated and handed me a mug of ale. I sipped it casually, then realized my friend was watching me expectantly.

"What is it?" I took another drink.

"At least tell me you let him down easy," Telken said.

I spat out the entire contents of my mouth, soaking the front of my shirt and sending a mist over poor Will. He started at the sudden shower, shaking the ale from his fur. I apologized to the little petiloos and dabbed him dry with my sleeve.

I gave a sidelong glance at Telken. "I don't know what you're talking about!" I looked around and noticed a few people stopped to stare at the spectacle I was making.

"If that's what you want me to think." Telken leaned back and took a long drink from his own mug.

"All right, fine," I whispered. "Just keep your voice down. How did you know?"

"Strongly suspected," Telken said. "He's always tripped over himself like an idiot around you."

"Lovely. Why didn't I notice?" I groaned and covered my flushed face with my hands.

"Too busy trying to live your life I suppose. Most women tend to notice when a man has eyes for her."

"I'm not most women."

"No." He shook his head and laughed. "That's how I knew you wouldn't have him."

"How's that?"

"Calux wants for a certain type of wife, one who will stay home."

"That's not what he told me. He said we could live in Faqur or travel the continent."

Telken looked at me as if I were a naïve child. It made my jaw clench, but I couldn't deny that I had very little experience when it came to such matters.

"I'd say when he said, 'travel the continent,' he means honeymoon before settling back in Faqur to start having babes. Calux comes from a very traditional family. They wouldn't stand for anything else."

I turned away and stared angrily into the flames. I was never more grateful for my instincts as I had been in regard to Seaman Calux. If I was a lesser woman, I might have accepted him out of charity or desperation and ruined my life.

Though Telken and Luc had very little interest in spending hours observing nature as I did, they took turns accompanying me on my outings over the next week in case Seaman Calux made the mistake of following me. As they explained, it was more for the sake of *his* life rather than my safety. They'd seen how deadly I could be with a sword. Thankfully, there was no need to be so cautious. The seaman was assigned to the cartographers in case they encountered any indigenous people during their mapping expeditions, so I saw him very little. I spent a lot of time at the lakeshore gazing across the vast expanse of the glassy surface and wondering what lay on the other side. It was too far to swim and too large to walk around in one day. I considered suggesting the cartographers choose the other side of the lake for their next project, but they were sticklers for their systematic approach, and they wouldn't venture in that direction in Artur knows how many weeks. I wasn't patient enough for that.

"Telken," I asked as we washed our faces in the lake after a long day. "How long does it take to build a canoe?"

He considered my question before saying, "Depends on how fancy you want to make it. Takes at least two weeks for something simple."

"Can you teach me to make one that will take me across the lake?"

"Sure, I can. Let's go up on the ridge and look for something suitable."

Telken explained the dynamics of building a canoe as we walked out of camp and toward the ridge of trees with axes in our hands. Will trotted and cavorted at my side with confidence now that his legs were stronger and he no longer ended up falling on his snout. His eye color changed to yellow, and he ate more solid foods. His bushy coat turned from a uniform dark gray to mostly shining silver with darker points on his nose, ears, paws, shoulders, and the tip of his tail—a stunningly handsome petiloos specimen, if I did say so myself.

When Telken and I reached the ridge and climbed up into the stand of trees, he explained we needed one that was straight and tall with a base measuring at least three feet wide. We quickly found an excellent prospect and felled the behemoth, taking care not to send too many other trees crashing to the ground with it. We cut a fifteen-foot section and left the rest to season. The entire process took several hours before Telken declared us done for the day. We carried back several logs for the fire and arrived at camp just as the evening meal was served.

With our bellies full, I took Will out of camp to relieve himself. I looked toward the green slopes leading up to the mountain on the other side of the lake. I was anxious to see what was over there, and the time required to complete my project didn't suit my perpetual impatience.

"Absalon informs me you've broken Seaman Calux's heart," Captain Romy's voice spoke unexpectedly behind me.

I groaned and couldn't bear to meet his eye. If a lake monster exists, this is the part where I hoped it'd surface to drag me under and put me out of my misery.

"Is Calux going around telling everyone?"

"No. He hasn't said a word. Mr. Crummin told the second mate."

Damn you, Telken.

"I wish he hadn't," I grumbled.

"It prompted my brother to alter the seaman's schedule and place him under his command."

"Thank Artur for him." I looked at the captain standing beside me scanning the lake and trying to repress a grin. "I'm glad someone finds all this nonsense amusing," I said.

"My apologies." Captain Romy pursed his lips to restrain a smile.

I studied his face, the expertly trimmed full beard, strong jawline, blonde hair tossing ever-so-slightly in the breeze. He caught me staring, and I hoped my expression was similar to the one I wore when contemplating a new species and not an adoring one.

"What are you thinking when you look at me like that?" he wondered aloud.

"Just trying to figure you out." I returned my attention to the lake. It wasn't a lie, but it certainly wasn't the whole truth.

"I always thought I was an obvious man to read," he said.

"You thought wrong."

"I'll try to make myself better understood in the future." There was an oddly hoarse tone to his voice. Was he falling ill? He appeared in good health, even in the waning light, though his eyes shone much too brightly. Maybe he had a fever? His cheeks didn't look flushed. Was I overanalyzing this? Probably. Despite my resolve to maintain a respectable persona, my heart folded at the way his blue-gray eyes reflected the ever-brightening moonlight. A splash and a yelp brought me back to reality, and I snapped my head toward Will. He ran to me, his front paws and nose dripping wet.

"Forgot you weren't a fish, did you?" I scooped him into my arms. He rubbed his face against my shirt and sneezed, his lip curled in indignation.

"I've enjoyed seeing him thrive. You should be proud of yourself," Captain Romy said.

"First Mate Romy thinks he's spoiled."

"Hasn't he earned it?"

"That's how I feel! Besides, how can anyone resist this face?" I held Will up toward the captain and pouted.

"The very thought is unfathomable, Miss Elejick."

CHAPTER 40

Telken leaned over the top of the log to inspect the leveled edge we'd painstakingly worked on for the last half a day after spending several hours stripping off the bark. It was too heavy to move in its present state, so we worked among the trees, the sounds of our chopping accompanied by the fluttering of leaves and chirping birds in addition to Will's cavorting in and out of the shrubbery. When Telken deemed the work acceptable, we heaved the log over until it was level side down and started doing the same to the other side. The work was intense, and my muscles ached terribly at the end of the day, but we were progressing at a satisfying pace. Two days into carving out the interior, I couldn't bear my own stench. Scrubbing a washcloth over my face and arms wasn't getting me sufficiently clean. I needed a bath.

I waited several hours after everyone went to sleep before poking my head out of my tent and checking to make sure no one lingered around the fire. The camp was dark, the fire out, and the only sound coming from the tents was snoring. I left Will asleep on his bed made from the ruff of a serarb and tiptoed silently around the tents and outbuildings. When I was well out of earshot, I rushed to the water's edge. In one hand, I clutched a nightgown and a towel and in the other a lump of soap and a hairbrush. I took one last look around before stripping off my clothes and stepping into the cold water. I gasped and sank lower, affording myself a little more privacy, then I sank deeper until I was completely submerged. The water wasn't as cold as the Rhyvor, but it wasn't exactly bathwater, either. I hastily washed, then allowed myself a minute to enjoy a languid swim. It felt wonderful to lie back and give my tired muscles a break, and soon all my worries sank into the depths. When I opened my eyes, I saw I was quite far from shore. I sighed and started swimming back, wishing I could stay longer or perhaps swim in the warmth of the daylight. But propriety was a dictator, and she was strict.

Moonlight reflected on the water as it rippled around my swimming form, glowing with a strange blue aura. I stopped and waited for the water to calm. The glow wasn't coming from the moon above but from something below. From the abyssal darkness emerged hundreds of tiny orbs shining bright blue. They floated toward the surface all around me, and I frantically swam for shore lest they turn out to be dangerous. Just my luck! Lake monsters actually *do* exist, and they possess terrible timing in the bargain.

The second my feet touched the rocky shore, I grabbed my nightgown and struggled to pull it on over my wet skin as I ran back to camp. My brain ceased rational thought, so I allowed my feet to carry me past the tents and other outbuildings toward the officer's quarters. My chest burned with the exertion, but I paid no heed to how tightly my throat constricted with each gasp of air. I threw open the door to the main room of the building, leaving it open to allow the moonlight to help guide my way inside. Papers fluttered to the floor as I dashed toward the sleeping area off the back entryway. The captain's bed was just inside and to the right. I swear I only knew because I helped build it.

I barely allowed my vision to adjust to the dim light before I reached out and shook his bare shoulder, hoarsely whispering, "Captain," past my raw throat.

He woke with a start, his hand shooting out to painfully grasp my forearm. I repeated myself, and his grip loosened. Though the darkness concealed my features, he no doubt heard the desperation and fear in my voice.

"Miss Elejick?" he whispered. "What's wrong?"

"Come," was all I managed. I tugged his arm.

He threw off the bedcovers and grasped the nearest items of clothing, a nightshirt and one of his navy-blue coats. He pulled on the nightshirt and followed me out of the building, keeping pace beside me as I sprinted back toward the lake. He asked what happened, but I couldn't answer. I skidded to a stop at the shore, my bare feet scraping against rocks, and searched the surface of the water for the glowing orbs.

"Miss Elejick," Captain Romy spoke between panting breaths. "What—
—"

"There's something in the water." I met his worried stare. I'm sure I looked like a lunatic with my bare feet, wet hair, and nightgown clad body revealing too much, the fabric clinging to my wet skin...But that wasn't important right now. I pointed to the water to direct his attention away from me. He took a few steps closer and said he didn't see anything.

"They were there!" I said. "I was swimming out there and they came up from below."

He glanced back briefly before turning back toward the water. "I told you not to go out at night."

I rolled my eyes. "I was in sight of camp. That's not the point." I walked up beside him and stared intently at the dark water.

"There!" I pointed at the blue glow several feet away. Captain Romy stepped back in alarm, and I grinned in vindication like an idiot.

"What is it?"

"I have no idea!" I beamed.

To my surprise, he walked a little way into the water, and it was then I realized he was also barefoot.

"Should we try to catch one?" he said.

Amyl's feathers! That was the loveliest thing I'd ever heard a man say.

"Let me," I said. "They didn't attack me earlier, so I think I'll be okay. And if they do become hostile, at least it will be a lowly sailor getting injured and not the captain."

He slowly turned his head and narrowed his eyes.

"Come on," I said. "Turn around."

He stepped back and met my eye with evident trepidation.

"I'll be fine." I gestured toward the bank a few feet away, and he obliged me by turning his back. My heart pounded furiously as I stripped off my nightgown and splashed back into the water. A glance toward shore assured me Captain Romy was still turned away, and I swam toward the uncountable numbers of glowing orbs. I treaded water over a swarm of them, but they were out of reach.

"I'll have to dive to catch one!" I called out.

"Miss Elejick, don't—"

I plunged into the cold water. I opened my eyes, and though the water blurred my vision, I could track the orbs bobbing around me. Without a second thought, I reached out and cupped one in my hand. It fit perfectly against my palm. I gently grasped it and kicked toward the surface. I broke out of the water into the cool night air with a gasp and held the glob of a creature over my head triumphantly.

"Got one!" I said.

Captain Romy stood at the edge of the water, and his shoulders sagged in relief when I appeared. He turned around as I swam closer. I emerged shivering from the water, my toes and fingertips numb from the chill in the air. I gently set the creature on the rocks, hastily toweled myself semi-dry, and pulled on my nightgown.

"All right," I said, my voice wavering, and picked up the creature. I held it out for the captain to see, and for a minute we regarded the strange, translucent form. It was soft and viscous, and when I poked it my finger bounced on the surface. The bottom part had tiny hairs that stuck to my skin, but it didn't hurt.

"Have you ever seen anything like it?" he asked.

"Never."

Tentatively, he reached out and ran his finger along the creature, inspecting the mucoid material it left behind. He asked me to turn it over. I obliged, and by the light of the moon, we inspected the clear projections beneath it.

"It's sticky," I said. "Like barbs on a blade of grass." I looked back into the water and watched the orbs drift with the motion of the water. "I wonder what they eat."

"Another time," he said.

I hitched up my hem with one hand and cradled the creature in the other. I waded into the water and lowered the orb. It glowed in the dark water as it floated away. I shivered and retreated to the shore.

"They're beautiful," I said through trembling lips. The night had become frigid, and I was acutely aware that I was barefoot and only wearing a nightgown. Captain Romy draped his coat over my shoulders, covering me in warmth. I tried to protest, but he clasped the collar closed so the garment enveloped me completely.

"You're shivering and your teeth are chattering."

Fair enough. I shrugged my arms into the sleeves and hugged myself, rubbing my arms to warm my numb fingers. Captain Romy retrieved my things and handed them to me, then motioned for us to return to camp. I took a step and sharp pain spiked through my right foot. My knees buckled.

"What's wrong?"

"I think I cut my foot." I seethed as the pain ebbed away. I tried to walk using just the tips of my toes, but I didn't make it very far.

"May I see?" I nodded and lifted my foot, bracing myself against his shoulder while he gently inspected it.

"There are a few scratches, but nothing deep," Captain Romy said. He probed the bottom of my foot with his thumb, and I dug my fingers into his back and winced. "I think you may have bruised your heel."

"Like a horse stepping on a rock?" I gritted my teeth.

"Precisely." He set my foot back on the ground. "Will you allow me to assist you to your tent?"

My eyes widened. Assist me…? Did he mean *carry* me?

"Um…I-I—" He stared at me quizzically as I struggled to form words. I wanted to say I can handle it on my own, but honestly, I didn't think I could. The thought of being in his arms made me feel strangely warm. It also made me feel helpless. The last thing I wanted was for him to see me as a lady in distress. On the other hand, it's a sign of a mature adult to admit when you need help, so what was the real harm? Also—

"Stop," he said firmly.

I jumped. "Stop what?"

"You're overthinking. Just let me help you. I won't tell anyone if it will make you feel any better."

I huffed. "Oh. Fine."

He moved to my other side and wrapped an arm around my upper back. "Put your arm around my neck."

Yes, sir.

He supported my weight against his side and used his body like a crutch as I limped forward. Oh, *that's* what he meant by assisting me. I admittedly was a little disappointed he didn't carry me.

When we reached my tent, I managed to hop inside and maneuver myself onto the cot. Will poked his nose out from his nest of furs and whined, and I whispered for him to go back to sleep. He complied with a yawn and snuggled back into his warm bed. The captain asked if I needed anything, and I was surprised he hadn't left.

"No. Thank you, sir."

With a perfunctory nod, he wished me goodnight and disappeared.

I fell asleep the instant my head touched the pillow surrounded by his distinct scent of sea water, clean wool, and well-worn leather. My dreams were filled with blue light, summer swims, and warm arms wrapped around me.

When I awoke the next morning, I was still wearing Captain Romy's blue coat. No wonder my night was so pleasant. I buried my nose in the collar, inhaled deeply, and sighed. I'd been reduced to a pathetic mess of a woman over this man. There was no use disputing the truth of my feelings.

I was in love with Captain Romy.

As foolish as it may seem, how futile, how doomed to disappointment I may be, I couldn't pretend any more. At least now I admitted it to myself, I could be more mindful, more careful about concealing my heart. I would keep our conversations brief and avoid any physical contact even if I were to break a leg. Definitely no more late-night frantic visits to his quarters.

I carefully folded the coat and tucked it in my satchel before leaving the tent in search of breakfast. I was starving after the eventful night before. Will bounded around my feet, equally eager to start the day. He looked like a perfectly miniaturized version of an adult petiloos, but though he'd started catching insects on the fly and digging up worms to snack on, he still relied on feedings from me and crew. He'd learned which of the men would indulge his begging and which ones ignored him, and he dashed to his favorites for morsels.

"Eat up, lass," Telken said as we ate. "We've a lot of work ahead of us. Took the liberty of packing some food so we can work through the afternoon."

"Perfect," I said. The more time spent away from camp, the better. "I'll catch up. Have an errand to run first." He grunted in reply, and I headed toward the officer's quarters with Will toddling after me, chewing the remains of his meal.

I heard several voices inside, and I wasn't relishing the thought of presenting Captain Romy's coat to him with his brothers looking on. I knocked lightly and entered before I lost my nerve. The three officers were gathered around a table with several sheets of paper shuffled aside to make way for their morning meal. The captain straightened when he saw me, the first mate eyed Will, and the second mate smiled amiably.

"Sorry to interrupt." I saluted. "I have that information you requested, sir." I stared pointedly at the captain. A confused look crossed his brow, but he followed my lead and rose.

"If you please." He indicated the direction of the quarters.

I could feel the other men's eyes follow us, but then Will did something to upset the first mate—probably sniffled or scratched at his ear—and he chased after the poor petiloos, yelling that animals didn't belong indoors. The second mate called after him to leave the creature alone, and I took the opportunity afforded by the distraction to remove the captain's coat from my satchel.

"I forgot to give it back to you last night," I whispered as I handed it to him. "Sorry."

"No apology necessary. I hope you were warm enough?"

"Yes, thank you." I shifted awkwardly, though he wasn't doing anything to make me uncomfortable besides standing there in his perfectly composed state staring at me. I had to get out of there. I saluted and bid a hasty retreat, almost pushing him out of the way as I left the building. I called for Will on my way out of camp, and he obediently followed. My heel was sore, but I limped to the ridge where I hoped to spend the majority of my time for the foreseeable future.

CHAPTER 41

We spent three days hollowing out the interior of the boat. It was now light enough for Telken and me to carry down to the lakeside to finish. A few crewmen came to inspect our work and offer advice, and even the second mate complimented our industriousness, stating that more should be made so others could boat across the lake. I wasn't a fan of this idea. I wanted to be the first, to have something that was mine, for as long as possible.

Once the sides of the hollowed-out canoe were about two inches thick and resembled a dried, curled up leaf, Telken and I braced a few pieces of wood inside and blocked the ends with flat planks. Next, we built up a large fire until it was very hot then lined it with stones. While we waited for the stones to heat up, we poured lake water into the hull, filling it up about halfway. Telken inspected the sides and bottom for leaks, though he assured me if there were any, they could be patched up. He declared the canoe fairly sound, and when the stones were hot enough, we wrapped our hands in leather so we could drop them into the water. Steam billowed out in waves with a satisfying *hiss*. We added more stones until the water boiled, then we covered the entire canoe with canvas. Telken explained this would soften the wood enough for us to complete the shaping of the craft.

After a while, we removed the canvas. Using a series of increasingly longer planks, Telken and I carefully stretched the once misshapen log into something resembling a boat. We dumped the water out and left the canoe in the sun to dry. Telken said this portion of the project might take several weeks and would act to strengthen the wood. That meant I would have to find something else to occupy myself with while I waited.

Will was two months old. I began developing his hunting skills by playing a sort of macabre version of hide and seek. I set traps to catch the rodents I'd seen his adult counterparts hunt, I marked a trail by dragging the creatures over the ground, then buried them for Will to find. I'd start by feeding him a morsel of the meat, and when I had his attention, I directed his nose to the ground. It wasn't long before he caught the scent, and I sat back to watch him track the area with his little black nose sniffing frantically over the dirt. I made notes in my journal detailing his quick ability to learn. Though he ended up giving up in frustration because he could smell the mouse but couldn't find it, the instant he saw me dig the carcass out of the earth, it was like a spark of understanding lit up his eyes. He let out a yip of excitement and nearly choked in his eagerness to eat the well-earned meal. Soon, he focused his attention enough to follow a trail without getting distracted and was finding his buried treasure within minutes.

We played other games together such as chase, wrestle with a stick, and a rudimentary version of fetch, but hide-and-seek-a-snack was his favorite. Unfortunately, his favorite game got him into trouble.

One morning I awoke to the sound of angry yelling, my eyes flying open as the hazy veil of sleep lifted. I rubbed my eyes and turned over in bed. Will was gone. I bolted upright to the sounds of heavy stomping, and I hastily dressed, not bothering with shoes or finishing buttoning my breeches in my rush to investigate. My heart sank when I reached the cookhouse and saw the cook waving a large wooden spoon, ducking and bobbing around the building chasing after my mischievous petiloos.

"What's going on?" I called out.

The cook fixed me with a dark glare and pointed accusatory at Will cowering just out of reach.

"That pest has snuck in 'ere and stolen a piece of meat that was drying out for jerky," he said.

Oh, dear.

"I'm so sorry!" I said. "He doesn't mean any harm. He must have smelled the meat and was playing a game. I promise it won't happen again. Right?" I raised an eyebrow at the little scamp emerging from the corner carrying a large strip of dried serarb. He laid it at the cook's feet and looked up at him with his head tilted as if to say, "You won this game."

"Get out!" the cook yelled, swiping at Will with the spoon. The petiloos took off into camp, and I ran after him with as much annoyance as the poor cook felt.

"Come back here, you little thief!" I growled.

The petiloos dodged around men coming out of their tents to see what the fuss was about. I left amused chuckles in my wake. A few voices called out to Will to run faster. Traitors!

Will ran toward the officer's quarters. I was sure I had him, but First Mate Evrard opened the door to step out, and Will ducked inside. The first mate grumbled inarticulately as I dashed after the scamp. I saluted him as an afterthought, and he didn't deign to upset himself over the situation. He was learning, too. Captain Romy was sitting at the table inside, and Will hid behind his boot like a coward.

"Apologies for the interruption, sir," I said before doubling over to catch my breath.

"Making mischief, are we?" Captain Romy asked the petiloos peeking out from behind his hiding place. He looked up at the captain in wide-eyed innocence.

"You have no idea." I crossed my arms and glared at the impudent beast.

Captain Romy reached down and scratched Will behind the ear, and I swear the little imp melted against his leg and gazed up at him with heavy lidded eyes. Oh, he was good.

I shook my finger at Will. "Don't pretend you're innocent."

The petiloos glanced at me casually as if to ask, "Who? Me?"

The captain stifled a grin, and I turned my fury on him.

"And don't *you* get suckered in by a cute face!" I regretted the words the instant they left my mouth. He was the captain for Artur's sake, not my brother or an errant child. He met my open-mouthed shock passively, and my heart thudded to a stop and I died.

I wished.

"I'm really sorry, sir, that was inappropriate—I should never have spoken to you in that manner…I don't know what I was thinking…Please forgive me."

"What happened?" he asked.

"Will got into the cook's dried meat. It's my fault, and I accept full responsibility for it. I've been teaching him how to forage for food and it's become his favorite game."

"Is that so? How have you been accomplishing that?"

"I've been burying mice and having him track the scent so he can dig them up."

"How clever. And he apparently thought he'd made the ultimate find?"

"I guess so." I narrowed my eyes at Will casually grooming himself.

"Can you assure me it will not happen again?"

"Yes, of course!"

The captain looked down and addressed the creature curled into a ball on the top of his boot. "Can *you*?"

Will tilted his head, yawned, then tucked his nose under his tail.

"That better mean *yes*," I said through gritted teeth.

"I'm sure he knows that if he continues to steal food, he'll make the crew so angry they will no longer give him scraps from their plates."

Will's head popped up and his eyes widened in astonishment.

"I'm sure he must know that," I said gravely. "Just as he must know that if the cook catches him in the food stores again, he'll be made into a hat."

Will let out a yelp of surprise and finally had the decency to look ashamed.

"All is forgiven." Captain Romy met my eye. "*This* time." Heat flushed my cheeks. His gaze flickered toward the floor, and the corner of his mouth twitched.

"You seem to have settled in rather comfortably, Miss Elejick."

"Why do you say that, sir?"

"You're barefoot again. And the top buttons of your breeches are undone."

"Amyl's feathers!" I gasped and turned around to fasten the buttons. I didn't think it was possible to be any more embarrassed than I already was, but I continued to amaze myself. I turned around to see Captain Romy struggle with every ounce of self-possession to keep from laughing, and I found myself equally amused with the situation. I had no such reservations as he. I doubled over laughing.

"That will be all, Miss Elejick. Dismissed," he said with a momentous effort to maintain a dignified air.

"Come on, Will," I said between fits of laughter.

The petiloos leapt to his feet and trotted after me as I left the officer's quarters with unrestrained mirth. I would like to think that the moment I left, the captain gave in to his urge to laugh. It felt incredibly therapeutic after stressing myself into an anxious mess over the last several weeks, and I wished for him to feel the same freedom. But as captain, he had to maintain a certain level of authority, and how could he inspire unwavering loyalty by acting childish, as First Mate Evrard would consider such behavior? Before this expedition was over I hoped to see Captain Lencius Romy laugh until he fell over, even if it meant breaking my own vow to keep as much distance between us as possible.

Once Telken decided it was dry enough, the ends of the canoe were capped off and we smoothed out all the rough surfaces to complete the hull. A brace was placed to support the hull and a seat carved to fit the shape of the boat and maintain stability. Any imperfections in the wood were filled with pitch and the entire boat was oiled. One of the other crewmen, an excellent woodworker, carved a pair of paddles. After almost two months, the craft was finally finished.

Although it seemed simple, Telken insisted I practice wrangling the canoe before setting off on the lake. He'd grown up in a fishing village along one of Faqur's rivers. "It's not like a rowboat, lass. Easy to flip over just by lookin' over the side." So we took her out for a couple hours and he showed me how to steer, how to switch the paddle from left to right and how to keep it balanced. Proud to say I only overturned us three times.

The entire crew, including the officers, gathered to watch Telken and me launch the small vessel. Despite my practice sessions, I worried it might sink the moment we hit the water. We set it down on shore and pushed it into the lake. Telken coiled the painter we'd tied to the bow and dropped it into the boat. A quick check of the interior assured me there were no leaks. Watching the canoe bobbing in the water made me giddy, like a stallion champing at the bit. Pride swelled within me at our accomplishment. Telken patted me on the back in approval.

"We've done well, lass," he said. "You could probably make one by yourself now."

A breeze pushed the boat sideways, revealing the name I'd chosen and painted myself: *Tenacity*.

"*Impertinence* would have been more fitting," First Mate Evrard muttered. I glared at him, and he raised his eyebrows to challenge me to argue otherwise.

I shifted my satchel and climbed into the canoe. I was eager to get underway, and I settled into a comfortable position and took the paddle Telken handed to me. If we started sinking, I was an excellent swimmer—if I wasn't in the middle of the lake. Will jumped gracefully inside and stationed himself at the bow as if he would direct our course. "Don't run us into a rock," I told him.

The captain stepped forward to help push the canoe away from the shore. I backpaddled a few deft strokes, came about, and aimed the bow toward the far shore.

"Safe voyage, Miss Elejick," Captain Romy called as I rowed away.

The lake echoed with the claps and cheers of the crew, but as the distance between us grew, the only sound was the slapping of the paddle dipping into the water, propelling us forward. I paused a few times to rest and enjoy the sunshine on my face, but the closer I came to the northern shore, the more excited I became. I pushed my arms to their limits of strength to reach it. Sweat trickled down my back and temples, and I scooped up a handful of cool water and splashed my face. The roar of the three waterfalls was loud, and drops from the spray reached me even at a fair distance away. I could just see the top of the mountain I'd glimpsed through the fog looming like a dark sentinel over the top of the waterfalls. It must be hundreds of miles away to appear so small.

When we reached the opposite bank, I cruised along the shore in search of a good place to put in—the bank was quite steep. I found a decent spot and propelled myself onto the bank, hopping out to pull the canoe onto firm land. Will bounded away into the long grass. I tied the rope to a large boulder to secure the craft. I scanned the horizon, shielding my eyes from the sun's rays. The ground swelled upward about a half mile away. I headed in that direction to take advantage of the elevated view it offered. The grass was just as green on this side of the lake, though tall in some places and short in others. Clusters of light pink flowers buzzed with bees. Will tried to catch one, but I sharply scolded him so he wouldn't get stung. A rabbit was frightened out of its hiding place, and Will gave chase. I sat on a boulder to rest and chew on some jerked serarb, waiting for Will to tire himself.

Will finally returned with his tongue lolling and an empty stomach, but he seemed pleased nonetheless. He collapsed heavily at my feet and panted, and I poured some water into my palm for him to drink.

"Wear your little legs out, young man?" I followed the water up with a bite of meat and gave him time to catch his breath before we hiked toward the hillside.

The petiloos pup tired and could go no further, so I carried him in my satchel, his nose sticking out to sniff the air as he watched the scenery. The roar of the waterfalls faded, replaced by the hum of insects and the delicate sound of grass swishing along my legs. The ground swept upward, and I climbed over thick clumps of grass and moss-covered rock. The angle became steeper and steeper, until I worried I'd end up climbing a precipice I couldn't descend. Just when I started considering turning back, the slope leveled out, and I crawled onto a smooth plane of ground lushly covered with emerald green grass.

"That was a bit of a trek," I said off-handedly to Will. I wiped the sweat from my brow. The petiloos sniffed the air, whimpered, and ducked his head into the satchel.

"What's the matter?" I stood and walked toward the edge and saw we were perched on the rim of a great valley carved out of the earth like a bowl. A ribbon of water trailed down the middle, blue like the lake behind me, with finger-like tendrils infiltrating the landscape. Far below, movement caught my eye. I squinted and tried to make out the shapes dotting the ground, but the sun dulled my vision. I rubbed my eyes and climbed a few feet down to get a closer look. I stood on a ledge overlooking the valley. Instantly I recognized the shapes I was seeing and sank to my knees.

Horses.

CHAPTER 42

A herd of horses. I attempted to get an accurate count and estimated at least fifteen with perhaps half as many foals. I chanced climbing down a little further, but the wind was at my back, and I didn't want to spook them.

In contrast to the long-legged, elegantly tall horses we bred in Praed, these were short and stocky, with bushy manes and low-set tails. They represented a spectrum of colors from bay to black to light cream. I sat and watched them graze for at least two hours, not bothering to take out my journal, content to merely observe. Will eventually became restless, so I reluctantly rose and scouted around the ridge for a place where I could descend into the valley on a future exploration.

I wore a ridiculous grin all the way to the boat. I let Will out to romp and watched him cavort with a fluttery winged insect as it landed on one flower then another. We shared the last of my dried meat then climbed back into the canoe. I paddled back at my leisure, a smile plastered on my face. The sun crested the sky and was descending toward the horizon. I lifted the oars and closed my eyes to enjoy the warmth on my face. Will started whining, and I peered at him irritably.

"You sure know how to ruin a moment," I said. He didn't feel the impact of my ire, but instead looked at me anxiously, then over the side of the boat into the crystalline water. Curiously, I leaned over the side and gasped, discovering hundreds of bobbing, translucent shapes in the water. They were no longer glowing blue, but they were no less intriguing. Again, I reached into the water without considering the consequences and scooped one up. Instead of poking at the soft, dome-shaped top, I ran a finger along the delicate projections on the bottom. A tingling sensation spread over my skin, and I rubbed my hand on my pant leg to relieve the irritation.

"Should we keep it and bring it back with us?" I asked Will. The petiloos tilted his head and whined at the strange blob in my hand. I looked down and saw the creature was already drying out in the heat. I returned it to the lake and watched anxiously for it to recover. When it began to undulate and move away, I breathed a sigh of relief.

"I guess that's one mystery that will stay that way for a while." I scratched Will behind the ear.

The light was fading when the canoe scuffed the shore. I jumped out as Telken came forward, and together we dragged the craft onto land and turned it over to keep moisture from collecting inside.

"Didn't think you'd come back," Telken said as we walked toward camp.

"I didn't realize you would watch out for me. I'm sorry if I made you worry," I said. My limbs felt boneless, and my eyes were drifting shut, but I was grinning like an idiot and already looking forward to tomorrow.

Later we sat before the fire, and Luc handed me an ale and tossed some food to Will. I drank from my mug until the contents were empty.

"Good trip?" Telken asked

"The best," I said with an air of satisfaction.

"Did you find a group of goddesses lying about in what nature gave 'em?" Luc chuckled.

"That's *your* dream, Luc. Not mine." I elbowed him playfully.

The dinner bell rang before I could elaborate, and we settled into the business of filling our bellies. I was in the middle of my second helping when Telken informed me the party First Mate Evrard sent back to Faqur with word of our safety had returned.

"They've been in with the officers ever since," Telken said.

"Is something wrong?" I asked.

"Nah." Telken waved his hand in dismissal. "Probably going over reports and other boring nonsense."

As if on cue, First Mate Evrard stalked toward the fire and started passing papers out to some of the men, and a murmur of excitement rose as we discovered they were letters. I watched eagerly as most of them received messages from home and listened to the increase in merriment as passages were read aloud. But the first mate repeatedly passed by me without placing anything in my hands, and I began feeling more and more despondent. The men who'd been gone these past months mingled with the others, but the second mate and captain were not among them. A sense of foreboding descended over me like a dark cloud threatening rain, sending my blissful mood into the gutter.

"Her Royal Highness, Princess Sulwen," First Mate Evrard announced from overhead.

I looked up hopefully, and he placed in my hands not one, but four letters, three bearing the Elejick family seal and the other the crest of Thistledon.

"Thank you," I said.

"You're welcome." He spoke in the kindest tone I'd ever heard from him.

I saved the three letters from Praed Castle for later, but I couldn't wait to open Lilias'. I broke open the seal and breezed over the sweet sentiments and hopes that I've had a safe journey to come straight to the point.

> *I am certain, dear sister, that you have impatiently skipped over most of my letter in favor of the information of which you so eagerly anticipate.*

She knew me so well.

> *I am happy to oblige you and announce the birth of mine and Andrew's first child, a daughter we've named Syrsha. We are beyond overjoyed at how perfect she is and could not have asked for a more beautifully healthy child.*

I cried with such overwhelming happiness I couldn't read past that line.

"Bad news?" Telken asked. I sensed the men around me didn't know what to do, and even Will looked at a loss and opted to nuzzle under my chin. Vaguely, I heard someone call for help, but I was so overcome with emotion I didn't think it was for me until I felt hands gently grasp my shoulders and give me a little shake.

"Miss Elejick?" Captain Romy's voice: I couldn't mistake the sense of panic in his tone. I looked up at him through a mist of tears, smiled, and held up the letter in my hand.

"Lilias," I managed. I swallowed and composed myself. "My sister. She had her baby after I left. I'm an aunt!"

His smile was so wide I even saw his teeth. If I wasn't such a mess and surrounded by fifty men, I would have been in real danger of doing something stupid.

"May I be the first to offer you congratulations then," Captain Romy said. "This calls for a celebration. Absalon!"

The second mate appeared beyond his shoulder.

"Yes, sir?" Absalon asked. "Is everything all right?"

"Bring my firkin of lavender mead," the captain ordered.

"I thought you were saving that for the conclusion of this expedition?" First Mate Evrard said.

"I found a better reason for it," he said as he regarded me. "The King and Queen of Praed have had their first grandchild." The last he said loud enough for everyone to hear, and there erupted a chorus of cheers and hurrahs as the second mate left to retrieve the requested libations.

I shakily rose to my feet and a mug was placed in my hand. I gripped it tightly to steady my nerves. The idiotic grin was back, but at least I was no longer crying. The second mate returned with a fanciful looking vessel already tapped. Each man stepped up to fill his mug. The captain filled his own cup, then poured a little into mine.

"It's very strong," he warned in a low voice. "Sip carefully."

Once everyone had their share, the captain raised his cup and asked for my sister's name.

"Lilias."

He stared at me blankly, and I rolled my eyes and amended, "Mrs. Wyrwyk."

"To Mrs. Wyrwyk!" Captain Romy raised his glass. The crew echoed my sister's name, and he tapped his mug against mine before drinking its syrupy contents. I took a sip first, and the sensation of savory floral and sweet coated my tongue. It was the most delicious drink I'd ever tasted, and I took another sip and closed my eyes to savor the feeling of it sliding over my mouth and leaving a warm trail down my throat.

"How do you like it?" Captain Romy asked.

I lazily opened my eyes and realized I was already having trouble focusing.

"I see how this could be a dangerous beverage," I said slowly.

In my periphery, I saw mugs being passed around, and I reached into the fray for more. The captain watched, but he didn't try to stop me. And why should he? I wasn't his daughter or his sister. I was a grown, independent woman! I took another sip and was again transported to a magical, soft place where everything was warm and delicious. My head was already becoming fuzzy, the same feeling I would get after multiple glasses of ice wine. This drink was strong indeed.

"Where does it come from?" I asked the captain in what I hoped was a language he could comprehend.

"It's my family's label," he said.

"My compliments." I was conscious of the fact that I'd drawn myself into a very erect stance, as if I was in a corset and mingling among a crowd in the Great Hall of Praed Castle. It was really the only situation where I overindulged in alcohol, so my mind apparently decided to place me in that scenario. There was even music, as the crew started playing in their combined joy of receiving news from home and being served quality alcohol.

"You were gone for a long time today," Captain Romy said over the lively playing and singing.

"Oh, I haven't had a chance to tell you! I made the most wonderful discovery. The best thing I could have found, actually. I'll be spending all my days over there from now on."

"Is that so?" He tilted his head. "Why? What did you find?"

I leaned forward and looked around as if what I was about to tell him was a great secret, cupped a hand over my mouth so no one could read my lips, and whispered loudly, "Horses."

"Horses?" His brow arched. "That is a momentous discovery, indeed."

"Momonon…moment… Um…good word." I sipped my drink again. "Just think what this could mean in considering this place as a potential colony." I chewed at my lower lip as I became lost in memories of Nettle and riding across the prairie.

"I agree," Captain Romy said. "I look forward to hearing about your observations. Let me know if you think these horses could be tamed."

I sighed. "You don't *tame* a horse." I blew a strand of hair out of my eyes. "You teach them that you're a team, that you're separate halves of a soul, that together you can become more. You can't tame something that powerful. You simply show them how to channel that strength into something meaningful." I met Captain Romy's eye. He appeared unmoved, but then I noticed he was standing very still and breathing rapidly. I stepped back, fearing I'd angered him, but before I could apologize, Telken came dancing up to me and held out his hand.

"Would you do me the honors, lass?" Telken asked.

"I'm afraid I don't know any Faqur dances." I gave an apologetic shrug.

"That's all right," he said with a bit of a slur. "Nothing fancy here. Just move about to the music!" I smiled, drank the last of my mug before setting it on the ground, and accepted Telken's outstretched hand.

The rest of the night passed by in a blur of dancing and laughter, and though I wouldn't be able to recall every detail, I didn't act in any way disgraceful or regrettable. Until I reached a hand toward Captain Romy and invited him to dance with me. He hesitated, and even in my inebriated state, my heart sank with disappointment. Second Mate Absalon accepted my hand in his brother's stead, but my mortification lingered throughout the duration of the evening. When I glanced over and saw Will curled up asleep next to the captain's boot, I decided it was probably best I turn in as well. I scooped up the petiloos without meeting the captain's eye and took off intently toward my tent, swaying only a little bit…at least so I maintain.

I was almost to my tent when I heard the captain call out my name. I froze and held Will close as I turned to face him, acutely aware that my inhibitions were dangerously low. Depending on how the next few minutes went, I would either be screaming or kissing him. Hopefully neither. There was a pensive look on his face when he came up to me, and I sensed there was something he wanted to say but for some reason he couldn't. Was I starting to figure him out? Leave it to the mead to open my eyes.

"Yes, sir?" I prompted.

"I hope I didn't offend you," he said.

"At what point would you have offended me?"

"I wasn't rejecting your offer to dance. I simply wasn't sure it was entirely… appropriate."

"Of course. I defer to your judgment." I tried to bow, but the motion made my head swim.

"I hope the rest of your letters bring you equal joy," he said.

I blinked, unsure how to respond. I'd been so ready to argue that I found myself completely without words.

"Thank you," I said. "If they do, would you happen to have more celebratory bottles?"

He smiled crookedly.

"That was my best one," he said. "You'll have to settle for watered-down ale in the future."

"Your best one? You didn't have to do that." My eyes misted over, and I stepped forward to rest a hand on his chest. "I truly appreciate it, sir."

He abruptly stepped out of my reach. "Goodnight, Miss Elejick."

"Goodnight." I ducked into my tent, tucked Will into bed, and fell over snoring within seconds.

When I awoke the next morning, I felt oddly refreshed despite overindulging the night before. Will was wagging his tail in anticipation of another adventure (or breakfast). I patted his head and scratched under his chin affectionately.

"Ready to watch the horses today?" He yipped, which I took to be a 'yes.'

I leapt out of bed and prepared for the day in record time. I caught sight of the letters lying unopened on the floor, and I gathered them up and considered whether to read them now or wait until evening. One letter was from Mother and Father, another a letter written jointly by my brothers, and the last was from Kyra. I opted to read the one from my brothers because it probably contained nothing but nonsense and teasing. If I read either of the others, I'd probably have a breakdown.

All four of my brothers added their own well wishes and hopes for my adventures laden with jesting, but I had to collect myself before leaving the tent because of a line from Alyx.

You must know how dearly you are missed, but this voyage you have undertaken has opened the country's eyes to the possibility of exploration and expansion. In pursuing your own destiny, you have also served the crown, for the council has decided to follow your example and assemble a team to venture east across the jungles of Vyt where it is hoped our allies there will assist us in funding the building of a fleet to be docked in the bay of Ilano for the purposes of mounting our own expeditions. Rian has volunteered to lead the team, and he leaves with our well wishes and hopes for a prosperous future.

I am very proud of you, Sulwen, and am, as always, your loving brother.
Alyx

It took several minutes before I was confident enough that my face wouldn't look like I'd been stung by a swarm of bees before finally stepping out into the sunshine. The air was fresh and warm, and the smell of food quickly superseded any longing for home. My heart swelled with pride at Alyx's words. Until that moment, I'd felt guilty leaving Praed and essentially abandoning my responsibilities there. But knowing that my actions spurned Praed's desire to look beyond our borders made those latent feelings melt away, and my chest lightened.

I ate hastily and commissioned the cook for a midday meal for me to take on my trip so I wouldn't have to come back, which he was all too happy to oblige me with.

"If it means keeping that dirty animal out of camp, then I'll pack you a feast," he said grumpily. I didn't issue the retort he deserved lest he decide to poison me.

Telken was helping me carry *Tenacity* down to the water when he asked if I'd seen the captain that morning.

"No." I shrugged. "But that's not unusual. Why?"

"After you went to bed last night, he stalked through camp in a blazing temper. I've never seen the likes of it from him before. Went right through us to the officer's quarters and hasn't poked his head out since. The first mate did a circuit of camp to make sure everything was in order this morning where the captain usually does that himself."

"Oh, no," I groaned. My stomach suddenly felt very heavy. Had I said something to upset him? I thought I recalled everything I said and did the night before, but now I wasn't so sure. "Does anyone have an idea what's wrong?"

"Besides maybe thinking he was regretting sharing his best mead?" He chuckled and shook his head. "Don't rightly know."

Perfect. Well, I didn't have time to dwell on what was bothering the captain and whether I had anything to do with it. We placed the boat in the water, and I was pushing off from shore before I could change my mind. Today was a glorious day, and I didn't want to ruin it by finding out I was in trouble. It was fortunate indeed that I planned to stay away from camp for the entire day. This made it easier to avoid the captain and a potential punishment that I honestly didn't think I deserved. After all, it was his family's mead that got me into the situation in the first place. If it loosened my tongue or lessened my inhibitions, the consequences would be worth it. The libations were quite delicious.

CHAPTER 43

I lay downwind from the herd in the valley, documenting the horses grazing several yards away. Fifteen adults and seven foals. Tails swished and flicked away buzzing flies, and a contented snort occasionally broke the silence. I found a spot out of the way so I wouldn't frighten them, though an ear swiveling my way suggested the animals weren't entirely ignorant of my presence. That might have been because Will was romping near me, pouncing on insects and sniffing for mice in the dirt.

"Could you try to be quieter?" I whispered.

The petiloos cocked his head and yipped. My heart clenched as I looked toward the horses, their heads raised and nostrils flared. A large chestnut with a flaxen mane falling in long locks took several steps closer and stomped a foot. His erect posture and commanding presence told me he was the stallion in charge.

"Thanks a lot, Will," I croaked.

Will ducked behind a tree as the horse tossed his head and pinned his ears. I groped along the ground and my fingers closed around a long stick just as the chestnut galloped forward with a short, high-pitched neigh. When he wouldn't relent, I jumped to my feet with a shout and swiped the stick through the air. The whip crack of the branch startled him into sliding to a stop. I continued smacking the stick on the ground, moving toward him to get his feet in motion. Mother taught me that if you control a horse's feet, you control the horse. He pinned his ears. I yelled and swiped the stick in a frenzy across the front of his body until he took off running in the opposite direction. He stopped several feet away and stared at me with his ears pricked. I ran forward and used the stick to get his feet moving again. This time, he galloped back to the group. When he raced by, the others ran after him, their hooves thundering over the valley. I stood catching my breath and watched the colorful procession fade into the distance. Will seemed to appear from nowhere and cowered behind my leg.

"You almost got us killed, do you know that?" I asked the petiloos. He had the graciousness to appear abashed, and I walked over to the meandering river to take a long drink.

After sharing a part of my meal with Will, I set off to track the herd again. They had stopped their frantic escape only a few miles away and were once again grazing, but the chestnut stallion was much more wary. I gave the herd plenty of space so the stallion wouldn't feel so on edge, but he soon realized I was nearby. Once again, he charged, and again I managed to chase him off and he moved the herd. This was repeated several times until I was so exhausted I could barely stand, let alone walk. The last time the stallion caught sight of me, I wasn't confident I could fend off another attack should he decide to charge again. He took a few steps toward me and lowered his head, ears pricked forward, and licked his lips. I gasped in shock. It was a sign of submission.

Taking a chance, I slowly turned my back on him and walked away. I heard his answering hoofbeats and froze. The hoofbeats stopped, too, and I turned to see the stallion regarding me placidly. We stared at each other for several seconds, then I backed away. He watched until I was quite a distance away, then turned and strode back to the herd which had been curiously watching our encounter. Not wanting to push my luck, I left the valley and returned to the boat.

I reached the opposite shore just as the last remnants of my strength vanished. I climbed numbly out of the boat and was useless helping Telken drag it onto shore. Even Will was subdued on the walk to camp and sat heavily before the fire. I ate in a daze, not acknowledging my friends, my eyes opening and closing slowly as the light faded.

"You look fully spent, lass," Telken said. He had to repeat himself before I realized he was speaking to me.

I nodded dumbly. "I think I walked enough to span the entire breadth of the island." I yawned, punctuating my statement. Will chimed in with a yawn of his own and stretched out beside me. He was asleep within moments.

"Lucky you were gone all day," Luc said. "The captain has been putting us through our paces."

Suddenly alert, I turned to Telken, "So, he finally came out of the officer's quarters?"

"Aye." Telken sighed. "And still in a state. I've never seen him so sour. Even the second mate stayed away from camp to avoid him."

I groaned in defeat. Captain Romy was angry, and I couldn't think of any other reason except it was my fault. It wasn't fair for the crew to suffer because of my actions, so I dejectedly rose to my feet, scooped up Will, and said, "I'll risk his wrath and go talk to him. It's probably my fault anyway." They chuckled but didn't try to deny it.

As I approached the officer's quarters, I rehearsed a speech of apology conveying my regret at upsetting Captain Romy and asking for forgiveness. When I was satisfied with the result, I took a deep breath and knocked on the door.

"I'm not to be disturbed," came the curt reply.

I was dumbfounded. I'd never heard the captain deny anyone entry into his quarters. He must be very angry indeed.

"Sir?" I called out tentatively. "Please, may I come in?"

Silence ensued. My cheeks flushed and my heart pounded deafeningly in my ears. I swallowed down a lump of emotions and lowered my eyes. I didn't know what I'd said or done, but whatever it was, it angered him more than the deceit I perpetrated when I first boarded *The Wayward Aymelina*. I had to fix this, even if he refused to see me.

"Sir," I said. "I heard from the crew that you've been in a dark mood they cannot account for, and I can't shake the feeling that I'm somehow to blame. I've wracked my brain trying to think of what I've said or done to offend you, but I confess I cannot recall it, and I have no excuse but to blame the drink. The crew can't be punished because of my actions. Please." I took a few breaths and cleared my throat before continuing. "Please forgive me," I whispered.

The silence that followed ripped my heart in two, and I held Will close to my chest to comfort me. Then the door opened, and the captain was standing there gazing down at me sympathetically. I looked up at him hopefully and was struck by how despondent he appeared.

"I regret that I have distressed you," Captain Romy said. "The fault is not yours. It is mine."

"Did you receive bad news from home?"

"No," he said. "All is well."

"Is there anything I can do?"

"No," he said with the barest smile. "The problem is mine to solve. I will not allow myself to become so overcome as to affect the crew from now on. You have my word." He reached over and scratched behind Will's ear. "You have exhausted him." His eyes met mine. "And you're about to fall over."

"Yes. With your permission, I'll head off to bed now."

"Such a thing does not require my permission." His tone wasn't cold, yet it wasn't quite kind either.

"Goodnight then, sir."

"Goodnight, Miss Elejick."

The door closed and I was left alone to contemplate the odd exchange. Captain Romy was clearly upset, and it worried me more than I could express. He was always so steady, so calm and collected. To see him unsettled was extremely distressing, but I had to trust his word that the issue would be resolved, and he would cease storming around camp upsetting the crew. I didn't want to have to worry when I was on the other side of the lake. There was too much for me to do. Wild herds of horses hadn't roamed Praed for centuries. If I wrote a book documenting their lives, it may help us better understand how our own horses interact. My work could end up in the library at Hrgun, maybe even taught in the natural sciences classes. I'd leave my mark on history, apart from the crown.

After the first encounter with the chestnut stallion, my subsequent visits went much smoother until he barely gave my intrusions a cursory glance and a flick of an ear. The mares followed his example and didn't bother about me as long as I didn't disturb their foals, who were too wary to come very close. After more than a week of observations, I managed to match the foals to their mares and noted a few yearlings that were starting to spend less and less time with the group. One day, the stallion completely ran off two of the younger horses, and I guessed they were males he didn't want to compete with.

I followed the young horses around the ridge of the valley where green hills jutted out of the land, creating a nest where the herd was protected from wind and rain. I struggled to keep the horses in sight as I climbed, but they pranced up the sheer hillside like deer. Will fared better than me, but my legs shook with fatigue by the time I reached the top. I braced myself on my knees to catch my breath. We'd reached the top of a plateau that stretched for miles. The horses were galloping and bucking ahead of me, sweeping toward the east. I gathered my strength and jogged after them.

The horses inevitably outpaced me, and I picked up their trail of hoofprints. After walking for miles, I started to worry it'd be nightfall soon and I'd have to turn back. The plateau abruptly sloped and dropped down into a meadow. Exhausted, I collapsed onto my backside, and Will sprawled over my legs, panting. The two young horses joined a herd of a dozen other males. They'd integrated into the group with ease, already grooming and grazing companionably. I scratched Will behind the ears and wondered how many other herds lived in the area. I looked toward the distant hills beyond the meadow. Could there be horses on the other side?

My shadow stretched out before me, and the air was cool at my back. The sun was setting, and soon it would be dark. Resigned, I headed back. I'd love to study the other herds, but the days weren't long enough. I could try convincing the captain to let me camp, but he wouldn't allow me to go alone. I'd rather focus on the main herd in solitude.

By the next week, I could distinguish each mare from the other based not just on coat color but personality. I named the stallion Sunset, and his favorite mare was a blue roan I named Matron. Her foal (who I called River) was a dusty gray with four high white socks. I bestowed a name upon each of them and spent more time in that valley than with people. A young bay mare danced around Sunset with her tail in the air, and I shook my head at her blatant flirtations. Her name was Flash, and she'd been prancing around the other mares as if she were the prettiest among them, though they ignored her completely. Matron bared her teeth when the young mare got too close, but Flash would toss her glossy black mane and gallop circles around them, her tail held high. She was magnificent to watch. Though she was as stocky and sturdily built as the rest of them, she moved with a grace only a Praed horse could match. The only herd members who bothered to acknowledge Flash when she felt the need to draw attention to herself were the foals. They leapt and bucked alongside her until she grew tired of their antics and settled in to graze. The pages of my journal were filled with observations I held close to my heart. Every day I left reluctantly, wishing I could move my tent into the valley.

Based on the long days and warm temperatures, I estimated that the island was in the height of summer. It wasn't as warm as the summers in Praed, but the weather was dry and pleasant. My skin went through several cycles of sunburn and healing, leaving more freckles scattered across my face and arms. Alone in the valley, I stripped down to my shirt and rolled up my sleeves and the legs of my breeches to stay cool. I hardly wore shoes, and I laughed inwardly at how decidedly un-princess-like I'd become. I glanced down at Will trotting up with a mouse hanging from his mouth. He'd started hunting for himself and insisted on presenting his prey to me as if to show off his skills, like he needed me to congratulate him before eating his meal.

"Very well done, sir," I said.

The mouse disappeared down his throat and he stretched out in the sun. He reclined in silence while I wrote in my journal, but after a few minutes he yipped and pawed at me.

"Am I boring you?" I asked.

Will fixed his yellow eyes on the horses in the valley then gave me a half-lidded stare, his ears slanted.

"Well, too bad," I said. "We're here to observe and record."

Will sighed, curled up into a ball, and tucked his nose under his tail. I ran a hand down his soft silvery fur, smiling at how much he had grown over the last few months. I rested my head on the lush earth and watched the slight breeze ripple his fur and drift over the valley, undulating the grass like waves. In the distance, I heard a nicker and contented snort as the horses grazed, their tails and manes lifting and falling with the wind. Before I knew what was happening, I fell asleep.

Something warm touched my head and blew air over the back of my neck. The haze of sleep slowly lifted as something pressed against my back. My eyes opened, and I remained perfectly still as I tried to see what was touching me. My hair was ruffled again, and Will yipped in alarm and leapt to my defense. There was a scramble of hooves, and I sat up as Will settled into my lap, his sharp teeth bared. A few feet away stood two foals, one a chestnut and the other dusty gray, both with four high white socks. Their nostrils flared, and their ears pointed forward in alarm. I covered Will's muzzle to muffle the sound of his growling.

"Hello there," I said in a pleasant tone. I held out my hand, and the chestnut foal bolted away. But the dusty gray, whom I recognized as Matron's foal, River, bravely took a step toward me. I kissed and coaxed, until his nose was just out of reach. Will whimpered worriedly, and I shushed him gently. River lost his nerve and cantered away, and I dropped my hand in defeat.

"Well done, Will." I gathered my things and prepared to leave, but as I walked away, I heard the patter of hooves. I turned and there was River, watching. I turned my shoulder to him, and he came closer. Will was frozen next to my leg, and I looked down to see River sniff at the little petiloos. Will lifted his lip to growl, but I sharply reminded him to mind his manners. I extended my hand toward the foal. He sniffed in my direction but didn't come close enough to touch. It didn't matter. I established my first contact with one of the wild horses, and I felt in my heart this was only the beginning.

"Some of us are starting to forget what you look like," Telken said the next morning as I stuffed food into my mouth in my haste to return to the valley.

"Sorry," I mumbled around a mouthful of breakfast. "I had a huge breakthrough yesterday. Two of the foals came close enough to sniff me over and one came back for more."

He laughed. "I have no idea what that means."

"It means they're becoming comfortable with me," I said. "Soon I might be able to touch one. Then who knows? Maybe by the time we leave here, I'll be riding one!" My eyes shone with excitement, which made my friend chuckle even more.

"Prefer horses to people, do you?"

"To be honest, they're a lot less complicated."

"Aye." He nodded in agreement.

"Are things here back to normal?"

"Oh, aye, lass. Captain's his normal steady self. Always meant to ask what you said to him, but never got around to it."

"Nothing very notable. I learned it wasn't my doing. That was enough for me."

"I didn't suspect it was, but I'm glad you found out for sure."

"Why do you think he was so cross?"

"There's not much I can think of that would unsettle a man that steady," Telken mused. "'Cept one thing that is."

"What's that?" I said around a mouthful of food.

"Isn't it obvious?"

"Enlighten me."

"A woman." He nudged me with his elbow and winked.

My eyes widened, then I shook my head and took a long drink to compose myself.

"A woman?" I repeated weakly. "What woman?"

"Oh, who knows. There's a few who tried to stake their claim before we left Faqur. He must have had a letter from one of them that didn't sit right. Who knows? Maybe it was a rejection to a proposal."

Before I could stop myself, I said, "You shouldn't gossip." My cheeks burned with fury and embarrassment. Of course, Captain Romy would have a multitude of ladies vying for his attention. He was a successful captain, presumably well situated, and undeniably handsome. Pain stabbed my heart. I'd been foolish to allow myself to fall in love with him. For all I knew, he had a longstanding engagement with a lovely Faqur woman he planned to marry once we returned.

"You're right."

I barely heard him through my grief.

"None of my business anyway," he said.

Chapter 44

Sunlight sparkled off the morning dew clinging to the grass after a steady rain the night before. It was the first time there'd been any substantial rainfall since our arrival, and the air was freshened with the cleansing water. Will sniffed around the grass, inhaled a few dewdrops, and sneezed, drawing attention to our position where we sat watching the horses. But by now, we were as common a sight as the birds skimming over the river. Though the herd grazed within a few yards of us, none of the adults came any closer. Sunset inspected me from a distance to assure himself I meant no harm, but never came within reach. The foals were a little more curious, but they kept a safe distance. Except for River.

After the day River sniffed at my hair and followed me on my way out of the valley, I brought hardtack to toss to him. I quickly learned that River's trust could be obtained through his stomach, and eventually he came running when he saw me. Yet he wouldn't take the biscuit out of my hand no matter how much I encouraged him. I decided to try a different tactic.

Instead of immediately offering food, I ignored him when he trotted up and walked purposefully to the river's edge. I removed my shoes, sat on a stone, and dangled my feet in the lazily moving water. River watched me in confusion, then pawed the ground in frustration. He snorted, and I casually glanced over my shoulder.

"May I help you?"

River huffed and trotted around the fringes of the shore, too timid to come closer to the water. Will splashed in the shallows trying to catch fish, his tongue lolling as he grinned playfully. River's ears trained on the petiloos and he watched the creature play. To my surprise, the foal tossed his head and pranced into the water after Will. Will was taken aback at first, but when satisfied the horse wasn't going to stomp on him, he continued the game. I laughed at the unlikely companions chasing each other around the water.

My stomach rumbled. I pulled my feet out of the water and the creatures followed me in search of a place to settle in for an afternoon snack. Will waited patiently for scraps, but River surged forward, practically shoving his nose in my lap for a morsel.

"No!" I held out a hand. The foal started and tried to come forward again, but I repeated myself more firmly. Once he maintained a respectable distance, I tossed Will a slice of meat and River a piece of hardtack.

After I'd finished eating, I rose and sought a suitable vantage to watch the herd. Will and River followed. I froze and turned my shoulder to the foal. He halted, and I slowly rotated until I met his eye and beckoned him closer. As if by magic, he followed the motion of my hand as if he were attached to a lead. I held out my hand when he came close enough to touch, keeping very still. He placed his velvety nose in my palm and inhaled my scent. I ran my hand up his face and rubbed circles over the small star on his forehead. He lowered his head contentedly, and I swept my hand further up his forelock and down his neck. I scratched at his withers, and he swished his tail happily.

"You like that?"

He leaned into my touch, and I rubbed his shoulder. A sharp whinny made me pull back, and I looked up to see Matron standing at attention a few yards away. She stomped her hoof, and River returned dutifully to her side. I sank to the ground, a beaming smile on my face, reveling in the progress I'd made.

I returned to camp earlier than normal, not wishing to push my luck. My friends were surprised to see me, but eager to engage in the games we used to play when I wasn't too busy. I had a sword lesson with Luc, learned a game involving throwing a ball to knock over a set of sticks, and played cards to win back the money I'd lost the last time I'd played with Telken.

"You're going to have to play better than that, lass." Telken won yet another hand.

I sighed in defeat, but it felt good to socialize with people for a change.

"Heard the trippers have about mapped the whole southern part of the island," Luc said. "And the notes from our wanderings along the river mean their work'll be done soon."

"Not soon enough," one of the sailors said. "Weather will be changing soon. We'll have to leave." The other men nodded sagely in agreement.

"How do you know the weather's going to change?" I asked. "It's been fine lately."

"A feeling," the sailor said without looking up.

I rolled my eyes but held my tongue.

"You think they'll hold a party for us?" Luc asked.

I quirked an eyebrow. "A party?"

"There's usually a big to-do at the end of the sailing season," Telken said. "Good food, good music, good company. It's Faqur's way of thanking everyone for their hard work."

"Everyone's invited," Luc added. "All the fishermen, sailors, officers, and all their kin."

"That sounds like fun," I said.

"Hope you brought a pair of dancing shoes," Telken said.

"What?" All the blood in my body drained to my toes.

"Dancing. Do you have it where you come from?" Telken said.

"Yes, of course. But remember I don't know any Faqur dances."

All the men looked up at me, and Telken sighed in exasperation.

"Lads, get the instruments."

The men retreated to their tents and returned with an array of musical instruments. They started playing a pleasant tune, and Telken explained the steps to a popular Faqur dance. I followed his lead, but it was difficult to try and watch his feet while concentrating on my own. In a hilarious turn, Luc stepped forward and took the lady's place so I could watch and mimic him. We must have looked ridiculous, but I was determined not to make a fool out of myself in front of all Faqur.

"May I be of assistance?" We looked up to see Second Mate Absalon smiling pleasantly at us.

Telken grunted and gestured toward me, and now I had a partner to dance with to practice the moves I was concentrating on so intently. Absalon was very helpful and encouraging, and we practiced until I felt confident enough to look at his face and not my feet.

"You're gettin' it, lass!" Telken said proudly.

I smiled and Absalon swept me across the grass, imagining a hall full of couples as we pretended to dance down a line. He was surprisingly light on his feet, and I learned another dance quite easily under my friends' tutelage. I passed down the line from the second mate, to Telken, to Luc, falling over laughing and enjoying myself immensely.

"It doesn't look like much work is getting done," a gruff voice spoke over the noise. The music ceased, and we all turned our wide eyes toward First Mate Evrard, glowering at us as if we were children caught out after dark.

"They were only having some fun," Second Mate Absalon said placatingly.

"Teaching the lady here how to dance in Faqur," Telken explained hurriedly. "For when we get back."

"I see," the first mate said dubiously. "Back to work with you all."

The men disappeared, and I went to chase after them when First Mate Evrard barked my name. I froze in my tracks and looked up at him questioningly.

"The captain wishes to speak with you."

I looked at the second mate, and his answering smile was reassuring. "Yes, sir." I followed the first mate, but instead of leading me to the officer's quarters, he brought me to the lakeside.

The captain stood on the shore looking out across the water. He turned at the sound of our approach. We'd barely spoken two words to each other since I knocked on his door many weeks ago. He looked more like himself today, the same composed, well dressed, and well-groomed captain. However, I detected a hesitancy in his eyes when he looked at me, and my heart squeezed painfully when I considered my suspicions that he was a betrothed man. Not that it mattered. It wasn't as if there was a future for us. But now I couldn't even dream.

"Miss Elejick," Captain Romy said.

I saluted. "You wished to speak to me, sir?"

"I thought to wait for you when you came back, but it seems you returned early today," he said.

"It was a good day. I didn't want to risk ruining it by staying longer."

"Explain," he said.

The first mate wandered away, and I found my feet carrying me to the captain's side. We gazed across the lake toward the valley, and I told him everything. I told him about my first encounter with Sunset, and though he started in alarm when I described how the great stallion charged me, I assured him I was perfectly safe. I told him my names of the mares and foals, about the day I awoke to find two nuzzling my hair, and my efforts to gain River's trust. I ended with the triumph of today, that I'd finally touched the foal. I let out a breath as I concluded my story. I'd rambled nonstop, gesturing wildly and expounding passionately in my excitement to tell him about the magnificent horses. All the while, he didn't say a word, not even to ask a question. He listened attentively, sometimes with his eyes on the horizon and sometimes with his focus on me.

"I must sound like a lunatic." I kicked self-consciously at a rock. It skittered across the ground and landed in the water with a *plop*.

"Not at all," Captain Romy said. "There's no shame in enjoying yourself or being passionate about your work. I can hear it in your voice. I've…er…" he hesitated, as if weighing his next words. "We haven't spoken in quite some time."

"That's true," I said quietly. "I hope I haven't been remiss in my duties."

"Not at all. But I would like more frequent reports of your activities. I don't wish to wake up and find that you've smuggled a foal into your tent." He peered at me out of the corner of his eye and smirked.

"I hope you think me smarter than that. A tent is way too small for a foal. He'd be better off in the officer's quarters." I grinned, and he turned away to hide his smile and stifle a laugh. I wished he wouldn't do that, at least when we were alone. But I understood he had to maintain boundaries, to preserve the distinction of rank. For here, I was no princess, and he was the ultimate authority.

"I would like to visit this valley of yours," he said.

My heart fluttered, and my breath hitched in my throat.

"Of course! Whenever you wish."

"I don't want to risk you losing what progress you've gained with your foal by intruding. When you think it best, name the day and I will join you."

"Thank you, sir." I was embarrassed, very aware that my gaze was much too soft, but I couldn't look away.

He held my gaze for a heartbeat…two…three—then he was very still again, the only movement the steady rise and fall of his chest. I couldn't read the look in his eyes. It wasn't anger but it wasn't contentment either. Then he blinked, nodded perfunctorily, and walked away.

Over the next few days, River became as constant of a companion as Will. They were equally fond of each other. While I made notes and drew pictures in my journal, they raced each other over the valley and played hide-and-seek. This was my favorite game to watch. Will could crouch low in the grass and be nearly invisible but when River tried to emulate him, it was just comical. When the sun was high and our bellies were full, we would lay in the grass together, Will curled up against River's neck and me resting my head against the foal's shoulder. We must have made a strange picture indeed, for a few horses would wander over to inspect us and shake their heads in bewilderment. The soft downy hair covering River's body was shedding over his face to reveal a beautiful shade of chestnut, and I suspected his true coat color would turn out to be a red roan.

Once River was completely comfortable, I began getting him accustomed to being touched all over his body, particularly the feet, girth, and ears. I didn't know if he would ever bear a saddle, much less a rider, but I wanted him to be familiar with feeling pressure in certain areas. I also wanted him to trust in his rider implicitly, so I led him over rough terrain, logs, and water to lessen his fear of these obstacles. One day, I brought a length of rope and ran it along his body, then fashioned a halter out of it and practiced placing it over his nose. It was a lesson in patience for both of us, although I never had a problem being patient with horses. From the moment I could ride, Mother taught me how to train horses, but I also relied on my instincts and read their body language. The day I slipped the halter over his head without so much as a flinch, I decided it was time to introduce Captain Romy to the valley.

Telken reported the officers were busy with the cartographers for most of the day, so it wasn't until after the evening meal that I finally had the chance to speak with him. I knocked at the door to the officer's quarters and was granted entry. I walked in on the officers finishing up their meal. I flushed red and offered a hasty apology for the intrusion.

"No need for that, Miss Elejick," Second Mate Absalon said amiably. "What can we do for you?"

"The captain asked for me to inform him when it might be appropriate for him to join me across the lake," I said.

"How is that your decision to make?" First Mate Evrard asked sharply.

"It's my boat," I snapped before I could stop myself.

"Miss Elejick," Captain Romy said in a warning tone.

"My apologies, First Mate Romy," I said. "I spoke out of turn." I met the first mate's eye, and to my amazement, he didn't seem very upset.

"When do we leave, Miss Elejick?" Captain Romy asked.

"In the morning. If that's convenient."

"It is," he answered without consulting his brothers. "Dismissed."

I darted out of the building before First Mate Evrard decided my outburst warranted further comment. I really needed to watch my temper, especially when provoked by the first mate.

CHAPTER 45

When Captain Romy joined me the next morning, I insisted on rowing the *Tenacity*. I momentarily panicked that the canoe might be too precarious with two people, but it was sturdily built and balanced well enough that we reached the other side of the lake without incident. After securing the boat, I led the captain to the overlook so he could view the valley in its full glory. His eyes swept the vast space, the meandering river, and the slope of the land leading to the triangular green mountain. Moving through the valley along the river in a procession was my beloved herd of horses.

"Impressive," Captain Romy said. "I assume you'll take me down for a closer look?"

"Yes, sir!" I said. I led him into the valley, Will bounding along in front of us. I no longer worried about keeping hidden or sneaking up on the horses since they'd accepted my presence. I strode confidently forward, and when we were so close you could pick out each animal, I brought my fingers to my lips and blew a short, loud whistle. Their heads came up, and River burst out from the middle of the group and galloped over. I worried he'd hesitate when he saw the captain, but he rushed up to place his muzzle into my open palm without missing a step.

"Impressive," Captain Romy repeated, and there was no mistaking how truly impressed he was.

I scratched River under the jaw and down his neck. The colt's lips twitched with pleasure.

"This is River," I said. "Come." I motioned for the captain to come closer, and the colt showed a touch of wariness and backed away.

"Turn your shoulder toward him," I instructed the captain. "And hold out your hand."

Captain Romy did as I asked, and River stepped forward, his curiosity winning over fear. He sniffed at the captain's hand, checked to see if it held any treats, then turned away indifferently when he found it empty. Captain Romy inched forward and carefully ran a hand over River's glossy neck. I rewarded the colt's compliance with a piece of hardtack, then he and Will ran off to play their games. We watched them frolic for a few minutes, and I snuck a peek at the captain's expression. He looked... relaxed. A contented smile graced my lips, and I sighed.

"I see Will has made a friend," the captain said.

"Yes. They are quite the pair."

His eyes scanned the herd. "They're much sturdier than I pictured. Why do you think that is?"

I shrugged. "They live on an island. Smaller horses require less food."

"An astute observation. Could their size also be an indication of what sort of winter might be expected here?"

An interesting idea. Winters in Praed could be very cold with months of snow, yet our horses were much finer boned. But our horses were also stabled, and these were not.

"Possibly." A sudden thought struck me, and my eyes flew to the captain's face. "Are we going to overwinter here?"

"I hoped to avoid it. We aren't prepared for a harsh winter."

"It's been a mild summer."

"Exactly my worry. If it doesn't get very hot in the summer, it can reasonably be guessed that the temperatures drop quickly."

"Perhaps."

"In any case, my goal is to leave within the next month or so."

"So soon?" My attention drifted to the herd. How could we leave so soon? I'd made so much progress, and there was so much more I wanted to do.

"Have you enjoyed your time here?"

I met his eyes again, and I found in that moment I could be nothing but completely honest.

"Yes. I've felt fulfilled here."

"I'm glad." He yielded a soft smile.

"I...I don't know how to go back to my life in Praed."

His smile faltered, and I turned away, afraid my face would betray my emotions. I couldn't do this anymore, couldn't bear to be near him knowing that when we reached Faqur, our paths would go in different directions. I could not serve *The Wayward Aymelina* with Lencius Romy as her captain, not while my heart beat his name throughout my body. I would have to go home and mend the pieces of my broken soul, to forget that he ever existed, if I was to live any semblance of a normal life.

"Is Second Mate Romy married?" Aside from Telken's speculations, there was little gossip about the personal lives of the officers. Perhaps I thought asking such a random question would lead to the captain confessing to a future bride. In which case, I could more easily proceed with the business of drowning in misery.

"Uh…no." His surprise was obvious. "Why do you ask?"

"Just curious," I said. "I don't really know anything about any of you, except of course your impressive military histories."

Captain Romy made a sound I could only interpret as a laugh.

"You've always been very blunt and overly curious."

"I don't mean to pry," I said. "You don't have to answer my questions if you don't wish to."

"I will answer provided I see no harm in it," he said.

"If I may speak freely—"

"Yes, please do, Miss Elejick. I know I can't stop you anyway."

My eyes flew to his, and I was relieved to find humor in his expression. He was teasing me, and I reveled in it.

"I'm surprised to hear of the second mate's singledom. He seems so amiable."

"He *is* amiable. To everyone. I suspect that's why he can't decide on a wife. Every woman has such endearing merits in his eyes he can't bring himself to choose, and he abhors the idea of paining any woman who might be pining for him but doesn't receive his attentions."

I couldn't help it. I laughed until I couldn't breathe.

"He is quite convinced of his own desirability then?" I said between breaths.

"Or the possibility of it. After all, you inquired as to his eligibility yourself."

"Not on my own behalf!" He narrowed his eyes, and I couldn't help rambling that I had no interest in Second Mate Absalon as a potential husband, though I liked him as a person and held him in the highest respects. His mouth twitched, and I suspected he was teasing me again. I glared at him and asked if all the Romy brothers thought so highly of themselves.

"We're not all as melodramatic as Absalon if that's what you're asking."

"Oh?" I hoped I sounded casual. If he tells me he's engaged or Artur forbid married, I'm hiking back to the ship tonight.

"Evrard married a very decent woman without worrying about potentially hurting anyone's feelings."

"What?" I couldn't hide how shocked I was at this revelation. Out of all the Romy brothers, he was the last I thought would've convinced some poor woman to marry him.

"You're surprised?"

"Yes. He seems so..." I tried to find the right words without sounding insulting, but all coherent thought escaped me.

"Taciturn?"

"Horribly repellent. Saddle sore would be more pleasant to deal with. Don't get me wrong. I like First Mate Romy, but I would sooner marry a dullard than him."

"Like Seaman Calux?"

"Exactly!" I clamped a hand over my mouth and stared at Captain Romy sheepishly. This time, there was no mistaking his laughter. I even saw his teeth.

"Don't stress yourself, Miss Elejick. I'm perfectly aware that my brother can be a difficult man at times. But he is a *good* man and a good sailor. And a devoted husband."

"I'm glad to hear it," I said. "Does he miss her when he's away from Faqur for so long?"

"I imagine so," Captain Romy said quietly. "But he doesn't speak of it, and neither should you."

"I won't. It must take a woman of strength to say goodbye to her husband without knowing when he'll return."

"I suppose it does. Just as it takes a certain strength of will for a man to say goodbye to a wife he loves with the certainty that he may *never* return."

"Do you know many such men?"

"Most of this crew as well as my brother. And many of the fishermen. Faqur is full of spouses who rarely see each other."

"That must be terribly difficult. I don't think I could be as strong as the women of Faqur."

"I don't blame you, Miss Elejick. I hear many of my crew speak of their wives with longing, and I greatly admire their fortitude. I think in many ways they're better men than I, for I never had the courage to take on a wife for the reasons we speak of."

There was a quickness to my breathing at his words. If he never took on a wife, then he wasn't married, nor could he reasonably be considered engaged. Though this didn't change our eventual outcome, at least I felt less a fool, however minuscule the amount.

"Miss Elejick?"

"Yes?"

"Are there more horse herds in this valley besides yours?"

"I found a bachelor herd, and I assume there are more family groups," I said. "But I've concentrated on this one since I've earned their trust. Why do you ask?"

Captain Romy pointed to the far end of the valley. Shielding my eyes from the sun, I followed his direction. An imposing cream-colored stallion was slowly approaching the herd. I'd never seen him before, and I instinctively took a step forward as if to intercede. Captain Romy grasped my arm to stop me.

Sunset noticed the interloper and took off after him. Both stallions arched their necks and touched nostrils, assessing each other. I clutched my hands to my chest as I watched, hoping that a little show of force would be enough to dissuade them from fighting. But the stallions were far from satisfied. A sharp squeal pierced the air and they stomped their hooves, kicking up dirt and startling the mares. They pranced around each other, their necks arched and their forelegs stepping high as they thundered around the valley chasing each other. They reared on their hind legs, hooves flailing and catching each other across the face, lashing out with bared teeth. Sunset appeared to have the advantage. He whipped around, kicking out at the cream-colored intruder, knocking him square in the chest. The rival charged forward, grasped Sunset by the withers, and pushed with his chest to knock the stallion off his feet. Before Sunset could regain his footing, the cream-colored stallion wrenched his jaws back and forth across his shoulders and rump. The attacker was relentless. He reared, and with a shriek that rang in my ears, he brought his hooves down on Sunset's head. The stallion collapsed, his knees buckling. The interloper pranced around him.

In my heart, I knew this was the law of wild horses, that it was nature's way of creating a strong species, but it didn't make it any easier to watch. Matron apparently felt the same, for she came to Sunset's defense with a mighty shriek. When she was within reach, the cream-colored stallion charged forward, grasped the top of her neck in his teeth, and shook. Her resulting shriek echoed across the valley, sending the other mares into a panic. A familiar whinny answered Matron's call, and to my horror, River raced to his mother's defense.

"No!" I shouted. I tried to intercede, but Captain Romy still held onto my arm. I struggled against him, but he wouldn't let go.

"Please!" I begged. "Let me go! I have to stop him!"

"You can't!" Captain Romy said. "You'll get yourself killed!" He wrapped his arms around me and pressed me to his chest. I couldn't move, so there was nothing for me to do but helplessly watch River attack the cream-colored stallion.

He valiantly squealed and reared into the air, kicking out at the intruder. Despite his bravery, he was no match for a horse four times his size. The stallion whirled around and kicked River in the ribs. When the colt was down, the stallion sank his teeth behind his ears and tossed him around as if he weighed no more than a feather.

I screamed, a sound exploding from the pit of my stomach and tearing out of my throat in bitterness and agony. Will ran into the fray to support his friend, but he was thankfully small and fast enough to escape the dangerous hooves of the cream-colored stallion when he stomped after the petiloos.

When the dust settled, the triumphant victor rounded up the mares, including Matron, and led them off across the valley. Captain Romy released me, and I ran to River. I slid onto my knees when I reached him and gingerly placed a hand on his chest. I barely breathed, my vision blurred, and Will's whimpers drowned in my grief. Captain Romy knelt beside me, and I looked up at him.

"Is he…?" is all I managed. I trembled so violently I could do nothing but stroke River's belly and hope there was still life in him.

The captain rested a hand over River's heart, then met my eyes solemnly.

"He's gone," he said.

To say my heart broke fails to describe the searing pain ripping through my chest, the wail of despair, and the torrent of tears flowing down my cheeks. I cried as if my own brother lay dead in the grass. It was the first time I would mourn so deeply.

I was barely aware of Captain Romy until he gently drew me against his chest in a comforting embrace. I don't know how long we remained thus, me crying like a baby, clutching at his coat and him rocking me in his arms. Slowly, my cries subsided, and my breathing returned to normal, but still Captain Romy held me, and I didn't pull away. I became self-conscious when his kind gesture made me feel something more than comfort. I extricated myself from his embrace without meeting his gaze.

I stroked River's neck and said, "We have to honor him."

"How do we do that?" Captain Romy asked.

"In Praed, if a knight's horse dies before him, the body is cremated in an elaborate funeral. The ashes are saved and buried with the knight when he passes. If they fall in battle together, they are either buried or cremated together."

"Do you want us to cremate him?" There was tenderness in his tone, and it was almost enough to make me break down in tears again.

"A lady's horse is buried," I whispered. "With gifts of great personal importance." I reached into my boot, removed the dagger from Mukahanu, and laid it on River's body.

"I'll go back to camp and bring back some shovels." Captain Romy got to his feet.

"You don't have to do that." I made to rise, and he placed a restraining hand on my shoulder.

"I'll be back as soon as I can. Stay here with him."

I nodded numbly and watched him leave. Then I curled up against River's lifeless body, Will tucked in my arms, and fell asleep for the last time next to my friend.

CHAPTER 46

A gentle shake brought me to consciousness. I blinked awake as remnants of dreams stripped from my hazy vision. The sounds of screaming horses echoed in my ears, and blood soaked the edges of my mind. I couldn't focus, so I closed my eyes again, but I was shaken with more urgency.

"Miss Elejick, wake up." I recognized the captain's soft cadence.

I sat up and rubbed the sleep from my eyes. I looked down at River's body and remembered Captain Romy had gone to retrieve shovels so we could bury him.

"I'll help you dig," I mumbled, rising shakily to my feet.

"No need. It's already done," he said.

"What?" I looked toward the ground and saw the substantial hole Captain Romy dug while I slept.

My shoulders sagged. "You didn't have to do that by yourself."

"I know. Let's move him."

Together, we dragged River the short distance and lowered him into the ground. My dagger was a poor offering, but I set the gift atop him.

"He deserves more than what I have to give," I said. "Were we in Praed, I could offer him jewelry and the finest clothes, but here I have next to nothing."

"Here." Captain Romy took my hand and pressed something against my palm. I opened my fingers and beheld the shining face of a compass.

"No." I tried handing it back. "It was your father's. I cannot accept it for this task."

"It has more value than all the jewels in Praed. Surely that makes it worthy enough to honor your horse?"

I was so taken aback I couldn't speak, but I could tell by the look in his eyes that there was no use arguing. Wordlessly, I lowered the compass into the grave, and together we covered River's body with earth.

"Do you say anything?" Captain Romy asked.

I fell to my knees and spread my fingers over the mound of earth, digging into the soft dirt. Captain Romy knelt beside me and rested his hand next to mine. Will set his paws on the grave and whimpered, then tucked his head between his legs.

"We commit you to the earth from whence you came," I began. "So that you may once again become a part of it. You will live on in our memories, and we will honor you by sharing stories of your bravery. Fly with hooves as swift as Amyl's wings into the kingdom of Artur and run with those who went before you. What is remembered shall never die." My throat tightened with grief, and I could speak no more.

"Well said, Miss Elejick," Captain Romy said.

When we walked out of the valley, I didn't look back, though there was a certainty in my heart that this was the last day I should venture there. The world could be incredibly cruel, and I'd witnessed the extent of its viciousness. I didn't think I could bear it if I had to continue observing such devastating events without being able to do anything about it. I didn't wish to repeatedly mourn nor risk my heart hardening.

I couldn't face Captain Romy as he paddled us across the lake. My eyes hurt from crying and my face felt puffy and raw. My nose was chapped from wiping it with my sleeve, and my hair was disheveled. I probably looked like a beggar. Will lay in my lap looking as mournful as I felt. I stroked his head and hoped he found comfort in it.

When we were almost to shore, Captain Romy asked, "Is there anything I can do?"

"You've done more than enough. Thank you, sir." I gave him a look I hoped conveyed my gratitude without being too pathetic. "I'm sorry if I've stained your coat."

He shrugged one shoulder. "It'll wash."

Telken and First Mate Evrard were waiting when we arrived and helped pull the boat ashore. I couldn't meet their eyes. I carried Will to my tent and didn't answer Telken's worried inquiries about my health. I spoke to no one, though my appearance elicited many questions, and ignored the concerned glances. I didn't shed my clothes when I ducked inside my tent. I curled up on my bed with Will in my arms and fell into an exhausted sleep.

I didn't emerge from my tent for hours, not even for food. Will left several times and returned once or twice with an offering of meat to try and tempt me to eat. I smiled and patted him on the head but respectfully declined his gifts of half-eaten rodents. Many times, my friends scratched on the outside of my tent to ask after me, but I either didn't answer or requested I be left alone. I felt no hunger, nor sadness, just emptiness. When I left my tent out of biological necessity, I wandered into the trees along the ridge and didn't come back until almost dusk.

Over the ensuing week, this is how I spent my days. I rose early, forced myself to eat a meager meal before anyone else was awake, then disappeared into the woods. I didn't so much as glance at the lake. I walked through the forest listening to the birds and the sounds of Will romping in the dried leaves and tried not to think about River. When I grew too tired to walk any further, I curled up at the base of a tree to sleep, then awoke and walked some more.

Rain fell more frequently, though not in the torrential downpours I was used to in Praed. During one of my walks, I was caught in a shower, and I turned my face to the sky to let the cool water cleanse my cheeks of tears and soak through my clothing. Though the rain ceased by the time I returned to camp, my teeth chattered. Not wishing to fall ill and further my misery, I approached the fire in the middle of camp and stretched out my hands to warm them. The men in my nearest vicinity fell silent, and I felt their eyes watching me. My temper rose, but I repressed the angry outburst threatening to explode from my mouth.

"Sulwen?" a voice said quietly. It was the first time Seaman Calux had spoken to me in ages.

"What?" I snapped.

"Is there anything I can do?" he asked. "To ease this melancholy you've found yourself under?"

"Yes. You can leave me in peace." I didn't have to look at him to know he was staring, probably pitiably. I didn't want his pity any more than I wanted his help. I wanted to be left alone.

"Of course. But please, should you need anything, know that I am at your disposal. As a friend." I met his gaze and saw only sympathy.

"Thank you." The barest smile graced my lips then faded.

One by one, nearly all the crew, even those who never cared for me, came forward with a similar sentiment. They couldn't know the nature of my sorrow, but nevertheless they banded around me in my time of need like I was family. The display of loyalty filled me with an intense feeling of belonging, a tie that I had only experienced with my own flesh and blood. Even First Mate Evrard expressed sympathy for my loss, an act which convinced me that underneath his gruff exterior, there was actually a human being capable of emotions. There was an explanation for his having a wife after all.

Without quite knowing how it happened, I found myself at the door of the officer's quarters and knocked before I could prevent it. When the captain called out, "Enter," I looked down at Will and told him to cause a ruckus if I became weepy. "I'll need a means of escape," I said. "He's seen me cry enough."

I pushed open the door, and when Captain Romy saw it was me, he quickly stood and took the few steps necessary to close the gap between us.

"Miss Elejick, how are you?" he asked.

"Better," I said.

"Would you like to sit down?" He indicated a chair.

"No, thank you. I just wanted to say again how much I appreciate what you did. There aren't many Faqur captains who would have gone through the trouble of burying a colt, I'm sure. You have done River a great service."

"I didn't just do it for River, Miss Elejick."

I dared to gaze up at him, and though his expression was passive, his eyes were strangely bright as they searched my face, for what I couldn't fathom.

"I find that I cannot go back there." My throat ached with the effort to keep from crying.

"That's understandable," he said. "I hope what happened hasn't altered your opinion regarding this expedition. You aren't regretting coming here?"

"No," I breathed, and a tear slipped down my cheek. I looked toward the table where several maps were laid out, some of the island and others of the surrounding area. They were a welcome distraction from my grief, so I wandered closer to inspect them. I touched the map of the island, running my fingers over the lake and the triangular green mountain. My pulse throbbed at my temples. I pushed the map aside and studied the others, one of which contained the islands we visited the year prior. I remembered the braxes and the Nakwacimek and smiled. How fortunate I was to be able to look back upon my life with satisfaction at experiencing these places, happy that I didn't keep to the castle or my own country. I traced the route we'd taken, noting that the area where we encountered the storm was notated in addition to the general location where we first fought the Burdeeds. My brows furrowed as I contemplated the map. A thought struck me I hadn't considered.

"What were they doing there?" I thought out loud.

"Who?"

"The Crif pirates. What were they doing way out there?"

"Patrolling the edges of their waters." His voice held a dark undertone.

I looked over the map more thoroughly. To the far east, there was Crif. To the north, the islands we visited. But to the south and to the west, there was nothing.

"What lies in this direction?" I pointed to the blank spaces on the map.

"No one knows. No ships have ventured that far."

My mind was spinning with an outrageous idea, an idea so impossible it wasn't worth speaking.

"May I borrow these?" I asked. "I promise I'll return them undamaged."

"Take all the time you need."

I rolled up the sections I was interested in and saluted before heading toward the door.

"Miss Elejick," Captain Romy called out.

"Yes, sir?"

"You're welcome." His expression was unreadable, his manner once again that of the stoic commander of *The Wayward Aymelina*. A smile flitted across my face, then I stepped out into the light misting of rain.

The maps were spread out on a makeshift table in the bunkhouse where I was consulting with Telken and several other seasoned sailors. Though I didn't voice my theory just yet, I wanted their help in estimating distances and their knowledge of the type of ship the Crif pirates sailed. I wanted to know how far they could travel, the amount of supplies they could hold, and so on. The men were extremely helpful, and I learned the ships the Crif sailed could carry enough supplies for the twenty or so men aboard to survive a considerable journey. However, upon further consideration, Telken informed me they never knew the Crif to travel as far as we'd seen them without having to stop somewhere to restock their provisions. This was the breakthrough I was looking for. I thanked the men for their help, gathered the maps together, and retreated to my tent. Three days later when I was confident of the argument I'd present, I gathered my courage and knocked on the door to the officers' quarters.

"Enter," came the response.

I took a deep breath and looked down at Will. "Wish me luck."

"Miss Elejick!" Second Mate Absalon exclaimed when he saw me. "How good to see you smiling again." It was true. I was beaming with anticipation and bouncing on the balls of my feet.

"I hope I'm not interrupting anything," I said.

"Not at all. Sit down if you please."

I didn't miss the look of annoyance on First Mate Evrard's face when his brother offered me a seat at their table.

"I prefer to stand, thank you, sir."

"What can we do for you, Miss Elejick?" Captain Romy prompted.

"With your permission?" I held out the maps and the captain made a space on the table for me to spread them out. "I've been studying these maps of the area where the Burdeeds captured the ship."

"For what reason?" First Mate Evrard asked, though his tone was not accusatory. He sounded curious.

"I've been speaking with some of the seasoned sailors about the nature of their boats, how fast they can go, how far they can travel, that sort of thing. I've made a few calculations and found where we encountered them is the greatest distance ever recorded in the history of our dealings. In fact, the battle where the last of their ships sank was only two-thirds this distance at most." I looked up to ascertain their receptiveness to this information. They were all listening with rapt attention.

"Intriguing, Miss Elejick," Second Mate Absalon said. "Please, do continue."

"Well, I wondered what they were doing out there so far from Crif." I looked from one man to the other, my eyes wide with unrestrained excitement. "I think they were looking for something."

"Looking for what?" First Mate Evrard asked. There was no mistaking the curiosity in his tone. "An island?"

"Bigger," I said. "It had to be worth five of their ships and a pirate leader to take them out so far." I paused for dramatic effect, relishing the fact that they were all fully invested in my speech. "I think they were looking for a new continent."

All three men's eyebrows shot up in unison, and I almost laughed at how comical their shared surprise was.

"For what purpose?" Second Mate Absalon asked. "They already possess quite a large one."

"My father told me that after King Karne was defeated, Crif divided into warring tribes. They fought over resources, especially after a drought lasting many years. The land is hot, it's covered in sand, and it's unforgiving. These factions value water over gold, and for a people so desperate for simple necessities, it stands to reason that they would be in search of a place where they wouldn't have to worry about such things. The risk of losing their ships outweighed the immense reward of finding a new home."

"She has a point," First Mate Evrard said, much to my utter astonishment. "We've never encountered the Burdeeds this far west. I didn't think about it at the time, but it's strange they were there to begin with."

Captain Romy worried the hair of his beard just below his bottom lip, something he did in moments of intense concentration.

"Absalon," he said. "Is it possible?"

The second mate shook with unrestrained giddiness. "I wish to make some calculations of my own. Forgive me, Miss Elejick, it's not that I doubt you."

"No offense taken, sir." If the second mate was devoting time to working out the problem, it meant he was taking me seriously. All of them were.

"We'll take this information under consideration. Thank you, that will be all. Dismissed," First Mate Evrard said.

It didn't matter they were sending me away. I took it as a sign they were eager to speak without me there. I saluted and all but skipped out of the room.

"Miss Elejick." Captain Romy's voice made me pause just as I reached out to open the door.

"Yes, sir?"

The captain's gaze met mine, and though he appeared as unaffected as always, there was an unmistakable glimmer in his eyes.

"Well done."

The smile on my face was so wide, my cheeks were sore the rest of the day.

CHAPTER 47

I heard no news regarding my speculation of a new continent. At first, I took this to mean the officers were debating the validity of my claim. But after hearing nothing for a week, I began having doubts. The weather was changing, the days were getting shorter, and soon there would be talk of returning to the ship and sailing back to Faqur. I wasn't ready to go back to Praed yet. I decided this would be my last voyage and I wanted to make the most of it.

My instincts proved correct when we were all summoned in front of the officer's quarters one gray morning. All three officers emerged, and a shiver ran up my spine as if portending something ominous. If I was one to believe in such nonsense.

"Able-bodied crew of *The Wayward Aymelina*." Captain Romy, encompassing all of us I was happy to note. "Your work here has been highly commendable and will secure your futures once I tell the Faqur Assembly how thoroughly you have furthered our knowledge of this island. Your dedication to this task has brought pride not only to your names, but to your captain. I am grateful for all of you." He paused to wait for the murmurs of appreciation to die down before continuing. "You have given much of yourselves as well as your time, and I cannot in good conscience ask any more of you. Effective immediately, we will begin preparations to return to the ship and sail to Faqur."

My heart sank as the men rejoiced, and a surge of temper rushed through me. We were going back? Without them telling me about it first? They waited until they announced our departure in front of everyone, for me to be humiliated, wholly unprepared. I could stomach no more underhandedness or the crew's joy. Without waiting to be dismissed, I turned around and forced my way through the crowd. I ran from camp and escaped into the forest.

It was petulant and childish of me to run away, but I didn't care. In a few months I'd leave all this behind forever. So what if I offended them now? Will appeared while I grumpily threw rocks at a knot in a tree. He'd been spending more and more time away from camp lately, and the thought struck me that I would soon be saying goodbye to him as well. I looked into his yellow eyes, his rounded ears erect, and his silver face tilted slightly as he regarded me. In my heart, I knew he belonged here, but a part of me wondered if I might take him back to Praed.

"Will." I pulled the petiloos close and hugged him tightly. He was almost fully grown and perfectly capable of taking care of himself. But was I capable of living without him? I was tired of losing. Couldn't I win just this once?

It was dusk when I returned to camp, fully aware that I'd been derelict in my duties. I clutched Will to my chest, unwilling to let him go. I ignored the smell of food and headed straight for my tent. Out of the darkness, a voice spoke.

"Miss Elejick, may I have a word?"

I whirled around to see the captain standing near my tent. He must have been waiting for me and did not look pleased. I followed him to the officer's quarters with growing trepidation, knowing I deserved the trouble I was in. He threw open the door, startling the first and second mates where they sat eating their meals.

"A moment alone if you please, gentlemen," Captain Romy said to his brothers.

Without a word, they stood.

"Of course, Lencius," Second Mate Absalon said. He gave me a pitying look, and my heart sank further. First Mate Evrard didn't look at me at all. The moment the door closed behind them, Captain Romy seared me with an angry glare.

"You left your work to other men," he said.

My cheeks flushed with shame. "I'm sorry. I'll work twice as hard tomorrow." There was no reply, so I tentatively asked, "Is there anything else?"

"Yes." His tone was clipped. "You left without being dismissed."

I buried my nose in Will's soft fur. *Don't cry, don't cry, don't cry.*

"You will conduct yourself as a member of this crew until we return to Faqur."

I'd never heard the captain so angry. I peered at him from between Will's ears and his dark glare filled me with fear.

"You will not disappear again. Am I making myself clear?"

"Yes." I gripped Will too tight, and he yipped. Captain Romy's eyes shifted to the petiloos, and his expression softened.

"You know you can't take him with you," he said, his tone gentler.

"I know," I whispered hoarsely.

"He belongs here."

"I know." Tears burned behind my eyes. "He belongs here, just as I belong in Praed, and there's nothing to be done about it."

Captain Romy's brow furrowed, and he regarded me with confusion.

"Is that what's bothering you? You don't want to go back to Praed?"

"It doesn't matter," I said.

Captain Romy sighed heavily. "Miss Elejick, I want you to know that my brothers and I believe the possibility of a continent located southwest of where we encountered the Burdeeds is high. However, the conditions for sailing in that area aren't favorable, and we are not equipped or adequately funded enough to make such a journey at this time."

"I understand," I said.

"Perhaps in another few years, the circumstances may be different."

I met his gaze and held it steadily. He still didn't seem ready to forgive my desertion of camp, but his anger had subsided.

"Perhaps," I whispered, knowing full well I would not be joining them. He looked disconcerted, but I'd lost all ability to care.

"You should be punished for your insubordination," he said.

My eyes widened and the blood drained from my face.

"But," he continued. "I think having to say goodbye to Will is punishment enough." He reached out and scratched under Will's chin.

"I don't know how to let him go," I said.

"I'll miss him, too."

"May I go now?" If I remained any longer, I was going to lose the battle with my emotions.

"Yes. You're dismissed."

Though I worked diligently the next day, it did little to improve my mood. The crew was extremely efficient, and whatever structures weren't permanent were quickly dismantled and camp was packed within a matter of hours. I couldn't blame them for being in a hurry. They were eager to return to their homes and families, and I listened to their exultations with attentiveness. On the inside, I couldn't be more lost.

"Was starting to forget what my wife looks like." Telken laughed while the last of the supplies were loaded onto carts.

"I didn't forget," Luc said. The two men jested amicably, but I only managed a smirk.

"It's a shame we can't take *Tenacity*," Telken said to me. "It was finely built."

"Yes," I said. "It seems everything has its place."

"Have you found yours yet, lass?"

"I don't know." I glanced toward the lake. "But for a moment, I thought I did."

"You're young." He squeezed my shoulder. "You've got time yet."

"Excuse me." I turned and walked toward the water.

"Don't take too long!" Telken yelled. "We're set to leave."

"I won't!" I stopped at the shoreline and became mesmerized by the three waterfalls feeding the blue lake. The sound drowned out thoughts of the future's uncertainty and the memories of heartaches I'd experienced. A few feet away, a fish jumped, and I watched the ripples expand and fade. I stepped forward, dipped my hand in the water, and watched the choppy waves I made collide with the ripples made by the fish. It reminded me of myself: a clumsy, awkward force trying to go against the laws of nature.

"Sulwen." I rose and turned toward Seaman Calux standing behind me. "It's time."

"I know." I looked back to the water. The disturbance I'd caused traveled in a wide arc across the surface of the lake and hadn't dissipated. Like me, it wouldn't stop until it was finished. "I'm ready."

Will trailed after me as we headed west toward the coast, and for two days I anxiously worried I would wake up and he'd be gone. But he remained by my side, and I began to formulate the perfect argument against leaving him on the island. He could eat the vermin on the ship. I would clean up after him. I would keep him away from the galley. He could be a source of entertainment on the long journey. He's small, so he barely takes up any space. I prepared a speech until I heard Will whine. I turned around to see he'd stopped several feet away.

"What's wrong, Will?"

He whimpered and looked behind him, turned back to me, then looked over his shoulder again as if to say we'd gone too far and should head back.

"No," I said. "We're going this way now."

He shifted nervously and took a long look back. Then I understood. This was his home, and he didn't want to leave. I took a deep, cleansing breath.

"It's all right, Will."

He cocked his head to the side and regarded me.

"You can stay. This is where you belong."

He yipped, then sat down. I wanted to rush to him and gather him in my arms for one last hug, but I resisted.

"I love you," I whispered. I turned around and walked after the crew hiking toward the coast. When I looked back, he was gone.

Instead of joining the men around the fire that night, I chose to take out my pent-up emotions by hacking at an obliging tree with my sword. I don't know if anyone heard, but no one came looking.

It rained the entire way back to the ship, and not a proper rain you feel completely validated hating. It was a blanket of mist that covered everything in a light drizzle, leaving droplets on your eyelashes and inexplicably soaking your clothing in seconds. I was perpetually chilled, but there was no sense complaining. Until we reached *The Wayward Aymelina*, this would be my permanent state.

"Haven't seen your little friend in a while," Telken said one evening by the fire.

"He's gone," I said flatly.

"Oh, I'm sorry, lass." He wrapped an arm around me. "It's for the best."

"I know. This is where he belongs."

"You did right by him. You should be proud."

I smiled. "Thank you."

From then on, I resolved not to allow myself to be mired down by depression. When the men sang songs, I either joined in or simply delighted in the music. I joined in the evening meal and rejoiced in their excitement to return home. I sparred with Luc and practiced Faqur dances. The distractions served to pass the time until we ascended a hill and looked down into the bay. There, moored offshore, was *The Wayward Aymelina* shifting with the movement of the sea. Seeing it again after so long was like looking upon an old friend, and my heart swelled with longing to board her. We were transported in groups on the dinghies, and I anxiously awaited my turn. When it was finally time to depart, I stepped into the dinghy, then took one last long look back. I said a silent goodbye before settling into the seat. I watched the shore shrink as we neared the ship until I couldn't bear the torture and turned away.

When I was once more on the deck of *The Wayward Aymelina*, I ran a hand along the railing and sighed at the feeling of the smooth, polished wood. I closed my eyes, and I swore I could feel the heartbeat of the ship. My breathing quickened, and my mouth opened slightly in awed wonder.

"Can you feel it, too?"

I smiled at the sound of Captain Romy's voice and slowly opened my eyes.

"Yes," I said, knowing intuitively what he meant.

He touched the railing reverently, and I felt a pang of envy. I wished I could feel such open admiration for a place as he did. Or maybe, I was jealous of the railing for receiving such a loving caress from his hand.

Easy does it, Sulwen. Heat flared to the tips of my ears, and I turned away before he read my thoughts.

"I'm sorry about Will," Captain Romy said. "I noticed he stopped following you, but I didn't want to bring it up."

"Thank you," I mumbled. "I couldn't pretend he didn't belong there."

"He owes his life to you."

"And I owe much of my happiness here to him."

He smiled down at me, and I couldn't help but smile back with unrestrained affection. I owed much of my happiness to this man. He'd shown me an entire world, allowed me passage on his ship despite being perfectly justified in hating me forever, and treated me as an equal. In a few short weeks, I would say goodbye. My smile faltered, and I tore my gaze away as the last of the crew boarded the ship.

"Time to go," I said quietly.

He left without a word, and the crew of *The Wayward Aymelina* lay aloft and loosened sails.

CHAPTER 48

It's astounding how quickly one settles into old routines and becomes lost in the mundane duties of life. Such as it was for me when *The Wayward Aymelina* exited the bay and made its way south along the coast back to Faqur. The misty rain settled into a fog that cloaked the island in gray, so I couldn't see the black shore. But I could hear the barking of the blubbery beasts lounging on the rocks. Their numbers sounded greater than before, probably due to the birth of a new generation. A dark head occasionally appeared along the ship, its large, black eyes watching us drift past. As we journeyed further, the noises of beasts grew dimmer, until the only sound was the lapping of water against the hull and the shouts of working men.

I kept myself busy spending as much time with my friends as possible. I devoted hours to Luc's lessons, informing him that his skills improved so much I wouldn't be surprised if he were the teacher on the next voyage. He was duly thankful for my praise, but his features fell as the weight of my words fell upon him.

"Me?" Luc asked. "What about you?"

I couldn't bring myself to give him a straight answer, so I shrugged and raised my sword. "Again."

The nights became quite cold, so I brought an extra coat with me to keep from shivering when I sat with Hrod in the crow's nest. The drop in temperature didn't seem to bother the old man. He leaned over the side gazing out into the night with his unlit pipe, his breath showing white against the black sea as he swayed with the motion of the ship. Most nights I regaled him with stories, but sometimes we simply enjoyed each other's silent company. It was easy to feel relaxed with Hrod. I never had the urge to prove myself through great deeds or feats of strength, and he wasn't loud and boisterous. I valued his insight and had no qualms asking for advice. Well, as long as it pertained to working on the ship or life in Faqur.

One evening as I watched Hrod pack herbs into a pipe he would never smoke, I broached a more personal subject.

"My sister had her first child," I said.

"A wonderful thing," he said without removing his eyes from the water.

"How did you know you wanted children?"

He glanced over his shoulder at me, then returned his attention to the waves reflecting the dim light of the moon after a cloud drifted away to reveal its glow.

"My wife told me it was time," he said. I laughed softly, and Hrod grinned widely as he lowered himself onto the floor of the crow's nest.

"Did you always want children?"

"It's not really somethin' I thought about, to tell you the truth. But when I saw my wife for the first time, such a pretty thing casting a net out into the shallows with her dress tucked up and her hair undone, well..." A wistful smile graced his lined face, and his eyes were suddenly far away. "I thought to myself, 'Hrod, if you let that girl get away, she's going to have another man's babes, and those babes are yours.'"

"So, she really had no choice."

"A woman always has a choice."

"Does she?"

"Oh, yes. Whether she's a fisherman's daughter or a princess."

"Sometimes I feel a princess has less choice than anyone."

"Your sister's husband...Did she want to marry him?"

"Yes, but—"

"And you, did you want to come here?"

"Yes," I grumbled. "But—"

"I admit not all royals are so lucky, but even if you were sent off to marry the King of Berg, you would've had a choice."

"What choice?"

"Simple, lad. Live or die."

"Not everything is that simple."

"No, but you gotta find the simple choices, even in a tricky spot."

"All right, Hrod." I felt a little bit cheeky. "What about a man who must kill another to survive?"

"That's not a difficult question. A man's life is precious."

"Which man's?"

He considered for a minute, then said, "Whichever one survives."

I covered my mouth to keep my laughter from echoing across the ship and prevent our merriment from waking anyone up.

"Fair. How about a less drastic scenario. This pretty girl you saw all those years ago. What made you decide to tell her how you felt about her?"

"I loved her, so I told her."

"That simple?"

"Told you it was."

My throat tightened. "What if she didn't love you back?"

"I'd rather mend a broken heart than spend my days wonderin' if it would've broken or if it would've filled with joy."

I fell into a heavy silence. I leaned back to gaze up at the sails billowing gently in the wind.

"I know you've had a picture in your head of what your life should be, lad," Hrod said gently. "But don't ignore somethin' different just cause it's not what you planned just to prove a point." I met Hrod's sympathetic stare and offered a weak smile.

"I just want to be happy," I whispered.

"That's what we all want, lad. The wisest people know what happiness looks like when they find it."

"Like you did?"

"Aye." He smiled so wide I could see the gaps where teeth once were.

As we neared the southernmost tip of the island, several crew members, including myself, noticed our course seemed off. Instead of rounding the edge of the island and heading east, we continued southwest. Despite our confusion, no one questioned the officers' navigational abilities. However complacent the crew chose to be, I was never one to remain willfully ignorant. I'm not ashamed to say I nosed around trying to piece together our destination, but without a map, I didn't get very far. I drew the line at asking the officers directly. I had spoken very little to them in general, and I wanted to keep our communications to a minimum. It was ridiculous, but I considered it a form of self-preservation. My ability to restrain myself from saying something I was sure to regret was waning, and I didn't want to be stuck on a ship with nowhere to run should I make a fool out of myself. So, I waited with the crew to see where this route took us. For three days, we saw nothing but sea, but on the fourth day, a voice cried from far above in the crow's nest.

"Ahoy! Land ho! Dead ahead!"

Land? We looked at each other in confusion. Gathering at the bow, we peered into the gossamer-like fog hanging over a heavily forested island. A rush of air escaped my lungs as if I'd been kicked in the stomach. Could this be the island that was home to the Nakwacimek?

Over the next few days, we navigated around the northern tip of the island and down the coast. I knew where we were, but I couldn't account for why. Last I heard, there was great urgency to return to Faqur. What changed? The crew seemed equally confused but didn't argue when ordered to drop anchor in a small inlet. The officers stood on the quarterdeck watching over the crew, and I summoned my courage to approach them.

"Sirs." I saluted when I climbed up the stairs of the quarterdeck. "Forgive me for asking, but where are we?"

"Where do you think we are, Miss Elejick?" First Mate Evrard said. He seemed irritated, but I didn't feel it was with me.

I looked toward the island, chewing on my bottom lip as I considered. "It appears to be the island of the Nakwacimek."

"Well observed, Miss Elejick," Second Mate Absalon said. "We thought a short visit would be good for continued good relations with the people here."

"That's wonderful." I couldn't hide my excitement. "How long are we staying?"

"Just for the night," the first mate said.

"Oh." I frowned. "Well, shouldn't we row to shore then?"

"Yes, we should." First Mate Evrard stormed past me to the main deck and ordered the dinghy prepared for departure.

I met Captain Romy's eye with a questioning look. He glanced away, and I was shocked to see his cheeks turn pink.

"Are you coming?" First Mate Evrard called.

Much to the first mate's consternation, I slid unladylike down the railing on my backside to reach the main deck. A small group of us rowed to shore, including Seaman Calux. I eyed him dubiously. He clutched the dinghy's gunwale until his knuckles were white.

"I hope you're as skilled with languages as Seaman Erec was," I said.

"He left his notes with me before he left Faqur," Calux said, his eyes never leaving the shore.

"I didn't realize the two of you were friends."

"Colleagues," Seaman Calux corrected. "We didn't know each other well enough to be called friends."

"Well, he was very instrumental in negotiating a friendship with these people, so don't muck it up."

He finally met my eye. His brow furrowed.

"You don't have to be so cynical," he said, his tone wounded.

I flushed and looked away in shame. He was right. I was being an ass, allowing my festering emotions to erupt in anger.

"I'm sorry," I said. "I'm sure you'll do fine."

"Are you angry with me? Because if that's the case, I'll leave you alone."

"It's not you." I sighed. "It's my own stupidity."

"Stupidity is out of character for you."

I gave him a wry smile. "You don't have to flatter me."

"I wouldn't dream of it," he said with an answering grin. "Is there anything I can do?"

"No. Nothing to be done."

We reached the shore, and I mulled over the conversation. I stepped off the dinghy and began walking toward the trees and felt Seaman Calux's hand on my shoulder. I turned abruptly.

"Is it...personal?" He struggled to speak the words.

"Isn't everything?"

"I want you to know." He took a step closer. "Even though you rejected me, I still consider you a friend, and as a friend, I'm willing to hear anything you may say."

"I appreciate that," I eyed him warily, "but there's nothing I have to say."

"Pardon the interruption, but we're on a tight schedule," First Mate Evrard said.

No *sorry* necessary, sir. The interruption is greatly appreciated. I followed the officers into the forest, and I overheard them wondering if showing up unannounced was wise.

"The last time we showed up in their village, we were nearly run off," First Mate Evrard pointed out.

"That was before they knew us," Second Mate Absalon said. "They're our friends now, especially after Miss Elejick killed that beast."

"How will they feel knowing their savior is actually a woman?" First Mate Evrard said.

"They already know," I said.

The officers stopped in their tracks and turned to stare.

"Well," I amended. "Noshluat does. I don't know about the rest of them."

"How?" Second Mate Absalon looked bewildered.

"I don't know." I shrugged. "Some people are more observant than others."

I brushed past them and walked on, hiding my smile. Their footsteps followed shortly thereafter, and I could practically hear their minds working out the confusing piece of information I'd just bestowed.

CHAPTER 49

We reached the outskirts of the village and approached unarmed, our hands clearly empty in case the Nakwacimek people didn't immediately recognize us. An alarm was raised once we were spotted, and it was difficult to tell if the people were running about in fear or excitement. We stopped and waited until the chief came out to officially invite us in. A young man stepped out from the tangle of curious onlookers. Mukahanu. He'd grown considerably in height and confidence. He strode toward us, but his eyes were fixed on me, his brows furrowed. Then his eyes widened, and a smile brightened his features.

"Nutamoson!" Mukahanu rushed forward and nearly knocked the wind out of me with his tight embrace. He was about an inch taller than I was, and the slaps he delivered to my back were strong. He let go but kept his arm around me and led me into the village, calling out to the people and pointing at me. I looked over my shoulder and saw the others of my party were uncertain whether they should follow. I frantically waved them forward, and they thankfully didn't hesitate.

"What are they saying, Seaman Calux?" First Mate Evrard said.

"Just a minute, sir. I read Seaman Erec's notes on their language and am piecing it together."

"Do it fast," Captain Romy said. It was the first thing I'd heard him speak all day. I glanced back. His eyes shifted between me and Mukahanu.

Calux translated. "I think he's saying that Nutamoson, the one who killed *nifo gomman*, has returned. He's asking for food to be brought."

"You *think*?" First Mate Evrard said.

"No, sir. I *know* that's what he said."

Poor Seaman Calux. You can't show an ounce of weakness with this lot.

We stopped before a fire being built up into a roaring blaze almost as tall as me. Standing in front of it was Noshluat, chief of the Nakwacimek.

He looked down at me, a twinkle of humor in his eye, and gave a kind, fatherly smile. He spoke, and Seaman Calux translated as efficiently as he could with everyone watching him.

"He wants to know if you still live in secret," Seaman Calux translated.

"No," I said with a lopsided grin. "Everyone knows I'm a woman now."

"Has this brought you trouble?"

"No more than usual."

There was a general ripple of laughter, most notably from the first mate. Typical.

"He says we are welcome at his fire."

Mukahanu slapped me on the back again and settled me into a spot near him and his friends. Seaman Calux was occupied translating for the officers as they conversed with the chief. I was left trying to guess what Mukahanu and his friends were talking about. Through a series of gestures, I deduced he was telling the story of the day we met. He self-deprecatingly demonstrated his horrible abilities at archery, and his friends laughed and jeered. When it came to the part where I saved him, they patted me on the back and grinned. Though they'd probably heard the story a million times, it was just as thrilling.

They encouraged me to tell a story, and I mimed the day I killed the beast. They clapped when I'd finished, and Mukahanu mimed the dagger and pointed to me as if asking if I still had it. My face fell and I turned away to hide the tears welling up in my eyes. Their voices faded and Mukahanu turned me to face him. He opened his hands and gestured toward me with a shake of his head.

"No," I said. "I don't have it anymore."

He repeated the gesture, and I gathered he wanted to know what happened. I leaned forward and dug a hole in the earth, made as if I was laying the dagger inside, then filled the hole back up. They considered the explanation, unsure of my full meaning. I proceeded to make the signs of a horse, though I don't think they knew what one was. I ran my hand across an imaginary mane, placed a hand against my heart, and deliberately placed my hand on the ground and kept it very still. Then I pretended to lift the fallen horse and lay it in the ground, then unsheathed an invisible dagger and placed it on top of it.

"To honor him," I whispered.

I don't know if they understood half of what I was trying to convey, but the meaning was clear enough. I'd buried the dagger with a dead friend, and by the solemn nodding of their heads, this was something they understood and respected. Mukahanu squeezed my shoulder sympathetically, then he handed me some food. I ate while I listened to them talk about more upbeat subjects.

When the ceremonial pipe was produced, I almost declined, remembering how ill I felt the day after smoking it. But fearing being rude, I took a few quick puffs and passed it along. The Nakwacimek inhaled deeply and languidly released a plume of white smoke from between their lips. Drums appeared shortly thereafter, and the women began dancing to the song. I became entranced by them moving to the beating drums in perfect rhythm around the fire. I was vaguely aware that my head bobbed in time to the music, and my thoughts were increasingly hazy. I was incredibly relaxed, my limbs heavy and warm, and my belly comfortably full of the hearty meal.

The song ended, and the women joined hands as another began. They circled the fire, pulling young men into the line. One reached out and took Mukahanu's hand, and as he joined them, he grabbed mine and pulled me into the dance. This time, I vowed to keep my hands to myself unlike the last time when I'd danced with Captain Romy. I didn't trust myself.

The evening ended much too quickly, and I stood by with an aching heart as Seaman Calux gave the Nakwacimek our final regards. Noshluat bid us farewell and said they would pray to the gods for calm seas. When the officers walked back toward the trees, Noshluat put a restraining hand on my shoulder and motioned for Seaman Calux to translate for him.

"He wants to know if he'll see you again," Seaman Calux said. I could see in his eyes this information was of interest to him as well, and though I didn't wish for him to be privy to my personal affairs, I had to be honest with the Nakwacimek chief.

"No," I said. "I believe this will be the last time we shall see each other."

"Will they not let you return with them again?"

"This is my choice," I said. "My sailing days are over."

"Is it because of a mate?"

I felt my cheeks redden, but before I could answer, the chief spoke again and Seaman Calux said, "Go away."

"What?" I asked.

Seaman Calux appeared just as confused, but the look of annoyance on Noshluat's face was priceless. He pointed at Calux then toward the trees and repeated the command to go away. Seaman Calux reluctantly backed away, and once he was at a respectable distance, Noshluat pointed to me, placed a fist against his heart, then made the motion I'd seen him use when speaking about the aforementioned mate.

I nodded. "I love a man, but he doesn't love me." I punctuated my words with hand motions I hoped the chief would understand.

He cocked his head to the side, pointed at me, then made a sweeping motion from his forehead to his eyes. I shook my head, uncertain of what he was asking. He made the motion for man, then pointed at me, made as if he was drawing words out of his mouth, and pounded a fist against his chest while shaking his head.

"No," I said. "He didn't *tell* me he didn't love me. I just *know* he doesn't."

He shook his head. I was about ready to call Seaman Calux back to translate and hang the embarrassment I would suffer. He made a series of signs, and I was shocked to realize he was telling me to confess my feelings.

I shook my head. "I can't."

He gripped my shoulder and gazed at me sympathetically. Then he repeated his plea and made a sign of farewell.

"Goodbye." I watched him return to the village.

I collected myself before walking into the trees, my mind full of Noshluat's assertions that I should voice my feelings. I suppose I had nothing to lose since I wasn't planning on coming back. Though I could face pirates and cat-like monsters, I was a coward when it came to matters of the heart. If I confessed to Captain Romy that I loved him, I would have to live with rejection for the duration of the trip. Even if I waited until we reached Faqur, I'd still see him at the celebratory ball and be reminded of my foolishness. No, there was nothing for it but to let things remain as they were. I noticed a figure in the waning light a few yards into the forest and stopped short, my hand instinctively falling to the hilt of my sword.

"There's no need for that. It's just me."

I expelled a *whoosh* of air at the sound of Captain Romy's voice.

"What are you doing?" I asked.

"Waiting for you. The others have gone ahead, and I didn't want you to have to walk back alone."

"How chivalrous of you." We headed in the direction of the ship.

"Actually, I was afraid there were more of those monsters out here and I wanted you to protect me." He cast me a sidelong glance.

I laughed. "Now *that* I believe!"

We continued in companionable silence, my heart content with the easy manner we found ourselves in. I'd succeeded in bringing out Captain Romy's humorous side, a triumph greater than defeating a Burdeed pirate.

"Is it true?" he suddenly asked, all signs of merriment gone.

"Is what true?"

"That you don't plan on returning to *The Wayward Aymelina* ever again?"

Seaman Calux, you are a rat who can't keep his mouth shut.

"I suppose Seaman Calux didn't waste any time in telling you that," I said irritably. "That was said in a private conversation between Noshluat and me."

"I don't condone him betraying your confidence nor his rushing off to inform me of what you said. I honestly didn't know whether to believe him. Which is why I'm asking you if it's true."

"It's true."

I couldn't bear to look at him, afraid of the disappointment or, Artur forbid, anger I might see in his eyes. I quickened my pace in the hopes we'd reach the others, effectively ending the conversation. But I couldn't outpace him, nor could I ignore the hand he placed on my arm to stop me. He turned me toward him, but I refused to meet his eyes, instead choosing to stare at the ground, the swaying branches of the trees, anything but him.

"Look at me," he ordered.

I complied and instantly regretted my inability to defy a direct order. Even in the near darkness, I could see the disappointment on his face, and my heart seized in distress.

"When were you planning on telling me?"

"I don't know." I couldn't trust my voice above a whisper, and I swallowed the lump forming in my throat.

"Can you at least explain why?"

"I cannot."

"Is it one of the crew? Is someone bothering you?" There was a dark undertone to his words, and I shivered despite the cool temperature.

"No," I said. "Everyone has been very supportive and kind."

"Are you homesick?"

"I do wish to see my family."

"But that's not why you won't come back?"

I could sense his rising frustration at my evasiveness, and the last thing I wanted was to have a fight with him. "We should return to the ship. It's getting dark."

"I know you've suffered losses," he continued. "And I can't promise that you won't suffer more on future voyages, but surely the benefits outweigh the costs?" There was an undercurrent of desperation in his tone that broke my heart.

"They do. That's not why I've decided not to return. Please don't ask me any more questions."

"If I have been remiss as your captain, I deserve to know it."

"No!" I cried, loud enough that several pairs of wings flapped out of the trees around us. "It would take a thousand lifetimes before I could adequately express how grateful I am for everything you've done."

I clamped my mouth shut before I could say more, then risked punishment for insubordination by walking away without being dismissed. His footsteps followed a few seconds later, but I didn't look back. He maintained a respectable distance until we reached the shore where the others were waiting, and I climbed wordlessly inside the dinghy. I flashed a dark glare at Seaman Calux before settling into my seat, and he at least had the decency to look away in embarrassment. I stared at my feet while we rowed back to the ship, and I didn't acknowledge anyone as I purposefully strode across the main deck and retreated into the lower quarters. A few crewmen called after me, but I ignored them, stepped into my room, and for the first time, locked the door. I promptly threw myself onto the bed and wept miserably, wishing that we were already back in Faqur so I could return to Praed and leave all this behind.

Over the subsequent week, I pretended everything was perfectly fine. I rose with the crew and performed my duties, sparred with Luc and some of the other crewmen, played cards with Telken, and waxed nostalgic with Hrod in the crow's nest. I followed orders when they were given, was polite when spoken to, and didn't argue, even with First Mate Evrard. I avoided the captain unless it was absolutely necessary to speak to him, and even then, I was dry and brief. He didn't bring up the subject of my departure. The closer we drew to Faqur, the walls I erected around my heart grew stronger and stronger.

The crew's excited anticipation was palpable, and the talk inevitably turned to the families they were eager to see again. They spoke of their wives and children, the comforts of a home-cooked meal, the pleasure of sleeping in their own beds, and being beholden to no one.

"Well, except my wife," Telken said with a nudge.

"Who do you look forward to seeing?" Luc asked.

"My niece first," I said. "Mother and Father second, my sisters third. My horse fourth. And I suppose my brothers."

"I'll miss that humor of yours, lass," Telken said. "Don't know what I'll laugh at until we sail again."

My heart sank at his words. I had to tell them. I couldn't leave them thinking they'll see me next year.

"I'm not coming back," I said.

The men fell silent and stared at me, some in confusion and others in sadness.

"Why not, lass?" Telken asked.

"I can't tell you that," I said. "I know that isn't fair, but I can't. Please know it's not because of any of you. You all have been wonderful friends to me, and I'll never forget you."

"We won't forget you, either," Luc said. He covered my hand with his. The rest of the men followed suit, resting their hands on my shoulders, arms, and head. Their display of support and affection was so overwhelming I nearly broke down.

"May the gods watch over you, lass. Wherever you go after this," Telken said.

The others murmured their assent, and they removed their hands. I was left with the feeling of profound calm, my soul filled with love and acceptance. I'd formed true and lasting friendships on *The Wayward Aymelina,* and I would be forever grateful for her.

CHAPTER 50

With a mixture of relief and sorrow, I stood at the railing of *The Wayward Aymelina* as she sailed into the Brasdemer Sound. The order was given to raise the sails, and I left to help the crew. The ship slowed as the sails were brought up one by one, until only the mainsails remained to steer us into the dockyard. From my position on the foremast yard, I saw news of our arrival had spread throughout the city.

Gathered on the dock was a waving mass of people. Their shouts and cheers grew louder as we neared, and we slowed to a crawl when the mainsails were ordered to be brought up. My heart thudded at the order to drop anchor. In the blink of an eye, we were in Faqur. My journey was over.

I spent an inordinate amount of time on the main deck helping to secure the rigging and cover the sails in preparation for the ship to overwinter. Once I ran out of things to help with on deck, I ventured below to find out if I could be of any assistance there. Everyone from the cook to the ship's surgeon had readied themselves days ago and had nothing for me to do. Many of the crew had already disembarked by the time I made my way to my private quarters and packed up the remainder of my things. They were eager to see their homes and families again. This would be the last time I would see *The Wayward Aymelina*, and I was determined to drag my feet. I snapped my trunk shut and took one last look around, trailed my fingers reverently along the wood paneling, and thanked the ship for protecting me during the long days at sea.

I opened the door and collided with Seaman Calux poised with his fist raised to knock.

"I'm so sorry, Sulwen!" He picked up my trunk. "Allow me to carry this for you."

"No need." I wrenched the trunk away with both hands and headed for the main deck. The air smelled of salt with a vaguely fishy undercurrent, and though the sun shone through the clouds, there was a light mist that hung about the ships and crowded streets.

"When do you leave for Praed?"

"I don't know."

"Wait." Seaman Calux grabbed my arm and pulled me around to face him.

"Let go of my arm," I commanded. He held my sword arm, so I couldn't reach for my weapon. I sized up the situation. If necessary, a swift blow to the side of the head with my trunk would do just as well.

"I just wanted to say goodbye," he said.

"Goodbye." I tried jerking free, but he squeezed tighter and drew closer.

"I won't forget you." His face inched toward mine.

I shoved the trunk into his gut, driving the air out of him. He struggled to catch his breath. I gritted my teeth, heaved the trunk back, and swung it at his stupid head. He raised an arm, and the trunk connected with a *crack*. He cried out, stumbled, and reached for me. He grabbed my sleeve, pulling me off balance. The trunk hit the deck. I drew back a fist, but a voice from behind stilled my movements.

"Let. Her. Go."

Seaman Calux's eyes widened, and he released me as if I were diseased. I whirled around. Captain Romy stared at the seaman with unconcealed fury.

Seaman Calux sat back, panting, and cradled his injured arm. "She…she attacked me."

"Why?" Captain Romy's voice was eerily calm.

"Um…" Calux's eyes darted to me, and he licked his lips. "I was saying goodbye."

"You were going to kiss me!" I jerked my fist toward him, and he flinched. "Without my permission!"

"Miss Elejick, you are dismissed," Captain Romy said. I reluctantly looked up into his blue-gray eyes. "*The Wayward Aymelina* thanks you for your service."

I lowered my arm and gave Captain Romy a short salute. I grabbed my trunk and walked toward the gangplank without looking back. I hoped Calux received a well-deserved punishment.

A cry came from the dock. "Sulwen!" I looked up and spotted my brother waving among the dwindling onlookers.

"Tyrnan!" I shouted. I raced down the gangplank and launched myself into my beloved brother's arms, hugging him as if he were the only thing securing me to the earth. "I'm so happy to see you."

He picked up my trunk, and arm in arm, we left the dockyard. I couldn't resist looking back at *The Wayward Aymelina* one last time. A shuddering sigh rippled through me as I turned away and allowed Tyrnan to lead us to the inn.

"I thought it would be a fine surprise if I came to collect you," Tyrnan said.

"I'm so glad you did. I missed you terribly. All of you."

"They can't wait to hear about your adventures."

"There were many! Kyra will be delighted to have new material for her stories."

We reached the inn and I was touched to find that Tyrnan secured not only the finest rooms, but had a bath prepared the instant he heard the ship was sighted. I don't think he was too offended that I abandoned him immediately in favor of the first hot bath I'd had in months. Once I was freshly clean and clothed in a robe fit for a princess, I joined Tyrnan at a table filled to the brim with steaming platters of fish and pastries, goblets of wine, and every imaginable side dish Faqur had to offer. We ate until we couldn't possibly fit another bite into our stomachs, then ate a little more just to be sure we were full. Properly satiated, we sat by the fire and watched the flames dance in the hearth.

"How is Lilias?" I asked.

"Doing well. Syrsha is crawling and eating some solid foods," Tyrnan said.

"Already?"

"She's almost eight months old, Sulwen."

"I've already missed so much."

"You still have time to get to know her."

"I know." I sighed. "From now on, my place is in Praed."

Tyrnan raised an eyebrow. "For good?"

"For good." I'd experienced tragedies, but I'd relive them time and again if it meant I could sail with Captain Romy with a cold heart. The moments of tenderness I'd glimpsed in his eyes could go no further. He was my captain, and he'd never allow a relationship to bloom between us. We'd be a distraction to one another, our work would suffer, and his reputation as a fair captain would shatter. To preserve his rank, we'd be forced to end our affair. For the sake of my sanity, I couldn't endure living on the same ship with the man I loved if he regarded me as a common sailor.

"Are you sure?"

"Yes."

"We've been through this before."

"This time, I really mean it. I cannot go back to *The Wayward Aymelina.*"

"Because you feel you've seen enough to be satisfied or because you're running away from something?"

I gaped.

"I'm not a fool," Tyrnan said. "You would spend your entire life sailing around discovering new places if no one held you back. So what is it this time?"

I shook my head and turned back to the fire. "It doesn't matter. When do we leave?"

"Tomorrow morning convenient?"

"No! We can't miss the Drop Anchor Dance."

"What's that?"

"It's held it every year at the end of the season for all the fisherman and sailors. I promised I would go. The crew taught me the dances and everything."

"All right then." Tyrnan flashed an indulgent smile. "The morning after the dance, we'll return home. Fair?"

"Fair." I rested my head on his shoulder and basked in the feeling of being loved, of having my family close. Though I dreaded the morning when I left Faqur behind forever.

Tyrnan failed to pack me any dresses suitable for a dance, so I applied to a dressmaker in town to have a simple, yet elegant gown fashioned for me in haste and at great expense.

"Is this really necessary?" Tyrnan asked dubiously.

"Ugh, you don't understand anything!" I rolled my eyes.

I really didn't care for Faqur's concept of ladies' fashion—way too much emphasis on the hips—but I was able to work with the dressmaker to design something to my taste. I thought about having it made in black fabric to match my mood, but I decided that would be a touch too morose. Instead, I chose a light blue, gauzy fabric that billowed and flowed like water in a cut I was certain Father wouldn't approve of. It revealed a lot of skin around the shoulders and chest. Even Tyrnan raised an eyebrow when he saw me wear it for the first time.

"Won't you get cold?" he said.

I elbowed him playfully. "Shut your mouth."

When we arrived at the Assembly Hall for the ball, it was already teeming with people. It was a pleasant sight to see everyone from the simplest fisherman to the richest noble gathered to celebrate a bountiful year. The room was brightly lit, and music echoed off the high ceilings. Dancers were laughing and enjoying themselves in the middle of the room while others mingled and drank wine along the periphery. Tyrnan and I were spotted the instant we entered the room, and a throng of people invaded our space. To my annoyance, most of them were interested in talking to my brother as opposed to me. I released his arm and snuck away so I wouldn't have to listen to the inane conversations that were sure to follow.

"As I live and breathe," a familiar and welcomed voice said from amongst the crowd of people. Telken approached with a lovely looking lady on his arm.

I took his hand. "I'm so glad I was able to see you before I left. This must be your beautiful wife. You didn't tell me you married a younger woman." I gave a saucy raised eyebrow.

"Oh, gods bless you, miss," the woman said. "I'm probably old enough to be your mother. I'm Linsy."

"A pleasure," I said. "Your husband has been a great friend to me."

"He may not be much to look at, but he's a good man," she said.

"Say that to my face, woman!" Telken said with mock indignation.

Linsy ignored her husband and looked around the crowded room. "We must find you a partner to dance the next one with." Her eyes lit up, and she waved someone over. A sailor I recognized approached us, bowed, and extended his hand. I danced with him out of politeness, though I couldn't remember his name. It was a lively dance with much clapping and circling, and once it was complete, I was nearly out of breath. Well, that's what I told the man when he asked for another dance.

"May I get you something to drink?" he asked.

"Yes!" I said, a little too eagerly.

Once he disappeared to fetch the drink, I wandered around the room, greeting the people I knew and nodding politely to those who showed me deference. Telken's wife seemed to take it as a personal affront that I wasn't dancing every set, for she found me walking alone and linked her arm with mine.

"Let's see if we can't find you someone else to dance with," she said as she scanned the room. I was about to say her assistance really wasn't necessary when she froze, her eyes fixed behind me.

"Seems someone's found you."

I turned, and there was Captain Romy, dressed elegantly in a black waistcoat trimmed with gold, a white scarf and breeches, and knee-high polished black boots. I noticed he was once again clean shaven.

"Miss Elejick, may I have the honor of the next dance?"

"Uh, yes."

He held out his hand, and I stared at it for a few seconds before I remembered I was supposed to take it. He led me to the dance floor, and I willed my heart to slow its rigorous pace. I was already breathing fast, and I tried to calm myself by inhaling slowly through my nose and exhaling out my mouth. When the music began and he reached for my hand, I stumbled. I recovered sufficiently enough that no one noticed, but my cheeks flushed for all to see. I passed it off as exertion from the exercise, but that was only a falsehood I told myself to bear the next several minutes.

It was a lovely dance that I'd particularly enjoyed learning. At times Captain Romy and I would be paired off as a couple and at others we joined the group in elaborate circles and exchanges of partners. I found myself unjustifiably jealous of every woman he clasped hands with, and I silently berated myself for being such an idiot. I managed to pull myself together and find joy in the dance, laughing as we twirled across the floor and marveling at what an accomplished dancer the captain turned out to be. I was sad when the song ended, but a thrill jolted through me when he asked if I might dance the next with him. I nodded mutely.

I moved through the next dance in a haze of euphoria. It was a slower song, almost mournful, and Captain Romy and I danced around each other as if a force kept us apart. But as the tempo increased, the steps brought us together, and I settled one hand in his and another on his shoulder. I couldn't stop smiling from my mouth to my green eyes for the rest of the dance.

When the last notes faded, it signaled the end of my time with Captain Romy. I couldn't meet his eye as I applauded the talents of the musicians. Nor could I look at him when he reached his hand out to lead me off the floor. I couldn't deny how bereft I felt when he allowed my hand to fall away.

"Your teachers would be proud of you," he said. "You danced very well."

"Thank you," I murmured. If he had more to say, I do not know, for at that moment, we were approached by a couple I barely registered through the fog of despair in my mind.

"Your Highness," the man said with a little bow. The haze lifted enough for me to realize it was First Mate Evrard, standing before me in his formal blue coat and white breeches.

"Sir." I smiled with genuine warmth.

"May I introduce my wife, Elizabel?" He brought forth a genteel woman with golden blonde hair, round cheeks, and sparkling blue eyes.

"It is such a pleasure to meet you at last," Elizabel said with a curtsey. "I've heard nothing but the highest praise of you."

"Oh, you are too kind." I hesitated, looking from the lady to her husband. "I'm sorry. I'm trying to think of something nice to say about your husband." To my relief, the trio understood and laughed at my joke, none more so than Elizabel.

"Come, Your Highness." She took my arm. "There are some people I must introduce you to."

I almost had enough willpower not to glance over my shoulder at the two Romy brothers. Hopefully, my companion didn't notice. She was busy talking about people she found interesting.

"That's Bruno Magnus," Elizabel said, pointing out a dour looking man with white hair and hollow cheeks. "He's the high councilman of the Faqur Assembly."

"Since the beginning of time?"

"You are such a wit!" Elizabel laughed. "You're not far off. He's served on the council for the last fifty years."

"Impressive."

"That decorated man next to him in the white coat is the Admiral of the Fleet, of course."

"What's his name?"

Elizabel looked at me in undisguised shock. "You mean you don't know?"

"I'm sorry, I don't." Had I just made a serious social blunder?

"That's Berin Romy. Father of Evrard, Lencius, and Absalon."

"Oh." I studied the man with greater interest. Of course, their father was the Admiral of the Fleet. There was an unmistakable family resemblance. He had dark blonde hair beginning to recede on top and graying at the temples. He was a few inches shorter than Captain Romy, but I could see where the captain inherited his blank stare. The high councilman was talking incessantly while the admiral stared resolutely ahead.

"Would you like me to introduce you?" Elizabel asked.

"Oh, I would not wish to disturb him," I said, my voice wavering.

"It looks to me as if he'd welcome the interruption, especially for an introduction to a princess."

"What if he disapproves of me?"

"My dear girl, there is no reason to make yourself uneasy. He's just a man. You've met plenty of those."

Just a man? This was the Admiral of the Fleet of Faqur. More importantly, Captain Romy's father. What if I did something stupid like open my big mouth and allow whatever I'm thinking to come tumbling out? *Best behavior, Sulwen.* I straightened my shoulders and reminded myself to act like a proper princess, not that it had worked in the past.

We approached the two men, and they paused when Elizabel spoke.

"Ah, Mrs. Romy, a pleasure as always," High Councilman Magnus said.

"May I have the honor of introducing Her Highness, Princess Sulwen of Praed," Elizabel said, beaming at me with pride.

"Your Highness." The councilman forced a smile and gave a miniscule bow. "We have, of course, heard much of you."

"I don't doubt it." I plastered on an overly bright smile. "You find me at a disadvantage. I regret I've only learned of your existence this very moment."

Elizabel feigned a cough to cover her laugh. I regret nothing.

"I hope you've satisfied your curiosity enough to return home and take your place at the castle," the councilman said.

"I find it interesting that you presume to know where I belong since I've yet to determine that myself."

"Did you find the sea to your liking?" Admiral Romy asked.

I noted the admiral's eyes were nearly the same blue-gray shade as the captain's. I blinked several times to banish those thoughts and gave him a genuine smile.

"I loved it, sir. I am so grateful for the opportunity to sail upon it," I said.

"Will you be joining us next season?" High Councilman Magnus' tone suggested he would rather I not.

I arched an eyebrow. "There's always a possibility."

The man reacted as flustered as I'd hoped.

I inclined my head politely and turned to Elizabel, bidding her to introduce me to some random person I picked out of the crowd. Once we were out of earshot of the two men, Elizabel leaned toward me and whispered in my ear.

"Evrard told me you weren't coming back. Was that not true?"

"It is true. But I wasn't about to give that odious man the satisfaction of knowing he was rid of me for good."

Elizabel did not hide her laughter.

CHAPTER 51

Once Elizabel felt satisfied she'd introduced me to everyone of note in the entirety of Faqur, she brought me out onto the balcony for fresh air.

"You must see the breathtaking view," she gushed. "There is nothing like it on the whole continent."

She was right. It was beautiful. We looked out over a cove tucked into the Brasdemer Sound. Water lapped gently against the rocky shore and fishing boats rocked lazily in the wind. I breathed in the refreshing salty air, savoring the memory I would take with me for the rest of my life.

"I think you are the bravest young woman I've ever met," Elizabel said.

"I'm not very brave. Foolish maybe, but I wouldn't say brave."

"You spent months among all those men. Is that not the very definition of bravery?"

I smiled. "I think most of them were afraid of me."

"Most men are afraid of a woman who knows her own mind."

"I hope you know I was only teasing when I said that about your husband in there. I really do hold First Mate Romy in the highest respect."

"Don't distress yourself, my dear. I know better than anyone how maddening Evrard can be. He is a good man, though."

"Did you know each other well before you were married?"

"I knew him by sight well enough," she said. "Everyone knew the Romy brothers. Their father was an extremely accomplished sailor who rose to the rank of captain at a young age, though not as young as Lencius. He married a councilman's daughter who bore him three handsome boys. All the girls adored looking at them. Absalon was really the only friendly one. Not that Lencius and Evrard were unkind. They just...kept to themselves. I had no reason to believe any of them knew who I was."

"What changed?"

Elizabel took a deep breath and said, "My mother died when I was a little girl, and Father worked long hours to provide for us. I have two younger sisters, and I looked after them when he was gone. One day, they wanted to see the ships, so I took them to the dockyard. My youngest sister slipped on the damp wood, and clumsy me tried to save her and ended up falling in myself."

"Could you not swim?"

"We live right on the sea. As children, we all learn to swim. Everyone in Faqur does. It's not easy to accomplish in a dress, but I was managing. I heard a splash and someone swam up beside me and lifted me onto the dock as if I weighed no more than seafoam. Evrard."

"How romantic."

"He asked if I was all right. Even called me by name. I didn't even know he *knew* my name. He gave me his coat and walked the three of us home. I was shocked when he returned the next day to inquire after me, but I suspected he only wanted his coat back."

"Typical."

"But then the most astonishing thing happened. He came back the next day, and the day after. Before I realized what was happening, we were courting. A year later, we were married."

"That's a lovely story."

"We've been married four years now. Evrard told me he admired me from afar months before that day, but he couldn't think of an excuse to speak to me."

"So, he orchestrated a fall into the water so he could save you?"

Elizabel giggled. "Evrard is not devious enough for that."

I took her hand. "I wish you both many more years of happiness."

"Thank you, Your Highness."

"Sulwen. Please call me Sulwen."

"What will you do now, Sulwen? Now that the voyage is over, I mean."

"I barely know. I'm sure I'll find some occupation to keep me entertained enough to stay home as my parents wish." I laughed, but my companion did not find the humor in my statement. She seemed distracted and fidgeted while we spoke.

"Do you think..." Elizabel glanced into the ballroom. "That you would consider marriage after your grand adventure?"

I frowned. "I suppose it makes sense, in practical terms. I spent the better part of two years indulging in my own whims, and I proved I'm a hard worker and can follow orders. And Artur knows I'm familiar with the intricate workings of a busy household."

I probably should have shut up, but my ire was piqued. "But I won't settle for a life where I am merely defined by these merits alone."

She stepped back as if I'd struck her.

"I—" She breathed, swallowed, and continued, "I didn't mean that you should settle. I just..." She turned toward the bay.

"I'm sorry." I hugged Elizabel's shoulders. "That was harsh and uncalled for. I'm too outspoken for my own good."

"I meant no offense." She offered a little smile. "I only...well, I apologize for my presumption."

"And I apologize for attacking you so unjustly. The subject of marriage is a sensitive one for me. I've always dreaded that my duty as a princess would lead to an arrangement that left me stifled. It's why I originally left Praed."

"I see. And has your opinion toward marriage in general changed at all?"

"I suppose it's the duty of a happily married woman to see everyone around her happily settled themselves. I don't object to marriage on principle, but I'm determined not to enter one of convenience. I want to be loved, to be desired as a woman with intelligence and spirit." I gazed down forlornly at the lapping waves and watched the dappled sunshine sparkle on the water. I squeezed my eyes shut, resolving that if Elizabel asked about the sudden appearance of tears I'd blame the blinding light of the fading sun.

"Are you thirsty, Sulwen?" Elizabel said abruptly. "I'm absolutely parched."

I nodded glumly and she left me alone on the balcony. I opened my eyes and watched birds dart over the waves catching fish. The sun was beginning its descent below the horizon, but there was still plenty of light to see the fluttering white wings. The boats creaked when the wind increased, tipping them back and forth on the rolling waves. I became so transfixed I almost missed the sounds of footsteps behind me.

"I was beginning to think you'd become lost," I called over my shoulder.

"Not lost, just delayed."

Captain Romy. I spun around and nearly lost my footing at the sound of his voice. He strode over and stood beside me, his hands resting casually on the balcony railing.

"I thought you were Elizabel. She was just getting something to drink." I looked toward the entrance to the assembly hall, but the lady was nowhere to be seen.

"I saw her inside. She's been detained."

"Detained?"

"The musicians started playing her favorite dance, and she dragged Evrard onto the floor."

"I see." I smiled sadly, wondering if my rudeness was the real reason she'd become 'detained.' "They seem well suited."

"They are." He smiled, faltered, and asked, "When do you leave for Praed?"

"In the morning. Tyrnan came to escort me home. Did you happen to see him inside?"

"I did have that pleasure. I asked him to give my compliments to your family."

I didn't know what else to say. We'd exhausted all my abilities at idle conversation, so I returned my attention to the bay and hoped that the silence stretching between us would either be interrupted or he would leave me in peace.

"I've met with the Faqur Assembly and presented all of the maps and measurements we collected over the last several months."

"Oh?"

"I also presented them with your observations."

"You did?" Our eyes met, and I gripped the railing to stop myself from trembling.

"Yes. Your notes on the plant and animal life are just as important to their decision."

"And what was their decision?"

"The Faqur Assembly declared their intention of establishing a colony on Safirelan. They are sending invitations to all the countries on the continent for volunteers."

"All the countries?"

"Yes. It is their hope to create an allied country where anyone might make a new start."

"That's wonderful!" I beamed. "And they're calling it 'Safirelan'? What does that mean?"

"Land of sapphire waters."

"Perfect." I smiled so wide my cheeks were getting sore. This was everything he had wanted, the pinnacle of his career he hoped for. But a glance at his hands had me concerned. He gripped the railing so tightly his knuckles were white. I had seen him do this before and couldn't account for it. I certainly couldn't now. He should be ecstatic. What wasn't he telling me?

"I—" He cleared his throat, then continued. "I have decided to join the colonists on Safirelan."

"What? You mean, leave Faqur? Forever?" I don't know why this news should make me so sad. It wasn't as if I was ever intending to see him again. But having him on the same continent somehow brought comfort in an otherwise heartbreaking situation. Now, I didn't even have that to assure me we both existed in the same world together.

He stared out over the bay and said, "I've spent most of my life on the sea."

Luckily he couldn't see the emotions I struggled to contain.

"I never considered retirement or leaving my home. But I've been inspired to start over. Safirelan is a chance to forge my own path, separate from my family name. Anyone may do the same. How exciting to start fresh, to make a life from scratch, without boundaries."

"Sounds familiar." I leaned against the railing and dangled my fingers in the breeze. "Do you ever wonder why I left Praed and snuck on board your ship?"

"I do."

"I didn't want to get married."

He looked at me, brows knitted.

I laughed and shook my head. "It sounds so stupid when I say it out loud. Mother and Father weren't pressuring me, but with Lilias married, I'd be expected to follow."

"Were you engaged?"

"No." I sighed. "Elizabel asked me how I felt about marriage, and I was irritated with her. It wasn't fair, but it felt like my adventures were over. That now I must be a pawn for the crown."

"It doesn't have to be like that."

I shrugged. "I'm a princess. I'll be married off, left behind to run a household, and raise children." I wanted to stamp my foot but resisted. "I don't want to be placed on a shelf like a trophy."

"I know how you feel."

He opened his mouth to say more, but applause from the Assembly Hall interrupted, signaling the end of a dance. People started milling around. We locked gazes, and he held out his hand.

"Come," he said.

I took his hand, and he led me to the far side of the balcony. To my astonishment, he vaulted over the railing to what I was certain was a painful, if not debilitating, landing. I rushed forward to see what became of him and saw it was only a few feet to the ground. He beckoned for me to follow, and I looked down at my attire in dismay.

"The only time I wear a dress in months, and I'm expected to leap over railings. Typical," I muttered. I hoisted myself onto the railing, gathered my skirts, swung my legs over the side, and dropped into his awaiting arms. He led me down a well-worn path toward the water's edge.

"Something tells me this isn't the first time you've made this escape."

"As a child, I was never very comfortable at social gatherings, but being the son of a prominent captain meant I had to attend all of them. I usually snuck away within the first hour until Father threatened me with a punishment of five lashings if I did it again."

"That sounds excessive."

"I don't think he would have followed through. The threat was enough to make me behave."

We reached the rocky beach below, and above us the dim sounds of the party could barely be heard. I watched the last of the seabirds return to their nests. The sun descended lower, leaving streaks of gold, pink, and red in its wake.

The captain joined me at the water's edge and sighed. "I don't want to be married for my name or wealth, either. I want a wife who isn't content to stay behind."

I froze, holding my breath, afraid if I made a sound I'd awaken to find this moment a dream.

"I want a wife who'll join me on adventures, whose spirit is as unfathomable as the sea. I want a wife..." Ours eyes met, and a shiver rushed through me. "Who makes me laugh."

The air *whooshed* out of me. I couldn't speak, couldn't move.

"Come with me." He cringed and shook his head. "I mean, will you come with me?"

"As a sailor?"

"No." He closed the distance between us and cradled my cheek in his hand, brushing away a tear I'd been unable to contain. "As my wife."

My jaw dropped and my heart raced wildly. This couldn't be real. Was he joking? I shook my head to clear my vision, and he tilted my chin so I'd meet his eyes, those beautiful blue-gray eyes gazing at me with all the warmth I'd been wishing for.

"Sulwen," he said softly. For the first time I heard my name on his lips, felt his touch on my skin. "You are the most courageous woman I've ever known. I've never met anyone with as much compassion for life and passion in their convictions as you. And no one makes me laugh as you do."

Something between a sob and a laugh burst from my lips. "Because I'm such a fool?"

"Not very often." He grinned. "I know I don't deserve you, but I promise if you'll allow me, I will devote the rest of my life to making you happy. Sulwen Elejick, will you marry me?"

"Do you love me?" I needed to hear the words, to know he felt as I did. My future happiness depended on it.

"Yes."

My breath hitched, and my heart swelled. All the obstacles I'd thrown between us fell away. I forgot about the crown, the differences in our births, and our duties to our countries. In Safirelan, I wouldn't be a princess, and he wouldn't be a captain. We'd be equals. The worries and what-ifs vanished, leaving just him and me, the only thing I should have been focusing on all along.

"Then *yes*," I said. "I will marry you." I threw my arms around his neck, and we held each other until the noises from above faded.

Eventually, I pulled away and met his gaze. My lips parted with my quickening breaths. He pressed a hand to my cheek, then caressed my skin until his fingers were in my hair. His eyes searched mine, and I finally understood. I closed the space between us, wrapped my arms across his shoulders, and pressed my lips to his.

It's funny what goes through one's mind during such an intimate moment. The instant I felt the warm pressure of Captain Romy's lips on mine, heat radiated from the tips of my toes to my cheeks, and I kissed him with a fervor equal to his own. A fleeting thought crossed my mind, making me laugh against his mouth. I remembered at Lilias' wedding when Merrin and I saw our parents fawning over each other and the revulsion we felt at the sight. How foolish I'd been then to think that kissing the man you love could be revolting.

"What's so funny?" His raw undertone made every nerve in my body tingle.

"Nothing," I said. "I'm just happy."

His arms tightened around me, and we seemed equally unwilling to release each other. He pressed his forehead to mine, and as my eyes slipped shut, he resumed kissing me, gentler this time, his lips moving softly across mine as if he didn't want to miss a single inch of my skin. He trailed tiny kisses along my jawline, my earlobe, and down my neck, nuzzling me as he reached the juncture of my neck and shoulder.

"I love you, Sulwen," he whispered against my skin.

"I love you, Lencius."

He made a sound somewhere between a groan and a sigh and managed to somehow hug me even tighter than before. My feet dangled off the ground, and I had no desire to come back to earth.

Night fell, and above us stars illuminated the sky. One of us would have to be an adult and make the decision to head back. There was an alarming amount of immaturity in the air. He gave no sign he intended to release me, and I wasn't about to pull away. He resumed his meticulous exploration of my exposed shoulder with his ardent kisses, and I shamelessly threw back my head to grant access to my collarbone. Despite the chill from the mist drifting off the water, my skin was feverishly hot, and my heart thudded as if I'd been running for miles. My feet finally touched the ground, but I still felt as if I were floating. I clung to Lencius for balance, my fingers buried in his hair.

"Are you determined to kiss every inch?" I asked as he began making his way up the other side of my neck.

"Yes," he said, his voice husky with emotion.

Something in his voice made my breathing raspy and my legs tremble. A small part of my brain screamed that if we didn't stop soon, we'd be in serious trouble.

I told that part of my brain to take a nap.

I started loosening the intricately tied scarf around his neck, when I realized someone was calling my name.

"Sulwen? Are you out here?" The voice was coming from directly above us, and it belonged to Tyrnan.

"I should go." We parted reluctantly.

"You leave in the morning?" he asked.

"Yes. Quite early."

"I'll follow you to Praed within the week." He kissed my hand and whispered, "I promise."

"Hurry. Before the snows come."

I left him in the darkness of the bay and allowed myself ample time to regain some semblance of composure before answering my brother.

He met me at the top of the path. "Where have you been?"

"Watching the sunset," I said, still catching my breath. "Are you ready to return to the inn?"

He eyed me suspiciously. "Any goodbyes you need to make?"

"I've already made them. Come." I linked my arm with his. "I'm exhausted."

Tyrnan glanced back once toward the bay, but to my relief, he didn't go down to make sure I'd been alone.

CHAPTER 52

On the journey back to Praed, I was the most pleasant I'd ever been in my entire life, which made Tyrnan highly suspicious. I couldn't stop smiling, I didn't argue, and I didn't complain about the rain and muddy roads. Every mile we traveled, Tyrnan became more and more disturbed.

"What's the matter with you? Have you contracted an incurable illness?"

"No!"

"Then why are you acting so weird?"

"I'm not! I'm just happy!"

"I've seen you happy. This is bordering on maniacal."

I punched him in the shoulder to make him feel better about my state of mind.

We ascended the White Mountain during a torrential downpour. The castle door opened to the warmth of the foyer, and Father pulled me inside and enveloped me in his secure embrace.

"I don't know how I'm going to manage doing this every year," he said. I breathed in his distinct scent of leather, polished steel, and musk.

"You can't have her all to yourself." Mother pushed her way through to hug me. "Welcome home, darling."

My brothers swarmed me with affection, but I had eyes only for Lilias and the adorable bundle she held in her arms.

"Welcome home, Sulwen," Lilias said. "Meet your niece, Syrsha."

"Oh, Lilias, she's so beautiful!" I stroked the soft, fine dark hairs on her head. She smiled a gaping, toothless smile as radiant as the break of dawn.

"Would you like to hold her?" Lilias asked.

"Will she let me?"

"We've told her all about her aunt so she would know you when you came home," Kyra said. Lilias held the little girl out to me, and I awkwardly accepted the baby without quite knowing how to properly hold her.

"Just tuck her into your arm like this," Lilias instructed. "It's easier now that she can hold her head up." Lilias' husband, Andrew, appeared behind her and smiled down at his infant daughter.

"Thank you," I said to him. "For making my sister a mother."

He blinked in surprise and looked at Lilias. She smiled sweetly, and I returned my attention to the child in my arms.

"We're going to have amazing adventures you and I," I whispered to my niece. "I promise."

At our family dinner that evening, I noted Rian's absence and asked, "Where's Rian?"

Khyr and Tyrnan chuckled, but a swift elbow from Alyx and a stern look from Father silenced them immediately.

"He's in Vyt," Mother said.

"Oh. I got Alyx's letter detailing the plans to confer with Vyt over the building of a fleet. Have Rian's negotiations been successful?"

Khyr snorted into his hand, and Kyra smacked him across the back of the head.

"We've had some favorable reports," Alyx said. "He's determined to remain in Vyt until the first ships are built."

"How long has he been there?" I asked.

"Six months," Mother said. "We have letters from him fairly regularly."

"How much longer is he expected to remain?" I wasn't sure when the colonists were expected to leave for Safirelan, though I assumed the ships wouldn't leave until the spring. I wanted to visit with Rian before I left.

"He hasn't been very clear on that score." Mother darted an annoyed glance at Father. Apparently, this had been a regular topic of conversation.

"It's because of that girl I told you about," Kyra whispered to me across the table.

"I see…Well, in that case." I said, "he's probably elaborated greatly in his letters to our brothers."

To my amusement, all three remaining princes dropped their silverware and stared at me like rabbits caught in a trap.

"After all," I continued casually. "Men do talk about such things to each other. If I'm not mistaken." I took a long sip of wine and set it delicately on the table before returning to my meal. My brothers looked at each other, then at our parents, flushing red and pretending nothing was amiss.

"Boys…" Mother's voice rendered them small children again. Fear passed over their features. "Do you know something we don't?"

Khyr said with a sideways glance at Tyrnan. "Well, *we* don't. But Alyx does."

Alyx narrowed his eyes at Khyr.

I took another sip of wine to conceal my reaction. Kyra beamed triumphantly and settled back to watch the scene unfold.

Mother's eyebrow lifted. "Alyx?"

"Rian went to Vyt because of a woman," Alyx blurted out.

My, how easy that was. I'd have to speak to Mother privately and learn how she accomplished such a feat with a simple twitch of an eyebrow.

"Of course, we know that. We're not blind," Father said. "Anything else to share?"

"He's wooing her," Alyx continued in a rush, "and doesn't want to leave without offering her his hand in marriage."

My jaw dropped. "Marriage?" I turned to Father. "Would you allow it?"

"It would be more suitable than the alternative," he said.

"Which is…?" I prompted.

"That no marriage takes place at all." He stared at me pointedly until I realized what he was inferring.

"Rian wouldn't do that. He may be an idiot about women sometimes, but he's never dallied with any of them."

Father continued to stare at me, so I looked to Alyx for confirmation. "Right, Alyx?" My oldest brother wouldn't meet my eye. I was ashamed that Rian turned out to be a scoundrel.

"He's certainly not as bad as some princes I've known," Mother said. "But he's certainly no innocent, Sulwen."

"If he's followed My'lan all the way to Vyt he must love her," Kyra insisted.

"Let us all hope so," Father said.

I saw sympathy in his eyes. Not for Mother, but for me. They knew who Rian was, and they still loved him regardless. But I'd just learned the truth about my beloved, handsome, strong, witty brother, and Father knew it broke my heart to hear it. To be honest, there was anger and pain, but it was fleeting. I'd learned men could be just as complicated as women, and it wasn't fair to judge them too harshly. Rian had faults like everyone else, but that didn't make him any less loveable. It did, however, secure him a sound match at swords when he returned.

Kyra bounced on the edge of the bed, reaching for my journals like a child receiving a sweet treat. She ran her fingers along the worn leather bindings with unabashed delight.

"I'm sure you'll find something to pique your interest." I climbed under the covers.

"Will you tell me one story before you go to sleep?" she pleaded.

I sighed. "All the stories are too long to tell."

"There must be one, or at least the start of one. Please?"

I couldn't deny my sweet sister anything, so scooted over so she could settle on the bed next to me.

"Do you remember me writing about the furry little wolf-like creatures in my first journals? The ones with the silver fur?"

"The petiloos?"

"Yes! Well, one day when I was out scouting, I found the body of one that had recently been killed. I don't know how it happened, and it isn't important. What matters is that I realized it was a nursing mother, and I was determined to find her pups. I searched with another sailor for a whole day and we found no trace of a den, so I had to leave until daylight. I spent the whole night worrying the pups wouldn't make it, but I didn't have the slightest idea what I would do if I found them. Anyway, the next morning, Captain Romy and I scoured the area looking for any signs of pups."

"The captain of the ship himself helped you?" Kyra asked, understandably surprised.

"Yes." I blushed. "Anyway, we searched for hours, until finally the captain found the den, and I had to dig my way inside."

"Were the pups inside?"

"Yes, but every one I touched had already died. Then I felt the last furry body tucked way inside the den. When it moved, I thought I would burst with excitement. I took the poor creature back to camp stuffed in my shirt, warmed it by the fire, and fed it an unnatural concoction of whatever I could find."

"Did it live?"

"Yes." A tear trickled down my cheek. "I stayed up all night willing him to survive, feeding it every few hours and making sure he stayed warm. I imagine it's close to what it's like having a human baby."

"If Lilias' experience is any indication." Kyra laughed. "Did you name him?"

"Will. I named him Will."

"What happened to him?"

"His home was on the island, so that's where he stayed."

Kyra squeezed my hand, and I kissed her on the forehead and bid her goodnight.

When I lay alone in the bed I'd slept in for nearly my entire life, I was amazed to discover how empty it felt. I'd always loved my bed, the vastness of the space, the softness of the covers, and the plush pillows. Tonight, it seemed too large and cold. I reached out and caressed the side where another person might sleep and wished Lencius was there beside me. It had only been a few days, but I was struck by how acutely I missed him. I couldn't imagine what the next week would do to me.

"The intrepid explorer and her trustworthy assistant hiked through the forest with easy grace, unaware that their every movement was being watched by the one-eyed beast that tried once before, but failed, to sink his teeth into our heroine's tender flesh. Suddenly, the birds ceased their twittering calls and melodies as if they, too, were an eager audience for the drama about to unfold. The beautiful explorer, always keen to the movements of animals and heartbeat of the forest, drew forth her sword and warned her assistant to be on his guard, for the silence of the birds told her that danger was at hand. He took the explorer

at her word and hid himself behind a tree just as a mighty beast sprang forth as if from the very earth to pull them into dark oblivion."

I leapt out from behind a cushion wearing a mask I'd fashioned to look like a less menacing version of *nifo gomman* and made a much more comical noise than the one that struck terror into mine and Seaman Erec's hearts. Syrsha giggled and clapped her hands. Kyra continued reading the story she wrote based on the true-life incident. I stalked over to my niece and pounced on her just as the creature in the story had. The sound of her laughter was music to my heart, and I tickled her belly to elicit more of the sweet sound.

Since returning to Praed, I'd devoted most of my time to forming a bond with my niece. I enjoyed every moment of our time together. She was sweet and inquisitive and so warm and soft to snuggle with. Even when she was tired and cranky or covered in a mess, she was perfect. Lilias invited me to Thistledon whenever I wanted, and I spent most of my days there.

I'd returned a fortnight ago and already started worrying why Lencius hadn't come as promised. I understood some things cannot always be completely in our control. So, I waited and trusted he would come, but when another week elapsed without the arrival of my fiancé, I could remain idle no longer.

Convention had never been my specialty even before my recent adventures. I'd grown in maturity and patience, but those attributes only lasted so long before I was tearing at the walls. My confusion over Lencius' absence evolved into anger and soon gave way to distress as I imagined something tragic had happened to my beloved. I resolved to defy decorum and sneak out of the castle once again (despite the torrential rains) and hasten to Faqur. Winter would come soon, so there was no time to dally. Like before, I prepared a canvas bag and boy's clothing in advance and chose to leave at night on Nettle. For the first time since returning, I noticed the contingency of guards roaming the halls had increased since my departure. During a break in the weather, my request to have my horse saddled was met with suspicion and accompanied by a groom. When I complained to Father, he was less than sympathetic. Regardless of my parents' support, they still prevented any unsanctioned travel. Father said if there was somewhere I wanted to go he would gladly escort me, but like a coward, I declined. I tried three times to escape the castle at night, even going so far as to fashion a rope from my bedclothes to climb out the window, but to no avail. For the first time in my life I was trapped— a prisoner in my own home.

When we hadn't put on a theatrical for Syrsha in a while, Kyra asked what was wrong, but I was too embarrassed to tell her of my wayward fiancé. I told her to write something particularly fantastical and we'd perform it at once.

One night when we were alone, Father asked if my tempered mood had anything to do with returning to *The Wayward Aymelina*. I was able to honestly reply, "No."

"*Will* you return?" he asked.

"I don't know."

I'd put my trust in Lencius, and he'd left me wondering and waiting. My family treated me like a wild colt because of his abandonment. I was flooded with irritation.

I rocked in a plush blue chair in the drawing room at Thistledon, clutching a teacup so hard my fingers ached. Lilias delicately sipped while peering at me over the rim of her cup. She settled it in the saucer and held up a plate of scones.

"No thank you." I clenched my teeth.

"Sulwen Elejick declining a pastry? You must be terminally ill."

I stopped rocking and snapped my attention to my older sister. In a perfect imitation of Mother, she regarded me with a raised brow and knowing smirk. My shoulders relaxed and I unceremoniously dropped my cup and saucer onto the table.

"What happened?" Lilias asked.

I wrapped my arms around my chest and sank into the soft cushions. "Promise you won't tell?"

Her brow furrowed. "If you wish."

I swallowed my pride and took a deep breath. "I…I've been snubbed."

"Oh!" Lilias coughed to cover a laugh and quickly composed herself. "Um, what makes you say that?"

"Isn't that the definition of being cast aside by your fiancé?"

"Fiancé!" Lilias dropped her cup, sending tea splashing over her lap. I jumped up and helped her sop up the mess with a handkerchief, but she waved me away. I'd never seen my normally stoic sister so flustered. Her cheeks were pink, and she couldn't seem to figure out what to do with her hands.

I backed away and fell onto my chair. Lilias pressed a hand to her chest to calm her frantic breathing. She locked eyes with me, then grabbed my knee and squeezed.

"Explain."

"I'm engaged to Captain Lencius Romy."

Her grip tightened.

"Ow! Calm down!" I tried to pry her hand away. She was surprisingly strong.

"Why didn't you tell us?" Lilias released me. I rubbed my sore leg—it would probably bruise.

"I wanted it to be a surprise! He was supposed to be here by now to secure Father's blessing."

"And when he didn't come? Why didn't you say anything? You know Father would have ridden to Faqur himself to find out what's keeping him."

"And I would have been mortified!"

"He could be ill or hurt. You don't know he's forsaken you."

"No, but if you'd been waiting for someone who supposedly loves you and they never came, would you rather be angry or sick with worry?"

"Neither."

I rolled my eyes. "Not helpful."

"Sulwen." Her voice gentled and she smiled. "You know Captain Romy better than anyone. Do you honestly think he's the sort of man who'd propose without the intention of following through?"

"No." I was embarrassed by how pathetic my voice sounded. I'd wanted to be angry with Lencius. If I hated him, it would make missing him easier. And I wouldn't spend my days watching out for his arrival.

Lilias poured herself another cup of tea and held out the tray of scones. I snatched one and nibbled at a corner.

"That's better." She smiled into her teacup and stirred in a lump of sugar. "He'll come. You'll see."

"Sage wisdom from an older sister?"

"No man would risk the ire of an Elejick woman by toying with her affections. Trust me. If he values his life, he'll come."

A bark of laughter escaped my lips. She wasn't wrong. The Elejick royal family were formidable indeed.

CHAPTER 53

After weeks with no sign of Lencius, the temperature began to fall. Soon, the long winter would be upon us, making travel treacherous. The emptiness in my heart was more than just a black void in my soul needing to be filled. It was a hollow, cold blankness, as if nothing had been there at all. My heart was broken, and I resisted my families' attempts to cheer me up.

The only comfort I found was with Nettle, and though the ground wasn't favorable for riding, I tore down the mountain in a wild fury. The poor groom ordered to accompany me didn't dare push his horse to such an extreme, so it wasn't long before I left the man miles behind. The feel of the wind and the rain against my face numbed my mind and made me forget *I* was the one being left behind. He'd promised me we'd face the world together. I'd never believed Lencius was capable of going back on his word.

I spent several hours each day pacing before the windows overlooking the front of the castle, in case Lencius happened to ride up the mountain. I rose early in the morning and peered through the frosted glass to search for signs of visitors. Seeing none, I would sit back on a bench against the wall and pretend to read while I listened for the sounds of hoofbeats. There were regular guests to the castle, even as the ground became covered with a thin layer of icy crystals, and each time I sprang to my feet to look down with unrestrained anticipation at the front steps. Each time I came away disappointed. He turned me into a moping fool, and it was becoming embarrassing.

"Enough." Mother's firm tone made me jump where I stood with my forehead pressed against the cold glass.

My hand flew to my chest. "You startled me, Mother."

She studied me, and I grew wary under her intense scrutiny.

"You've spent hours looking out the window," she said. "What are you waiting for?"

"Nothing. Just lamenting the cold weather. I haven't been able to ride."

"A fact I also regret, but this window doesn't face the stables."

"I don't understand what you mean." I turned back to check the road again.

"Sulwen, talk to me." Her voice was not gentle. She'd been very patient while I wallowed in self-pity, and now her patience had run out.

"Mother." My throat tightened with restrained emotion. "Please don't press me."

She turned toward the window, her chin raised as she regarded the frost sparkling on the windowpane. When our eyes met, I knew from the set of her mouth and the determination in her gaze that whatever she said next must be obeyed.

"Come with me," she said.

She swept from the room, and I hurried after her. I asked where we were going, but she didn't answer. She didn't need to. It took seconds for me to recognize the well-trod path to the stables. I fell in step beside her, nodding at the stablemaster when we entered. The aisleway stretched before us, the air warm and smelling of straw. Stablehands paused to bow as we passed, and horses stuck their heads over stall doors and nickered for treats. Mother ignored them all, not breaking her stride until she came to a stall near the end of the row. She rested her arms on the stall door and leaned over to look inside. There was a wistful smile on her face, and her gaze was tender.

"How is she today?" she said. Her tone was soft, almost reverent.

I stepped closer, though I almost felt like an intruder. Of course I knew which horse was housed in this stall. A man poked his head up and smiled at Mother.

"The cold's been rough on 'er," he said. "But that tonic you gave me 'elps. Just finished rubbin' 'er down."

"Thank you, Hayden."

The head groom tipped his hat and opened the stall door for my mother. She nodded as she rushed inside, leaving me with Hayden. Tall and broad chested, he'd worked at the stables of Praed Castle since before I was born. His short brown hair was peppered with gray, and the lines at the corners of his eyes were deeply furrowed. His large hands were calloused, but they tended to the horses with gentle kindness. He was the only person trusted to care for Mother's beloved mare, Promise.

He took his leave, and I inched around the doorframe. Mother cooed as she lovingly stroked the length of the mare's head. Once, she was a stunning dappled gray, but now she was mostly white, the only dark points on her lower legs. She'd lost muscle definition over her topline, but she was in remarkable condition for her age, nearly thirty. Though it was partly due to Hayden's expert care, the credit fell to Mother. She knew more about caring for horses than anyone at Praed Castle, and her methods not only kept Promise alive, they helped the old mare thrive.

"You've been wallowing," she said. Her tone was calm, quiet, as if to keep from upsetting the mare. "If you tell me what's reduced you to this person we barely recognize, perhaps I can help you come back to yourself."

I tangled my fingers in Promise's mane, and the walls I'd carefully constructed broke. I wept into the soft strands, and Mother stroked my hair and rubbed my back. The tears eventually ran dry, and I inhaled the comforting scent of a warm horse and released a ragged breath.

"Oh, Mother," I said. "I feel so lost."

She brushed away a strand of damp hair from my forehead. "What happened, my love?"

"Before I left Faqur, Captain Lencius Romy asked me to marry him."

Mother's gasp quickly turned into a smile. "What was your answer?"

"I said *yes*."

"Oh, Sulwen, I'm so happy for you." She hesitated, her expression darkening. "But he hasn't come to ask for your Father's blessing."

"No, he hasn't."

Her eyes softened. She wiped a tear from my cheek.

"Did he give you any indication of when he would come?"

"He told me before I left he would follow me within the week."

"I'm sure there's a perfectly rational explanation." Promise snorted and shifted as if she didn't agree. Mother ran a soothing hand down her neck and patted her withers.

"That's what I told myself at first. It's been almost a month." I rested my cheek against Promise and wrapped my arms around her neck. Mother told me once how she'd confided in horses as a child, preferring their company over people. *Horses keep your secrets*, she'd said. *You can tell them anything and they won't judge, argue, or try to fix things. Sometimes, it's nice to talk and have someone just listen.*

"I can make some inquiries in Faqur. Find out if anything happened requiring his staying there?"

"That would look odd."

"Do you love him?"

"Yes!" The word burst from my chest like the splintered pieces of my broken heart. Promise pricked her ears forward but didn't startle. She was steady, like Mother.

"Does he love you?"

I hunched my shoulders. "He said he did."

"Then you cannot give up." A steadfast resolve transformed her features. "Even if you have to travel back to Faqur yourself to discover what has kept him."

"I tried. Father's tightened castle security." I rolled my eyes. How was I to remain a miserable mess if Mother kept trying to fill me with thoughts of things that could not be?

"How long have you loved him?"

"Longer than I care to admit," I said. "By the time I was being arrested for fraud, I was more than halfway to loving him. I cannot fix the exact moment I knew for certain, but I've loved him for most of this voyage."

"And you never suspected he loved you, too?"

"Not at all. He maintained a respectful demeanor and made no indication of his feelings until we were in Faqur again." A thought struck me, and I pursed my lips.

Mother parted a few strands of Promise's mane and braided them. "Well, it's only right that he waited. He was your captain after all. It wouldn't have been proper for him to make his personal feelings known."

"No, it wouldn't." A smile spread across my face, and I breathed, "The compass."

"What compass?" She pulled one of the ribbons out of her hair and weaved it into the strands of Promise's mane.

"Remember when I told you about the horses on Safirelan? Beautiful, strong horses with flowing manes and thick bodies? Well, I befriended one of the foals, a colt I named River. I loved him." I took a deep breath to steady my voice before continuing. "One day a rogue stallion attacked the herd, and River's mother was threatened. Even though he was still small, he tried to protect her and...and he was killed."

"Oh, Sulwen! I'm so sorry!" She gripped Promise's mane and her green eyes shimmered. The mare curled her head across Mother's back and blew out a warm puff of air. The pair were bonded in a way I could never imagine. I loved Nettle, but what we shared was a dim glow compared to the intensity burning between them. I'd jokingly asked Father once if he was ever jealous of the way Mother doted on her horse, and he'd smiled in that secretive way of his. *How can I be?* he'd said. *I brought this on myself.*

I combed my fingers through Promise's mane and braided another ribbon into it. "Captain Romy saved my life. If he hadn't been there, I would have chased after that stallion to try and save River. It was so vicious it probably would have killed me, too."

"Then we owe him our gratitude."

I ignored Mother's comment. I didn't want her to feel gratitude toward Lencius. If he came to Praed, I wanted my parents to give their consent without feeling they owed it to him. "I told Captain Romy we had to bury River and honor him with gifts. All I had was a special dagger. I wished I had all the jewels in Praed to place in the grave with the colt. When I told Captain Romy, he produced a compass that had been a gift from his father. I didn't know then that his father was the Admiral of the Fleet."

"A very generous gift indeed." Mother gave a knowing smile.

"He must have loved me then, to sacrifice something so precious."

"I have no doubt. If you want my honest opinion, I dare say he loved you the day he arrived at the inn and presented you with commission papers under your proper name."

"Oh, Mother," I breathed. "What should I do?"

"Once whatever is keeping Captain Romy away is resolved, what do you want him to find when he arrives in Praed? A frail, shadow of a woman, or the bright, exuberant, playful, and sarcastic Sulwen he fell in love with?"

I set my jaw firmly and answered, "I want him to see that even in his absence, I can be strong and trust in his loyalty to me."

"Well then." Mother raised an eyebrow in a silent challenge. "Prove it."

With the power of my stubborn will, I rose to the challenge laid forth by Mother and rallied my spirits. I banished all dark thoughts from my mind and heart and devoted my time to making my niece happy. Kyra wrote a delightful theatrical based on the Crif pirate attack on *The Wayward Aymelina*, and I was excited to bring it to life for Syrsha. Minus the death and gore, of course.

Lilias came for a visit to the castle, I suspected to cheer me up. We whisked Syrsha away to the living room where Kyra and I had fashioned a makeshift sailing vessel. I was to play the villainous pirate, Syrsha was the captain, and Kyra the heroine of the hapless ship. We made a hat for the little girl out of parchment, but she ended up chewing on it and Lilias insisted we take it away. We settled for a black coat we found in one of Alyx's old baby trunks to symbolize her status as captain. Kyra dressed in breeches and a worn shirt while I wore a crafted hat, old dressing gown, and rubbed soot on my face to symbolize a scruffy beard.

"The black-hearted leader of the pirates boarded the ship without provocation, threatening the lives of the precious crew sailing under a white flag on a mission of peace to bring the Princess Leela to her new home in the distant land of Philandra, where it was said resided the most handsome prince in all the known worlds," Kyra said, her voice commanding.

Lilias, in the role of the beautiful princess, lay her fingertips upon her forehead and sighed as if the journey were indeed interminable.

"Avast, ye men! There sails *The Courageous,* a ship whose captain is foolish enough to breach our borders," I said in a gritty voice. "Aboard is said to be the greatest treasure in all the land, and I intend to have it for my own!" I made a show of climbing up the side of a hull, then jumped with a flourish before my niece's eyes. She giggled and clapped, then stood and bounced on her chubby legs in excitement.

"Ho there, villain!" Kyra called as she drew her wooden sword. "Get thee off my ship at once and I may spare your life!"

"Never!" I drew my own weapon. "I know you have a princess of the most enchanting beauty on board, and no one will stop me from taking her!" Syrsha squealed with delight as Kyra and I clashed wooden swords, and Lilias asked if there was no one who might save her from witnessing such a distressing scene.

A page entered, interrupting our play. "Your Highness," he bowed.

"Yes?" the three of us said in unison.

"Excuse me. Princess Sulwen?" he amended.

"Yes?"

"The king and queen request your presence in the drawing room, Your Highness."

"What did you do now?" Kyra teased.

"I'm sure it's nothing." I hurried out of the room. "Don't start without me!"

I followed the page to the drawing room, silently rehearsing the lines of our play. I gave no thought to what Mother and Father might want. I'd done nothing wrong, and my mood had improved, so there was no need for a heart-to-heart regarding my fragile state of mind. I was announced before I entered the room, which I found odd given it was just my parents. With my mind still focused on my lines I strode in saying, "I hope this won't take too long because I was just about to take the princess hostage." I glanced up and froze.

Beside my parents, there was a third person present in the room. My wooden sword clattered to the floor, and everyone stared at me in silence. I struggled to process the identity of the man standing next to Father.

Lencius.

CHAPTER 54

He looked terrible. Never had Captain Lencius Romy looked anything less than completely composed and meticulously dressed, no stitch out of place, no trace of dirt soiling his polished boots. Never, that is, until that moment. His clothes were soaked through. His arms hung limply at his sides, hat dangling in one hand, accompanied by the audible drip-dripping of water trickling off his sleeves. Mud streaked his legs above his calves, and his hair was unkempt and sticking out at odd angles. He looked as if he'd ridden in the rain for weeks.

He regarded me sorrowfully, his eyes red-rimmed and feverishly bright. I'd never seen him come so close to crying before, yet I couldn't will myself to move. He swallowed and winced as though I was somehow causing him pain with my continued silence.

Mother rose from the settee where she'd been observing the scene.

"You were missed," she said to Lencius in a low voice.

His eyes barely alighted on her before settling back on me.

She moved to Father's side, and I couldn't help but notice his thunderous expression. He must have determined that Lencius was the cause of my recent melancholy, and fury was written on his features. Mother took his arm and pressed a hand to his chest, diverting his attention to her. I couldn't see her face, but Father took a step back after meeting her eye, and I had the sense that she just saved Lencius' life.

Lencius took a step toward me. When I didn't move, he took a few more until he was within arm's reach. I barely breathed, afraid that if I suddenly moved, I would awaken from this dream.

"I'm so sorry," he said.

I could hear in his voice how sorry he truly was. The sound of it pained my heart so acutely I rubbed a hand across my chest to ease the tension.

"I promise I would have come sooner if I could, but my father had an episode and became very ill."

"Is he all right?" I was relieved that there was a good explanation for his absence and yet terribly worried over the admiral's health.

"He is now." His eyes softened. "We weren't certain he'd survive. Then High Councilman Magnus died, and all of Faqur was in an uproar."

"How awful!" Even after such a short acquaintance, I didn't like the high councilman, but I didn't wish him harm.

"Because of my rank in the fleet, it was my duty to oversee the council in the interim between Magnus' death and the election of a new high councilman. There was talk of giving the position to me."

"Do you want it?"

He blinked, clearly not expecting I would ask this question.

"It's not something I considered," he said.

"But do you want it?"

"I have made other commitments." A smile tugged at his lips.

"I hope you didn't decline on my account."

"I admit I did consider your feelings when I declined the offer."

"I wish you hadn't. I wouldn't wish to come between you and any ambition you wanted to pursue."

His brow furrowed, and he appeared quite mournful at my words.

"We made plans together," he said. "I didn't want to alter them without speaking to you first. Is it no longer the case that our future destinies are entwined?"

I was shocked at his question. What an absolute idiot.

"Nothing has changed between us, you dolt! Whether we live in Safirelan or Faqur, it makes no difference. I would follow you anywhere. No matter where your ambitions take you, wherever you feel your career most fulfilled, that is my place. With you."

He let out a sigh of relief and touched my cheek tentatively. I could no longer resist the longing pulling me to him. I wrapped my arms around his waist and snuggled against the wet fabric of his coat. His arms came tightly around me, and though the dampness from his clothing soaked into mine, I didn't relinquish my hold. I forgot Mother and Father were in the room, forgot about my sisters and niece waiting for me, and forgot about all the doubt and uncertainty hanging over my head. The world around us disappeared, and I breathed in the distinct scent of Lencius underneath the rain and dirt. My heart resumed its normal beat as if it had been lying dormant since our parting, and warmth spread throughout my body.

"Did Father give his consent?" I asked.

"No," he said. "They had you summoned after I asked."

"What?" I exclaimed and pulled away. I stalked over to where Mother and Father stood on the other side of the room and stared at them.

"Well, Father?" I said. "Are you going to continue torturing us, or will you give us your blessing?"

"He left you without any idea of his whereabouts." His voice was dangerously low. "It nearly broke you."

"Surely, you can forgive him if I can?" Father was extremely protective of his children, and I knew he couldn't stomach the treatment I had borne regardless of Lencius' excuse.

His eyes fixed on Lencius. "His reasons are understandable, but was he so busy he couldn't be bothered to send you a letter?"

Mother stared at Father with one eyebrow raised. "I seem to remember you leaving me without sending any assurances of your safety."

"I was at war!" Father said.

"Before that." Her tone spoke of grievances long past.

Father's lips pursed and his jaw flexed.

"These circumstances are very different," he said.

"Perhaps, but in each case, a man was gone, and a woman was left having to trust he would return."

Father narrowed his eyes at her suspiciously. "Did you know about this?"

Mother became preoccupied with her shoes. "Not the whole of it."

I stepped in before their quarrel escalated. "I asked her not to say anything. Please, Father." He returned his attention to me. "Let us focus on the future. Do you have any objections to Captain Romy aside from the circumstances surrounding his absence?"

Father's cerulean stare met my fiancé's, and I was proud of my future husband for not shrinking at my father's fierce glare as most others did.

Father sighed heavily. "No," he grumbled. He looked at me and his gaze softened. "Sulwen, I trust your judgment. Do you believe you will find happiness with this man?"

I smiled. "He is where I belong."

Father smiled tenderly and brushed a tear off my cheek. Though I felt his consent was imminent, there was a small matter I couldn't keep a secret. If I waited until after Father gave us his permission to marry, it would appear very underhanded, and I wanted his blessing after he was fully informed of all the facts.

"There's something you should know," I said. "After we are married, we plan on living on the island we explored this summer."

Mother's hand flew to her heart. "What?"

"Faqur is establishing a colony on it. They are seeking volunteers from every country. Have you not heard about this?"

"Some," Father said, his tone again hard as stone.

"How long will you be gone?" Mother asked.

"I don't know for sure." I looked toward Lencius. "It may be that we make a permanent home there. But I promise to visit as often as possible."

"And we can certainly visit you, can't we, Risteard?" Mother gazed sympathetically at Father. My parents loved all their children, but everyone, including Mother, knew Father and I had a special bond. The thought of my leaving pained him, and though I regretted causing him distress, I wouldn't alter my plans. Mother surreptitiously took his hand, and I impulsively reached out and took the other in both of mine and kissed it.

"I will, of course, accept whatever you decide," I said with more poise than I felt. My knees were quaking, and my pulse throbbed in my veins. "But is there anything else I can say to help you come to a decision?"

"Your conviction is all I require," he said. "You have my consent."

In the next instant, I was in Father's arms thanking him profusely.

"Why don't you show Captain Romy the library?" Mother said. "He can warm himself by the fire."

I kissed Father on the cheek, hugged Mother, then grabbed Lencius' hand and led him out of the room before he had a chance to thank the king with a respectful bow.

Once we were alone, Lencius confessed, "That was more frightening than facing Crif pirates."

I led him down the corridor toward the library and said, "You did well. Most people bend like a sapling in a windstorm when Father looks at them with such disdain."

"Does he hate me, do you think?"

I waved my hand flippantly. "He'll get over it. Otherwise, he wouldn't have given his consent." I pushed open the library door and proudly presented the beloved room filled with books and large, plush settees before a warm fire.

Lencius' eyes roamed the room. "Impressive."

"Mother worked hard to restore this place after King Conall destroyed it. She wanted it to be inviting and comfortable for anyone who may wish to read. It holds almost three times as many books as it did before she was queen."

"The queen is fond of reading then?"

"Very much. So is Father."

"And yourself?" He smiled over his shoulder.

"I think Kyra is the fondest of reading—oh, *Kyra!*" I'd left my sisters wondering what happened to me! I started toward the door.

Lencius grabbed me by the shoulders to stop me. "Will you sit with me for a moment?"

Something about his tone quickened my breathing, and I nodded mutely. I led him over to a couch where I sat at a respectable distance. For about three seconds. I couldn't stand being separated from him, even by a few feet, so I scooted closer on the pretense that I wanted to be nearer the fire. I felt his stare as I reached my hands toward the flames. I avoided his gaze, fearing if I saw the same look in their blue-gray depths as that day on the shore of the Brasdemer Sound, there would be flames in other places besides the hearth. A bit of luck saved us from going too far last time.

He ran a finger down my face where it was covered in soot. "What is this?"

"Oh, we were putting on a play for Syrsha. I can't wait for you to meet her." I wiped the dirt from my face. "She's visiting the castle with Lilias today." Our eyes met, and a contented smile spread across his face. I answered with one of my own, and he took my hands and kissed each knuckle tenderly.

"I missed you," he said hoarsely.

"I missed you, too." Each touch of his lips sent waves of warmth through my body. "Is your father really recovered?"

"Yes," he said without pausing in his systematic kissing of my hands.

"What about the rest of your family? Are they well?"

"Yes."

"Do they know about us?"

"I believe they had some inkling when I told them I was leaving for Praed the moment all was settled within the council."

"Was it a very trying journey?"

He peered up at me over the tops of my hands, and my lips parted at the intensity in his eyes.

"I nearly exhausted five horses to get here," he said.

"Only five?"

He lowered my hands and leaned forward. His lips softly met mine, and the last of my resolve melted. I buried my fingers in his hair, determined to give in to the passion rising within me. Lencius' kisses remained tender, his lips brushing against mine almost chastely. He was holding back, which left me both frustrated and relieved. Then I felt the barest caress of his tongue against my bottom lip, and my resolve not only disintegrated, it was as if it never existed. I crushed my mouth against his and kissed him desperately. He answered my passion with equal fervor. His hands tangled in my hair, then roamed down my back, pulling me so close I was practically in his lap. I shifted to face him more comfortably, then deftly unbuttoned his coat and shoved it off his shoulders. He shrugged out of the damp garment and let it drop to the floor. He lifted me so he could swing his legs onto the couch. I hovered over the top of him, our kissing building in intensity, until my instincts completely took over. Without conscious intention, my hands settled on his chest and moved toward his waistband. In a haze, I pulled on the tails of his shirt to free them of his breeches, but he grabbed my wrists to stop my movements.

"Sulwen, stop," he commanded, his voice raw.

"Why?" I tried controlling my breathing, our gasps filling the stillness.

"Because I don't want to give your father further reason to hate me."

I laughed, knowing he was right. I stretched out beside him, lay on his chest, and listened to his heartbeat slow from a frantic pace to an even rhythm. He ran his fingers through my unrestrained hair.

"I thought about something while you were away," I said.

"Go on." He lazily twirled locks of hair into tight coils, then released them and watched the firelight play off the copper strands.

"I want children."

"Good." He kissed the top of my head. "So do I."

"No." I propped myself up to look him in the eye. "I mean, I want children right away. I don't want to wait."

He smiled gently, and his eyes were soft. "Are you sure? There's no rush."

"I know." I teased the buttons at his collar. "But spending so much time with my niece makes me long for children of my own. It's as much of a surprise for me as I'm sure it is for you, but I'm ready to be a mother."

"I'm not surprised. I've seen your great capacity to love." He brushed my cheek with the back of his hand, and memories of Will and River flashed in my mind. He'd been closer to me than anyone and saw my devotion to those beloved creatures. "I will endeavor to give you children as soon as possible."

"I'm still going on adventures. Children won't stop me."

"I'd be shocked if they did."

"You won't stop me?"

"I'd be a fool to try."

We remained in our loving embrace until we decided it would look rather suspicious if we didn't resurface. I tucked my hair back into my hat while Lencius donned his coat, and together we left the library. Lencius placed one last kiss against my forehead before we were seen and whispered that he loved me.

"I love you, too." I linked my arm with his. "Now, come and meet your future niece."

CHAPTER 55

When I returned to my sisters, they didn't notice our unexpected guest at first. Lilias was fussing with Syrsha's costume and Kyra was about to deliver a reprimand for my long absence as I walked through the door with Lencius.

"It's about time," she said. "Our predictions of what you might have gotten in trouble for were becoming more and more elaborate."

Lilias was first to notice him and pinched Kyra's arm. Kyra squirmed in protest, then looked up. Her jaw dropped. Her eyes darted from me to Lencius then back to me.

"Lilias, Kyra," I addressed my sisters. "May I present Captain Lencius Romy."

Lencius bowed respectfully.

"This is an honor." Lilias rose gracefully. "We've heard nothing but the highest praise of you. Right, Kyra?" She nudged my dumbstruck sister with her elbow. Kyra blinked and shook her head.

"Yes," Kyra said. "I've read all Sulwen's journals. She only had good things to say about you. Mostly."

"Mostly?" Lencius said.

My face flushed, and Lilias glared at our sister.

"Don't embarrass Sulwen like that, Kyra," Lilias whispered.

Syrsha toddled up and broke the tension with her delighted giggles. I scooped her up and presented her to her future uncle.

"This is the darling Syrsha."

"A pleasure." He took the little girl's chubby hand and bowed over it.

"I hope this isn't a brief visit," Lilias said. "You *will* be staying in Praed for some time?"

Lencius and I looked at each other, and I couldn't hold back a smile.

"I think this visit shall be a long one," he said.

Our engagement was announced at dinner, and the news was met with nothing short of exuberance from the entire family. Their shouts of surprise were quickly followed by congratulations, and Lilias immediately started inquiring about the wedding plans. I shrugged noncommittally and admitted I hadn't considered anything yet.

"There is much involved in planning a wedding at Praed Castle," Lilias said. "One can never start considering too soon. Spring will be here before you know it."

Spring? I met Lencius' eyes across the table, and I was certain his thoughts mirrored my own. Neither of us were interested in waiting that long.

"We want to be married after the first snow," I said.

Silence followed my declaration. Everyone stared as if I'd gone mad.

"Travel will be very difficult for guests by then," Mother argued.

"But not impossible," I said. "We needn't have a very large wedding. Only close friends and family."

Lencius nodded in agreement, but the others were not convinced.

"Of course, the number of guests is your choice, dear," Mother said. "But that's still a long way to travel from Faqur in the winter. And your aunt and uncle will be coming from Hrgun, which is just as far."

"Maybe we should write and tell them to start their journeys now, so they arrive on time," I suggested. Mother wasn't amused.

"Is there a reason you're in such a hurry?" Khyr whispered in my ear. I elbowed him so hard I probably bruised a rib. He doubled over the table and sheepishly tried to compose himself while Lilias glared at him. She'd obviously heard his inappropriate comment.

"I think a winter wedding would be absolutely enchanting," Kyra said. "Everything all white with snow, crisp air, blue skies, maybe even a flurry or two. It sounds like a fairy tale."

I smiled appreciatively at Kyra's enthusiasm. She winked across the table at me.

"Then it's settled," Alyx said, though I suspected in Mother's mind, it was anything but.

Alyx raised a glass. "To Sulwen and Captain Romy's winter wedding celebration. May our clothes and our kumis warm us." There was an answering reply from everyone around the table, even a reluctant smirk from Mother. The rest of the meal passed without a repeat of the drama my siblings managed to thwart.

That evening, I drafted a list of everyone I wished to invite plus allowing space for Lencius' intended guests. Then, I wrote a letter to my absent sibling, Rian, informing him that if he was any sort of loving brother, he would leave Vyt this instant and attend my wedding. I didn't know if the letter would reach him in enough time, but I wanted him to feel how important it was that he be there. My family was my world, and now my world was growing, and I wanted everyone I loved to share in the joy.

I caught my breath after a match of swords in the courtyard the next afternoon. We'd had a blessed break in the weather, and my brothers and I disappeared outside to enjoy our good fortune. Yes, I abandoned my fiancé. To be fair, he was busy writing letters and divulging every single detail regarding the proposed new colony to Father. That alone could take hours.

"You're getting sloppy," Alyx said.

"I'll admit I'm out of practice," I said. "But I'd hardly call that sloppy."

"You dodged when you should have parried. Are you becoming timid?"

"No!" I shouted and raised my sword. I channeled every ounce of strength I possessed and pressed my attack with ferocity, putting weight into my forward blows and keeping my feet moving. The clang of blade against blade punctuated our fight as Tyrnan and Khyr cheered us on. However, my focus was fixed on my brother, who stared at me with a stoicism matched only by Father. With a growl, I swiped across his midsection. As he leapt backwards out of the way, I paused, raised my sword, and swiped down and across his torso. He deflected with an upward blow, exposing his belly. I drove into him with my shoulder. He was knocked off balance, but he didn't fall, and the momentum I built up served to doom me. He stepped to the side, sending me tumbling forward. Before I recovered, he kicked me in the backside, sending me face-first into the snow.

Alyx knelt beside me. "Yield?"

"Yield." I said, then surprised him with a snowball to the side of the head. Despite this act of hilarity, Tyrnan and Khyr were uncharacteristically quiet. Alyx and I sensed the shift of mood and saw Lencius standing over us.

"Lencius!" Alyx helped me to my feet. "We were just sparring. Alyx always wins."

"I see." He held Alyx's gaze, his face expressionless, and I frowned at his odd behavior. "May I?"

"Of course!" I readied myself to spar with him, but he extended his hand out for my sword. My brow furrowed, but I shrugged and handed it to him.

"Alyx, may I borrow yours?" I asked.

"He's going to need it," Lencius said, his eyes fixed on my eldest brother.

My jaw dropped. It wasn't just the gap in their ages nor experience. Alyx was the crowned prince and future king. One didn't simply draw their blade against him. Alyx raised his sword in salute. Astonished, I had to dive out of the way at the sudden clang of their first blows. I settled in next to Tyrnan and Khyr, the three of us sharing a wide-eyed glance, then returning our attention to the pair.

The opponents were remarkably well matched. Alyx had been training since he could lift a sword, and I imagine Lencius had as well. However, my fiancé had the advantage of real combat, and he smoothly parried every attack and anticipated every trick Alyx could throw at him. But my brother was a quick study, and it wasn't long before he was deflecting the captain's attacks with ease.

"This is the greatest thing I've ever seen," Khyr whispered as the pair continued fighting. "Your fiancé is amazing."

Tyrnan didn't share Khyr's enthusiasm. He trembled beside me, no doubt because he still regarded the captain as a superior and feared we'd all be in trouble if he lost. Sweat poured down Alyx's temples, and Lencius appeared to have the upper hand. Then my fiancé did something unexpected. Just as it seemed he would claim victory, Lencius brought his sword up in a salute then swiped it downwards, signaling a draw. Alyx acknowledged him, then smiled tremulously.

"Well met," my brother said. He shook the captain's hand.

After that, my brother and fiancé spent a lot of time together, and though their budding friendship warmed my heart, it also struck me as odd that only days prior, they'd been clashing swords. I asked Lencius why he challenged my brother, and he merely shrugged and said he felt it was the fastest way to get to know him.

"Is that why you challenged me on *The Wayward Aymelina?*" I asked.

"Partly," he said.

"And?"

"I learned you were worth knowing better."

Two months later, snow blanketed Praed, covering the prairie in pure white interrupted by the occasional carriage tracks and hoof prints. The preparations for our wedding were nearly complete, and all that was left was to welcome the guests as they arrived. Unfortunately, Admiral Romy's delicate health prevented his ability to attend. I offered to have the wedding postponed so Lencius' parents could be there.

"That won't be necessary," Lencius said.

"But they're your parents. Don't you want them to see you married?" I asked.

"They will. When we visit them in Faqur before we leave for Safirelan."

"You know what I mean." I smirked. "You want them to be at the ceremony, don't you?"

"Of course. But our marriage is not contingent on their being in attendance. The only two people I care about being present are you and me."

"There's no need to worry on that score." I wrapped my arms around his neck. "Even the leader of Burdeed pirates couldn't keep me away."

I hadn't seen my Aunt Ula, Uncle Finton, and my cousins since Lilias' wedding. I nearly wept when Merrin emerged from the carriage looking more lovely than when I'd last seen her. There was a confident rise of her chin, and her skin was a shade darker, probably because of her travels. She laughed when I embraced her so tightly her feet lifted off the ground.

"I missed you so much!" I said. "I want to hear everything about your journey."

"In time," she said. "For now, I want to hear about you. I heard you didn't turn out to be as clever as you thought and got caught."

I recalled my revelation to the first mate in Tyrnan's hospital room. "My own fault," I said.

I led her up the front steps of the castle. I'd abandoned Lencius to greet Merrin, and he was currently being introduced to my aunt and uncle. Cale and Kormac already looked bored and wandered off with Tyrnan and Khyr.

"Lencius." I tugged at his sleeve. "I would like you to meet my cousin, Merrin."

He smiled down at Merrin politely, but she wasn't content to do the same. She took his hand and shook it warmly, told him it was a pleasure to meet him, and wished us a happy marriage. He acknowledged her platitudes then became distracted by a question posed by my uncle. Merrin and I fell behind as the group entered the castle, and she stopped once we were in the foyer.

"What is it?" I asked.

"He's very handsome." She kept her voice low.

"He is," I said, flushing a bit. "Don't sound so surprised." I smirked, and she stifled a giggle. "He's also very intelligent, kind, and an accomplished captain."

"I don't doubt it." She struggled to maintain her composure.

"So, there's no point in implying I'm only marrying him for his looks."

"I would never think that."

"Or because he has the most amazing blue-gray eyes."

"Farthest thought from my mind. I think more highly of you than that."

"I'm also not only marrying him because his kisses are intoxicating."

"Sulwen!" Merrin glanced around the room. "That is an unbecoming thing for a princess to say."

"A princess, yes, but not a sailor." I raised my chin and haughtily marched through the foyer. We didn't make it very far before we were rendered incapacitated by throes of laughter.

A carriage bearing the remaining two Romy brothers and Elizabel arrived the next morning. It must have been quite a sight for them to see the entirety of my family poised on the steps of Praed Castle to greet them. Well, everyone except Rian, whom I had yet to hear from. I wanted to impress upon them how fortunate an alliance their brother was making. We were certainly an imposing scene. Mother and Father were elegantly dressed, their crowns glittering in the cool winter sunshine. Behind them were all my siblings in descending age, including Lilias and her husband, and behind them were my aunt, uncle, and cousins. The servants were dressed in their best attire, and knights flanked the road leading to the castle. Father thought the showing rather extravagant, but I argued there was no better way to impress my new in-laws than a show of solidarity.

Lencius stepped forward as the carriage came to a stop, and Evrard Romy emerged critically eyeing the scene.

"You're certainly marrying up," Evrard muttered. "You know the whole of Faqur should be in attendance at your wedding." His attitude clearly showed his disapproval of our hasty marriage.

I gritted my teeth. A look from Kyra annoyed me further, for it was clear everyone heard his comment.

"Oh, leave him alone," Elizabel said as she alighted. She took a deep breath and let it out slowly in satisfaction. "The air is so pure here." She took her husband's arm.

Absalon Romy was the last to exit the carriage, and his characteristic cheer softened my mood. Lencius presented the three of them to my parents, and after they showed their due respect, I stepped forward.

"Welcome to Praed," I said. My nerves were rattled.

Absalon smiled and bowed. "An absolute pleasure, Your Highness. I cannot tell you how delighted I was to hear of your engagement."

"Please, call me Sulwen. After all, we are going to be brother and sister soon." His smile widened, and I couldn't help but hug him. He'd always been very kind, and I was equally as excited to have him as my brother.

"I'm so happy for you, my dear," Elizabel said. She embraced me. "It's absolutely beautiful here. I've never seen so much snow!"

"We get a lot of it in Praed. It's actually quite mild right now." I turned to the first mate. We scrutinized each other suspiciously.

"I almost couldn't believe it," Evrard said.

"What's that? That your brother was marrying a princess?"

"No, that he was marrying *you*."

My jaw clenched. Absalon and Elizabel admonished him. But a gleam of mischief in his eye suggested he didn't disapprove of the match.

"Are you going to welcome me as your new sister or not?" I asked.

He smiled, really smiled with his whole face. When he hugged me, I nearly fainted.

CHAPTER 56

Father and I skirmished earlier in the day over the manner of the meal that evening. I wanted a private family dinner, but Father maintained that our distinguished guests merited a celebration in the Great Hall. I appealed to Mother since she hated these boisterous affairs as much as I did, but she sided with Father (traitor!). In the end I conceded, and we planned a feast in the Great Hall.

Shouts arose from outside and an uproar circulated throughout the hall. Father sprang to his feet, as did Alyx, their sword hands twitching. The doors to the Great Hall opened, and a man with long, dark hair and a bright red, robe-like tunic strode inside. The hall fell silent, and I cried:

"Rian!"

I jumped to my feet, my chair clattering to the floor. I rushed to my long-absent brother and launched myself into his embrace. People watched and murmured, and I distantly heard Mother explaining that her second eldest son had returned.

"I didn't want to miss my sister's wedding," Rian said in my ear.

"I didn't think you'd make it in time."

"I might not have, had I not intercepted your letter when already on my way home."

I pulled back to look up at him. He was smiling, and I found that despite the truth I'd learned, I still adored my carefree brother.

"We'll talk later," he said. "Would you care to introduce me to your betrothed?" He cast a look at the sumptuous feast laid out on the tables. "Also…I'm starving."

I laughed and brought him to the head table. He embraced Mother and all his siblings in turn, shook Father's hand, and accepted the introduction of Lencius and his brothers with unmatched charm. The evening passed much more pleasantly with Rian there, and I realized how acutely I'd felt his absence. Our wedding wouldn't have been complete without him.

"We honestly didn't think Sulwen would make it out of Faqur after we heard who the chief prosecutor was," Rian told the table.

"What do you mean?" Absalon asked.

"Oh, Rian, don't!" Aunt Ula warned.

"Sulwen and Gerrid Ekhane have a history," Khyr said.

I turned to him. "You weren't even born yet!"

"Gerrid and I got into a bit of a scrape when we were children," Tyrnan explained. "It didn't end well."

"In fact, the last time we saw the young master, Sulwen was attached to his calf by her teeth," Alyx finished. "She wasn't even two years old!"

The table erupted in laughter, even Evrard Romy.

"I think he may still bear the scar," Merrin said.

"It was an impressive bite," Uncle Finton said. "His mother was worried it would become infected."

"I wouldn't have been surprised if it did." Aunt Ula smirked. "She ate a lot of sweets that night."

"No thanks to you," Mother admonished her.

The carefree manner of the conversation was bolstered by the steady flow of wine and kumis. It was one of the most delightful evenings I'd spent in the Great Hall. I was sorry when the end of dinner was announced, and everyone rose to go their separate ways. But the hour had grown quite late, and only a few minutes in the drawing room with the ladies had me yawning.

"Go on to bed," Mother said, brushing a stray lock of hair off my face. "You're exhausted, and there's still much to be done before next week."

The following week marked the date of our wedding, and I smiled wistfully before dragging myself from the room.

Even though I could barely function, I sought out the library where the men gathered before joining the ladies. I crept silently into the room and ducked behind a bookcase, cautiously searching the faces for the one I sought. There he was, Rian, casually leaning against the fireplace, the red fabric of his tunic reflecting the dancing flames. The others spoke in low tones and mostly had their backs to me, so I gave a stealthy wave to get his attention. To my dismay, he didn't notice, and I rolled my eyes and looked for something to throw. I pulled a pin from my hair, aimed it at his thick skull, and flicked it. It struck him just above the eye, and I covered my mouth to keep from laughing. He looked up and saw me, shook his head, and set down his glass of equi.

"If you'll excuse me, gentlemen," Rian said. "It seems I have a previous engagement." He gestured in my direction, and everyone turned to look. I bowed elaborately, and Rian graciously held out his arm. I found Lencius' eye before we turned to leave, and I winked at him.

"You wanted to speak to me?" Rian asked as we strode down the corridor.

"I wanted to know how the negotiations in Vyt are going."

He raised an eyebrow. "Shouldn't you be tucking in your fiancé?"

"Now, Rian, that is inappropriate. Some of us still possess moral fortitude."

He had the decency to look away in shame and didn't do me the discredit of denying any rumors.

"He seems nice," Rian grumbled.

"He is, but I would like to talk about you."

"Go on."

"Kyra and Lilias told me about My'lan."

"I'm sure they did."

"Is she the reason you went to Vyt?"

"No." He answered much too quickly. A long sigh, then, "Well…she wasn't the *only* reason."

"I'm not here to judge you, Rian. Artur knows I'm the last one to do that. I just want you to be happy."

He grinned, his green eyes serene.

"She is the most beautiful woman I've ever seen. But more than that, she's passionate. About her people, her country, music, and dancing. She dances so gracefully it's like water flowing through a river. She's the epitome of kindness, but that frightens me. I fear she's only kind to me because she's kind to everyone."

"You fear she doesn't hold you in any particular regard?"

"Exactly. There were moments I thought it, others I was sure of it, so sure I nearly declared myself, but then I was so afraid she would reject me I said nothing. I'm a coward."

"No, you're not! You're just as vulnerable as everyone else. I was just as scared as you."

"What changed?"

"One of my dear friends said he'd rather declare his feelings and risk rejection than say nothing and live wondering what might have been. You have to decide for yourself which is worse."

He lapsed into quiet reflection. I leaned my head on his shoulder. We stopped at my room, and I kissed him on the cheek and told him whatever happens, it brought joy to my heart to have him in Praed for my wedding.

"Father says you'll be leaving afterwards and might not return. Is that true?"

"It is." The prospect no longer held any remorse, fear, or trepidation for me. I eagerly anticipated starting my new life with Lencius on Safirelan, and I only hoped all my siblings could feel such happiness.

"I shall come visit you someday." He flashed an impish grin.

"I hope you both will." He flushed an endearing shade of crimson. My brother was truly in love. I was astonished but said nothing for fear of embarrassing him. I went to bed laughing to myself about the unexpected surprises life can bring.

"If you break her heart, my father will kill you," I heard Rian say to Lencius on our wedding day.

"Rian! Leave him alone!" Alyx admonished.

"It's true, isn't it?"

"Well…yes, but you shouldn't scare him like that."

Lencius gave an answering chuckle and assured my brothers he had no intention of disgracing me. "And if I fail as her husband," he added, "I would welcome the king's wrath myself."

I smiled and stole away before I was seen, fearing Molli's consternation for my tardiness.

Mother entered the room as Molli affixed the last of my curls to the top of my head. She waved Kyra toward the door.

"Just me?" Kyra asked. "Does Lilias have to leave, too?"

"No," Mother said. "Go outside and let Father know that Sulwen will be out in five minutes."

Kyra rolled her eyes, but she complied. The moment the door closed behind her, Mother took my hand.

"I have an idea what this is about," I said, unease rippling through me.

"My mother wasn't around to talk about my wedding night," Mother said. "But I'm here for you should you have any questions."

I looked to Lilias, and my sister smiled warmly. She didn't seem traumatized from her pre-wedding night discussion. I took a deep breath and met Mother's green eyes.

"I understand the basics. I know it may hurt. What I really want to know is, what do I do if I disappoint him?"

Mother's smile widened, and her eyes held a hint of amusement.

"You won't," she said with conviction.

"But I don't know what to do."

"Lovemaking is in your blood. Your body will help you. Listen to it."

I smiled, and she leaned over and hugged me. Lilias wrapped her arms around both of us, and shortly thereafter, I walked out of the castle and into the courtyard for the last time as Sulwen Elejick.

I wore a white gown with long sleeves trimmed with fur, the bodice sparkling with tiny bits of crystal so I glittered like stars when the sun shone upon me. Over my gown, I wore a thick, light blue wool cloak elaborately embroidered with entangled white branches. In Faqur, Lencius told me, brides wear a veil over their faces until the couple are declared married, whereupon the groom ceremonially removes it, symbolizing the lady's transition from daughter to wife. In accordance with his traditions, a gauzy white veil was draped over my face. As in Ilano, the men of Faqur bestow a ring upon their brides, but it wasn't expected that I would give one back.

Torches flickered in the breeze, and Elejick family banners rippled around the courtyard. Lencius stood before me in his black coat trimmed with gold, his medals and commendations hanging prominently across his chest. His white breeches blended in with the stark scenery, and his sword hung sheathed at his hip. His brothers stood in their finest beside him, and both smiled when I approached. Just as I took Lencius' hands, snow began falling in large, beautifully delicate snowflakes. From the corner of my eye, I saw Mother opening her mouth to catch a few. My eyes darted to Father in time to see the smile he sent in her direction.

"A lasting relationship often begins under circumstances that will test the boundaries of not only your connection, but of your own fortitude,"

Father's voice echoed in the stillness of the wintery morning. "It is from these trials that we arise better than we were, and the resulting foundation becomes strong enough to endure whatever hardships might befall you. There is no better place to start a marriage than in friendship, and how fortunate these two people are to have a comradery that will see them through the long years to come." Father didn't dwell on platitudes that marked most Praed and Ilano weddings. He spoke truly of our hearts in a poignant way I loved. He knew our minds, and he knew I didn't care for long speeches. He didn't care for them either, and we both appreciated the ability to say so much with so few words.

"Lencius Romy of Faqur, Captain of *The Wayward Aymelina*, do you take Princess Sulwen Elejick of Praed as your wife? Do you vow to cherish her uniqueness and support her in the life you will forge together?"

"I will," Lencius said.

"Princess Sulwen Elejick of Praed, do you take Lencius Romy of Faqur, Captain of *The Wayward Aymelina*, as your husband? Will you promise to build upon the foundation the pair of you have established and remember to bend when necessary?"

"Yes, I will," I said.

Father nodded toward Lencius, and my fiancé held out his hand to Evrard, who placed a dark metal ring in his hand.

"Sulwen," Lencius said in a low voice. "You have brought more light into my life than all the sunrises I've seen on the open sea. I promise I will spend the rest of my days endeavoring to make you as happy as you've already made me by becoming my wife." He slipped the ring onto the third finger of my left hand, and the look in his eyes told me how deeply he meant those words.

"Will you laugh at my jokes?" I arched an eyebrow.

He smiled. "Yes."

"Then we'll be all right."

The people nearest to us laughed, and Father gave me a sidelong glance. He seemed to hesitate, as if he wasn't yet willing to let me go.

"I now pronounce you husband and wife," Father said in a rush. "You may seal your vows with a kiss."

Lencius took hold of the bottom of my veil and tossed it back over my head. Then his lips were on mine, and even the hurrahs of the courtyard couldn't drown out the pounding of my heart and the mingling of our breaths. I would have been content to remain kissing him forever as snow fell around us, but Mother's voice whispered in my ear that there would be plenty of time for that later. I blushed furiously and drew away. Lencius proudly led me back into the castle on his arm.

I'll admit the rest of the evening was a blur of dancing, drinking, laughter, and stories told by my brothers attempting to embarrass me in front of my new relations. But I wasn't going to allow their childishness to affect me. I shrugged them off and danced with anyone who would stand up with me, including my new brothers-in-law. Elizabel laughed when I extended a hand to Evrard, but I would not allow him to refuse me. Absalon was an absolute darling, dancing with me multiple times and telling Lencius he'd married the most adorable gem of a woman. I knew I liked him.

Lencius smiled more that evening than I'd ever seen in the whole duration of our acquaintance, teeth showing and all. I took full credit for his merriment. The only moment of dread came when Grandmother approached with all the dignity due her station. I tried to make a hasty exit.

"Sulwen," she called out.

I froze in my tracks and turned to face her.

"A word, darling."

"Yes, Grandmother?" I asked with the falsest smile I'd ever conjured.

"I don't know if I approve of my granddaughter marrying a man who isn't from Praed." She cast a disdainful glance toward my husband. "But I will allow that he comes from a distinguished lineage and seems to appreciate the honor marriage to you has afforded."

"Thank you, Grandmother." I counted it a sign of personal growth that I didn't goad her into a fight over the matter. Instead, I kissed her on the cheek and wished her good health before sneaking away.

The room had begun spinning when I felt a tap on my shoulder. I turned around, and Mother stood behind me with a beautifully tender smile.

"Sulwen," she said softly. "It's getting very late."

I understood her meaning immediately, and I was shocked to feel no fear or trepidation, merely excitement.

"Should I go get Lencius?"

She smiled at me the way she used to when I was a child asking a silly question with an obvious answer.

"I'll have him sent up in a few minutes. We need to prepare you for bed first."

Both Mother and Molli readied me for bed, and there was no mistaking the wistful expression on both their faces. I was no longer a little girl, and these careful ministrations would soon be performed by someone else in a distant land. Molli said nothing as she met my eyes in the mirror, but I felt her pride and well wishes clearly enough in her steady gaze. Mother dismissed her once I was in my nightgown, and I expected her to ask if I had any last-minute questions. But she merely held my hands with an enigmatic smile until there was a quiet knock on the door.

"Remember what I said about tonight?" she said.

"Yes. Let him in."

Mother nodded and opened the door to my husband. The door shut behind her, signaling the last time she would look upon me as her maiden daughter. In the morning, I would rise a wife, and I was eager to learn what my body had to teach me.

&PILOGUE

I insisted on rowing *Tenacity*, much to my husband's consternation. It was a delightful surprise to find the canoe hadn't wasted away but had survived to be repaired and resealed. The sound of the oars cutting into the water was punctuated by the quiet grunts of exertion I tried to conceal. But Lencius was no fool. He fixed me with a stern glare I ignored, my gaze on the diminishing size of the stone houses lining the lakeshore behind us.

The strength in my arms was nearly sapped by the time we reached the opposite shore. I jumped out of the boat and could barely pull it onto the bank.

"Stop," Lencius commanded and started to rise. "I'll do that."

"Stop mollycoddling me! Be careful before you fall." I reached out, and with a great flourish, he deposited eighteen-month-old Reyvan into my arms. The little girl squealed with delight when I tossed her in the air then tickled her belly.

Anxious to run free, she squirmed out of my arms and toddled through the long grass toward the upward slope of a hill. I watched her red-haired head bob up and reveled in the shine of the copper strands as she picked flowers. Lencius came up behind me and kissed my neck just below my earlobe, and I smiled in pleasure at the touch of his lips against my skin.

"I won't ask if you're up to walking this far," he said.

"Good." I peered at him out of the corner of my eyes. "Because you should know perfectly well that I'm capable of such a hike under any circumstances."

"I brought some food if you get hungry."

"Good man." I kissed him before chasing after Reyvan. She laughed when I swooped down and pretended to miss catching her. About halfway up the hill, her little legs grew tired, and Lencius picked her up and set her on his shoulders. My back was sore by the time we reached the top of the hill, and I stretched languidly as we looked down into the valley.

"Horsh!" Reyvan called. She pointed at the shapes moving about and grazing on the lush grass.

"That's right, honey," I grinned up at the toddler bouncing on her father's shoulders. "Those are horses."

I accepted Lencius' offered hand and we climbed down the trail into the valley of wild horses. We took a break to enjoy a quick meal before ambling closer to the herd.

I recognized the cream-colored stallion immediately and scowled at him. My heart seized at the memory of his violent attack on the herd, and Lencius wrapped an arm protectively around my shoulder.

"Do you see any horses that might remember you?" he asked.

Reyvan took a few tentative steps closer to the herd.

"A few," I said absently, keeping an eye on our daughter.

A whinny pierced the air, and hooves thundered toward us. Lencius grabbed Reyvan and shielded her in his arms as a blue mare trotted toward us with nostrils flared and ears erect. Behind her, a cream-colored colt followed looking just as curious.

"Hello, Matron," I said warmly. The mare took a few hesitant steps closer. I'd never been close enough to touch her in the past, and it seemed that wouldn't change. She snorted, turned to leave, paused to look at me for a last lingering moment, then galloped away. Reyvan protested being restrained and Lencius put her down. I glanced at her wide, light blue eyes staring after the mare, her hand clasped in her father's. I followed her gaze and saw the colt hadn't retreated after his mother, but instead was regarding my daughter. She giggled and reached out for him, and to my surprise, his ears pricked, and he took a few tentative steps forward.

"Let her go," I whispered.

"What if he hurts her?"

"He won't. Trust me."

Lencius reluctantly released her, and she toddled toward the colt. He wagged his tail and lowered his head to sniff her outstretched hand. She lay her tiny fingers on his soft muzzle, and my heart nearly burst at the wide smile on her face.

"Give his head a little scratch," I instructed my daughter. "Gently."

She stretched her arm up and patted the colt between the eyes, then ran her fingers through his forelock. Lencius was poised to grab her if the colt made a move to harm her, but I remained relaxed as he lowered his head and blew out a huff of air. Reyvan giggled as her hair lifted with the horse's breath, and her little nose scrunched up as she babbled.

A cry from the herd caught the colt's attention, and he leapt sideways and bolted to his mother's side with a buck and a sharp whinny.

"Horshy, Fa-Fa!" Reyvan said excitedly as she pointed toward the herd.

Lencius lowered himself to her level and listened to his daughter's incomprehensible mutterings as she waved her hand toward the horses. I wandered off in the direction of a mound of earth I hadn't visited since I'd last set foot in this valley. A few of the horses watched me warily as I walked by, but even the stallion found my presence not worth bothering about.

Grass covered the grave since I'd last been there, but I would never forget the spot where we'd laid River to rest. I knelt on the ground and placed my hand on the rounded earth.

"Hello, River," I said. "I hope you're running with your ancestors and eating until your belly bursts. I've seen your mother, and she's well." I turned and glanced at the cream-colored colt. "You seem to have a brother."

Reyvan and Lencius joined me, and my daughter tucked herself into my side.

I wrapped an arm around her and continued talking to the colt. "This is my daughter, Reyvan. I wish you could've met her. You may have even carried her on your back." Lencius sat on my other side and rubbed circles in my lower back. I leaned into his touch.

"Do you regret giving me your father's compass to bury with him?" I asked.

"No."

"Did you love me when you offered it as a tribute?"

"Yes."

I pulled a babbling Reyvan into my lap. With careful deftness, Lencius reached over and took her from me and let her bounce on his legs.

"You don't have to do that," I said, summoning all my patience. "I know my own limits."

"I know." He launched Reyvan into the air higher and higher and she laughed merrily. "But protecting you makes me feel like I'm being useful."

"You were useful." I kissed his cheek. "I wouldn't be in this state if not for you." I rested a hand on my swollen belly to punctuate my point, but my husband wasn't as amused as I was. He was very watchful, ensuring I was adequately fed, rested, and protected. Though it warmed my heart that he cared so much, his hovering could be stifling.

"I don't know how many times I can do this." He sighed and lovingly ran a hand over my abdomen. I chuckled at his dramatics. Constantly worrying over my health put a strain on his sensibilities. Lencius by nature was a man who took his responsibilities very seriously, and there was nothing he regarded more importantly than his pregnant wife's health.

"Don't worry," I said. "I don't intend to have as many children as Mother."

His eyes widened comically, and I couldn't help but tease him.

"Well," I amended. "I may change my mind after child number three and elect to have ten." I couldn't stop myself from laughing at his blank expression, but I was silenced by an onslaught of ardent kisses.

"Be careful," he said hoarsely. "Or I'll hold you to that threat."

I settled into the crook of his shoulder and closed my eyes as the summer sunshine warmed my body. The sweet voice of our first born resonated in my ears as I dozed, and I sighed in contentment. Before long, a little warm body snuggled next to mine, and under a blue summer sky, Reyvan and I napped under Lencius' watchful eye and protective embrace.

That night, as I sat before the flames in the hearth we built ourselves, I pored over a ledger I'd meticulously kept since we started building a home on Safirelan. The ledger contained the names of every family, their children, and the location of their holdings. It was my hope that if we started from scratch, we would maintain a count of everyone living, and eventually dying, for all posterity. It would be an arduous task, but it was an opportunity to keep busy and fulfilled. Though there was much involved in establishing a colony aside from the obvious of building houses for people, in my current state of rotundness, it was difficult for me to perform any manual labor or remain standing for hours. Anything I could do seated was a blessing.

Lencius kept busy helping to oversee construction of necessary businesses including a blacksmith, hospital, and the beginnings of a market. A council was established within the first months of our arrival, and now, more than a year later, there was talk of making my husband something called a 'governor.' A colonist from Hrgun, who studied different systems of government, explained that a governor acts as the leader of the people. Though he may seek advice from a council, they ultimately followed his authority. It was basically like being a captain, but instead of commanding a ship, he would command a colony. Lencius didn't speak of this possibility very often, I expect because a part of him simply wanted to live in peace. A part of him would honor the role should it be bestowed upon him. Personally, I felt my husband was the only logical choice. He had years of experience leading people, was fair, level-headed, and widely respected. He also had impressive royal connections.

"She's asleep," Lencius announced, settling down beside me.

"I hope she didn't give you too much trouble," I said absently, my eyes locked on my notes.

"No more than her mother."

I peered at him, a reluctant smile tugging at my lips. I'd successfully taught my husband how to jest. Sometimes I regretted it, but I had to admit, he was good at riling me up.

"Do you have much work left?" He eyed the papers in my hand. There was an edge of anticipation in his voice, as if he were waiting for me to be finished so he could tell me something.

Intrigued, I closed the ledger, folded my hands over it, and gave him my full attention. "Was there something you wanted to discuss?"

He placed a hand on my growing belly, a look of contentment on his face as he gently caressed my body. I moved his hand to a different part of my stomach, and a bright smile lit up his face when he felt the child within roll around inside me.

"At the meeting last night they asked me to be the governor." He continued to rub my belly.

"What did you say?"

"I told them I'd consider it." His eyes met mine. "I wanted to discuss it with you first."

"I think it's a wonderful idea. It's the best decision for Safirelan in its infancy."

"It would take me away from home more than I'd like."

"I know." I covered his hand with mine. "But it wouldn't take you too far. We'll find ways to keep ourselves occupied during the day, and we'll be waiting for you to come home every night."

His free hand slid over mine and squeezed. In his eyes, I could see how torn he was regarding this decision. I smiled encouragingly and asked, "If it was just you, would you accept the offer?"

Without hesitation he answered, "Yes. But—"

"Then you should accept." I stretched out my back and declared I was going to bed. He stood to help me out of my seat, and we walked arm in arm to our bedroom. I could practically hear his mind turning. He said nothing until we were tucked securely under the covers, his arm wrapped around my midsection possessively.

"If it starts to become a strain, I'll resign," he said.

"Deal." I snuggled closer to him.

Our lives had been incredibly hectic and exciting since the moment we exchanged vows. I wouldn't have it any other way. I couldn't stay idle for long, a quality my husband shared, so the adventure we found ourselves in was well suited to our personalities. I recalled Tyrnan cautioning me not to fall in love with Lencius and how angry his presumption made me. Later, after our engagement was announced, I asked why he thought I needed a warning.

"Because." He shrugged. "He was clearly perfect for you."

My idiot brother was right, but I'll never give him the satisfaction of telling him that.

PRONUNCIATION GUIDE

People:
Risteard ~ Rihst-ERRd
Alyx ~ like "Alex"
Rian ~ like "Ryan"
Tyrnan ~ Tirr-nen
Lilias ~ Lih-lEYE-us
Sulwen ~Sulh-when
Khyr ~ kIRR
Kyra ~ kIRR-uh
Wyrwyk ~ wurr-wIK
Lencius ~ len-SHus
Romy ~ Rahm-ee
Noshluat ~ nAHsh-loo-aht
Mukahanu ~ mook-aw-hA-noo
Nutamoson ~ noot-aw-MOH-sun
Nakwacimek ~ nahk-WA-si-MEHK
Zubhod wa Mara ~ zoo-BAHD wa mar-ah
Calux ~ kal-UHx
Reyvan ~ rAY-vehn

Places:
Praed ~ like "bread"
Kuste ~ koost
Faqur ~ fahk-OOR
Ilano ~ ih-LAHn-oh
Safirelan ~ sah-FEER-ih-laan

Things:
Nifo gomman ~ nee-foh goh-maan
Aymelina ~ aye-mah-leen-aa
Petiloos ~ peht-ih-loo

ACKNOWLEDGMENTS

This is a story that combines my love for *The Princess Bride, Pirates of the Caribbean,* and *Twelfth Night*. One of my favorite tropes is the girl dressing as a boy and accidentally falling in love with someone strictly off limits. Add a dash of high seas adventure, fencing, fighting, escapes, true love, and miracles, and you have my best work to date.

Once again, a lot of research went into writing this book. I love deciding to write about something I know absolutely nothing about, and sailing is no exception. True confession: I've never stepped foot on a sailboat. But I've seen enough pirate movies to think it couldn't be *that* hard.

Dear reader, it was in fact *very* hard.

I didn't want to slap phrases in your faces and drag the story down in vernacular. I needed just enough knowledge to make the story believable yet keep it moving. A huge thanks goes out to my editor, Ron, for knowing more about the parts and types of ships than Google. He's the reason this story seems plausible.

But I'll still never master lay vs lie.

A loving thank you to my number one fan, Mom. Your support has kept me writing since before I could hold a pen.

Oh, yeah, thanks husband 😊

Without you, I'd miss all those glaring grammatical errors. Thanks for man-checking, being a stunt man, and reading my books more than I do. XIXO.

My readers are fantastic. Thank you for reviews and texts telling me how much you enjoy my stories. I may never be a bestselling author, but I'll always be a grateful one.

Special shout-out to the writing community across all my social media platforms. It's been wonderful getting to know you!

About the Author

Mandy is a Certified Veterinary Technician specializing in small animals on the Oregon Coast. When she's not saving lives, she's weaving tales of strong women using their intelligence to pursue incandescent happy endings. This is the third novel in her *Daughters of Riverstone* series. She lives on the Washington coast with her husband and their four children. Besides leaning uncomfortably over a computer screen, Mandy enjoys camping and hiking with her family, reading, and drawing maps of her world.

You can find me on the following social media platforms:
Facebook - @RiverstoneSaga
Twitter - @RiverstoneSaga
Instagram - @riverstonesaga
YouTube - Riverstone Saga
Goodreads Author Profile

Please consider leaving a review! It helps readers find their next exciting book!